BROKEN BONDS

To Steph, ♡

Erin O'Kane

ERIN O'KANE

Contents

The Brides of Darkness Prophecy	ix
Prologue	1
Chapter 1	3
Chapter 2	12
Chapter 3	21
Chapter 4	32
Chapter 5	48
Chapter 6	57
Chapter 7	68
Chapter 8	82
Chapter 9	95
Chapter 10	103
Chapter 11	117
Chapter 12	128
Chapter 13	141
Chapter 14	152
Chapter 15	165
Chapter 16	180
Chapter 17	193
Chapter 18	209
Chapter 19	229
Chapter 20	242
Chapter 21	251
Chapter 22	263
Chapter 23	275
Chapter 24	290
Chapter 25	299
Chapter 26	312
Chapter 27	323

Chapter 28	339
29. Three months later	355
The End	359
Author's Note	361
About the Author	363
Also by Erin O'Kane	365

Kingdom of Broken Bonds
The Brides of Darkness
Book One
By
Erin O'Kane

Copyright © 2024 Erin O'Kane

Kingdom of Broken Bonds

First publication: 2024

Editing by Elemental Editing & Proofreading

Formatting by Kaila Duff

Cover art by DARK IMAGINARIUM Art & Design

All rights reserved. Except for use in any review, the reproduction or utilisation of this work, in whole or in part, in any form by any electronic, mechanical, or other means now known or hereafter invented, is forbidden without the written permission of the author.

This is a work of fiction. Any resemblance to places, events or real people are entirely coincidental. No part of this book may be used to create, feed, or refine artificial intelligence models, for any purpose without written permission from the author.

erin.okaneauthor@gmail.com

Written by L. Guyatt as Erin O'Kane

Dedication

*To my bestie and constant cheerleader, Katie.
I couldn't do this without you and your crazy ass sending me aggressive praise.
Everyone needs a friend like you.*

The Brides of Darkness Prophecy

Seven lands, seven brides.
Lands united, peace will reign,
Harbour this warning if you are out for your own gain.
Without the brides, it matters not what is planned,
For the deadly war will destroy the land.

The firstborn will take the lead.
Silver surrounds her,
as bright as the hope she helps take seed.
Thirst for blood will twist the tide,
A macabre warning for those who wish to kill the bride.

Wings of fury and fire of power,
This bride's fate will come to pass in the final hour.
Honour and pride burn in her soul,
Will she be ready when the reaper comes
Ringing out his death toll?

With the sound of the sea in her heart,

The Brides of Darkness Prophecy

The third bride will have a broken start.
Shattered,
She will be forced to make a choice,
That could tear her world apart.

The fourth has unimaginable power,
but is cursed by others, turning the bride sour.
Isolated, shunned and betrayed,
she does her duty with no joy in her heart,
and along with the souls she carries, her soul will slowly depart.

Tame the beast, tame the bride.
Tiptoeing the line of control,
number five will struggle to keep hold of her soul.
Claws and teeth can kill,
But betrayal will destroy someone faster than any dagger will.

Phases of the moon rule number six,
And sneaky as a fox she likes to play tricks.
Yet she will surely need to grow,
Quicky,
As her land needs her more than she will ever know.

The final bride will be the saviour of the plains,
If only she was given control of the reigns.
Protection becomes detainment,
Hidden away and unable to take her rightful place,
This will spell doom for the entire race.

Seven lands, seven brides.

The Brides of Darkness Prophecy

The brides of darkness will soon rise.
Unified, they will bring peace to all,
So beware those who wish it to fall.
Seven lands, seven brides.
Without them, no one survives.

Prologue

The War of Drathlor was long and ruthless, the citizens of the land slaughtered purely due to their race. The streets were paved red with blood, and the screams of our young were a constant song of despair. So many were killed that we wiped out bloodlines that were around since before records were even kept.

We were on track to eliminate entire races, until King Drath unified us and stopped the massacre. We are now bound to him out of respect and gratitude. To keep the peace, he split the land of Drathlor into seven regions to suit each race. Since then, each region has promised one of their newborn females as a future bride.

Seven lands, seven brides. The lands were at peace, or so we were all told.

I always knew I was promised to another since the day I was born, my path already decided. However, a yearning in my heart and a whisper in my ear tell me that I'm meant for so much more than being a trophy wife.

Chapter One

The wind is bitterly cold as it whips around my body, making my already cool skin prickle. Wrapping my arms around my middle more out of comfort than against the weather, I continue to stare over the cliff as the sun sets above the ocean. Even as I close my eyes, the sound of the sea crashing upon the rocks below and the scent of salty water fill me with a familiar longing. It's so fierce that I wince at the sensation, wishing I didn't have to leave.

My long, silver hair is unbound, blowing around my face, the delicate strands dancing on the wind. I'll have to fix it before I leave and make myself look more presentable, although this is the least of my worries.

Despite the fact that I have been spending half of the year away from my home ever since I was old enough to walk, it never gets any easier leaving this all behind. Here, I can be myself, surrounded by my people and the land I was born in.

"You look like you belong in one of those dramatic romance novels you enjoy reading so much."

The voice takes me by surprise, something I will never admit aloud. It's one that is as familiar to me as my own. A true smile stretches my lips as I take Felix in. He towers over me, his body frozen in time, the bite scar on his neck glimmering slightly in the light of the setting sun. He must have been in his early twenties when he was bitten, although I have no idea how old he is now. I've known him ever since I was a young girl. He has warm hazel eyes and slightly wild, light brown hair. He's never been able to tame it, the slight curl in the strands giving it a life of its own. His clean-shaven jaw is strong, yet he still has a boyish look to him that detracts from the fact he's a vampire.

"Ah, but in those books, the princess is always kidnapped by the monsters." Shifting my weight, I place my hands on my hips. "You're forgetting that I'm no princess. I'm one of the monsters." I flash my fangs in demonstration, my eyes twinkling with humour so he knows I'm not threatening him.

His smile widens as he shakes his wayward fringe from his eyes. "You're not a monster, you're a softie at heart."

Raising a brow, I make it clear that I think he's talking shit. "Oh yes, a softie who enjoys snacking on humans." I simply let myself enjoy this moment the two of us can share before everything changes. "Have you forgotten who I am?"

The comment was supposed to be a joke, yet I regret saying it as soon as it leaves my mouth, all humour draining from his face as he takes in those last words.

"No, I've not forgotten." His eyes land on the mark around my neck that signifies exactly who I am and the promise of what I will do. Sighing, he shakes his head. "Are you ready to leave? The horses are waiting."

Regret floods me, and I know I should say something. In fact, I'm desperate to say something and wipe that resigned expression from his face. When I open my mouth to do so, though, nothing comes out. The weight of my responsibilities sits heavily on me, the burden mine and mine alone.

I've already said my goodbyes to my father, the only family I have left, and that was quick and stilted as usual. Due to the nature of my role, I don't have many friends here, so I spent many evenings down in the stable with my horse, Shadow. Felix was the stable hand, and we formed an unlikely friendship. Although we've been seen together, our relationship is frowned upon. A full-blooded vampire such as me shouldn't be lowering herself to spend time with one of the changed—him.

Our land of Trador is ruled by vampires. There are other denizens who live here too, as well as the humans spread across the continent like ants, yet it's the vampires who are in control here. Everything here is run through a strict hierarchy, even within our own race. There are two types of vampires in Trador who live very separate lifestyles —those of us who were born into it, and as such, we're part of the higher society that runs the land, and the changed, who were once human and had their blood drained by a vampire. It can be a tough experience, and many don't make it through the process. However, if they do live, they wake up as one of us.

This is the main difference between us as a race. Born vampires grow, whereas those who were changed stay frozen in time, forever the same as the day they were bitten. As a population, there are many more of the changed than us who were born into it, yet we have powerful gifts that help us stay in control of the land.

Unfortunately for the changed, they are treated with the same derision as the humans. Personally, I've never understood why there's such a stigma with the changed.

They are still part of our community and should have the same rights. Their place in society is a strange one, as not even the humans like them, making it difficult for them to settle. I've always thought it was odd, since they *were* once human, yet as soon as they are reborn, they are treated as other.

Taking a deep breath, I glance out over at the ocean once more, pointlessly wishing I could escape what's awaiting me by sailing far away. That is not what the Fates have planned for me, however, and the tingling mark around my neck reminds me of this. When I turn back to Felix, my expression is neutral and doesn't give away a single hint of my true emotions.

"I'm ready."

He looks at me for a moment, *truly* looks at me as if he's able to see straight through my mask. His gaze is so intense that I think he's going to call me out on it, but instead he simply nods, his brows furrowing.

We walk together across the clifftops in silence and inland to the castle. It's beautiful to look at, if not a tad dramatic, which sums up our race perfectly. Lots of tall, spiralling towers reach towards the sky, with large windows glistening in the setting sun. This is my favourite time to view the castle, when the orange and pink hues of the sunset highlight the details that are hidden at night. Oh, the castle is stunning in the dark, since it was built this way for that very purpose, the stone glimmering like starlight. Even so, there is something softer about it in this light, showing a different side of our otherwise volatile nature.

Figures begin to come into sight, their dark forms still as they wait beside several horses just outside the castle gates. Something flips in my stomach, and I force myself to stop for a moment. Frowning at the unfamiliar feeling, I take several deep breaths and try to wrangle the anxiety into submission, pushing it down low in my stomach. This is not like me. I've never been one to feel trepidation or be anxious about my role, yet this time, everything is different.

"You look pale," Felix comments quietly. "Do you wish to feed before we leave?"

Usually, I'd make a joke about always looking pale, since it's one of our key features as vampires, but I'm not in the right mood to joke, especially as I think over his question.

"Are you offering?"

My question slips out before I have a chance to stop it, the surprise in my voice making it clear that his offer was unexpected. Feeding from another vampire is risky, and often only done as an act of subservience or between lovers. Offering your neck to another shows a great deal of trust and loyalty.

I've never fed from Felix, and while I'd be lying if I said I've never fantasised about it before, it's not something I ever expected to happen. For him to offer now, just as I'm about to leave my home for the next six months, there has to be a meaning behind it, right? My fangs ache in my mouth, saliva pooling at the very thought of biting into his strong neck. Hunger rises within me, my every thought narrowing down to feeding from him. I bet his blood tastes amazing.

He flashes me a cheeky grin, cutting through my internal ramblings. "You are always welcome to feed from me, Thea. However, I was going to suggest calling for one of the volunteers."

Of course he was. There is always a steady supply of blood in the form of human volunteers—gone are the days when we had to hunt for our next meal. I want the earth to open up and swallow me whole. It was stupid of me to think that he was suggesting anything else, and my embarrassment is enough to make my pale skin flush.

Laughing in a way that I hope doesn't sound forced, I attempt to play off my comment. "Oh, I know, I was just joking with you."

His expression tells me that he doesn't believe me for a second, so I plough on before he can comment and call me out. "Anyway, I fed last night, so I'll be fine for the journey."

Something about Felix has always made me feel comfortable around him in a way I've never felt with anyone else. I've known my duty since I was a child, and the weight that responsibility carries makes it difficult to make friends. There is a certain way I am expected to behave and carry myself, something that is as easy as breathing to me, yet Felix manages to break my composure with a twitch of his lips. One of the reasons we've been friends for so many years is because he can see the true me beneath the mask of responsibility.

Not giving him the chance to comment, I roll my shoulders back and brush my hands down the front of my riding jacket, the garment fitting like a second skin. Combined with my leather trousers, the deep red colour of the jacket with black trim makes me look like the lady I'm supposed to be. Walking towards my waiting escorts, I reach up and pull my hair into a simple braid.

"Thea, wait a second. I have something I need to tell you," Felix calls out from behind me. Not slowing my pace, I turn and look at him over my shoulder, taking in his expression. Whatever he was going to say is quickly wiped away, his face hardening as his eyes shift to something beyond me.

Frowning, I face forward and discover one of my escorts closing the distance between us. It's Geoff, my stern but fair attendant. He looks exactly the same today as he did the first time I was thrust into his arms as a child.

I've spent more time with him than my own father, and I can't help but view him with affection despite the fact that he's perpetually wearing a frown and his presence indicates that I'm leaving once again. He might pretend otherwise, but I know he feels fondness for me, not that he would ever admit it aloud. His frame is slim, and the lines on his face show his age, but he isn't frail. No, I've seen him take out threats faster than I can blink. For a born vampire to show signs of age, they must have lived for centuries, and while I've never dared to ask Geoff how old he is, I suspect he's lived for hundreds of years.

Felix appears at my side, and I raise a brow at his tight expression. The two males have never been friendly, but I'm surprised by Felix's obvious display of dislike towards the older vampire. Geoff believes in the hierarchy that states the changed are below us, so unless he needs my friend's services, he won't acknowledge him. Felix, on the other hand, thinks Geoff is a pompous ass.

"Miss Anthea," Geoff greets, dipping his head. His hair is silver, like mine, and tied at the nape of his neck with a black cord. His vivid blue eyes scan me from head to toe, assessing my choice of outfit for the journey ahead. "Are you ready to depart?"

A small smile graces my lips as I tilt my head to one side. "Geoff, after all these years, are you still insisting on calling me Anthea?"

He raises one silver brow. "That is your name, is it not?"

A flicker of amusement rises within me, but I'm very aware of the other escorts waiting for us. They may be several meters back with the horses, but their enhanced hearing will pick up every word we whisper. Holding back the instinct to smile, I mimic his actions and raise my own brow.

"Only the king and my father call me Anthea. Thea is my preferred name, you know this." If it had been just the two of us, I might have said this teasingly. However, that is not the case, and I need to shift my behaviour back to what is expected. This isn't usually so difficult, but I suspect that the circumstances of my latest journey are making it harder.

Something changes in his eyes, as though he can see right into my mind and sense my turmoil. "If no one followed the rules, we would live in chaos, Miss Anthea." His tone is sharper than usual and holds a bite I wasn't expecting.

This isn't about my name, but the situation we all find ourselves in. He's not speaking this way to be cruel, he's simply reminding me of my responsibilities—as though I need the reminder, because that's all I've been able to think about this last month since I received my summons.

He seems to realise he snapped, and his expression softens. Had the rest of the riding party been standing with us, he wouldn't allow this moment of weakness. It's only there for a second, but I see it, acknowledging it with a dip of my head. My heart clenches tightly in my chest, and I take a deep breath as I work on building walls around myself.

Geoff takes a step to the side and gestures to the horses. "If you are ready, we should leave."

I look over my riding party and see all of the usual people who accompany me on these journeys. Four guards stand next to their horses, and a stable hand waits with Geoff's horse and Shadow. That's when I notice a spare horse, a beautiful grey mare with dark dappling on her back legs. She's fully saddled and waiting patiently with the others, not needing anyone to hold her in place.

I slowly walk over to the beautiful horse, holding my hand flat for her to scent me before I stroke the soft velvet of her nose. "Who is this horse for?"

Others will join me throughout my stay, such as ladies-in-waiting, assistants, maids, and my weapons trainer, but they travel separately in carriages, not arriving until several days after me. Therefore, it doesn't make sense that someone would be joining us now.

Shadow whinnies behind me, jealous of the attention I'm paying to the grey mare. I turn to roll my eyes at her and almost crash directly into Felix's chest.

"That's what I was trying to tell you," he comments quietly, his soft eyes exploring my face for my reaction. "I'm coming with you this time."

My heart hammers, and a pulsing ache forms in my temples as I process this news. Felix has come with me on my trips several times over the years, and honestly, it helped me get through the rough, lonely months away from my home. He's been my rock and a glimmer of light in the darkness, so the fact that he's coming with me should bring me joy, but this time, everything is different.

This time, I'm finally going to see my mate—the male whom I'm going to marry in a matter of months.

Chapter Two

The ride through Trador gave me a much-needed reprieve by helping me avoid any more awkward conversations and forget the twisting unease in my stomach.

Tradorian horses are different from the ones the humans like to breed. Their legs are longer and more powerful, making them one of the fastest creatures on land. Their features are sharper, and a row of spikes protrudes from their spine, rising above their mane and stopping by their shoulder blades. Due to these differences, it takes care and enhanced reflexes to ride one without being thrown off or impaled. Shadow would never allow me to fall, but her speed makes all other thoughts fly from my mind. Riding her has always made me feel free, and it's the only time when I can forget who I am. Today, it feels different, and I'm unable to enjoy the ride across the mostly flat, barren land that makes up Trador.

My purpose has always been clear—I am to represent my kingdom and be married to my mate, one of King

Drath's sons. As a child, I loved the idea that I would get to be a princess one day, and that this special destiny was mine and mine alone. However, as I grew up and saw my peers begin to flourish and grow into ladies who chose their own destinies, my purpose began to feel more restrictive. I have never resented my fate, but I will admit to some jealousy over the course of my adolescence. As I became an adult, my future was something I accepted, and until now, I have been waiting for the king to decide I am worthy.

That time has finally come.

Having already travelled for over four hours, we are on the last leg of our journey. An hour out from our destination is a trading post and the last signs of civilisation before the huge walls that surround Drathlor City. No one dares venture too closely to the walls, and those who do never return. Even here, at the outpost, the humans and handful of changed vampires look ragged and hold a fear in their eyes you don't see in other citizens of the land. This has always been my least favourite part of the journey, as we swap from horseback to riding in a carriage.

King Drath decreed that all of the chosen females had to arrive via carriage when called back to the city, so this small trading post is where we do exactly that. I hate riding in the carriage, it feels so confining, and I wish I was out on Shadow's back, feeling the wind in my hair. Much to the disgust of my tutors, I've always had a wild streak they've not been able to tame. As I grew, I began to see the consequences of that behaviour, and I learned to hide it. No matter how much I hate riding in this carriage and wearing my hair in a neat braid, I do as is expected of me.

I know better than to push the king on issues such as this.

Taking a deep breath, I look down at the scroll on my lap, my eyes scanning the letters without really seeing them. I've memorised every word of the summons, having read it many times.

I've waited for many years, always being told that when the day came, I'd be whisked away to meet my mate and become his bride. Now that it's here, I find that I'm not ready, but not because of a lack of training, no, I know exactly what's expected of me. The things that circle in my mind now are the questions that no one could have prepared me for—questions about... feelings. As a race, vampires are very good at keeping their emotions hidden, and it's frowned upon to be overly emotional. The excitement in starting my new life isn't here, pulsing in my chest as I expected it to be. Instead, I feel nauseous, confused, and full of trepidation. Is it normal for me to feel this way?

One thing that has also been playing on my mind is that Felix is going to be here, and I can't place my finger on why this is disturbing me so much. I never expected him to be there on my wedding day, and certainly not like this. As my friend, I should be happy that he's going to be present on one of the most important days of my existence, yet here I am, feeling conflicted.

Geoff sits opposite me in the carriage, staring out of the window with a distant expression, also lost in his thoughts. As my escort, he has to travel with me and attend me as an advisor, tutor, and father figure, and I can't help but wonder if he's finding this whole experience as uncomfortable as I am. Taking in his expression, I doubt it. Geoff is a stickler for the rules and hides his emotions better than any vampire I've ever met.

Returning my focus to the window beside me, I run my gaze over the barren landscape as the carriage races over the dry, dusty plains. All of our guards are riding alongside the carriage to keep us safe from the many threats that prowl the land, and I know Felix is out there with them.

Before the war, it never used to be this way, and our land was green and prosperous, with towns lining the borders between our neighbouring kingdoms. After the war, the life was stripped from Trador. Even now, I can see the burnt, dilapidated ruins from what must have been an old town, a reminder of the cost we all paid during the war.

The continent of Drathlor is made up of eight kingdoms, the largest of which is Drathlor City. The name makes it sound like it would be small, and I don't know why they chose to call a whole kingdom a city, but the main city alone is enormous, and almost as large as half of Trador. I've never seen the rest of the land that Drathlor City stands in, and strangely, no one ever speaks of it, but it extends into a huge mountain range known simply as the Border. No one has ever been able to give me an explanation of the name or what it's supposed to border.

The city is home to King Drath and his court, where he rules over us all, while the remaining seven kingdoms are spread out like a fan around Drathlor City. There are seven main races, other than humans whom we share our continent with, and each race rules their own kingdom—merfolk, witches, beasts, shifters, centaurs, dragon folk, and, of course, the vampires, whose land is in the middle.

Each kingdom has their own king or queen who rules them, and generally, they reign peacefully and dole out justice within their own lands. However, King Drath has overall supremacy when it comes to what happens on the continent.

He was the one who united the races and stopped the great war, and as such, each land promised one of their females to him. These females are to marry one of the citizens of Drathlor City at the king's discretion, spending half the year in his court until that time. It is because of this that I travel to Drathlor City every six months and spend the remainder of the year within his castle.

As a child, I was taught what was expected of me as a future bride, but now that I'm older, I see it for what it is—a way of controlling my kingdom. By never being allowed to spend more than six months in my homeland, it makes me different from my peers and difficult to establish meaningful relationships. I'm never fully trusted by those in Drathlor City due to my ties with the royals of my country, yet because I spend so much time in the city, there are those in Trador who believe I'm nothing more than a spy.

By having a permanent hold over me, King Darth has a constant, not so subtle threat over my people. If Trador were ever to rebel against Drathlor, my life would be forfeit. Although it would be easy for my people to kill me to break this hold, they can't due to the prophecy.

Just as King Drath was attempting to unify us, a prophecy was unveiled. A seer from each of the races received the message at the exact same moment, speaking in unison on the battlefields.

Seven lands, seven brides.
    Lands united, peace will reign,
    Harbour this warning if you are out for your own gain.
    Without the brides, it matters not what is planned,
    For the deadly war will destroy the land.

The firstborn will take the lead.

Silver surrounds her,
as bright as the hope she helps take seed.
Thirst for blood will twist the tide,
A macabre warning for those who wish to kill the bride.

The prophecy goes on to describe the other brides and their struggles, along with a warning that if we don't complete our destinies, our races will suffer for it. I am the eldest of the brides, so it was clear that I am the first bride. My silver hair was another dead giveaway, along with the warning about a thirst for blood. As a vampire, we are the only race to drink blood, so there was never any doubt that this would be me.

My verse protects me, not only because of the prophecy as a whole, but due to the specific line at the end warning those who want me dead. Hence why my people still accept me within the kingdom, albeit reluctantly. Without me, they would be destroyed.

I've had a long time to mull over the prophecy, having heard it many times during my life. All angles and choices of words have been examined, and many scholars have theorised regarding its meaning, yet no one really has any answers. It makes me believe that someone is out to kill me, so I've spent many years learning to defend myself.

During my times at Drath City, the other brides and I have always been kept separate and encouraged not to mingle. We had lessons together as younglings, but as we grew, we were separated more often until the only time we were able to mingle was at official events. I would see glimpses of them in the castle, but other than a few words of greeting to each other, we quickly moved on. I've never quite understood why this is the case when we're supposedly going to maintain peace over the land together.

However, I've never spoken out over this rule, and becoming close with them has always been a risky move. Brides have died over the years. It seems the prophecy protects us, but only the ones who are chosen. Initially, it was assumed that all of the chosen girls would be the same age, but the prophecy never specified *when* the girls would be chosen. When one of the girls dies, another is chosen in hopes of her being the one. Of course, there are a few exceptions, such as myself. The prophecy is very clear that I need to stay alive, so I am guarded at all times for my own safety.

Due to the curse of their responsibility, the brides from the beasts tend to die quickly after they reach adolescence, unable to control their inner animal. Several of the other brides have also been unstable over the years, so it's generally safer to stick to myself.

"Are you ready for what awaits us?"

My advisor's voice breaks through my thoughts, bringing me back to the present. I glance over at him, surprised by the question.

"I'm well aware of my responsibilities, Geoff, don't fret."

His expression softens slightly, something I've rarely ever witnessed from him. "Of that I have no doubt, Miss Anthea. I was merely checking on your emotional well-being."

Disbelief strikes me mute, and I can only blink dumbly as I try to process his words. Amusement works its way through me until a smile begins to pull at the corners of my lips.

"Oh, Geoff," I coo, leaning back in my seat as I take him

in, still bowled over with surprise, "are you worried about me?"

He scoffs, his usual stoic expression returning, yet there's still a twinkle in his eye that gives him away. "Worried that you might trip over your large feet and embarrass our entire land."

I can't help but chuckle quietly. I tripped over my feet one time when I was being presented to the king as a child, and Geoff has never let me forget it. Pressing my hand against my chest, I feel my heart beat sluggishly. "I didn't realise you cared so much."

His expression turns serious, all traces of humour gone. "You have been my charge your entire life. My only purpose is to train you and make sure you complete your fate. Don't confuse my sense of duty for care."

He might sound like he's scolding me, his tone snappish, but vampires aren't the most affectionate of creatures, and I've learned to spot the signs of hidden emotions. He might pretend otherwise, but Geoff cares more than he outwardly shows and would ever admit it. In fact, showing emotions in Trador is akin to showing weakness, so he's probably offended that I'd even think this of him. Besides, it's better that people believe he doesn't care for me anyway—it's safer for both of us.

Before I can say anything or tease him further, he sits upright in his seat, his shrewd eyes narrowing on something outside the carriage. "We're at the gates, prepare yourself."

We're here.

Nerves try to claw their way up my throat, constricting tightly so any noise I might make would simply come out as a strangled cry. No, I have to control myself. Taking a deep breath, I focus on pushing my emotions back and presenting the stoic expression that is expected of me. This is more difficult than usual, thanks to the myriad of thoughts and emotions that circle in my mind like a hurricane.

I will not let them destroy me.

With that thought, I close my eyes and will myself into a sense of calm. Once I've achieved it, my eyes open, and I meet Geoff's gaze, nodding once.

Chapter Three

As the first bride from the prophecy, I am the first to marry, but there is also another, very specific reason I'm getting married now. King Drath's youngest son, Prince Havoc, is my true mate.

True mates are rare in our world, and as such, they are honoured and prized. They are a partner who is tied to your soul and predestined to be by your side for eternity, and it is something that many can only dream of. I discovered that Prince Havoc was my mate about a decade ago during one of my six month visits.

As a rule, the princes are kept away from the brides, only seeing them on official occasions we were required to attend. Our eyes met for the first time at one of these events, and the connection snapped into place between us. Although I had never felt anything like it before, a surety had blazed through me in that moment—we were mates. Every time I've seen him since, it was always from a distance, and I was unable to keep my eyes from him. Even though this was over ten years ago, I've still not been officially introduced to him, and part of me wonders if I'll actually get to meet him before our wedding day.

The fact that we are mates has been taken as a sign from the stars that we're from the prophecy, and the marriage must go ahead at all costs. It certainly makes things easier for the king, as we're already predestined, and he has to do little with finding the right male to match me with. He also takes great pride in the fact that one of his sons is chosen, and takes every opportunity to remind us all and use it to affirm his status as king.

I wish I could view this as they do, that it's an honour to be fated, but it feels more like a vice around my chest, getting tighter and tighter with each passing second. My choices have been stripped from me ever since the day I was born, and this is yet another I have no say in.

It's strange to know that I have a mate and to feel the pull towards him, yet I have no emotional attachment to him. I don't know this male, and any thoughts of a fairy-tale wedding died with my childhood when I was ripped from my mother's arms to be brought to Drathlor City without her.

Unlike the rest of my people, I have always struggled to maintain distance and the mild mannerisms of the vampires. As a child, I was impulsive and wild. Emotions would build up within me so strongly that it was a struggle not to let them out. My tutors would tell me that it was not our way to be so liberal with our emotions, their disappointment clear on their faces.

Others began to notice my lack of control, and whispers began to circulate. My mother eventually pulled me aside and explained that what I was experiencing were feelings, and that vampires keep theirs hidden. I once asked my mother if everyone had feelings like I do and just didn't let them show. She told me that I was special, that I had a gift and experienced things others couldn't, and that I shouldn't tell anyone else and had to keep them hidden as best as I could.

At the time, I was proud of my emotions, even though I had to keep them hidden. Now, though, I know it isn't a gift, but a curse, a constant burden that I attempt to keep locked away.

The carriage suddenly jerks, jolting me from my thoughts as we enter the tunnel that leads to Drathlor City.

The magic in the gates lets us through, shutting firmly behind the carriage and sealing me off from my homeland. There are seven of these gates, one leading from each land into the city. Once on Drathlor land, the changes are immediate. Although the land is mostly empty, the grass is green, and plants grow tall. The few wooden buildings we see as we travel down the brick road are well maintained. The river flows to the right of the carriage, the water clear and teeming with fish. Even the ground beneath us seems to thrum with energy, just another reason why we continue to follow King Drath. For some reason, beyond the walls of the city, our lands are slowly dying. They have been for a while, like the life is being sucked from them, which is part of the reason that our main cities are on the coastline.

Within a few minutes, the houses begin to appear around us, and before long, we're in the city proper. Despite the sun having long been set, the streets are bustling with people. Most of the humans who live here will have retired for the night, but other denizens of the land are only just waking.

As a born vampire, I am actually a living being, unlike

the changed. Because of this, I have needs like any living creature, such as sleeping. I can go much longer without sleep than most, and I only need to rest for a far shorter amount of time before being back at full strength. The sun doesn't affect me like it does with the changed either. While they can only cope for very short amounts of time under direct sunlight, I am able to spend a full day without dying. However, I wouldn't come out completely unscathed, and it would leave me drained of energy.

We're only minutes away now, our guards and escorts leading the way on horseback. Geoff is sitting upright with a neutral expression, brushing down his immaculate maroon jacket and dark trousers. Looking out the carriage window once more, I see a large, looming structure ahead.

King Drath's castle.

Right in the centre of the city, the King's abode is huge, the complex larger than my whole city back in my land. Large, imposing walls surround it, containing its own city within. The lords, ladies, and those with higher social status live in the massive houses on the manicured grounds leading up to the castle. Here, they are able to go about their lives without having to regularly interact with those they consider lower than themselves. They also benefit from being close to the king. Not only is it easier to separate the classes this way while rewarding those loyal to him, but the king is also able to keep an eye on the nobility.

Over time, I have noticed that although the city looks as though it's thriving from a distance, there are signs of depravity if you know where to look. Even now, as I glance down a dark, hidden alley, I see bodies leaning against the wall—alive or dead, I'm unable to tell at first glance, but from the hunched over figure of a vampire covered in blood,

I'm guessing that if they aren't dead, it won't be long until they are. Guards line the streets, keeping order, yet I notice they are simply moving anyone who looks out of place, ensuring the streets appear more in order than they are.

One can't simply hide poverty and pretend it's not there. All cities have a poor area to them, and the one I'm from is no exception, but there's corruption here that always makes me uncomfortable. I've spent enough time here over the years to notice the difference.

We're allowed through the gates, and our journey up the winding road to the castle is uneventful. While I've done this trip many times over the years, apprehension has its grip on me. I'm not sure what to expect this time. Feeling eyes on me, I glance over to see Geoff's frown, sensing the difference in me. He looks as though he wants to say something and is trying to decide how to word it when the carriage pulls to a stop.

The door opens, and a tall male stands in the doorframe, bowing stiffly at the waist. Something about him tells me that I've met him before, yet I can't place where I recognise him from. There's nothing remarkable about his appearance, and if not for the subtle glow of his eyes, I might have mistaken him for a human. I know all of the footmen and king's messengers, and I am sure he's never been in one of those roles before. Perhaps he's been promoted?

Geoff climbs from the carriage before turning back and offering me his hand. This is a tedious tradition, but one he's insisted on maintaining while we're here. I am perfectly capable of climbing from the carriage myself, and the look I give my escort tells him that. Of course, Geoff is the master of being emotionless, and he ignores me, assisting me down the single step and onto solid ground.

"Lady Anthea, welcome back to Drathlor Castle," the male greets, his face as expressionless as Geoff's. "I am Warren, and I shall be acting as your aide and the link between you and the king."

An aide and link to the king. I've never been assigned one of those before. I assume the change is due to the fact that I'm about to marry his son. Nodding as though I was expecting this all along, I clasp my hands in front of me.

"Thank you, Warren. Am I to meet with my betrothed now?"

This question makes my chest clench with apprehension, which takes me by surprise. Why am I so anxious about meeting the man I'm about to marry? I'll have to meet him sooner or later, and I would rather our first meeting not be at the altar.

It seems that I worry for nothing, though, as Warren eyes me up and down with a look of distaste, obviously finding my riding gear inappropriate for a meeting with the royals. "The king thought you might like the chance to freshen up first."

"How thoughtful." The words sound drier than intended, not quite able to hold back my sarcasm. "Are the other brides here yet?" Perhaps I can meet with some of them and see if they know more about what's going to happen.

Warren looks disapproving again, only this time it is not aimed at me. "All but the lady from Barheer."

This doesn't surprise me. Barheer belongs to the beasts, and of all the races, they are not known for their promptness, and their feral natures make them unreliable at best. Not to mention, like vampires, the beasts often prefer to travel in the dark.

Humming thoughtfully, I glance at Geoff, silently checking that everything's in order. At the slight dip of his head, I clear my throat and clap my hands together expectantly. "In that case, I shall retire to my rooms."

"Very good, my lady." He seems pleased to get rid of me, a slight spring in his step that wasn't there before. He crooks his finger, calling someone forward. I'm not able to see anyone in the gloom, but a figure hurries towards us. "This is your attendant. She will help care for you while you are here."

Stepping closer to the aide, Geoff places a hand on his arm and guides him towards the side entrance of the castle. "Warren, I have several matters I wish to discuss with you regarding Lady Anthea's stay."

I take a deep breath and turn to see Felix and several attendants are already caring for the horses and moving the carriage now that it's no longer needed. Two guards remain with me, and for a crazy moment, I consider how easy it would be to disable them and flee. I'm fast and smart, so I think I could get into the city proper without any incidents, but then I would need to make alliances to help hide me...

What am I thinking?

If I flee, I'll damn my people. Where are all these traitorous thoughts coming from? I've never felt like this before. Squeezing my eyes shut, I work through the breathing exercises one of my tutors taught me to help calm my emotions.

A quiet cough has my eyes flying open, and I'm spinning before I even realise what I'm doing, dropping into a defensive position.

"Oh!" A petite female shrinks back from me, her eyes going impossibly wide at my show of aggression. Her long, blonde hair is pulled back into a neat braid, exposing her pale skin. Her almost black eyes would mark her for one of the changed, even if her scar wasn't visible to all.

Sighing, I stand upright and press a hand to my temple. "Apologies, I was lost in my thoughts," I explain quietly, not expecting much of a response from her given my previous interactions with maids.

"Greetings, Lady Anthea, I didn't mean to startle you," she replies, recovering quickly. Her voice is steady, but I don't miss the slight tremble in her hands as she gestures to the doorway behind her. "If you are ready, please follow me to your quarters."

Although I've been visiting the castle for half of my life, and I certainly don't need a guide, I keep my thoughts to myself, nodding and gesturing for her to lead the way. Feeling bad that I frightened my attendant, I try to make up for it with some light conversation.

"Please, call me Thea."

One of my guards coughs in disapproval behind me at the informality in which I'm speaking with the female, but I ignore it. Social classes have always seemed strange to me, and I have never understood why someone of a lower class is considered less than someone from the higher classes.

"Thank you, Lady Thea."

I roll my eyes at her reply but fight the twitch of a smile that's trying to appear. We walk the rest of the way in silence until we reach the suites where my entourage and I will stay. All of my escorts, teachers, and guards stay in adjoining suites, a large central dining room connecting them. It's safer for us this way, keeping all the vampires in one place and easier to protect.

When I come to the city, I am always attended to by a vampire, specifically one of the changed, and it's always piqued my curiosity. Are the other brides attended to by one of their own race? Where is the king finding all these vampires to work here?

All races are welcome to call Drathlor City home, and while some vampires decided to settle here, it was predominantly the changed who made the move. Even then, not many decided to leave their homelands. Merfolk is another race that there aren't many of in the city, mostly for practical reasons, but their faith calls for them to be close to the sea. As Drathlor City is landlocked, that doesn't make it particularly habitable for anyone from Corallina.

Passing the shared living quarters, I follow my attendant into my suite. Made up of three adjoining rooms, it looks exactly as I left it. A lounge with long, comfortable day beds are placed by large windows, all of which are covered with a screen to stop the sunlight from coming in while still allowing me to enjoy the view. Bookcases line the far wall and is one of the other things I like about my six monthly visits. There is so much information waiting for me between those pages, and I can't wait to be alone and dive in.

To the right is the archway that leads to my bedchambers. Slowly walking through, I marvel at the huge bed that takes up half the room. I've slept on it many times, but I still can't get over how big it is. I could have three large males in the bed with me and still have space—not that anything like that could happen while I'm here, sharing my quarters with my guards.

Finally, on the other side of the room, is the doorway to my private bathroom. The bath is a beautiful sunken tub surrounded by sparkling tiles, and it's deep enough that I can fully submerge myself.

"I have everything set out for you," my attendant says.

"Please let me know if you need anything changed, and I'll be sure to do that for you."

Pulling my gaze from the obscenely large bed, I turn to take in the young woman. It's impossible to know how old she really is, but she looks like she was barely out of her teens when she was changed.

"I've not seen you here before. Where is my previous maid?"

The vampire who attended me for the last few years on my visits was also one of the changed, and she was so terrified of me that she barely spoke a word. I never even knew her name.

My new attendant looks uncomfortable, shifting her weight from foot to foot. "Unfortunately, my lady, she was found guilty of treason and was put to death. I am your new attendant."

Treason? The girl could barely look at me without shaking, and they are saying she committed treason? Unless she was an incredible actress, something doesn't seem right here. I know better than to say anything though. Until I can be sure of my new attendant's alliances, I have to assume her loyalties are with King Drath.

Due to this, I let her comment slide with a humming noise and quickly change the topic despite my burning curiosity about my previous attendant.

"Well, new attendant, do you have a name?"

Her discomfort quickly dissolves, and a small smile lights up her face. "Yes, my name is Bright. My mother said that my personality reminded her of the sun."

Bright. Yes, the name suits her. Although her emotions are composed, there is something sunny about her that makes me want to spend more time in her company. It might seem like an odd name for a vampire, but as one of the changed, she will have carried over her old attributes from before she died.

My gaze shifts to the garment lying on the bed, my brows rising in surprise. It seems that Bright has an eye for clothing, and the dress she picked will make me look like a queen.

Chapter Four

I have to give it to Bright, she knows how to pick an outfit for the occasion. The dress she managed to magic from somewhere is gorgeous and fits like a dream. It also fits with the style and fashion that the vampires prefer, without making me look out of place in a formal setting.

Vampires are pretty vain and find no shame in their bodies or sharing the forms we were born with. Because of that, it is common to see us wearing form-fitting and revealing clothing, showing off as much of our pale skin as possible. The lighter the hue of our skin, the more beautiful an individual is considered. I've been blessed with a creamy complexion that appears both pale and flawless, but a little warmer than the marble-like effect some of the vampires possess.

The top of the dress consists of a strapless corset, the plunging neckline displaying a generous amount of cleavage and the tattoo around the base of my neck that tells all exactly who I am. Delicate silver twists of metal have been shaped and linked together, then fixed onto the bodice in a beautiful design that looks both like a delicate floral pattern and armour. The lavender colour compliments my skin beautifully, the fabric darkening as it travels down my body until the bottom of the skirt is a deep, rich purple.

The skirt, mostly consisting of layers of purple mesh, gives my hips a curved shape. Paired with the long slit up to midthigh, I feel both feminine and fierce.

My silver hair hangs freely down my back, and a silver circlet sits upon my head. I don't bother to cover my face with powders and potions like some do, wanting my skin to remain as pale and smooth as possible. Instead, I swipe some mascara across my lashes and tint my lips with my favourite blood-red gloss.

I look like a warrior princess. The thought makes me smile.

I'm still looking at myself in the mirror when there's a knock on the door. Bright excuses herself to speak to the new arrival, only to return moments later, dipping into a curtsy.

"Lady Thea, your attendance has been requested on the patio for tea with the other brides."

My brow rises, the only outward emotion I allow, demonstrating just how surprised I am by this invitation.

The brides are rarely allowed to mingle, and now they are actually creating opportunities for us to meet. This has to be due to the upcoming wedding. Other than the humans, the rest of the denizens of this continent are long-lived, meaning that nothing happens particularly quickly. We age slowly and hold grudges for a long time, which makes us reluctant to act rashly. This means that everything is meticulously planned and has a reason behind it. The brides suddenly being thrown together isn't just a casual decision.

Wary at this sudden change, I smooth my expression and dip my head in agreement. Thankfully I'm already dressed, and when I step out into the shared living space, I find Geoff waiting for me. He obviously had a chance to change as well, his dark green jacket fitting like a glove and his hair slicked back. He appraises me just as I assess him, and other than a tiny nod of approval, he says nothing about my gown.

Bright approaches with a purple cloak that matches my dress, the silver fastenings at the neck giving the appearance of a choker rather than clasps. It sets off the whole outfit, and I feel ready for battle, my dress as my armour.

Geoff dismisses Bright with a wave of his hand, not bothering to look at my attendant as he offers me his arm. "I can take it from here."

From the corner of my eye, I see Bright simply curtsy and scurry from the room, seemingly not offended by the casual disdain my escort held towards her. Unfortunately, this type of behaviour towards the changed is not uncommon in Trador, and from the fact she didn't bat an eyelash at her dismissal, I'm guessing it is the same here.

I rest my hand over the top of his arm, and we're ready to go. Two guards accompany us, stepping ahead and opening the door for us, only for a familiar figure to stumble into the doorway.

"Felix," I call out in surprise, happiness lacing my words.

He looks dishevelled from travel and getting the horses settled, his clothing dusty and smelling slightly of horse, yet he still looks as handsome as ever. I've made a mistake, though, in allowing my pleasure to be witnessed, especially by Geoff. For most races, they wouldn't question the warmth in my voice, yet for vampires, I practically just shouted my affection for him. In the safety of my lands when it's just the two of us, I allow myself to be freer with my emotions around him. However, here, affection can be dangerous, and I need to remember not to act too familiar with him. Clearing my throat, I work on keeping my expression neutral, acutely aware of Geoff watching from my side.

He begins to smile in greeting when he finally realises what I'm wearing. His heated gaze travels the length of my body as he assesses each inch of me. "Thea..." He trails off, seemingly lost for words, and gives a slow shake of his head. "You look stunning." His lips curve up into an appreciative smile.

His reaction does something funny to me, and the feeling of butterflies taking flight in my stomach makes me giddy. I have no idea how to respond, especially with the audience we currently have.

Thankfully for me, Geoff takes that concern from me by releasing my hand and taking a step in front of me, blocking Felix from my sight. "Yes," he snaps, "and she's about to be late. Move."

I've never seen Geoff like this before. He's a master of controlling his emotions, and while I've seen him irritated and irked, he's never appeared this frustrated. In a way, he's almost acting defensively towards me, as though he's trying to protect me. This makes no sense though. He knows I'm perfectly capable of protecting myself, and he certainly wouldn't need to keep me safe from Felix of all people.

"Of course," my friend replies, looking contrite as he sketches a half bow and hurries out of the way. As we pass him, he gives me a wink so I know he's not been deterred by my stern guardian.

This time, I'm able to keep myself composed despite my amusement and keep my gaze ahead, guided away by Geoff.

The guards walk ahead of us, leading the way and acting as my protectors. The hallway is deserted. This part of the castle is a new addition, as are the quarters of the other brides, and it's located away from everyone else, connected to the castle proper by a long, thin bridge. There is one way in and out of my quarters, and as such, it's rare to see others in the hallway unless they are specifically coming to see me. Any who are afraid of heights would be unable to pass, the covered bridge connecting us to the castle high enough to make even me nervous.

We walk in silence, but I sense something brewing within Geoff and know it's only a matter of time before he says anything. We are almost at the bridge when he finally speaks again.

"If the changed boy is going to be a problem, I can see that he's removed from his duties." He speaks as though he's discussing the weather rather than the fate of my friend.

My stomach twists with a ball of emotions I don't know how to cope with as I turn my head to look at him and force a small smile onto my lips. It's the last thing I want to be doing right now, but if I can play it off lightly, then it might stay that way, and my escort will drop the subject.

"Geoff, he didn't mean to get in our way. He had no way of knowing we were leaving at that very moment."

"Do not play dumb with me, Anthea. I wasn't born yesterday." The look he gives me is scathing. He and I both know that the issue isn't Felix's timing, but our reactions to each other—reactions that neither of us were able to hide.

Not having anything to say to his comment that won't offend him or make me look like an imbecile, I simply stay silent, my dress swishing quietly in my wake. This was one of the most important things I've learned in my training—if in doubt, stay silent.

"Dalliances you had back in Trador is one thing, but you are about to be *married*. Not only that, but to the son of the man who could see to our ruin."

Raising my brow, I give him a look. He's going a little hard considering all I said was Felix's name. Everything he says is true, but all of this was triggered by a *smile*. Is there something more here I don't know? Are our relations with the king so weak that a simple smile could shatter it all? Dread settles in my stomach, and I try to push it aside. There is no point in jumping to conclusions nor panicking unless I'm given a reason to.

"Don't you think you're being dramatic?" I finally ask, desperate to end this conversation. "You're acting as though I stripped naked and fucked him in the corridor for all to see."

A hand whips out and stops me in my tracks. I frown down at the arm restraining me then turn my attention to Geoff. He looks as serious as ever, his expression telling me not to try and fool him. "I saw how you looked at each other. You're not nearly as good at hiding your emotions as you should be." Finally, he releases my arm and sighs, pressing his hands to his temple. I wait patiently, studying the empty hallway. "I'll drop this for now, Anthea." His voice carries a warning as he continues. "However, at the first sign of him being inappropriate with you, he's gone."

I know a threat when I hear one. Vampires aren't known for their forgiving natures or doing anything by halves. When Geoff said Felix would be gone, he meant for good. The thought of my friend being killed sparks an anger in me so strongly that I'm snarling before I know what I'm doing. My fangs lengthen, and my senses heighten at the threat, unable to distinguish between the threat of harm and an actual attack.

He crosses his arms over his chest, disapproval radiating from him. "This is exactly what I'm talking about, Anthea."

I'm overreacting, and I'm not even sure why I reacted so fiercely. There have been reports of vampires going feral when someone they love is hurt or threatened, but Felix is my friend, not a relative or lover.

"He is my friend. You won't lay a finger on him." My words are muffled thanks to my extended fangs, and slowly, my rage begins to calm and my body returns to normal. I'm still on edge, but I work hard at making sure my outward appearance is unruffled.

Geoff waits until I'm composed once more before speaking again.

"As long as you don't lay a finger on him either, then he will be fine." He snorts and shakes his head. "I thought you knew better than to make *friends*." He says the last word with disdain. "It will only end in heartache."

As we step off the bridge and into the warmth of the castle, Geoff effectively ends the conversation. There are too many listening ears here, and neither of us want to risk this getting back to the king. There's an energy in the hallways that almost makes them seem alive. Maids, servers, and other palace workers move through the halls with purpose. I'm used to them ignoring me, since I'm not an unusual sight here, yet today, I feel their eyes following me.

Ignoring it, I continue to follow the guards and focus on getting through the next hour with the other brides. I know the way to the patio, having been there before, and recognise that Geoff is just for show. The other brides will also have their chaperones and escorts with them.

Light chatter reaches me as we approach the wing of

the castle where the patio is situated. The stone walls open up so I'm completely surrounded by light. Why they chose to call this place a patio is beyond me, as it's totally enclosed in glass. Suitable for all weather, the dome-like structure glistens with magic imbued in the glass, lighting the area like twinkling stars. Despite the fact it's still dark outside, there is plenty of light to see with. Glancing up at the sky through the glass roof, I assess the position of the moon. The sun will begin to rise soon, and the view from here will be stunning. Built on a cliff edge, the structure is attached to the castle by only one wall, magic keeping it firmly attached. While terrifying, the view is astronomically gorgeous thanks to the glass wall.

A large table has been set up in the centre, its metal legs intricately twisted to create a pattern before disappearing up and under the tablecloth. Atop the table are several stands brimming with cakes, sandwiches cut into small triangles, and pieces of cooked meat. Steaming pots of tea await us, although I spot a wine glass full of red liquid that I know has been procured for me. Everyone else will be sipping tea while I dine on blood. It used to bother me that I was served blood in clear glasses at the banquets I attended, as it made me stand out. Nowadays, though, I have no such qualms.

Fully entering the patio, I spot four of the brides sitting at the table, their chatter dying down as I enter. I know them all by name, even though we've had little time together over the years. With an uncertain future, I made it my business to know who was part of the prophecy with me.

"Lady Anthea Rose of Trador," my guard introduces, his voice ringing around us.

Celest, the only princess amongst us, smiles and

gestures for me to come closer. "Lady Anthea, please join us."

At the invitation from the princess, Geoff moves over to stand with the other escorts, giving us the semblance of privacy.

Glancing around the table, I nod in turn to the females in greeting. Lady Ember from Brimstone is at the far end, and working around the table is Princess Celest of the shifters, Lady Mallory the reaper from the witch realm of New Spellman, and finally, Lady Bliss, who represents the merfolk of Corallina.

It seems that the new representative for the beasts has not yet found her way here, and given that she was the last to arrive, this is no big surprise. What does surprise me, however, is that Meadow of the centaurs isn't here yet.

"Anthea, a pleasure to see you, especially with such a joyous occasion just around the corner," Lady Ember comments with an edge to her voice as I take the seat beside Bliss, where my wineglass is waiting.

I'm pretty sure her mood isn't aimed at me, but the situation, because Ember is the second bride of the prophecy. It's not always easy to tell with her, as sharing the spirit of a dragon seems to make the whole race quicker to anger.

I sense tension, and I think I know why. For such a long time, we've all known of our fate, but it seemed so far away. With me being the first to wed, I'm setting off a chain of actions that was only a distant promise. Ember will be paired soon, and as a dragon, I know it goes against the customs of her people to have an arranged marriage, especially to someone outside of their race.

"Joyous, of course," I reply, keeping my smile tight. My eyes flit to the pretty porcelain cups and matching saucers on the table, and I note the effort that's gone into preparing this for us. "This little tea party is... unusual."

"The prophecy is now in action, so there is no point keeping us apart any longer," Bliss speaks, her voice like the twinkling of windchimes, captivating and inviting.

Everything about Bliss is seductive, from her gorgeous looks to the scent of a fresh ocean breeze. However, all of that is nothing compared to her voice. As a siren, her song is her weapon. The land of Corallina is filled with creatures of all types, shapes, and sizes, unlike the other lands.

Even now, away from the water, her sparkle hasn't dimmed. Her shimmering silver-blue hair frames her heart-shaped face perfectly, and her slim frame is draped in thin, gauzy fabric that shows off her body almost as much as mine. It shimmers in the light, a mixture of blue, purple, and silver. Her neck is adorned with pearls and matches the diadem she wears. In certain lighting, you can see the iridescent scales on her skin, but it's her pointed ears and webbed fingers and toes that truly mark her for what she is.

Of all the brides, she is the closest thing I have to a friend amongst them.

She represents all of the merfolk and other creatures that reside within the oceans and lakes. Many of these are unable to leave water, and some are bound to the body of water they inhabit, dying if they leave. Sirens can walk on land and live within solid houses, yet being away from water for too long will weaken them, and eventually, they will die.

Celest shakes her head, the small beads attached to her headdress clattering together with the movement. "I still don't understand why we were ever separated in the first place." The princess of the shifters is someone I know little of. All I've been able to gather over the years is that she's able to shift into a large feline and is part of the ruling royal family in their land. She's a little younger than those of us currently in the room due to the first bride of theirs dying from an illness in her childhood. This sometimes shows in her actions and thoughts, but I don't doubt that some of it is pretend.

"The king didn't want us becoming conspirators and finding a way around the prophecy," Ember snaps, bumping her hands on the table. Dragons, much like the shifters, transform into dragons, shedding their human skin. However, they are not tied to the phases of the moon like shifters.

Princess Celest looks fully human when not shifted, whereas Ember has the typical fiery red hair, deeply tanned skin, and a ridge of small horns that travel from between her brows and disappear into her hairline. Add this to the nails that look suspiciously like claws, and you could never confuse her with a full-blooded human.

A very unladylike snort comes from Lady Mallory, the reaper from the witches. The witches are renowned for their experiments, both in science and magic, and have discovered some great and powerful things that help us all. Because of this, they are generally well respected and thought of. Lady Mallory is a different matter altogether, as she is a reaper. Death magic is rare and doesn't manifest in a witch until they reach puberty. By that stage, it was too late to choose another bride, and she became one of the most feared females in the land.

"As if that would stop us." She rolls her eyes at the thought. "My people have been looking for ways out of the prophecy since it was announced. There is no way."

A heavy weight seems to settle over us with that depressing news. I've always known there was no way out of this fate for me other than death, yet if anyone was ever going to discover a way to break the prophecy, it was the witches. If Mallory says it can't be done, then I believe her.

"Where is Meadow? She's usually so prompt," Bliss comments lightly, glancing around the room as if the centaur is hiding behind one of the potted plants. She is obviously not here, but honestly, I'm just thankful for the change of topic.

There's a lull in the quiet conversation by the doorway where our advisors and escorts wait. I don't really pay it any mind until one of the advisors coughs, and we all turn to look at him.

A tall, stern-faced male with a small ridge of horns across his forehead looks over each of us, his hands clasped behind his back. "Meadow of the centaurs will not be joining us."

He's obviously Ember's escort and one of the dragons, his facial features giving him away. I've never had much to do with him in my time here, and I don't remember his name, but he has always been fiercely protective of Ember, and I keep an eye on him because of this. I'm confused why he's the one telling us this now though.

"Is she unwell? Has someone called for a medic?" Celest asks lightly, like she's asking after a distant relative. You would never have thought that we've all been through this journey together from our aloof reactions to each other. That is exactly what the king wants though, to keep us divided.

"You misunderstand me," the dragon escort retorts, his patience wearing thin. "The centaur is not coming for her yearly visit."

Silence meets his declaration, and it's clear I'm not the only one who is surprised. Glancing at Geoff, I see that even he's taken aback by the news. The dragons are not known for their humour, but I wait for him to crack a smile and tell us all he's joking.

We're not given a choice about whether we attend. In fact, it's continually made very clear what would happen if we *don't* follow the rules and spend six months of the year here. We all know the consequences and have been raised for this very purpose, so how is it that she's not here?

I glance over to where Ember sits, trying to see if she knew any of this beforehand, but her expression tells me this is news to her too. Before any of us can begin speaking, he sighs and addresses us again, realising he's going to have to provide more information than that.

"I received a message from her guardian just before we left our chambers to come here. There has not been any time for me to divulge this information until now."

I know for sure that the king will already know this information. Why did the centaur guardian send a message to him though? The centaurs and dragons are neighbours, their lands bordering each other, so they could have a closer bond because of this.

"How is this possible?" Mallory asks, her face set in a frown. "We have never been given an option on whether or not we attend before."

The dragon ambassador looks uncomfortable but doesn't shy away from the question. "From what I gather, the centaurs have decided to break away from the king. Not sending their representative was the first step in this."

"They are breaking away?" Bliss asks. "This will result in war. The king will not stand for this."

I can see why he's uncomfortable with this knowledge. It could be seen that the dragons agree with their neighbours about breaking away because they knew about it first.

Bliss is right though. Is this why the wedding has been called for now, after so many years? The king knew there was discord in the realms and talks of the lands taking back their power, so he's starting the prophecy as a reminder to everyone.

We're all here to make sure a war doesn't occur, and now the centaurs have decided they don't want to send their representative. Everything we've worked for, every birthday and holiday that I've missed because I've been here as required, was all wasted because of this one decision.

I shouldn't jump ahead. Things may not be as bad as they first appear. The king has diplomats for this very reason, and I'm sure they can come to a resolution that doesn't end up in innocent blood being shed. Even if the king did declare war over this, my people should be safe. We have nothing to do with what's happening.

"This is all I have been told. I'm sure the king will address the issue in due time," Ember's advisor comments, effectively ending the conversation with a sharp look in the direction of the guards standing by the doors.

Geoff appears uncomfortable with this information, and although he makes it look as casual as possible, he slowly walks over to me until he's standing behind my chair. To my eternal surprise, he lays a hand on my shoulder as a silent statement. This simple action tells me a lot. He's silently warning everyone in the room he would protect me, as well as warning me in the same breath that we might be in danger. I don't think he suspects that anyone in this room would try to hurt me, but it's a reminder of our roles here. Rebellion from one realm is dangerous, as it makes others believe that it could be an option for them too.

A flurry of activity happens around the door, and we all turn towards the sound, our movements jerky and on edge from what we just learned. My heart speeds up, adrenaline pumping through my body, and I clench the edge of the table tightly, ready to fight my way out should I need to. The other brides seem to have the same reaction. Bliss is halfway out of her seat, and I notice the princess's eyes are glowing as she holds back her spirit animal.

We seem to have overreacted, though, as several guards stop in the doorway and part for Hect, the advisor for the beast's chosen female. I've seen him many times over the years with his different charges, so I'm able to recognise him instantly—not that it would be difficult to guess where he's from. With a body like a bear covered in long fur from head to toe, he looks every inch the beast he is. Large horns extend from his forehead, yet his eyes are filled with a human-like intelligence.

"Lady Terra from the land of Barheer," he announces in a crisp voice, always surprising me with how civilised he sounds. I shouldn't judge by appearances or the stereotypes of their race.

Intrigued by our newest bride, I shift my attention to the female walking in behind him. She's younger than the rest of us but not a child like the previous beast representatives were. I would guess she's around twenty or so. They've obviously chosen a female who was already of age to represent them this time around rather than the children who usually arrive. Perhaps she might actually survive long enough to see out her part of the prophecy, her maturity helping her control her inner beast.

Her smooth, ebony skin seems to glimmer slightly, as though she has a golden sheen covering her. The land of the beasts contains creatures of all types, and I have no idea what Terra is. Long dark hair hangs down her back, with several braids decorated with tiny golden beads and hoops in it. Peeking through the hair atop her head is a pair of horns like that of a bull, which also have a golden sheen that I don't believe is from makeup. They look as sharp as daggers, and she holds her head high as she walks, secure in the knowledge that she's a walking weapon. The rest of her body gives nothing else away, but I swear I see her shadow moving independently to her.

Shadow stealer.

I've never met one before, but I've heard of them. They have the ability to trap someone's soul in their shadow and then steal it, feeding on it to sustain them. She's a dangerous creature to be around, and from the tension in the room, everyone else can feel the terrible power she leaves in her wake.

"Sorry I am late." Her voice is low and carries a note of authority, like she always knew she would end up here. "We arrived a short time ago, and I was famished, so I was just finishing my meal."

Now that I know what she feeds on, it makes her statement a little terrifying, but I give away no hint of my discomfort. Taking the seat opposite me, she sits down with a small smile, looking around the table expectantly.

"Which one of you is the lucky female to marry first?"

Chapter Five

As I stride through the castle corridors with Geoff at my side, I'm glad for the guards surrounding us. Usually I hate the constant escort I have here, yet after the news we were just given and Terra's arrival, I feel uneasy—not to mention the strange atmosphere that seems to fill the air like an invisible fog, making rational thought harder to reach.

The staff that passes us in the hallway watches me with a strange confidence that they don't usually possess. Instead of lowering their eyes, they meet my gaze and nod their heads, almost as though in respect. I'm not sure what has changed other than the fact I'm about to marry the prince. Has that shifted their attitudes towards me?

There is something more going on here, and everyone seems to know it except for me. I will find out what it is and rid myself of this awful uncertainty, but for now, I'm just glad we left the strange tea party on the patio and put some space between myself and the others. While I was already feeling out of sorts with the knowledge of my impending marriage with a male I've never met, knowing there's unrest in the other lands is unsettling. Too much is changing all at once. Does it have to do with the prophecy, or is everything we know beginning to fall apart?

Geoff and I have been maintaining our usual silence since we were summoned from the patio to meet with the king, yet I'm unable to hold my questions back any longer.

"Did you know anything about that?" Although I keep my voice low, there is more anger in my tone than I had intended and it takes me a moment to reign it in.

Geoff eyes me with displeasure. "The centaurs or the shadow stealer?"

"Both," I grit out through clenched teeth. We're supposed to be a team, and if I learn that he knew about the centaurs, I'm going to struggle to keep my composure. That sort of information is not something to keep from me. I need to know everything that involves the prophecy, especially as I'm about to fulfil my part of it. My head is pounding, and my fangs ache in my mouth, a sure sign that my body is priming itself to fight. I didn't even drink the spiced blood in the glass at the tea party, something I'm now regretting since I'm going to need all the strength I can get to make it through today.

"I heard that the new bride from Barheer was powerful and older than the previous representatives, but I had no idea what she was. I'm surprised that the king allowed it, to be honest, since they are dangerous creatures to have around." Clucking his tongue in disapproval, he shakes his head, keeping his gaze straight ahead. "Many have been put to death over the years. I was not aware that any of their kind remained."

The power of the shadow stealers is addictive, and no matter how innocent they begin, their hunger for souls grows over time, until they tear through villages and towns, ravaging them and leaving the dead husks of their victims behind as a calling card. That sort of power made them good assassins, until they turned on their employers. Eventually it was decided they were too dangerous, which is why there aren't many left.

Why has the king decided to allow her to be one of the brides? If she lost control and slaughtered half the castle, it would be devastating. However, having a shadow stealer on hand would be useful for the king, not to mention a huge deterrent for other lands to think about taking back control. He must have a way of controlling her.

I believe his explanation, but he's not yet answered the most important question. "And the centaurs?"

As I look at him, I notice the small signs of tension in him, such as the tautness he carries in his jaw. His eyes flick around us, surreptitiously looking around to see who is within hearing distance. "There have been rumblings from them for quite a few years, but no one ever thought they would be stupid enough to break off from the king."

While I can understand why he doesn't want to talk about this now, what I don't understand is why I was kept in the dark. Incredulous, I shake my head. "Why am I only just hearing about it now?"

"It was kept quiet to ensure that rebellions didn't break out, especially since none of us thought the centaurs would do anything so rash." The note of distaste is the only outward sign of Geoff's feeling towards the centaurs' actions. Clearing his throat, he turns his attention to me, taking in my appearance. "Are you ready for this meeting?"

I wonder what he would do if I suddenly told him I wasn't ready and I didn't want to do this—not that I would ever do that. This is about more than just me, it's about the prosperity of my people. Still, I can't help but wonder what his reaction would be.

Not long after Terra joined us, a messenger arrived with a missive from the king, requesting my presence immediately. No one offered me their best wishes or any form of luck, but the looks they gave me conveyed their understanding and silent support as I went to greet my fate.

"Of course, this is what I've trained for my whole life," I reply smoothly, the words coming easily as I respond exactly as I've been taught over the years, not letting a hint of my apprehension show.

A meeting with the king can only mean one thing. I'm going to meet my mate for the first time. Geoff informed me on the carriage ride over that the first time we met would be supervised, and after that, there would be a time for us to meet alone and get to know one another.

I would be lying if I said I wasn't a little excited to meet my mate. I've seen the bond between true mates in the past and am excited to have a connection so pure between myself and another, knowing for certain that the other person is a hundred percent made for you.

"Good," my advisor replies after a long moment, his look assessing. "Remember everything we taught you. I will be there if you need anything."

This is uncharacteristically nice of him, and it helps to reassure me. He might be stern, but he's been the only constant in my life. Not even my own father treats me with fondness.

I take a deep breath, feeling my lungs expand, and hold it for a second, clearing my mind. With a slow, smooth exhale, I allow all of my negative emotions to leave with the air I expel from my body.

I am ready for this.

As we've moved through the castle, I have noticed that there are less and less people in the hallways, indicating we're getting closer to the king's office. Guards appear as we turn into another corridor, and I know we're here.

We stop outside of the heavily guarded door, and one of the guards goes inside to announce our arrival. I take a moment to glance around at the opulence surrounding me. Even without the six fully armed guards stationed outside, it would be impossible to mistake this wing of the castle as belonging to anyone other than royalty. The door is wooden and intricately carved with representations of each race, and it makes me wish I had more time to study the depictions. Rich woven rugs line the hallway, which is much larger and better lit than the other corridors I've traversed so far. Windows line the wall, allowing the pink light from the rising sun to illuminate the space.

After only a moment, the guard slips through the doors and bangs his staff on the ground, an action the others repeat. If one didn't find the synchronised sound intimidating as it echoes in the hall, then the golden sparks that burst from the bottom of their staffs would be enough to put anyone on edge.

"The king is ready to see you," the first guard announces, and with a wave of his hand, the huge double doors to the king's office open independently.

Shaped like a semicircle, the king's office is more like a miniature library, bookshelves covering every spare inch of the curved walls. Directly opposite the doors is a huge bay window, filling the room with light. The tiled floor is spotless, and the heavy drapes around the windows are neatly tied back with golden cords. In the centre of the room is a large desk with a throne-like chair behind it. My eyes pass over the stacks of books on the king's desk, and I can't help wondering what he's reading.

Four large, plush chairs are set up in a semicircle facing the desk, one of which is already taken by one of the king's advisors.

Of course, the only thing that is left is the king himself, who stands by the window, watching the sunrise.

"Your Majesty," I greet, dropping into a deep curtsy as Geoff does the same from behind me. Protocol dictates that we hold our gestures of respect until the king acknowledges us, and I've heard rumours that he's made some people wait for hours before allowing them to stand. However, while I hold my curtsy, I allow my eyes to flick up and take in the figure of the king.

No one is quite sure what race King Drath is. I've heard whispers that he's a hybrid of several races, and that's why he is so powerful. A lot of his kingdom is made up of the other races who have decided to leave their homelands behind.

He has a large build that is all muscle. His golden, mane-like hair travels down his back, and the only thing keeping it in order is the golden circlet he wears. There is a feline look to his face that I've never quite been able to place, and his almond-shaped eyes have a slitted pupil rather than a circular one. Sharply pointed ears poke from his hair, and the nails on his hands are more like claws. I have no doubt that he could gut me with one slash of his wrist. He appears to be middle-aged, but I have no idea what his true age is. The power he exudes would make me think he's far older than he appears.

The king continues to stare out of the window, his eyes locked on something I'm unable to see from my angle. There's a yearning in his expression that I doubt he meant for us to see, and with a sigh so quiet I almost don't hear it, he pulls away from the window and faces us.

"Greetings, Anthea, Advisor Geoff."

Straightening from my curtsy, I ignore my protesting leg muscles and dip my head to him in reverence. The king smiles, watching me with keen eyes, and there's no sign of the quiet, thoughtful male I saw just a moment ago.

"It is an exciting time for our lands as we form a union that will bind us together in peace and prosperity." He smiles as he speaks, but it looks more predatory than welcoming. "You are the first bride, so many eyes will be on you, and as such, I need everything to go smoothly. This wedding has to go ahead."

The weight behind his words and the silent order is loud and clear. I have no say, and if I want my land to thrive, then this is what I must do. Thankfully, I have been trained for this since birth, so I don't blink at the order.

"Of course, Your Majesty," I reply as expected. In my mind, however, I'm going over his words, reading more into it since I learned of the centaurs. Talk of bringing us together just makes me think that my original thought was right. The wedding is taking place now because of the unrest with the centaurs. By giving the citizens something to be excited about and showing the eager participation from the vampires, it will distract from any talk of rebellion.

"Good," he purrs in satisfaction. "The fact that you are true mates with my youngest son... I'm taking it as a sign from the universe that we are going to beat this prophecy." He signals to his advisor who stands and slips from the room through a side door.

"Anyway, enough of that," the king continues. "I suppose it's time for you to meet your mate." His eyes glisten.

My heart clenches painfully in my chest, and a strange feeling builds in my stomach—one that I can't decide if it's excitement or nerves.

The side door opens again, and the king's advisor leads the way, followed by three males. One must be the prince's advisor, as he is much older than the other two and is wearing the king's colours of gold and red. He steps to the side to allow the prince and his companion to enter the room.

My gaze should go straight to my mate, after all, we're destined to be, however my eyes get stuck on the other male. Tall and broad shouldered, the male is grace personified, his every move fluid and smooth. His face is beautiful in a way I've never seen on a male, and his pointed chin and bright eyes make him look mischievous. I've only ever seen glimpses of this male before. Finnik is the prince's best friend and constant companion, as he tends to stand back in public. His dark hair looks as though someone has been running their fingers through his locks, and there's a slight wave to it that only makes his mischievous expression all the more obvious. When I look at his ears, I feel like my heart has stilled in my chest, and I glance at his face to confirm what I suspect.

Fae. He's fae.

How did I not notice this before? Now that I'm close, it's so obvious, even though I've only ever seen one of the elusive creatures before.

There's a pulling in my chest, and I finally give into the feeling and meet the angry, golden-eyed stare of the prince —my mate. It is the strangest feeling to be drawn to him in such a familiar way despite never having even spoken to him.

From the small glimpses I've had of him, I've always

known he's handsome, and now, seeing him face to face... He's gorgeous. Even scowling, he still looks regal and princely. I want to say something, to greet him or drop into a curtsy, but before I can, he bares his teeth in a snarl.

"Take this disgusting creature away. I will *not* marry."

Chapter Six

Those words rock me to my very core, my soul screaming within me at the rejection. I stumble back a step as pain rips through my chest, feeling as though my heart is trying to tear itself apart. It is agony unlike anything I've ever experienced before, and a part of me I didn't know existed withers within me at the harsh words. A pained gasp escapes me, and I press a hand against my chest in the hopes that it might stop the pain and hold me together.

Geoff is there in an instant, his hand on my shoulder as he steadies me, his fangs flashing in the light. I've never seen him so angry before, and if it didn't feel like I was falling apart, then I'd marvel at this side of him. My eyes are locked on the prince, looking for any reason why he would reject me like this, but all I see is hatred. I'm aware of other people in the room, yet my entire focus is on my mate.

"What is the meaning of this?" Geoff demands, his steady hand against my shoulder the only thing that's keeping me grounded. Without it, I think I would disappear in the pain of the rejection.

"Son, we have spoken about this." The king's power fills the air, breaking through my daze enough for me to notice the anger lacing his tone.

The prince looks away to glare at his father, and I'm finally able to break away from his stare and inhale a huge breath of air. I hadn't realised that I was holding my breath. No wonder my lungs were screaming and I was light-headed. Attempting to regulate my breathing, I look between the king and his son who are having a quiet, hissed conversation. Their emotions are written across their faces, both of them not accustomed to hiding feelings like vampires. I can see the similarities between Prince Havoc and the king, both of whom possess golden hair, yet the prince's locks are shorter, the perfect length to run your fingers through, and his eyes are a startling blue, the colour of the sky in full summer.

I feel so lost. It's becoming clear that this isn't the first time the king and his son have had this conversation. Drath must have thought his son would fall in line once I arrived and everything was set in motion, but it seems to have done the opposite.

That connection the prince and I share twinges in my chest, and I wince at the feeling. Prince Havoc's head whips around to look at me, accusation turning his expression dark. He turns back to his father. "No, I won't do this, Father. I refuse."

The king's body seems to swell at the refusal. "She is your mate."

His voice is deadly calm, and he says this as though that reason alone is enough. It should be enough. That is the surety of what the bond offers, so why is the prince denying it?

"I don't care. This is *wrong*. *She* is wrong." His voice

gets louder with each statement, hitting me like a dagger to the chest.

"Havoc," the fae says quietly from his side, a note of caution there as he glances towards me, all signs of playfulness long gone.

"No, Finnik." The prince gestures roughly towards me, his teeth bared like he's going to try and bite me. "I will not be tied to a *creature* like her."

He wants to bite? Well, I know all about biting, and he can bring it on. I will not continue to stand here and be insulted. The pain still pulses through me, but I remind myself who and *what* I am, and I can push it aside and focus on my anger instead. He sounds like a petulant child trying to get out of doing his schoolwork, and I'm about to give him a dose of the truth that will make him see me differently. I'm not some meek and mild lady from their court, I am a vampire, and we do not take insults like this lying down.

"Like it or not, prince, you are tied to me," I state, my voice strong as I channel my anger forward. "We are mates. I know you can feel the connection, the pull between us."

He can't deny the truth of my words, and for a moment, he simply glares at me. I wait for him to tell me I'm wrong, but he surprises me by turning back to his father, ignoring my comment completely.

What an ass.

"It doesn't have to be this way." Stepping closer to his father, he tempers the anger in his voice, trying to reason with the ruler. "Marrying her won't stop the centaurs from rebelling."

This is confirmation of what I feared. They are speeding up the marriages in hopes it will bring unity to the lands and stop rebellions. Geoff stiffens beside me, and I know he made the connection too. The state of peace across the lands must be far more fragile than I realised.

"For the sake of the prophecy and the fate of our kingdoms, I suggest you choose your next words carefully." The king is clearly furious, his words biting as he glares down at his son. "Leave us. I need to speak with Lady Anthea, and I think you need a reminder of exactly who is in charge here."

Stiffening at the dismissal, the prince spins on his heel and leaves the office via the door he arrived through, not so much as glancing in my direction. The bond pulses in my chest again, creating a wave of pain and dizziness at the cruel rejection. The prince's advisor hurries from the room without a word, and the fae glances at me once, his brows furrowed as he walks out.

Geoff looks murderous at my side, glaring at the king as though he is personally responsible for every vile word the prince spewed. His mouth opens, and I prepare for him to demand answers from the king, but he seems at a loss for what to say. Honestly, I don't blame him. Neither of us expected a reaction like that, and now everything I've prepared for is dead in the water.

"Please, take a seat." He gestures to the chairs opposite the desk, his face weary. It's strange seeing someone so powerful looking so... weak. That is the only reason I slowly walk over to the chairs. All I want to do is retreat to the dark, gorge myself on blood, and hide until the sting of being refused eases. However, I know I need to hear the king out, and while Prince Havoc might not care about the future of his people, I do, and I can't just abandon them.

Geoff takes the seat next to me, his anger radiating from him, but he keeps his mouth shut, watching the king with a wary expression. The king's advisor, who has remained silent during this whole interaction, continues to do so, and it's easy to forget he's even here.

"My son is struggling with this transition," the king begins, leaning against the edge of his desk as he faces us. "He seems to think there is something wrong with the brides, and that they are tainted and will destroy us." Pulling an expression that indicates exactly what he thinks of that belief, he slowly shakes his head. "He's always been reluctant to act out his part in the prophecy, but until recently, I had no doubt that he would go ahead with it. Then, when we announced the marriage between you two, he seemed to change. He has always had an attitude, but he would never act as he has today. For that, I can only apologise. I think fear is making him act like this. You need not worry though, he will do his duty, and I know I can trust you to follow your destiny."

Havoc kept saying I was wrong, that I was a creature. I assumed he meant because I was a vampire, but if the king is to be believed, then it could be because I am one of the brides from the prophecy, in which case, he would feel the same way about all of the brides.

"Of course, Your Majesty," I reply as expected of me, my voice surprisingly steady. Making the most of that miracle, I do something that's *not* expected of me, and question the king. "What will happen if he refuses the match?"

"That will not happen," he assures me, giving me a smile that is supposed to reassure me. However, I am an expert at reading hidden emotions, and I can tell he's furious at his son and unsure of what will happen. "I will arrange for you to spend some time together so you can get to know each other. He will come to his senses. You are a beautiful female, he would be a fool to turn you away."

I was ready to leave the king's office peacefully, but that

final comment causes my hackles to rise. Of course the only factor in a marriage is how beautiful the bride is, and because I fit that category, I would make a perfect wife. It has nothing to do with my intelligence or skills with a blade. His son is a fool because he could miss out on having a gorgeous female such as me on his arm. My sarcastic thoughts are so loud in my mind, I almost expect him to hear them.

He most likely didn't mean it that way, but I can't help myself. Females are treated equally where I'm from, but I know that's not the case in most of the lands. Clearly the king has the same attitude. Females are for marrying and breeding, that is all.

Tilting my head to one side, I narrow my eyes ever so slightly, and I see Geoff stiffen in his seat. He knows exactly what's coming, having watched over me my entire life, yet there is nothing he can do to stop it—not without causing a scene.

"Even a *creature* such as me?" I ask sweetly, putting emphasis on certain words to make it known I've not forgotten what the prince said about me.

The king stares at me in surprise, one of his brows rising. He's likely trying to figure out if I'm asking a serious question or if I'm making a dig.

"Anthea," Geoff cautions quietly beside me, attempting to rein me in before I can get us into trouble. Needing to pull the king's focus from me, my advisor clears his throat. "Your Majesty, are you able to offer me assurances that this union will continue as planned? My king will be most upset when he discovers what has happened here today."

This certainly gets the king's attention. Honestly, I'm surprised. I've heard Geoff speak like this to leaders and

Kings before, but never King Drath, the ruler who holds the safety of our land in his hands.

"Need I remind you that I want this prophecy fulfilled just as much as you do?" King Drath replies gruffly, his intense gaze trained on Geoff. "Everything will happen as planned."

Geoff bows his head deeply, assured for the time being. "Yes, of course, Your Majesty."

Releasing a huff of air, the king rolls his shoulders and shakes out his hair before brushing down the front of his royal red and gold robes. He glances over his shoulder, spotting the glowing top of the rising sun.

"Get some sleep, you must be exhausted after the long trip. The sun will be up soon, so you can avoid the hustle and bustle if you go now. The ball will be tonight, and all will go to plan." Gesturing towards the exit, he makes it clear that we're to leave him in peace, thinly veiling it with the excuse of avoiding others.

After everything that happened, avoiding the other brides and hiding in my rooms until sundown sounds perfect. Standing, Geoff and I bow our heads and leave the office without any further instruction.

My guards meet us outside the office where they've been waiting in the corridor, eyeing the king's guards with suspicion. They have never trusted the castle guards to keep us safe, frequently telling me those males will only ever look out for the king. They fall into formation around us, and we make our exit, leaving the royal wing of the castle and entering the main corridors.

Due to the sudden foot traffic, neither of us say anything, walking in companionable silence. However, in my mind, it's anything but quiet. My thoughts spin around and around, twisting in on themselves and distorting until I don't know what's real and what's a figment of my overactive imagination. Did the prince reject me because he thought I wasn't good enough, or is my mind exaggerating? On the outside, my face is a mask, not moving a single muscle as we walk back to our wing. I'm afraid that the slightest movement will crack it, and my calm outer façade will crumble.

I cannot afford to fall apart here. I am stronger than this.

After what feels like the longest walk I've ever taken, we arrive at the bridge separating my rooms from the main castle. I imagine if anyone were to look out now, I would look like a ghost, my pale skin glowing in the low light of the dawn, my hair and dress billowing around me as I walk.

"Well, that didn't go as expected." My voice is quiet as I break my silence now that we're back in the deserted corridors. Despite myself, I'm unable to hide my disappointment, and I have to grapple with the emotion before the rest of my tangled feelings force their way out.

"Prince Havoc is an entitled fool," Geoff spits, still furious. "He can't just *refuse* to marry you—not when the prophecy insists you marry. He is your *mate*, it is his responsibility and duty. If our realm falls, his will too." He's practically shouting now, which I've never seen from him before. I didn't even know he was capable of experiencing emotions like this.

We get back to my rooms, the guards opening the doors for us to pass through. Back in our space, I feel more comfortable and know we can't be overheard, but it's not home no matter how we try to pretend otherwise. Kicking off my heels, I groan with relief and reach up to remove the circlet in my hair. I'm ready to fall into bed, and with the way I feel, I will swan dive in and surround myself with cushions. If I don't remove my shoes and jewellery now, then I'll be sleeping in it.

"We should strategize and come up with a plan."

Groaning, I turn around and see my advisor pacing the length of the shared living space. This is how he manages when situations go wrong, but I don't have the energy to sit around and discuss my rejection in detail.

"Geoff, I'm exhausted, and my heart feels like it's been stabbed. I need to sleep."

He looks at me for a moment, on the edge of arguing with me. However, hearing the plea in my voice, his expression softens, and he sighs, rubbing a hand across his face. "Fine, get some sleep, and we'll plan when you wake."

Turning, I hustle towards my rooms, my dress swishing around me when Felix steps into my path.

"Thea..." He trails off when he sees my face, obviously sensing my dejection. He's at my side in a second, clasping my shoulders. "What happened?"

I know that if I talk to him, I'll end up breaking down, and that's something I won't do in front of my guards and escorts. Instead, I pull away from his hold and gesture for him to follow me into my bedroom.

He frowns, clearly confused why I would need to speak to him in my room, but he immediately follows, shutting the door quietly behind him.

I stand in front of the mirror, my back turned to him as I attempt to suppress my pain, my eyes stinging with tears. "The prince doesn't want me." It's supposed to sound casual, a fact that's not tearing me up inside. What actually comes out is scratchy and strangled. "He thinks I'm a disgusting creature and refuses to marry me."

"Oh, Thea." He steps up behind me, placing his hand

on my shoulder, and looks at me in the mirror. "You are beautiful inside and out, don't let him tell you otherwise."

Tears track down my cheeks at his sweet words. I don't know why I'm so upset, but there is something about Felix that makes me feel more real, and I become more vulnerable and honest about my feelings. It's the complete opposite of what our kind believes.

Felix makes a noise of comfort and wraps his arms around me. I'm expecting a hug, but when he lifts me, I don't protest, instead leaning against his chest. He carries me over to my bed and gently places me down, pulling the sheets over me even though I'm still dressed.

I don't know why I'm crying. I've never been one to cry over a male before, and as I consider it, I realise that I'm not sad he doesn't like or want me. That doesn't bother me. I know others find me attractive. He doesn't have to find me attractive to marry me. While it stings that he already decided that he didn't want me because of my race, that's not the reason for my tears. I can't do anything about the fact that I was born a vampire, so yes, I'm offended at his blatant dislike of my people.

However, what truly makes me upset is that I'm not good enough. If I was a better first bride, he might have liked me and at least given it a go for the good of our people. Rejecting me means the prophecy won't come to pass, and my people will die. War will ravage our lands, all because the prince said no.

Felix shuts the blackout curtains and turns to leave. Something akin to panic forms in my chest, and I reach out before I even realise what I'm doing.

"Don't leave."

Felix freezes, his expression torn. "Thea, I don't think that's a good idea."

Rejection stings again, and pain laces through me, causing me to wince as it steals my breath. I couldn't be like this with anyone else, they wouldn't understand, and Felix is one of my closest friends. I need him right now. When I wake up, I'll be back to my normal self and make a plan with Geoff and the others. Here and now, though, I need to be vulnerable.

"Please." My voice cracks. "Just hold me until I fall asleep."

I see the moment he decides to stay, something in his eyes shifting. He approaches the bed, pulling the sheets tightly around me and climbing on. My rational mind is telling me that if I was found with another male in my bed, it would spell bad news for all of us, which is why he's lying on top of the covers, using it to separate us. My rational mind is currently *not* in control, however, and it just feels like more rejection.

I stop caring as soon as he wraps his arms around me though, his muscular body pressing against mine. The covers do little to stop me from feeling the ridges of his muscles.

"I've got you," he whispers, pulling me close.

Something in my chest loosens, and for just a moment, the pain from the prince's refusal eases. Felix smells like home, and with him close to me, it doesn't take long for me to fall asleep.

I'm not sure when he left my rooms during the day, but when I wake up from nightmares of being rejected over and over, he's no longer at my side. Tossing and turning, I try to go back to sleep, but the words from the dream echo in my mind.

Not good enough. You're not good enough.

Chapter Seven

The welcome ball, held once every year at the beginning of the brides' six month stay, is something King Drath has hosted for the last five years, and it is opulent to the extreme.

Originally, the king started it in preparation for when we are officially introduced to the kingdom as the chosen brides. However, it would be next to impossible for someone *not* to know who we are thanks to our upbringing. It did give us the opportunity to practice attending an event with so many creatures from different realms, as we've mostly been brought up in isolation away from everyone else.

Tonight's ball, however, will be different, as it is the first where one of us will be announced as an intended bride.

The other brides and I currently wait in a small room adjoining the ballroom. Our escorts and advisors stand off to the side, talking in low voices but never taking their eyes from their charges—all except Geoff, who is at my side, brushing his hand down my outfit and rearranging my skirts for the hundredth time. His unflappable demeanour isn't present tonight, and it's strange seeing him on edge like this.

"You know what you have to do. You have trained your whole life for this."

This is not the first time I've heard him say this, and I am sure it won't be the last. I believe he's trying to give me a pep talk after my disastrous meeting with the prince, but he's wrong, I *don't* know how to deal with this. Never in my whole time of training did I consider that the prince wouldn't want me at his side.

Movement catches my eye, and I look up in time to see someone walking towards me.

"Lady Thea," Bliss greets brightly. The other brides have kept their distance, most likely because of the tension rolling from myself and Geoff.

"Bliss." I dip my head in return, forgetting to address her formally.

From anyone else, they might not notice the slipup, but I am a stickler for getting titles right, and Bliss knows this. Raising a brow, she tilts her head, her eyes becoming more assessing as she looks me over.

"Your dress is stunning," she comments after a few heavy seconds pass, a hint of jealousy in her voice.

She's right, it is a beautiful garment. The dress is the colour of autumn leaves, starting with brighter colours at the shoulders and bodice, and slowly transitioning into burnt oranges and deep reds at the bottom. Hundreds of tiny fabric leaves have been bound together over pads to form epaulets, which exaggerate the shoulders of the dress. Small twists of stiff brown fabric made to look like branches have been curled and attached to the epaulets, giving it a dramatic, imposing effect. From a distance, they looked like armour, but as you come closer, you can see the movement of the individual leaves.

Skintight sleeves the colour of egg yolk end in delicate points by my fingers, with glittering details catching the light depicting falling leaves. My bodice is a mixture of oranges and reds, blending into each other seamlessly. The front panels of the bodice are decorated with swirls of golden embroidery. In comparison to the rest of the dress, the skirts are relatively plain, with layers of different coloured gauzy fabric that shift with each move, flashing a different autumn hue. However, what brings the two pieces together are the red embroidered leaves and vines creeping down from the bodice to the skirt. It looks as though the dress is alive, the vines growing on the fabric.

My dress for the ball was organised months ago, and this design had originally been picked as a representation of my transition from a lady of Trador to a princess of Drathlor. It was a beautiful idea. Wearing it after being rejected by the prince, however, changed the meaning behind it for me. Now, I feel like one of those autumn leaves, full of life but slowly losing my life force and becoming obsolete.

"Thank you," I reply with a small, tight smile, hoping she's not able to see past the dress and into the despair inside me. "You look beautiful tonight."

I mean it. Her hair is pulled back and pinned up with seashells, and she looks ethereal. She wears minimal makeup, only some gloss on her lips and a swipe of mascara to exaggerate her lashes. Her dress is one-shouldered in design and fairly simple, and it's a mix of gauzy fabrics that look like sea foam, swishing like a gentle wave as she moves.

Waving off my comment, she looks at my face as though

she's searching for something. "This night is about you. How did your meeting with the king go?"

While she's the closest thing I have to a friend here, we still don't know each other much thanks to being kept apart, which means I don't know how much I can trust her with.

Everyone will know sooner or later. Will Prince Havoc reject me in front of everyone tonight, or will the king make good on his promise? Either way, my life is not going to turn out as expected. My options are dismal. He will either refuse our bond and everyone will know, or I will be married to a male who hates what I am. Even just knowing this starts the painful throbbing in my chest. It feels like an open wound. If I'm feeling this bad, then it *has* to be affecting him too, even if it's my second-hand pain. He can't be completely spared from this agony.

Geoff is looking at me sternly, and I know he wouldn't want me to say anything to Bliss about what happened. Keeping my gaze away from him, I take a deep breath and meet her questioning eyes, needing a female friend to support me.

I turn away from the other brides and guide her to follow me, not wanting to announce my troubles to the others. "The prince is refusing to marry me."

Geoff makes a small noise beside me, disagreeing with my choice to share my news with the siren. I don't regret my decision, though, as I see emotions flitting across her face.

Whatever she was expecting me to say, this clearly wasn't it. Confusion, anger, and second-hand pain are written across her features, open and easy for me to read. Her whole posture changes, seeming to become bigger as she takes a step closer to me. I think she might be trying to protect me from the others, and I can't put into words how much I appreciate her.

"Thea..." Her voice trails off. At first I think it's out of sympathy, but I quickly realise she isn't feeling sorry for me, she's anticipating what the pain of the experience must be like and how that's hurting me. "I thought that perhaps you were having doubts about marrying him. I had no idea that *this* was what you were dealing with. Can I do anything for you?" she asks, and before I can even reply, her expression shifts again, and indignation colours her face. "He's your mate, he can't just say no. What happens now? Oh, if I get my hands on him..." She seems angry on my behalf, and that affirms something inside me. Seeing her reactions lets me know that what I'm feeling is valid. While it doesn't take away the pain, sharing this has relieved some of the burden from my shoulders.

"I don't know. The king said he would talk to his son and everything would go ahead as planned." Shrugging, I glance over my shoulder at the other brides. They have been sending a few curious glances my way, but I'm sure none of them can overhear our conversation.

"But... he's your *mate*," Bliss continues, flabbergasted by what she learned, "not just a random male the king paired you with. How could he just refuse you? What about the prophecy? It makes no sense."

I have no way to explain any of it to her as I don't understand it myself. The one surety I had was that I was going to be marrying my mate, and that everything would work out because I would have his unfailing support at my side. "I know."

My head pounds and my stomach cramps uncomfortably with my stress. I'm starting to regret the fact that I turned down a feed earlier, my stress making it harder to control my baser instincts. While blood feeds and nourishes me, it also helps me keep my feral side at bay and calms me in general—something that I could really use right now.

The door that leads into the ballroom swings open, and a tall male enters. Glancing around, he seems to do a headcount before nodding to himself and clearing his throat. "The king is ready for you. Please line up."

We all start to move, knowing what's expected of us. Being the first bride, I'm expected to take my place at the front of the queue. Ember, Bliss, Mallory, Terra, and Celest will all line up behind me in order of the prophecy. Usually Meadow would take the final spot as the last bride, but today it is just the six of us. Will the king address the issue?

"If you want me to drown him for you, just let me know," Bliss whispers as she passes me to line up. If I wasn't feeling so raw, I might have taken her up on the offer, although the scary thing is, I think she would actually do it.

Moving into position, Geoff offers me his arm, and as the doors swing open, we step into the ballroom. There is no time to be nervous, and I know better than to look around. Instead, I keep my gaze ahead and shoulders back. With the dramatic dress, I look like a queen, so I adopt that persona so no one can see the damage their prince caused in my heart.

"The first bride, Lady Anthea from Trador and mate to Prince Havoc."

The announcement fills the room, and I feel hundreds of eyes on me, all assessing. Quiet murmurs surround me, yet I ignore them all and continue walking through the space until I reach the king's dais. The king watches me with interest, his expression approving as he takes in my fierce outfit. All of the princes are at his side, including my mate, but I refuse to look at him. Dropping into a low curtsy, I feel Geoff bow beside me.

"Welcome, Lady Anthea. Please stand."

I'm glad he doesn't make us wait long, the weight of the dress making it difficult. He gestures for me to move to the side, and I do, knowing I'm expected to stand to the right of his throne while he greets the others.

"The second bride, Lady Ember from Brimstone."

The announcement causes attention to shift from me to the dragon representative. She looks fierce, a dragon walking in human skin. Her dress is tightly fitted and looks like thousands of tiny black scales all overlapping, only flaring once it reaches her knees, the heavy fabric then falls back behind her to reveal her legs.

When she reaches the king, she curtsies, and the king dismisses her. She joins me, and so the routine continues.

"The third bride, Lady Bliss from Corallina." Bliss smiles as she glides through the ballroom, her dress swirling around her. I swear I can smell the scent of the ocean and hear the call of gulls, but when I pay closer attention, it disappears.

"The fourth bride, Lady Mallory from New Spellman."

Wearing a simple black dress, the witch looks bored with this whole affair. Mallory has never been one for extravagant dresses, preferring the simpler clothing many of her people choose to wear.

"The newest bride, Lady Terra from Barheer."

It's no surprise to me that this announcement causes a murmur of conversation throughout the room as Terra makes her way towards the king. She wears a dress of deep green and has vines and dark purple flowers wrapping around her torso. At first glance, it seems like a very feminine and unlikely choice for the beasts, yet I examine her dress closer and see the flowers are deadly nightshade.

"Finally, the sixth bride, Princess Celest."

There are whispers in the hall as the nobility realises that one of the brides is missing, as well as the fact that the centaurs have no representative here. As I glance around, I see that there aren't actually *any* centaurs in attendance. That's strange. While there are never many of them here because of their love of open spaces, there are always several centaur nobles who stay here. Is that because of the talk of rebellion? Did they leave, or were they forced to go?

The princess ignores the whispers and makes her way to the king. Her dress is a little like a toga, the blue fabric draped around her to create delicate folds and pleats, the rest of the fabric trailing behind her. Bells, gems, and jewellery are artistically draped around her too, and each step she takes creates a quiet jingle.

With all of us standing in line to the king's right, we look out at the nobles. Males and females from the realms fill the hall, although the majority of them are the same unknown race as the king.

Everyone's attention returns to King Drath as he stands from his throne and opens his arms wide. "Welcome, one and all, to the official welcoming ball."

A low, excited murmur fills the space. This is all a game to them, seeing which bride will be paired off with whom. I can't really blame them when that is exactly what the king wants—distract them from the destruction the prophecy promises and any whispers of rebellion, and instead dazzle them with glimmering dresses and grand balls. Even the way we are displayed under spotlights for everyone to see takes away our personal lives and turns us into property.

"We have waited a long time for this moment, and I can now announce that the prophecy is in motion. Please welcome our brides and applaud their dedication."

Applause fills the room, and the excitement rises so

much I can feel it in the air. The hair on my arms stands on end, and all the attention is making me uncomfortable.

The king waits until the clapping dies down, then he continues to speak, his expression settling into a frown. "As you might have noticed, the bride from the centaurs is not here. It is something we are dealing with, so there is no need for concern about her part in the prophecy."

That's it? That is all he is going to say, simply that they are dealing with it and to cast it from our minds? Surely they can't expect this to be enough of an explanation.

He claps his hands together loudly and smiles once more. "On to more exciting news. Our first pairing will happen at the end of the month between Lady Anthea and my youngest son, Prince Havoc."

He sounds so proud, and this time the applause seems warmer, more genuine. The nobility seems to be fond of the prince and pleased for him that he found his mate. If only they knew. They also don't seem to be concerned over the missing bride, taking their king's word and following blindly.

He turns slightly, not looking away from the crowd of nobles before him, and gestures for me to come to him. Receiving the same gesture to come forward, Havoc reluctantly climbs from the dais to join us. He stands only inches away from me, close enough to touch. It takes all of my willpower to keep looking straight ahead and not reach out and give into my needs. The bond twists in my chest, and I lose my battle, turning my head to gaze up at him. I feel like I'm holding my breath as I wait for his reaction. He looks over at me, giving me an assessing appraisal. His gaze lingers on my chest, and I see a flicker of interest in his eyes. However, when he looks at my face, he grimaces and looks away.

A lance of pain threatens to take me down, but I manage to stay upright, only a grimace pulling at my face. I want to scream and yell, to rip at my hair in my agony and make him see what he's doing to me.

That is not the way of the vampires though. Somewhere in the darkness behind me, I feel Geoff's stare and use that to strengthen me, attempting to channel his cool demeanour.

Hundreds of people are watching us, clapping and murmuring about what a wonderful pair we make, yet there's a particular set of eyes that burn against my skin. Managing to keep my frown from my face, I look up and follow the heat of the gaze. The lights in the room are positioned so the dais is lit up, casting the rest of the hall in darkness. It shouldn't be possible, but I'm able to pick out one person in that darkness, and somehow, I know exactly who it is just by their silhouette—Finnik, the fae best friend of the prince.

When my eyes adjust to the light, I can just about make out his expression. He's watching with a frown, his disposition rigid and cold. It seems that he dislikes me just as much as his friend does. Have they had conversations about how much they hate me, planning ways to get Havoc out of marrying me? I don't know why that annoys me so much. After all, I have no proof that is what they have been doing, and I am basing my assumption of his dislike on his current frown.

Fae are mysterious creatures, and no one is quite sure where they came from. There are theories that they were here before the other races colonised the land. The other theory is that they come from lands beyond the mountains. Behind Drathlor City is a treacherous mountain range that is unpassable. Anyone who has tried either had to return, or they were never seen again and presumed dead.

Fae abilities far suppress our own, so it wouldn't surprise me if they were able to traverse the mountains. From the stories I've heard, they are vicious and fiercely protective of what belongs to them, including those they consider family. If Finnik adopted the prince into his circle, then I am going to have to watch my back.

"I pronounce the ball open, enjoy your evening!" the king announces, startling me back into the present. "The prince and first bride will begin the first dance."

The prince grumbles under his breath, and I watch as his posture stiffens. While I don't quite make out what he says, I do hear several expletives that would make many females blush. However, I'm not any random female, I am the first bride. Fragile females don't last in this role, which has been proven from some of the previous brides who died before they could fulfil their destiny.

Smoothing out his features, he offers me a gentle dip of his head as is protocol. As I place my hand in his, I'm grateful for the curtsy I'm expected to give, as it gives me the excuse to lower my face. The feeling of his skin against mine causes the bond to do a cartwheel in my chest, and it's not a comfortable sensation.

I don't understand it. I crave his touch, yet it is more like I've been starving for years and am craving anything I can get. Everything will settle down. At least, that's what I keep telling myself.

Leading me out onto the dance floor, the prince places his hand on my waist. His expression seems to be back under control, his face blank as the music starts and he leads me into a simple dance. His touch is light and almost non-existent, making his discontent clear to me.

I can only imagine what we look like to everyone watching—the perfect fairy-tale match, a true mated pair and the first to help complete the prophecy. The music swells, my skirts shifting around me in a flurry of colours. We speed up, the prince's grip becoming firmer as he moves us into more complicated movements. When I spin on the spot, I must look as though I'm on fire, being consumed by the bright autumnal colours. We have only been dancing a short time, and I sense something strange happening—I am beginning to enjoy myself.

What is even more surprising is that Havoc isn't watching me with hate-filled eyes anymore. While it might not be declarations of love, it could be a start.

Feeling more confident, I meet his gaze. "I am surprised that you decided to turn up. You seemed confident you weren't going to marry me earlier."

It comes out sounding more accusatory than I meant it to, and I regret saying it as soon as it leaves my mouth. Any hint of warmth disappears in an instant, a scowl replacing it.

"Nothing has changed. I am only here for my people."

What in the underworld does he think I'm here for? Does he really think that I want to leave my home and people to come here every six months, where I'm treated like a social pariah and taught how to be the perfect bride? Funnily enough, that isn't the life I would have chosen for myself. If he gets the impression that I do want to be here, then I've done my job well.

Hearing that your mate is only dancing with you because he believes his people will suffer if he doesn't is a blow to my confidence, but I will not let him know it. My entire life has been dedicated to serving my people, and he is spitting on my sacrifice.

"Do you think I wanted this?" I hiss furiously, trying to

keep my feet moving in time with the flowing music. "The only reason I agreed to marry a stranger is because I am trying to save my people." He has to understand that, since that is why he is here too. Is his bond not aching, begging us to be together?

Scowling with disgust, he drags me to a sudden stop, and I stumble into him.

"I don't care what you want." Grabbing my shoulders, he roughly pushes me away from him. "You are *wrong*, I can't even stand to touch you."

With a scowl, he backs away and stalks off the dance floor. The music screeches to a halt, and everyone watches me with wide eyes, taking in as much of the drama as they can. While Havoc's words were whispered, it feels as though he just announced to the whole room how much he despises me. This only gets worse as the gossip starts.

You are wrong.

There is something about me so bad, so *wrong*, that he can't stand to be with me for more than a few minutes, even for the sake of his kingdom. My touch repels him. This isn't just some misunderstanding or mild dislike. He hates me, and my soul feels like it's fracturing in response. Breathing becomes difficult, the vice tightening around me making me feel as though I'm about to shatter into a thousand pieces.

I don't care for him, and I certainly don't love him. I was not brought up to whine and mourn over males who have no interest in me. I am better than that. The bond between us is undeniable, though, and it is tearing me apart. If he won't acknowledge it, then how are we going to get through this? My soul is tied to him, and no matter how much I tell myself I would be better off without him, the bond is telling me otherwise.

Everyone is watching and talking about me, but the

pain in my body from the rejection is making it impossible for me to focus. I just stand here and attempt to keep myself together. I'm alone out here, the voices blurring into one and ringing in my ears.

I need to hold my head high and walk from the dance floor like nothing happened. There is so much more at stake here than me, I just need to get through this agony.

A figure suddenly appears in front of me and pulls me against him, positioning my hands on his shoulder and moving me across the floor in a dance. My body falls into autopilot, automatically following the male's lead. The pounding in my head eases slightly, and I feel like I'm able to focus on the body I'm pressed against.

Part of me already knows who it is, the otherworldly energy he gives off a dead giveaway. The haze of pain lifts, and I'm able to lift my head to meet my saviour's eyes.

It's the fae. Finnik.

Chapter Eight

"Finnik." My choked gasp causes his hazel eyes to drop to mine. Before now, he had been looking over my shoulder, taking in the reactions of those in the ballroom. That is no longer the case. Taking me in with a sweeping glance, he ends at my face, curiosity written in his expression.

I use this moment to examine him in return, never having been close to the fae before. From a distance, I wasn't able to see the mixtures of greens and browns in his irises, all shifting so they never appear the same at any one moment. There is a beautiful depth to them that I could lose myself in.

"So you are the one causing all the problems around here." There is a mischief in his expression that I can't quite put my finger on, making it difficult for me to decide if he's joking or not.

I'm not the one who just publicly rejected his mate in front of a whole ballroom of people. The prince seems determined to cause as much drama as possible around our union, whereas I have always done my duty. I don't have the strength to say that to the fae, though, my soul aching and broken in my chest.

"He rejected me, again." I hardly recognise my own voice, the stranglehold on my throat making speech difficult.

Why am I telling him this? Not only did he witness both episodes, but he is best friends with the prince, so his alliances are clear. Could it have something to do with the fact that Finnik's presence seems to help me function despite the internal torment I'm currently experiencing? Or is it because he's the first person to come to my aid after the prince left?

Either option could be possible, or it could simply be that I am turning into a person who shares all of their thoughts aloud as they experience them. All I know is that he is here now, helping me. I have never seen him dance before, so I imagine this is going to start some gossip that he jumped in to dance with me when the prince stalked off. There is also a high possibility that he stepped in to help his friend save face.

"He has not officially rejected you, there is still a chance the two of you can work through this." Lifting his chin, he focuses on the people around us once more, and I realise with surprise that other couples have joined us on the dance floor.

An ember of hope sparks to life inside me as I consider his words. Havoc and I could still make this work. I haven't failed my people yet.

"You would be feeling a lot worse if he rejected you like that."

The comment is said conversationally, and I think he means it as a comfort, but it feels more like a threat. Honestly, I'm more taken aback by the fact that I could feel any more wretched than I already do.

"This pain gets worse?" Any worse, and I think it would kill me.

He sighs and gives me a look of what I think is supposed to be sympathy. It is gone in a flash, though, and replaced by a smirk, his perfect dark brows creasing. "You are the one from the prophecy, not him." His face is close now, his stare intense. "Pull yourself together and get through this."

The advice isn't said to be kind, and there is zero warmth coming from him, but he's right. This isn't about Prince Havoc, it's about completing my destiny as one of the brides. My focus becomes clearer, and I study the male before me.

"Why are you helping me? He's your friend."

The more I think about it, the more I realise he's potentially creating problems for himself. He could be seen as going against his friend, dancing with the bride he rejected.

"He's like my brother," the fae says with a dip of his head, "but I don't always agree with his decisions." The music fades, and the dance comes to an end. Partners move around us, preparing for the next dance, and he stops us short, locking eyes with me once more as he gives me a short bow. "Enjoy your evening, Lady Anthea."

"It's Thea," I call out, but he's already halfway across the ballroom, disappearing into the shadows created by the alcoves and bright lights. He's probably on the lookout for Havoc. What will he say to him?

It doesn't matter, and I won't waste any more time stressing over the prince this evening. No good can come from it, and there are no solutions that I can manage for this evening.

Funnily enough, I find that Finnik's words have a positive effect on me, and I am able to straighten my back and hold my head high. I don't have the ability to shift my face into a mask of smug indifference, so I settle on a neutral expression as I make my way back to Geoff, who is waiting for me.

Standing in a line with the other advisors that mirrors the order of the brides, Geoff dips his head in greeting, stepping up to my side as I return to my place. Despite the cool aloofness he portrays, I can feel his anger, and I brace myself for his disapproval.

"That was an interesting first dance." He doesn't take his gaze off the twirling couples on the dance floor, his lips pursed and hands clasped behind his back. Geoff is not one to make a scene, so the fact he is even mentioning it now means that heads will roll.

I also watch the dancers, needing to keep up the pretence that everything is fine and going to plan. Keeping my voice quiet and even, I explain, "I did what I could. The pain—"

His gaze jerks to mine, cutting me off with the intensity of his stare. "You did your duty. It was the prince who failed you." Slowly, as though remembering where we are, he returns to watching the nobles milling around the ballroom. "Our king *will* hear about this."

The promise in his words both terrifies and reassures me. You do not mess with Geoff. He may seem like a calm escort and advisor, but he is also one of the best swordsmen I have ever seen and is fiercely loyal to his king and kingdom. There was a reason he was chosen to watch over me.

Knowing that he has my back in this and is furious on my behalf is... gratifying. I have someone who supports me, not to mention Felix. I can only imagine his reaction when he discovers what happened tonight. A pang in my chest makes me wish he was here, only it was made very clear that assistants and anyone who was not a noble was not invited.

It is probably for the best, as he would threaten to tear out the prince's throat for the way he treated me.

My stomach clenches painfully, and I know I will have to feed soon. Vampires are able to go days without feeding, but the longer we go without, the harder it is to control our baser natures. The strain that Havoc's rejections has put on me is making it harder to curb those desires.

Movement from farther down the line catches my attention, and from the corner of my eye, I spot Bliss making her way towards me, her escort following dutifully behind. While it is not forbidden for us to move about the hall, it is frowned upon. Personally, I believe it is another way to keep us separate, as we are much easier to control than if we were to band together.

Standing next to me, she places her hand on my arm. Thankfully, Ember, the second bride, is currently on the other side of the room being introduced to several of the nobles, so she is unable to hear us.

"Thea, is everything okay? Your dance with the prince looked a little... strained."

Bliss already knows about Havoc's first rejection of me, hence her concern for me now. However, here in front of everyone, especially with Geoff at my side, I don't want to speak about this newest episode while we could be overheard.

"Just a little case of cold feet I believe," I reply with a tight smile, hoping she reads between the lines and realises what I'm trying to tell her. "All will be fine."

Nodding slowly with understanding, the siren examines my face. "It was kind of Finnik to step in and dance with you."

Kind. Her comment makes me want to snort, yet I know what she is asking. Curiosity flashes in her eyes, and I wish I was able to speak with her candidly. The fae has never shown an interest in dancing with anyone before, so for him to step in is monumental for the castle gossips.

"Yes, he is a knowledgeable dance partner," I reply easily, implying that I was able to gain information from him during the dance. This makes it appear that the fae and I were having light conversation without it seeming suspicious that we were talking. However, while I did manage to get a little information from him, and I would have liked more, I feel a little steadier knowing what I do.

"Anthea, the king wishes to have a word with me," Geoff tells me, cutting through my conversation. "Will you be okay here on your own for a few minutes?"

We both know I won't be on my own, the constant presence of the guards surrounding me like a bubble. "Of course," I reply, surprised to see genuine concern in his eyes.

Bliss steps closer as soon as he steps up onto the dais with the king. "Are you okay? Genuinely, I mean. I know vampires are not very big on sharing their feelings, but I am worried. There was a moment when you were on the dance floor when you looked like... You looked unwell, Thea. Pale, even for you."

I could pretend that I am fine or play down the whole incident. That is what would be expected of me, but I'm hurting, I'm exhausted, and I need a friend to talk to.

"He rejected me again." I look away, not wanting to see her expression as I share everything. "What you saw on the dance floor was the bond indicating it was unhappy."

"Do not worry, Anthea," a voice says, making Bliss and I turn. It's Ember, her face the picture of smugness. A male just escorted her back towards us, but before she could get far, another stopped her. Not only is her new suitor handsome, but he is also one of Havoc's older brothers. Fantastic. "At least one of us is suitable for the princes. You won't see me shirking my duty." Winking, she links her arm with the prince's, and he leads her away, whispering something that makes her laugh aloud.

Bliss bares her teeth at the dragon shifter as she struts past us, hissing in warning. I sometimes forget how terrifying she can be. She's always dressed in bright colours and adorable outfits, looking beautiful without even having to try, but the heart of a siren is a wicked thing, cursed with an insatiable hunger.

We watch Ember as the prince leads her into a dance, the two of us scowling at how perfect the two of them look together. It makes me feel sick.

"The prince will be in for a big surprise if he is paired with her," Bliss comments with a shake of her head. "She is vicious."

I can't say I disagree. Dragons are known for their fiery tempers and strong wills. There is a lot I would like to say about this potential pairing, but I wouldn't dare do it when anything I say could get back to Ember.

"I'm sure he knows what he would be getting into if he chose to marry one of the dragons," I say as diplomatically as I can.

We stand together in companionable silence for a little while, watching the comings and goings of the dancers. Most of the brides are asked to dance, but for some reason, no one comes to dance with Bliss. Usually she is one of the most popular, and I start to suspect there is a reason she's not being asked. I keep watch from the corner of my eye, and it's not long before I notice her baring her teeth at any male who walks in our direction. They wisely turn on their heel and walk away, not wanting to invoke the wrath of a siren.

Raising a brow, I glance over at her. "Are you scaring off your suitors?"

Unlike me, the rest of the brides are not yet paired up with their future husbands, so these balls are the perfect opportunity for them to meet males. Some believe the prophecy will somehow make it clear which male will be the perfect match, another reason why all the brides are invited to attend.

"I don't feel like dancing. Besides, I want to spend more time with you." She shrugs it off like this is no big deal, as though she isn't sacrificing this time she could be using to find happiness.

"I appreciate it, Bliss, but you shouldn't hold back because of me." Placing a hand on her wrist, I wait until she turns to look at me before speaking again. "Please, you should dance. It would look strange if you didn't."

She knows that what I say is true. Others will begin to notice the two brides who are standing together and not dancing. It might make them suspicious that we are planning something. Besides, she enjoys this part of being a bride, and holding her back for my own comfort is selfish.

She slowly nods in agreement, yet her concern is still visible in her eyes. It is not long before another male walks over and asks her to dance. Smiling brightly, she accepts, but just as she's being led away, she glances over her shoulder at me. "My offer still stands. You say the word."

Her comment has the desired effect, and a small smile pulls at my lips as I try to restrain my humour. Her offering to kill the prince, while fun to think about, isn't something that would solve my dilemma.

Alone once more, I watch everyone in the ballroom. Much of my life has been spent alone, so I don't mind not having anyone beside me. It means I can relax a little. My gaze wanders across the room, and it's only as I begin my third circuit of the room and the ache in my chest becomes a throb that I realise I'm looking for two people in particular—Havoc and Finnik.

Frustration courses through me, and I focus on that rather than the pining sensation in my chest. Neither of the males seem to be in the ballroom, and I should be grateful for that. While the initial pain of being rejected has eased a little, it has only been replaced by a yearning feeling, which only frustrates me more. Where I would usually enjoy this time to myself, my pent-up feelings are beginning to become overwhelming. My gums ache with the desire to feed, and I need to distract myself before I give into my cravings.

As if summoned by my thoughts, a stranger appears in front of me.

He's beautiful in an exotic way I've never seen before. He has pointed ears and slightly feline features like one of the fae, but his olive skin and the way that he holds himself gives me the impression that he's something else. What I know for sure is that he isn't from around here. His blond hair hangs down to his shoulders, with streaks of gold woven through it as though he's spent a lot of time in the sun. His clean-shaven chin is pointed like that of the fae, and his light blue eyes are piercing as he greets me with a wide smile. The thing that makes him stand out, however, is the tattoo that cuts through the centre of his face, from forehead to chin, then disappears below his neckline. The ink is gold and appears to shimmer, becoming clearer in some lights and almost disappearing in others. They seem like glimmering symbols, and it makes me wish I understood what it says. It is just as beautiful as he is, the swirling symbols so delicate.

The stranger says nothing to me, but his smile is wide and charming, numbing some of the pain of my earlier rejection. He offers me his hand with a flourish, and I see the same golden tattoos on his hands. These swirls and patterns look beautiful, but they give off a vibe that warns you not to mess with him. He doesn't seem like he wishes me harm though, so I take his proffered hand and follow him out onto the dance floor.

Bowing gracefully, he waits for me to finish my curtsy before pulling me against him and leading me into a dance. I'm immediately swept up into the steps, enjoying the feeling of being pressed against him despite the fact he's a complete stranger. It doesn't feel awkward at all, and whoever taught him to dance did an amazing job, every step smooth and graceful.

I have had lessons since I was old enough to walk, so I am proficient in most dances, but as he leads, he makes it seem as easy as breathing. My heart lifts in my chest. He feels like a balm against the wounds to my soul, and I want to stay pressed against him until he takes away all my pain. Our eyes stay locked together as we dance, and something hums with happiness within me. This is more like what I expected a mate bond to be like, not the shambles that mine is.

The song ends, and we slowly drift to a stop, other couples moving around us as they exit the floor and choose their next dance partner. With my heart in my throat, I reluctantly start to step back, knowing it is expected of me to return to my place. Dancing multiple times with the same person is frowned upon, especially when you have a mate.

"I suppose—"

He presses a finger against my lips, stopping anything else I was going to say. His expression is intense, saying a thousand things that words could not express. I have no idea who this stranger is, yet I feel like I have known him forever.

Music starts again, the violins lulling us into another dance. Without another word, we waltz across the floor. We dance and dance, one after another, never saying a word to each other, communicating through the movements of our bodies. I know I should stop and allow others to dance with me as is expected, yet I can't find it in myself. This is the first time I have felt happy in a long time.

A shadow appears over my shoulder, and the male slows me to a stop, a frown marring his features. Blinking back into reality, I find myself also frowning. What is the reason for the abrupt ending? Turning, I find Prince Havoc standing directly behind me, his eyes locked on the stranger.

"Your kind is not welcome here."

For a moment, I think his harsh words are aimed at me, extending my public humiliation, but I push through my initial panic and see that he has not once looked away from my dance partner, his body practically vibrating with anger. Is this because I've danced multiple times with him? Is the prince jealous? A twisted part of me is happy that the prince might be experiencing jealousy and that he's finally feeling something towards our bond instead of ignoring it.

The rational part of my mind recognises that a fight might be about to break out. Others in the hall seem to have realised the same thing and have stopped dancing to watch the drama unfold. I need to do something before this gets out of hand.

Taking a step towards Havoc, I soften my frown. "Prince Havoc, we were just dancing, he hasn't been improper—"

Kingdom of Broken Bonds

"Hush, mate," Havoc replies, cutting me off harshly.

The use of the word "mate" is like a slap to the face. What an insult. After rejecting me twice, he's happy to call me mate now that another male is interested in me. Even now, he still won't look at me. I can feel the calming presence of the stranger behind me, and his hand lands gently on my shoulder, squeezing it in comfort as he senses my indignation.

Havoc watches the move with narrowed eyes. "How dare you come here? Leave before I have the guards remove you."

Something in the atmosphere changes, becoming charged. I turn so I can see both the stranger and the prince, shocked when I see the change in the unknown male.

The stranger looks angry now, his posture changing. He appears as though he wants to snatch me away from the prince, yet he doesn't say a word. Baring his teeth, he makes a gesture towards Havoc that I get the distinct impression is a threat before turning his gaze to me. His eyes soften a little, but his expression is no less fierce. Taking my hand in his, he bows deeply and slowly kisses the back of my hand, his eyes locked on mine.

Straightening up, he gives me one last intense look before turning on his heel and striding towards the exit.

My heart thumps, and before I know it, I've taken a step forward as if to follow him, but a hand on my wrist stops me —Havoc.

"Wait!" I call out, shaking off the prince's touch. I don't follow the male, not wanting to make things worse between my mate and me, but I can't let him go, not until I know one important detail.

The male pauses and glances at me over his shoulder.

"What is your name?" I ask.

He smiles, his eyes sad. "Eli," he replies, his voice rich and velvety.

His expression is one of surprise, and a slow smile pulls at his lips, making him look like the happiest male in the realm. "My name is Eli." His eyes glimmer with promise. "I will be seeing you soon, princess."

He stalks from the room with a swish of his cape, my heart thumping in my chest as I watch him leave, wondering what in the world just happened.

Chapter Nine

Cursing under my breath, I hiss with pain as I try to remove what feels like a thousand pins from my hair. Every single one seems determined to get caught and tangled until I have a knot the size of an egg on the back of my head.

I'm grateful to get out of my elaborate clothing and just crawl into bed.

However, before I can do that, I have to feed. My dress wasn't too difficult for me to take off, so I slipped into a comfortable sleeping gown before I began to work on my hair, avoiding the fact I'm desperate for blood. Is it a stupid thing to do? Yes. The cravings won't go away by themselves, but the thought of leaving my rooms to track down someone to feed from after everything that's happened tonight is enough to make me shudder.

What an awful fucking night. Nothing went as planned, and I ended up being the centre of all the drama, something I hate. After Eli left, Finnik arrived to quietly escort the prince away, and I was once again left alone on the dance floor. Thankfully Geoff came to my rescue. The ball was mostly over by that point, so it was acceptable for us to make our escape.

Everything about me feels off. My body feels heavy and cumbersome, and my mind is slow, like I'm wading through treacle. Some of it is because of what happened tonight, but I know some of it is caused by my thirst.

A knock sounds at the door, followed by the light squeak of hinges as it's opened before I have a chance to say anything. I turn in annoyance, prepared to snap at whoever has decided to enter without waiting to be called in, but when I see the figure in the doorway, I hold my tongue.

Felix.

"Thea? Are you okay? I thought I would come and see..." He trails off as he sees my state of undress, and if he were able to blush, I'm sure that's exactly what he would be doing right now.

"I feel like this is becoming a habit of yours," I joke and gesture for him to come farther into the room. For anyone else who just walked straight into my room, there would have been hell to pay, yet my annoyance fizzled away as soon as I saw who it was. Am I just exhausted, or is it because I *like* him seeing me this way?

"What can I say? I just can't stay away from you," he teases, a smile pulling at his lips. It doesn't reach his eyes, though, and his expression quickly shifts to one of concern. "I heard about what happened at the ball."

I shake my head, my fingers still tangled in my hair. "It was a mess, Felix, and I don't know what to do to fix it." My voice becomes tight at the end of my comment as emotions rise that I don't have the energy to deal with tonight. Clearing my throat, I drop my gaze and walk to the mirror, using it to give me an excuse to move away from him.

"He's a fool," Felix snarls, showing a rare flash of anger. "Any male would be lucky to be mated to you."

My heart thuds painfully in my chest. I'm grateful for his comment, and I believe he means it, yet it just makes me feel worse. There must be something about me that turns the prince off. He even said he won't mate with me because of what I am. If any male would be lucky to have me, then something truly awful must be causing the prince to reject me.

A small, fractured part of me wishes Felix was my mate and not the prince. We would make a great team, and if we were fated, then no one could complain that he was one of the changed. Any relationship between a born vampire and a changed one would be frowned upon, so for me, a bride who is fated to another, it could never happen.

Not paying attention to the pin in my hair, I yank it too hard, cursing at the sting of pain and the knot that now has an even tighter grip on me.

"Do you need a hand?" he asks, and I see a trace of humour in his reflection.

"Yes please," I say with a sigh, dropping my arms defeatedly as I sink onto the end of the bed, turning enough that he's able to access my hair.

Walking over, he gets to work on untangling my hair. He's good at this, and I suppose part of that is thanks to his work with horses. The man knows how to use his hands. The gentle motions are strangely relaxing, and I close my eyes, enjoying his quiet company. After an unknown amount of time has passed, I feel his hands slide into my hair, and he begins to massage my scalp. The feeling is blissful, and my head falls back as pleasurable sensations work their way through my body. My fangs extend, heavy and tender in my mouth thanks to the endorphins flooding my body.

"You're pale." His voice is quiet and close—close enough that I can feel his breath against my skin. "You should feed."

The suggestion sounds seductive, and while I'm sure he doesn't mean it that way, the hair on my arms stands on end. Slowly opening my eyes, I get a glimpse of us in the mirror—me on the edge of the bed with my back arched and head thrown back in bliss, and him with his hands gently moving across my head and neck.

We look like lovers.

I sit up abruptly and look away from the mirror guiltily. Needing some space between us, I stand and stride to the bathroom. I run the cold tap and splash my face with icy water, hoping it will shock some sense into me.

"I know," I call out, finally answering once I manage to get myself under control. Slowly padding back into the bedroom, I groan as I run my tongue over my exposed fangs, trying to ease the ache. "I'll need to track down someone to see if there are any volunteers available."

Finding a volunteer at this time of night is not going to be easy, and the thought of having to leave my room in my current state is enough to bring tears to my eyes.

Seeming to realise how close to the edge I am, he steps forward and places a hand on my arm. "That's going to take too much time, you need it now." His eyes sweep across my face, probably noticing all the signs of my thirst taking its toll on me. "Feed from me."

I step back in shock. For vampire kind, we only really feed off another vampire in acts of loyalty or for pleasure during sex. Emotions and feelings are heightened when we bite someone, and it's easy to get carried away, especially if we are in dire need of feeding. Trust is a huge part of feeding from another vampire, as we are making ourselves vulnerable to the other. Felix's trust in me is shocking.

"Felix..." My words trail off, as I have no idea what to say to him. I want to reject him and accept the offer at the same time. Would this change our friendship, or is this a casual offer that doesn't mean anything to him?

As if he can sense my concerns, he raises both hands. "Nothing sexual has to happen. This is purely for food and something you need sooner rather than later. I can see how much strain you are under. You need to be at full strength."

I feel myself wavering, being convinced by his arguments. I won't pretend that I don't want to drink from him, I have always wanted to taste him, but it can be addictive feeding on our own kind. While I know I should say no, I *really* want to say yes.

"If you're sure..." I trail off, my eyes already locked on his neck. My willpower isn't strong, but I have to hear his consent before I do anything.

Since the changed are the dead brought back to life, their hearts don't beat. Because of this, their blood is rich in flavour, but not as powerful as if I were to drink from a born vampire. Human's blood is watery, but it does the job and provides the nutrients we need.

We pride ourselves on our restraint, and as such, born vampires only feed on volunteers, never the unwilling. Most of the changed follow the same rules, yet there are some who enjoy the thrill of the hunt. We compensate our volunteers financially, but there are also certain benefits of feeding a vampire, mainly the immense pleasure that our bite causes.

"I'm sure. Let me help you."

He sits on the edge of the bed, and as soon as he finishes

talking, I'm in his lap, clinging onto him like a baby monkey. He chuckles quietly and wraps his arms around me, holding me close. I need no encouragement, and I thread my hands into his hair, tilting his head to the side so I can get a better angle on his neck. Lowering my face, I take a deep breath, inhaling his sweet scent and nuzzling against his skin.

Running my tongue over the patch of skin, I feel for the bouncy sensation that tells me I've found an artery. I open my mouth and sink my teeth into his neck.

The taste of his blood hits my tongue, and I groan with pleasure. Thick and fast, the life sustaining liquid pours down my throat, and somehow, it tastes just how I always imagined Felix would taste. He tastes like home.

He groans, his back arching. "Thea," he moans, my name sounding like a prayer on his lips. "More, take more."

His ragged pleas only spur me on, and I release some of the stranglehold I have on my inner demon. My instincts have always been feral, more so than other vampires I know, and I've always felt like I was one feed away from madness. As such, I've had to learn to control that side of me with an iron fist, never letting myself get as worked up as I have tonight.

His cock strains against his trousers, and before I can stop myself, I grind against it, arousal flooding through my veins, taking away all sensible thought.

My stomach is full, and I somehow manage to pull myself away from his neck, only to press my lips against his. He freezes then groans and kisses me back. His lips move against mine, his blood now coating both of us. I need more. I need him. Something to fill this hole inside me that Havoc created.

"We should stop," he whispers reluctantly against my lips.

I press myself against him instead, lifting one of his hands until it rests on my breast, needing to feel his touch. Rolling my hips, I grind against him, trying to ease the ache between my thighs.

"Thea, no. Stop."

His words feel like a bucket of cold water has been thrown over me, my arousal and need immediately vanishing.

"You don't want me." It's not a question or an accusation, just a dejected realisation. He only offered to feed me, and here I am, grinding against him like a sex starved hooker. He specifically stated that there would be no sexual stuff, yet I allowed myself to get carried away. He's one of my closest friends, and I might have torn that relationship apart.

It is just another rejection, and after the last few days I've had, I'm struggling to take it with dignity as is expected of me. Mortified, I slide off his lap and start to walk away from the bed, needing to put as much space between us as possible.

"I absolutely want you." His arm flashes out as he grabs me, stopping me from escaping. I could pull away from him, I'm strong enough, but something about the tightness in his voice stops me from leaving. I turn to face him.

His eyes examine my face, taking in my emotions that I'm struggling to hide away. "I want to fuck you so badly that I'm hating myself for saying this, but you've had a shit night. Your betrothed embarrassed you, and the blood was making you horny." He squeezes my arm to take the sting out of the reminder. "You know how much trouble you would be in if anyone found out we slept together. I'm not saying I don't want to, I'm saying it's complicated and we need to work things out."

Stepping closer, he looks down at me with an intensity that causes my entire body to tingle. I can sense his barely contained lust, and it makes my heart beat faster.

"When we do have sex," he continues, "it will be because you want *me*, not because you've been rejected and need comfort."

He says it gently, but I still feel the burn of his words like an accusation.

"I'm sorry," I say quietly, realising what an idiot I've been. Everything he said is right, and I could have just screwed up our friendship. What in the underworld has gotten into me? I was on a blood high, and I was going to just use him for sex because my feelings were hurt. Feeling like a terrible friend, I squeeze my eyes shut and rub my temples to ease the pounding headache building there.

"Never be sorry." Pulling me against his chest, he wraps his arms around me in an embrace and kisses the top of my head. "I'm always going to be here for you."

Chapter Ten

Breakfast is tedious. I lean back in my chair, one arm propping up my chin and the other clutching a wine glass containing watered-down blood. I stay silent as the others chat.

Thanks to my hangover from drinking too much blood last night, I feel as though I've been run over by a carriage. Apparently too much time passed between feedings, and the stress of the evening gave me a pulsing headache. This has put me in a foul mood—not to mention that I'm still mortified over my behaviour in my room. I've not seen Felix since he left last night, and I'm not sure if that is a blessing or not.

Geoff has been giving me strange looks all morning, but I don't have the energy to fight with him about any of this, especially when I'm surrounded by my fellow brides. Why I'm being forced to take part in the morning ritual with them when I don't eat, I don't know. Perhaps it's a penance for everything that happened last night. While it wasn't my fault, I am sure there will be some sort of consequence.

My breakfast invitation arrived at first light in the form

of an envelope being slid through the bottom of the door. One of the guards found it and brought it straight to Geoff, who in turn came to me. He explained that I was to join the other brides in the glass room I'd been in the day everyone arrived. It was made clear that this wasn't optional, and they expected to see me there at eight.

The sun is still rising in the sky, and thanks to the mountains that surround us, I have been shielded from its rays, but things are about to get uncomfortable.

None of the ladies ask me about what happened last night. In fact, they mostly avoid talking to me altogether. Bliss has been shooting concerned looks in my direction ever since I arrived, but because we don't want to give away the closeness of our friendship, she says nothing, attempting to brush it off. The others aren't stupid, however, so I am sure they are picking up on something between us.

Breakfast seems to go on forever. How long does it take for someone to eat a bowl of fruit? I contemplate if walking out would be worth the king's wrath when a lull in the conversation seems to fall upon us.

"Lady Thea, it seems as though the prince can't make up his mind about you."

Glancing up, I find the bride from the beasts, Terra, watching me with a serpentine smile. She tilts her head to one side, mock sympathy pulling at her features. "I find that so strange when you were blessed with a mate bond, yet he still does not want you. That must be difficult for you."

So they noticed. I suppose it would have been pretty hard to miss last night's spectacle. I was hoping that the part about Havoc not wanting to mate wouldn't have spread yet. I'm not just going to confirm it since I have a reputation to uphold. Plus, I don't want to give her any more ammunition to use against me.

Forcing myself to relax in my seat, I take a sip from my glass and tilt my head in question. "What do you mean, Terra?"

The other brides sit in silence, watching us as we swap barbs across the table. I don't know this new bride, but from what I've seen, she is as bullish as the horns growing from her skull. She looks annoyingly perky this morning, a healthy glow painting her cheeks whereas I feel two steps away from death.

"Was the little standoff in front of everyone last night not enough to tell you, Thea?" Shaking her head, she clucks her tongue with disappointment. "I heard you were more observant than that."

I am not in the mood for this, and she is clearly trying to pick a fight and has chosen me as her target. Well, she chose the wrong day to mess with me. Anger flits through my body like a hot ember, igniting as it moves through my veins. Usually, I am better at controlling this part of myself, yet everything has just become too much.

"I think what she means," Mallory intervenes, shifting in her seat, "is that we have all heard of your... teething problems with Prince Havoc, and his behaviour last night only confirmed it."

I glance over at the witch, and she smiles at me sheepishly. It's fleeting, yet it's more emotion than she's shown to me in our previous interactions. Why is she acting this way? Is it simply to stop an argument, or for another reason?

Ember snorts, her dragon flashing in her eyes. "He publicly left you on the dance floor, that seems pretty clear to me."

"Then, when you were dancing with the handsome stranger, he came and declared that you are his mate. He doesn't want you, but he doesn't want anyone else to have you either," Princess Celest adds slowly, as though she's figuring it out as she speaks. She looks a little worse for wear this morning. At least I am not the only one feeling the effects of last night.

"He did seem jealous," Bliss chimes in. "He is probably struggling to get used to the fact that he won't be a bachelor anymore. You could see how much he wanted her though."

My friend is clearly trying to comfort me without giving away that she's completely on my side. At the moment, that is the least of my problems, and having a friend fully in my corner is something I could use. I can see where she's going with her comment though. She is trying to get the others to think along the same lines. If the prince is jealous, then that means he must have at least *some* feelings towards me, which in turn could lead to other, deeper feelings.

"Don't worry about me, ladies, I have it all under control." Raising my glass to my lips, I take a long sip of blood, wishing I felt as confident as I sounded about this.

All I want to do is crawl back into my bed and pretend last night never happened, both the disastrous ball and when I mounted my best friend and made a fool of myself. Unfortunately, that doesn't seem like it's going to be an option.

"Tell me, what was going on with the prince's friend? The fae who danced with you once Havoc left?" Mallory asks, something sparkling in her eyes that makes her seem far too interested in the fae. "I heard he doesn't speak to anyone but the royal family."

Where are they hearing all of these rumours from? Clearly I need to socialise more if I want to know what's happening around me. The witch bride hasn't said much, but she's more alert now that we're on the subject of Finnik. Why does that awaken my anger again? Finnik is not my mate, so I can't be jealous. I must be frustrated with all the questions, that is the only option that makes sense.

Lowering my glass to rest on my knee, I clear my throat. "Finnik was just dancing with the mate of his friend, finishing where the prince was unable to."

Terra raises a brow, the corner of her lip turning up. She doesn't believe a word I'm saying. "Unable to, Thea, or unwilling to?"

"Terra," Bliss chides, turning towards the female. "We should be supporting everyone around this table, not gossiping and attempting to tear each other down. This is going to be difficult enough." Anger flushes her skin, causing her scales to appear more iridescent, catching the sunlight that's now shining down on us. "You are new to this, so you don't know how much pressure we are under. Thea is the oldest of us all and has been training for this her entire life. You should show some respect."

Whoa.

I see my friend in a new light. Clearly she's had enough of the new bride. I'm even more surprised when several of the others hum and nod in agreement. Some of the tightness in my chest eases a bit knowing I have her support. I hadn't realised how much I needed this, her publicly standing up for me, and everything she said is true. We are going to have to support each other to survive the prophecy.

Movement by the door catches my attention, and I spot Geoff pulling away from the other advisors and making his way towards me. Reaching my side, he bows stiffly to everyone at the table and then turns his full attention to me.

"I'm sorry to interrupt your breakfast, Lady Anthea, but your presence has been requested by the king."

My heart sinks. I knew this was coming sooner or later. Perhaps this is just a ruse to get me away from this conversation. Hope flutters in my stomach, yes, that could be it. "Yes, of course."

Placing my drink on the table, I dip my head in farewell to the others, but I don't bother to speak to any of them as I turn and follow my attendant into the main stone castle. I rub my temples now that I've left the brightness of the glass room.

My four guards surround us as we walk. Glancing around the hall to check that no one else is around, I tilt my head towards Geoff and smile slightly.

"Thank you for rescuing me."

"Don't thank me yet," he drawls. "I didn't make it up, the king wants to see you to discuss what happened last night."

Perhaps I was better in that glass room after all. Am I walking to my doom? The king is not known for his leniency, and after everything that happened last night, I might be the one to pay.

"Am I in trouble?" All light-heartedness has gone, and my voice is flat.

My advisor seems to grow in size beside me. "You did nothing wrong. I won't let anything happen to you."

"Oh, Geoff, you do care," I coo playfully as I press my hand to my chest. Teasing my stern escort has always been something I've enjoyed, and I know he secretly likes having someone to banter with. However, part of my teasing is covering up the fact that I am actually touched by his words. I don't think he would appreciate it if I pointed it out.

Rolling his eyes, he releases a long-suffering sigh. "I spend more time with you than your own father does. Of course I care."

I'm dumbstruck. Those are two words I never expected

him to utter, even in my wildest dreams. Geoff is a master of controlling his emotions, one of the best I've known. He's never spoken of feelings like this before, and hearing him say it now easily confuses me. Is he just messing with me, his own idea of a joke? Perhaps he's trying to help me relax before we see the king so I'm not too stressed for the meeting.

My face must convey my surprise, because he shakes his head when he glances at me.

"Do you really think I would have stuck around if I didn't care for you? Leaving my home every six months and not returning for half a year? I hate this place," he grumbles, glancing around the dark corridor.

The castle is very grand, yet it lacks any touch of warmth, which I find amusing seeing as we are a race who feels very little. Back in Trador, our palace is richly furnished on the inside. Tapestries and paintings decorate the walls, and chandeliers and exquisite sculptures fill the halls with light and beauty. I remember the first time I noticed the differences between the two as a child. I hadn't understood how they were both so different.

He makes a good point though. I don't get a choice about coming here, and because he's never let on that he hates it, I assumed he enjoyed being in the city. He is always telling me that it's an honour to support his kingdom in this way. If what he said is true, then he suffers through all of this because of how he feels towards me.

"Yet you do it anyway." My voice is full of quiet gratitude as I watch the man who has been more of a father to me than my biological father.

"For you, yes." He glances over at me once more, his expression softening for a half second, and then a ghost of a smile appears on his lips.

Of course, it's gone in the next moment, and no one would ever know the two of us just shared a moment. We reach the corridor that leads to the king's office far too quickly, and I feel queasy, not knowing what's waiting for me behind those doors.

Geoff nods in greeting to the guards at the door, and one of the king's guards pulls away from the others, knocks, and steps inside the office, most likely announcing I have arrived. We are not left waiting long. The guard returns and opens the doors for us with magic, gesturing for us to enter.

The king is sitting in the chair behind his desk. He looks tired. Did he not get any sleep last night either?

A sharp tug in my chest informs me Havoc is here, and sure enough, when I glance up, I find him leaning against the door on the opposite side of the room, looking as though he has been dragged straight out of bed to attend the meeting. None of his usual style or finesse is present, just him. Seeing him like this without his smart suits, crown, and perfect hair, he looks... ordinary. He is still handsome, and that pull between us is ever present, yet he doesn't emit that sense of entitlement royalty often carries.

There is a light knock on the side door, and at the king's call, it swings open to reveal Finnik. Excitement tingles in the centre of my chest as my eyes land on the fae, tracing every inch of his body. He's attractive, no, he's gorgeous, and I struggle to keep my eyes off him, especially after last night when he stepped in at the ball. There's a sense of danger around him, like he could kill within a second, and for some reason, in the light of day, that only makes him more attractive to me.

Where have these feelings come from? Am I just latching on to him because of Havoc's rejection and his swoon-worthy act of dancing with me when the prince couldn't finish? No, I shouldn't be doing this. I'm due to marry his best friend, and here I am, lusting after another male like a horny teenager. I need to focus on working with Havoc to sort through our differences and complete my role in the prophecy.

However, no matter how much I tell myself this and believe in the plan, I struggle to pull my gaze away from the fae as he strides across the room. He's the opposite of the prince, looking immaculate in a navy blue jacket without a wrinkle to be seen. Taking his place beside the prince, he immediately meets my gaze. His expression doesn't change, but there's an intensity in his demeanour that holds me in place, and I don't want to blink in case I lose it.

Havoc notices the way I look at his friend, and when he glances at the fae, he must see something in his expression that he doesn't like because he frowns. The urge to jerk my head away and look elsewhere is strong, but that will only make me appear guilty. There is nothing wrong with looking at his friend, and that is all I'm doing, so I won't act like I have been caught out.

I turn my attention fully to the king, and I find him watching us with his own frown, his face weary. Trying to ignore the two males on the other side of the room and the feelings they invoke inside me, I think of all the people back in Trador who are counting on me.

A heavy silence weighs on us as the king watches, the atmosphere taut like just before a thunderstorm. Will we survive the deluge?

"I have called you all here because of what happened last night." Another heavy pause ensues as the king puts his thoughts into words. It gives me hope that he's not furious, his voice calm. He is known for his strict punishments, even for his own people, and leniency is not something that is ever used to describe King Drath, so the last thing we want is him to be angry.

"It was an utter disaster," he growls, destroying my hopes of a calm, rational conversation. Surging up from the desk, he whirls around and snarls at his son. "What was going through your mind? My advisors are now questioning if we were right about the prophecy. You are making me look weak." While his direct attack is aimed at Havoc, I get the distinct impression that Finnik and I are included in this too.

"Father, I don't want to marry her. You know what I think of the *brides*." He shudders as he speaks, yet I can see he's trying to keep his temper in check, making out as though *he's* the reasonable one.

If I didn't know that it would get me into hot water, I would shake my head, and from the corner of my eye, I can see the minuscule movements of Geoff's. Well, I am glad we are on the same page about this. The prince is only coming off as entitled, his opinions apparently more important than everyone else's.

King Drath appears dumbstruck. "You don't *want* to marry her?" His entire body seems to swell with anger, his teeth gritted as he attempts to control it. "You don't get a choice."

Anger transforms Havoc's face, and I see a hint of that otherness coming through, separating him from the humans and making him supernatural. "Father—"

Striding towards his son, the king cuts him off with a gesture, stopping only inches from the prince. Glaring down at him, he shakes his head firmly. "No, Havoc! She is the one from the prophecy, and you are her true mate, which means you are to be her husband and help fulfil that prophecy." Seeing the stubborn set of his son's jaw, Drath sighs and runs a hand over his face. "Are you unable to feel the bond? Is there something wrong with it?"

"There is nothing wrong with the bond," I call out, my voice sharper than intended. I wasn't going to speak at all, but I will not let this be blamed on anything or anyone other than Havoc. "I can feel him and his hatred for me. Every second, I feel like a part of me is dying because he still denies the bond. If I can feel it, then so can he."

The prince looks at me as though I betrayed him, and Finnik is staring at me as though he's only just seeing me for the first time.

Nodding solemnly at my assessment, the king sighs again, but his determination is strong. "You don't have a choice in this, Havoc."

Geoff takes a step forward, his hands clasped behind his back as he addresses the two royals. "Do it for your kingdom, because if you don't, then we shall all perish."

Although Geoff promised he would protect me from the king's wrath, I'm still surprised by his words. For the closed-mouthed male who prefers to help from a distance, this is practically him shouting. It gives me confidence and has a greater effect on the room as a whole, because he generally only speaks if he has something really important to say. He's right though, and I watch the king nod in agreement.

"Do not let your selfishness destroy us all, son." The king speaks in a low, but even voice, the anger all but gone. "You have to at least *try*."

I can see the battle raging in Havoc's eyes as he tries to put his sense of duty over his own needs. I'm starting to view him in a different light, and it's not a flattering one. I've dedicated my entire life to this cause, and if I fail, the other brides won't stand a chance. All of my own desires and thoughts have been put aside for the good of my people, and he can't do the same because he doesn't like the brides cursed by the prophecy.

A growl that sounds animalistic rumbles through his chest, but he screws his eyes shut in frustration. When they open, they are glowing, locked on his father and purposely not looking my way.

"Fine, I'll do it, but only if she stays away from the cursed one," he demands. "May I leave now?"

The king sighs. "Yes, you may go."

The prince is out of the room before his father has even finished speaking, his movements a blur as he puts as much space between us as possible. Once again, he doesn't even look at me. The bond twinges in my chest at his obvious hatred towards me, and I fight to keep any discomfort from my face. Finnik turns to leave, following his friend, but unlike the prince, he does look at me. His gaze is hot on my skin and so intense that it leaves me feeling all out of sorts. I can't tell what he's thinking, and for some reason, that bothers me.

When he leaves, I'm finally in control of my thoughts again, and I go over the last words the prince demanded. The cursed one? What was he talking about? Who is this cursed one, and why am I supposed to stay away from them? Is he referring to the other brides? That seems like an odd request.

My confusion must show on my face, because the king makes a quiet noise of frustration. I turn to look at him and am surprised by how weary he appears. The strong, unageing king who battled to rule over us all appears... old.

"Anthea, how much do you know about the cursed?" he asks, confirming my theory.

"Nothing, Your Majesty," I reply, a delicate frown

pulling at my brows despite my best efforts to keep it under wraps. Even Geoff looks confused by the question.

Drath nods, striding back over to his desk and leaning against it, crossing his arms over his chest. "Last night before you left, you were dancing with a male—golden hair and a golden tattoo down the centre of his face."

His face appears in my mind, my heart doing a summersault in my chest as I realise whom he's talking about. "Eli." His name sounds like a breathy gasp, and the king's frown deepens. I hadn't meant to speak his name aloud. I usually have better control over myself than this, so I'm surprised by my outburst.

Stress. That's it. The stress of today and last night must be wearing on me.

"Yes. Eli." He says the name like a curse. "Eli is from a group of fae who have been cast out of their homeland beyond the mountains. They have committed a crime and are cursed as part of their punishment. The tattoo relates to whatever act of treason they committed and is a constant reminder to them of their treachery."

This is the first time I've ever heard of a land behind the mountains. Sure, I assumed there was *something* beyond the mountains and that they didn't just fall off into the sea. Occasionally a fae would turn up, but I had never known that there was a whole land of them on the other side of the mountains. I suppose that makes me naive, yet no one has ever spoken about it. I don't understand why it would be kept a secret, so I assume no one knew about it.

With Eli's face still imprinted in my mind, I remember the swirling shapes that made up his tattoo and how I thought they were beautiful. The gold glimmered and almost appeared to shift in the light.

If what the king said is true, his tattoo is a curse for

committing a crime. Eli's tattoo was right down the centre of his face, even his lips shimmered with the patterns. There is no way to hide a mark like that, meaning that everyone who sees him will know what he is. What did he do to get cursed like that? He seemed so surprised when I spoke to him, and the happiness in his eyes warmed my heart. It would make sense that anyone who knows of the cursed would treat him differently, which could explain why his face lit up when I spoke with him.

"You should stay away from him. Remember your place and the part you play in our survival." The harsh way the king speaks to me causes the image of Eli to vanish from my mind.

"Of course, Your Majesty. I would never do anything to jeopardize the safety of my people."

How dare he assume I would act as selfishly as his son when I have done nothing but prove my trustworthiness since day one. I almost snap at him, but a gentle hand on the small of my back reminds me whom I'm speaking to.

"Good, you may go now. You have the rest of the day to spend as you wish. Just stay within the castle grounds."

With a bow, I turn and stride from the room, heading straight back towards my own quarters, Geoff on my tale. He can sense my mood and wisely doesn't say anything. It will only be a quick stop in my room so I can change out of my dress and into training gear. It's time for me to do some training.

I need to stab something with my blade so I don't use it on anyone else.

Chapter Eleven

Whirling around in a flash of steel and fangs, I slash my blade down on my imaginary foe. I leap forward into a roll and avoid their blow of retaliation, barely touching the ground before my feet are back under me and I'm spinning with a snarl on my lips. The target I've been practicing on is looking worse for wear. While it's designed to withstand the strength of supernatural creatures, vampire strength and my current frustrations are putting it through its paces.

The soldiers in the training yard all stilled when they saw me striding in, clad in dark leggings with a tapered overskirt, which is open in the front to allow for movement, and a vest that I use to train in. It is not all that unusual to see females dressed this way for sparring or travelling back home in Trador, but in Drathlor it is frowned upon. Females are expected to be in skirts and dresses, especially females of status. As a bride, others seem particularly shocked by my clothing. Clothing that reveals a female's legs is distracting and provocative.

When I'm training, I honestly don't care if my legs

distract males, only that I can move around and protect myself as necessary. If they get distracted by it, then that is not my problem, and they should train harder to develop stronger discipline. Anything that might benefit me in a fight is something I'm going to use to my advantage.

When I first arrived in the training grounds, I brought their training to a stop. However, I ignored them and pulled out a dummy target to practice with and jumped straight into my drills. Now that I have been here for the last two hours, I only get passing looks from them.

I know the other brides can fight, we were all given basic lessons together, but some of them choose to wield their abilities over their skill with weapons. As a vampire, my abilities come in the form of strength and speed. Because of this, I have honed my fighting abilities so my body is as much of a weapon as my blade is.

Back on my feet, I whip around and throw my long, wicked dagger, hitting the centre of the target with a satisfying thud. A grim smile pulls at my lips, and I stride forward, retrieving my blade and sheathing it at my thigh.

Leaving the training circle, I grab my bow where I left it leaning against the low fence surrounding the grounds. It takes me a matter of moments to strap my quiver to my back and set myself up at the archery targets. Positioning myself in front of the target, I begin around halfway on the track, notching an arrow and stretching the string.

Each target has a track set in front of it, with several marks painted onto the ground to identify how far away you are from the target. Most would begin from the first or second mark, but I have destroyed too many targets by shooting too fast and hard, so my warmup shots are farther back where many of the beasts begin.

Lining up my shot, I take a deep breath in and focus

entirely on the centre of the target. With a slow exhale, I release the arrow. It embeds in the middle of the target. Good. I take a few more shots, and all hit home. I step forward to retrieve my arrows before setting myself up several marks back. I go through the same process, slowly working my way back along the track, the distance increasing with each shot.

I'm on the second to last mark, the colour of the rings blurring together. My bow whines as I pull the string back, arrow notched and my target lined up in my sights. I force myself to still, my focus locking me into place so I can make the shot.

Breathe in.

Hold.

Release.

The thud of the arrow makes me smile. I can't determine if it hit the bullseye or not, but it's certainly in the centre ring. I have been working on my shooting from a distance. While I have the strength to manage it, my accuracy from such distances is not as good.

Awareness returns to me, and I become cognisant of a presence behind me. I whirl with my fangs bared, my blade in my hand as I bear down on whoever snuck up on me.

They either have a death wish, or they are trying to hurt me. In my experience, it's always the latter.

However, when I lock eyes with the male behind me, I only just manage to pull back from a killing blow.

Finnik.

What in the underworld does he think he's doing getting so close to a training warrior? I've seen the muscles in his arms, which someone doesn't get from just attending meetings. He trains a lot from the look of it. He should know better than to sneak up on me. If I hadn't managed to pull back, then I could have killed him. There's a part of me that rebels against that thought, but I push it aside and focus on my anger.

"Are you trying to get yourself killed?" I yell, not caring who might overhear. Speaking to him like this could probably get me executed, thanks to his close relationship with the royals, but in this moment, I don't care.

Finnik doesn't deign to reply, only stepping past me to peer at the target. His scent is crisp and fresh, the sort of smell that makes you want to roll around in it just so you can hold it for a second more. It is addictive—not that I would tell him that. He looks immaculate as always. I'm sure I look like a mess after two hours of training, and my scent will be anything but addictive.

Trying to calm my breathing, I watch him incredulously. There is something about him, an otherworldly aura that he carries around with him, and a presence that suggests pride and ego play a huge part in his personality. Despite not being from the kingdom, he moves around as though he owns the land, like he deserves to be here.

"It is impressive."

His comment takes me by surprise. I thought he was going to refuse to acknowledge me. Now that he has spoken, though, I don't know what he's referencing.

"What is?" I ask abruptly, not addressing him formally. If he wants to sneak around and be obscure, then I am not going to pander to him.

He finally looks at me, a glimmer in his eyes and a half smile pulling at his mouth. I don't know if all fae carry the same devilish look or if it is just something he mastered, but I get the sense he's amused by this whole interaction. "Your Highness."

"What?" I lower my bow, confused by his words. Is he

addressing the prince? Looking over my shoulder, I see we are alone, so that can't be the case. He's not addressing me, and I doubt a male like him would ever deign to admit I hold a position over them.

Clucking his tongue, he crosses his arms over his chest. "I think you mean, 'What, Your Highness.'"

Raising a brow, I give him a disparaging look as I realise what he's implying. "Just because you spend time with royalty does not make you one too."

"I know that." Rolling his eyes, he takes a slow, predatory step towards me. "I am, in fact, royal. I am a prince where I am from."

He carries himself like a royal, and his ego makes more sense now that I know this little snippet of information. If he is a prince, then why is he here? Does he not miss his family and homeland? I might have asked him this if it wasn't for the smug expression he wears. If he is expecting me to bow and scrape now that I know he's a prince, then he is about to be disappointed.

"Ah, but you're not there anymore, are you?" Something about him makes me want to push back and verbally spar with the fae prince, especially when he stops just inches from me.

His eyes narrow at my comment, his voice lowering. "I am currently your only ally when it comes to Havoc, so you might not want to offend me."

I scan him from head to toe. "Is that a threat?" My expression makes it clear that I find him lacking. Really, there is nothing lacking about Finnik. He's gorgeous and carries a grace that should be impossible, but I would rather die than ever admit that to him.

"Oh, it's a promise." He grins, but it's wicked, and two sharp fangs protrude from his mouth.

Huh, impressive. Fortunately for me though, I have my own. Grinning back, I let my fangs extend over my bottom lip. "I shall look forward to it then, Your Highness," I say mockingly.

He laughs, a short burst that seems to take him by surprise.

I raise my bow again and aim at the target, pretending his presence isn't a distraction. "What is impressive?" I ask, not taking my gaze from the target as I refer back to his original comment.

"That you can actually fight," he comments lightly. "You are not the pampered princess I thought you'd be."

Releasing the arrow, I wait only long enough to confirm that I hit the centre of the target before turning to look at the fae once more. "Your first mistake is assuming I'm a princess. I'm not. Secondly, all of the brides can fight, not just me." He's trying to get a rise out of me, I can see it in the mischievous gleam in his eyes, yet I can't seem to stop myself from biting back. "Plus, if you think that was a compliment, then you need some serious help."

I don't know why he's riling me up so much today when I am usually so good at blocking out others. A vampire trait is appearing cool and collected on the surface, but I'm struggling around him. I blame it on the events of the last few days causing my patience to be thinner than usual.

"No, the other brides can defend themselves long enough for their guards to step in and rescue them," he corrects, and annoyingly, he's right. "You might actually stand a chance against an attacker."

I snort. "Stand a chance? I think there is something wrong with your eyes, *prince*."

I am one of the best fighters in our land, my father ensured I had the best trainers available. My lessons were split between learning about court and what was expected of me and fighting lessons. These sessions went way past just self-defence, and I learned to love the burn of my muscles as I trained.

"There is nothing wrong with my vision." His expression is serious now, all traces of humour gone. "You are fast, and your aim is accurate, but training against imaginary foes is not the way to get a true indication of a fighter's worth."

His comment stings, but I know he's right.

Slinging my bow over my shoulder, I stalk towards the targets to retrieve my arrows, not wanting him to see the frustration burning in my eyes.

"I make the most of what I have," I call back to him, knowing he can hear me despite the distance. "No one will train with me for fear of hurting me."

A curse of being one of the brides. I am tiptoed around by most, fearing that I will get hurt and be unable to fulfil my part of the prophecy. In more recent years, my training has consisted of fighting against targets or soldiers far below my skill level. It isn't ideal, and I have fought with my trainers over this many times, but the answer is always the same.

"Then they do you a disservice." He starts to unbutton his jacket, and I watch him with raised brows. While I don't want to agree with him, I have been held back, and I know I can do more.

"What do you think you're doing?" Cocking my head to one side, I watch him roll up the sleeves of his shirt, admiring his thick, muscular arms.

"I'll spar with you," he replies.

Choking out a laugh, I shake my head with disbelief. "You have to be joking."

He wants to spar. Here, in front of everyone. A fae

prince. Their skills with a sword are legendary, but I am pretty sure I can hold my own against him. Princes don't get their hands dirty though, so I can't quite work out why he's doing this.

His fingers pause in rolling his sleeves so he can look up at me, his expression flat. "Do I look like I jest?"

No, he doesn't. In fact, he looks deadly serious. Shaking his arms out and rolling his shoulders, he unbuttons the top two buttons of his shirt to allow for more movement. Striding over to the weapons rack, he selects a sword, testing its weight and taking a few practice swings.

Excitement courses through me at the thought of sparring with him, where I can prove my skills and cut him down a few pegs—not to mention being able to fight against someone who isn't going to take it easy on me.

I left my sword in my room, not thinking I was going to need it, so I stride over to the weapons rack, ignoring how close that puts our bodies. His stare is hot on my skin as I examine the swords. None of them are as good as my blade, but they will do. Testing the grip on one, I go through a quick sword drill, confirming that this blade is acceptable for the purpose.

Without a word, I stride past him and into the practise ring, his smug smirk burning my pride. I will soon wipe it from his lips. He follows me, only stepping back when we reach the centre of the ring and take our places opposite each other.

"First to land a death blow wins the match."

Nodding my agreement, I surge across the ring, my steps kicking up bits of sand and grit in my wake. Speed is one of my strengths, so I'm going to take full advantage of that, hoping to catch him off guard.

He seems to be expecting this, though, and dodges to

the left, slashing his sword down towards my exposed back as I burst past him. Throwing myself into a roll, I feel the air move above me as I narrowly avoid getting cut. He might hold back a death blow, but he is clearly in this to win and doesn't mind wounding me in the process.

Good, I don't want him to go easy on me. When I win, I want it to be because of my own strength and skill.

Back on my feet, I whirl and raise my sword just in time to block another killing blow, the clang of metal ringing out around us. Feinting left, I duck to my right and swing towards his exposed side with a burst of vampire speed. I'm too fast for the eye to track, and I'm pretty confident that I'm about to win. However, his sword meets mine, and he manages to shove me backward. I stumble for a second but quickly regain my balance. He's on top of me though, taking advantage of my brief unsteady steps. He pummels me with blow after blow, moving impossibly fast, and I'm only just able to stop them from landing on me.

Disbelief runs through me. How is he so good and so fast? Are all of the fae this fast, or is it just Finnik? I might not win this fight. That thought causes a wave of anxiety and annoyance. If I start thinking like that then I've already lost.

Baring my teeth, I shove him back and manage to catch his arm with my blade. It's a shallow cut, barely anything really, but my instincts instantly take over. Whether or not I want to, I have no choice as I drop my sword and grab his arm, the scent of his blood driving me wild. In the blink of an eye, I've gone from fighting to holding his arm with a vicelike grip, rubbing my cheek against his skin like a house cat. Blood trickles down, and I press my tongue against his arm and lick along the path, groaning at his taste.

I have never tasted anything like it. I feel euphoric,

strengthened in a way I never knew was possible. It's addictive, and I want to sink my teeth in and encourage the blood to flow.

The cool metal of a blade presses against my throat, not enough to pierce the skin, but enough to get my attention. My mind finally wins the battle against my instincts, and I remember that I was in the middle of a fight. Shit.

"I win." His voice sounds tight, and I'm gratified to hear he's breathless. Good, I might not have won, but I made him work for the victory.

I don't blame him for the sudden tension in his body. He has a vampire ready to suck his blood without permission. Had I been one of the changed, then I might not have been able to hold back. As it was, the only reason I didn't bite him was because of the sword pressed against my jugular.

Releasing his arm, I take a step back, licking my lips and savouring every last morsel of his blood. I'm already missing it, but I tightly grab those urges and push them deep down within myself. With a deep breath, I meet his gaze, not sure what is going to greet me. He's probably furious at me for not having better control over myself. However, when my eyes meet his, I am surprised to see confusion looking back at me.

At first, I thought he tensed up because of what I was doing, but examining his expression and body language, I wonder if it is actually because he enjoyed it. A vampire's bite is euphoric. However, I only licked the blood that escaped the cut, no matter how much I had wanted to lock my lips around the wound, so he wouldn't have experienced that euphoria.

My thoughts are interrupted as he clears his throat and returns his sword to the weapons rack.

"You are skilled," he calls out, glancing at me over his shoulder. "But you rely on your speed too much. Against a fae, you would never stand a chance, not to mention the blood. That was a complete distraction for you and *will* get you killed in a fight."

While I have always struggled with the beast within me, I have trained to fight against the instinct to feed when blood is exposed since I was a small girl. My control is better than that, so what is it about his blood that made me lose that hard-won control? My ego burns, not just at losing against the fae, but at showing my weakness. Thinking over his words, I frown at one of his comments.

"Against a fae, you would never stand a chance."

The only fae I have ever met are him and Eli, and while I have heard tales of other fae in the kingdoms, they are rare. Why would he bring up the fact I wouldn't win against a fae unless it's something that I should be focusing on?

"Am I likely to have to fight against the fae?" I watch him closely as I ask the question.

His face shuts down, giving me nothing to go on. That in itself is an answer. There is more going on than what they want everyone to believe. Sighing, he shakes his head, his gaze intense. "I will train you. Meet me here an hour before sunrise."

Clearly, I get no say in this. "Tomorrow morning?" I ask to clarify. While I'm surprised at his offer and don't particularly relish the idea of training with him after what happened today, I can reluctantly agree I need more practice.

"Every morning," he replies, and with that, he strides from the area, leaving me watching his retreating back, wondering what just happened.

Chapter Twelve

Hot water streams down from the showerhead above me, causing me to moan with pleasure as it washes over my sore, aching muscles. I've not felt this exhausted and sore for a *long* time, and part of me can't help but wonder if that's because I haven't been training as hard as I should have been back in Trador.

Rubbing my hands over my body, I wash the sweat and grime from my skin. Most of the castle denizens will only just be waking up for the day, yet I have been awake for hours. I don't mind the early start, as I only need an hour or two to recharge, so I was already up and dressed when I was expected to meet my new fae trainer.

As I expected, training with Finnik is a nightmare. He was harsh and uncompromising this morning. Gone was the mischief from his eyes, and it was replaced by a harsh taskmaster. To my surprise, he took me to a quarry just outside of the castle grounds and had me climbing sheer rock faces with nothing but my hands, destroying boulders with my fists, and throwing huge chunks of rock as far as I could manage.

When I complained that I thought we were training with blades, he told me that working on my strength was just as important. Only expecting my abilities to help me is lazy, and I need to work them just like any other muscle. Sparring would come when he thought I was ready.

I am already dreading tomorrow morning.

Today, I am meeting with Havoc, just him and me. I'm not quite sure how I feel about it, but I am filled with trepidation. Considering how hostile he's been towards me so far, I'm not expecting anything different from him. Even so, I am determined to make every effort. No one will be able to accuse me of not trying to uphold my role.

I finish cleaning myself and dry before the maids come in to help me dress. Choosing a gown of deep red, I watch myself in the mirror as the young females flit around me. The bodice is low and form-fitting, as is the preferred style in Trador, with a loose gauzy skirt, allowing for full movement. There is a slit in the fabric up to my thigh, and I wear leggings beneath the skirt because I don't know what the prince is planning for us today. Floaty, off-the-shoulder sleeves finish the look, exposing the mark on my neck. My silver hair is dried and brushed, left down as I requested, with only a band of bronze flowers woven around the crown of my head.

A knock on the door has one of the maids scurrying to open it, and through the mirror, I see Geoff step into the room.

"Lady Anthea, are you ready?" he asks as he straightens from his bow.

"Yes, let us go," I reply with a tight smile, my words far more formal in the presence of the maids. There is no doubt in my mind that everything they see and hear is reported back to the king, so I will not give them any reason to doubt my intentions.

Walking through our suite of rooms, I don't see any sign of Felix, and I feel disappointed. Seeing his happy smile would have helped reassure me as I step into this day of uncertainties. I nod in greeting to my four guards who are on duty today and let them lead the way.

As usual, our section of the castle is deserted, and we only start seeing signs of life once we cross the thin bridge separating us from the main part of the palace. Most of the windows here are tinted, allowing vampires and other creatures of the night to fit around the schedule that the king keeps. The only one that isn't tinted happens to be the patio where the other brides and I meet. Back in my homeland, we mostly hold court and live life in the evenings, but because most of the world is awake during the day, we have learned to adjust.

Geoff and I say nothing as we walk. While it isn't all that unusual, I get the feeling he's as tight and wound up as I am today. He poured a large portion of his life into moulding me into the perfect first bride, and nothing is going to plan. He would never blame me for that, he knows how hard I have worked—how hard we have both worked.

My guards lead us into a part of the castle I have never been before—the royal wing. Curiosity burns in me, and despite my trepidation, I can't help but examine everything with quiet fascination. Like the rest of the castle, the hallways are large and open, but the pillars that hold up the walls are made of a type of marble I have never seen before. Veins of sparkling blues and greens glisten as we pass, almost as though they are lit from within.

We are just about to reach the day room when I hear two low voices. I'm not sure what makes me do it, but I throw out my arm to stop Geoff in his tracks. The guards instantly stop with us, glancing around to check for threats and waiting for further instruction. Geoff glances down at my arm, frowning as he looks up at me, ready to snap at me for touching him. When he sees the look on my face, though, he stays silent, his eyes going distant for a moment as he extends his hearing.

"Havoc, you have to do this," a familiar voice chides. "Think of your people."

Finnik. Even if I didn't recognise his voice or feel that strange pull towards him, there are very few people who would talk to the prince that frankly. It would be a death sentence for anyone who wasn't part of their inner circle.

"Do you think I would still be here if I wasn't thinking of them?" the prince hisses, his frustration clear. "I would have jumped on a ship and sailed as far away from here as I could have as soon as I discovered I was her mate."

The bond in my chest weeps at his harsh words. Biting down on my lip, I force myself to stay silent despite the agony. Am I really so bad that he would abandon his kingdom to avoid having to know me? I still don't understand his aversion to me, and usually I would cut my losses and move on, but I can't. We are tightly bound, and there is no way around it.

Finnik sighs, and I hear the weariness in his voice. "The gods have decided your fate, my friend. There is no changing it, not without dooming us all."

With the fae's hearing, he must have heard that I'm here, yet he continues speaking, meaning that for some reason, he wants me to hear this conversation.

I hear a snort followed by the sound of striding footsteps. For a moment, I think he is about to leave the room and find me huddled in the hallway, but I hear him spin and return in the other direction. Pacing, he's pacing.

"I do not believe in your gods." Havoc sounds as though he's about to lose his temper, but he surprises me by sighing. "I *will* find a way out of this without dooming my people. Have faith in me."

That is what he's been spending his time doing, trying to find a way out of having to be my mate. Anger washes through me as I push away the sadness that threatens to overtake me. How dare he? He thinks I'm not good enough for him and that he can just toss me aside. If it weren't for the prophecy, then I would be in the first carriage back to Trador.

"I always do, Havoc," the fae replies, and despite sounding muffled from being on the other side of a wall, I can still hear the warmth in his voice. The two of them seem to really care for one another.

Finnik clears his throat, and I hear movement in the room. "Your bride approaches."

Well, that's my cue to stop eavesdropping and enter the room. I share a look with Geoff, and he wipes the look of frustration from his face before he gestures to the guards to lead us forward once more.

Rolling my shoulders back, I take the few steps to the door that separates us. We are quickly met with Finnik as he opens the door.

Without waiting to be invited in, I step over the threshold, knowing Geoff is following close behind. I give Havoc a tight smile and dip into a curtsy. "Good morning, Your Highness." My greeting is polite and follows protocol. I will not have anyone saying that my manners were what caused the prince to push me away.

Straightening, I glance over to the fae, his hands clasped

behind his back. "Finnik," I say with the slightest dip of my head. My entire body aches because of what he put me through this morning, and I'm still feeling sore about it.

"Lady Anthea, Geoff," Havoc greets sharply. Leaning against a desk, he looks like every female's dream of a handsome prince, his blond hair lightly tousled and his royal jacket pristine. "Anthea, I thought we might get some fresh air and go for a ride."

The fact that he wants to go for a horseback ride when the sun is up and going to be at its warmest in a couple of hours just goes to show that he either doesn't care about my comfort or he is so self-involved that he hasn't thought about it—not to mention the fact that he sounds less than enthusiastic about it.

"Your Highness," Geoff begins, stepping forward, a frown marring his features, "the morning light will make it very uncomfortable for Lady Anthea, what with her being a *vampire* and all. Perhaps a more appropriate activity could be arranged."

"Oh." He looks at me, his expression one of surprise, but his eyes hold a smug gleam. He knows exactly what he's doing. He's testing me. "Maybe we should cancel the—"

"A horseback ride sounds lovely," I reply, stopping him before he can get too far. The sunlight won't kill me, and I will not let him use this as an excuse to get out of spending time with me.

"It won't be too uncomfortable for you?" His question is said through clenched teeth as he attempts to keep his expression neutral.

"I think you will find that there isn't much I wouldn't do for my people." The retort is barbed, and I see it hit home. I really shouldn't be baiting him, but I just can't seem to help it. I am really starting to dislike my mate.

"Havoc," Finnik warns from his side.

Smiling at me through bared teeth, the prince ignores his friend, balling his hands into fists at his sides. "Wonderful, let's go."

As I climb up onto Shadow, I am suddenly very glad that I chose to wear leggings under my skirts. Side saddle has never been a position I adopted. When I ride, I want to *ride*. I love feeling the strength of my horse beneath me as she moves as fast as the wind.

Felix places his hand on my leg as he helps me adjust my stirrups. We are so close that our faces almost bump into one another. Chuckling quietly, I move back and watch the smile on his face. I love his smile. It literally lightens my day. If only I was going on this ride with him and not my moody mate.

My friend opens his mouth to say something but decides better of it, his smile becoming sad. Rumours travel quickly in this castle, and he's clearly heard about the animosity between the prince and me. While he knows not to believe everything he hears, it's clear just by looking at my mate and me that something is not right.

"Are you ready?" Havoc asks impatiently, sitting atop his white stallion.

Biting back a cutting remark, I take a deep breath, share a look of exasperation with Felix, and straighten in my saddle. I take the reins and gently nudge Shadow into a slow walk, steering her towards the prince.

"Of course, Your Highness."

Without replying, he clucks his tongue, and his horse starts to walk. Shadow matches his speed without me having to direct her until we're walking side by side. This gives me the perfect chance to admire his horse. Tall and proud, the pure white stallion practically gleams in the light of the rising sun. It must take a lot of grooming to keep him in such good condition. Next to Shadow, they look like a perfect couple.

I don't think it's a coincidence that my black mare is the complete opposite of his white stallion. It is as though fate brought them to us as a visual representation of us.

The sun has peaked over the top of the castle, and its rays are warm on my skin, feeling both comforting and uncomfortable at the same time. If I stay out in the sun for long, then it will drain me, making me weak, but there is enough shade created by the trees that I should manage without too much discomfort. Honestly, it's so nice to be outside, enjoying the breeze against my skin and being away from the stress of the castle, that I barely even feel the irritation of the sun. Shadow trots beautifully beneath me, needing little direction from me as I bask in the beauty of the land around us.

The parts of the land closest to the castle are manicured and hold an array of flowers and exotic plants. However, the farther we explore, the less pruned the land is, as though nature is taking back the space for herself. It's perfect.

I have no idea how long we've been out exploring in silence, but I feel comfortable with the prince like this. He seems lost in his own thoughts, and a contemplative quiet has descended over us. After what must be at least ten minutes, I decide to break the silence.

"The grounds are beautiful," I comment softly.

From the corner of my eye, I see him startle, but he seems to relax as he follows my gaze to a row of wildflowers that creates a bright splash of colour.

"Yes," he agrees. "Although I don't get the chance to come and admire them often."

Noting a slight tinge of regret in his voice, I decide to broach the subject of the two of us. "Perhaps we can arrange to have our wedding out here? That way you can admire it for the entire day."

I hope he will see the effort I am putting in to try and make this work for both of us. However, I see him stiffen, his expression changing to anger. I misjudged and pushed him too far, erasing any progress I might have made earlier.

Tightening the reins in his hands, he jerks his horse forward until he moves into my path. Shadow stops abruptly so as not to crash into him, rearing up in the process. Thankfully I'm holding on tightly, so I don't fall, keeping my seat as she returns to the ground. Havoc knew what he was doing when he blocked my path, and from the furious expression on his face, I know he has something to say.

"I. Will. *Not*. Marry. You." Each word is spat out, full of venom, as he holds my gaze. He wanted to look me in the eye when he told me this, that's why he stopped us. Is he trying to get his message across, or is he just trying to dig the knife in and make this hurt more?

"Why?" I ask, my chest constricting with the pain the bond is causing. "Why do you hate me so much?"

Growling, he tilts his head up and stares at the brightening sky. He looks as though he's attempting to put his thoughts together, so I say nothing, giving him time to formulate an answer. I'm furious and done with his attitude, so even if I have to wait all day, I am not leaving here without knowing what the hell I have done to upset him so badly.

He drops his head, and his eyes gleam as he meets my stare. "It's not you I hate. Just what you are."

I think he's attempting to apologise with that feeble excuse, his shoulders shrugging as some of his anger drains away. That is what all of this is about, his dislike of my race? He cannot put up with marrying a vampire to save the kingdom.

I shake my head, needing clarification. "You hate vampires?"

"No, although I wouldn't say I think much of your kind." He takes a deep breath, shaking his head. "I belong to the Brothers of Change."

I hiss at his comment about disliking vampires, unable to let that insult pass. My attention quickly shifts, though, as he mentions the group he's part of. The name sounds familiar, but I can't remember where I heard it before. What I do know, however, is that it gives me a strange, wary feeling.

"Who are the Brothers of Change?"

He lifts his chin and meets my gaze. "We are a group that doesn't believe in the prophecy and thinks that the brides will actually bring about our downfall. We think we can break the curse by adopting change and rejecting the prophecy."

I stare at him in open-mouthed shock for a moment. Is he serious? This has to be a joke. I remember my father telling me something about a group that was going around, trying to brainwash people into rejecting the prophecy, but never in my wildest dreams would I have thought my mate would be one of them.

"What you are saying goes against everything we believe, everything we have all worked for over the last several centuries. What evidence do you have that the brides will doom us? The only way for that to happen is to ignore the prophecy!"

I can't believe I'm having this conversation with him. Prophecies have been a part of our culture as far back as our records go, and we have always paid them heed. When this one was announced, all the kingdoms immediately adapted to ensure everything was in place for the brides to be selected.

Havoc is living up to his name, believing a group of fanatics who have decided they can change the world without following the prophecy. Personally, I believe he's only listening to them because he doesn't want to be fated to me. This gives him a way out, and they managed to talk him into believing it. I'm interested to see what evidence he has to back up his belief.

"You wouldn't understand," he scoffs, his face contorted with anger. "Besides, you are one of *them*, you would try to convince me that you're right."

Nothing. He has nothing, no proof that the prophecy is wrong and that there is another way to break the curse. Even if there was another way, why risk it when we already have a plan?

"Is that really reason enough to doom our people? Are you really so selfish?" I ask with bewilderment, shaking my head with disbelief. My anger builds again, the darkness within me rising, and it takes everything in me to wrangle it under control. I try to put my thoughts into words. "The last thing I want to do is marry you, Havoc, especially after you have demonstrated how selfish and cruel you are. However, this is my fate, *our* fate, so I will see this out to the end."

Unable to face me any longer, he grits his teeth and looks away. I suppose my remarks hit home, but he seems to be sticking to his convictions. What I need to know now is how many others think the same way. From the way the king has been encouraging him to marry me, I would say he still believes in the prophecy, but I have to know for sure.

"Does the king believe this bullshit? Finnik?"

My question might be a little forceful, but I think it's justified after everything. I'm also not sure why it feels so important to know Finnik's stance, but I wait with bated breath for the prince's answer.

Blowing out a sharp breath, he stares at the treeline with a pissed off expression. "No, I'm the only one."

A weight lifts from my shoulders. I tell myself it's because I don't have to fight against the king or the other royals about the prophecy, but I know it's really because Finnik hasn't been brainwashed.

This whole conversation has left me exhausted, and I just want to go back to the castle and hide in the darkness, letting my sensitive skin recover from the sun and my bruised heart recuperate.

"So where do we go from here?" Even my voice is weary. We're at an impasse, neither of us willing to change our views on the situation. Something does have to be done for the good of the kingdoms though.

He finally glances back at me, and I see something in his eyes that looks like hope. "I'm trying to find a way out of us marrying that won't hurt my people in the process."

My eyebrows shoot up at how blasé he is about this. "Oh, it's alright to hurt me though?" Laughing without any hint of humour, I sit back in my saddle and look at him like the stranger he's turning out to be. "Do you not feel how painful it is each time you speak of rejecting me?"

Regret and frustration seem to war for dominance on his face, and he drags his hands through his hair. Annoyingly, it only makes him more attractive in a rugged, dark prince way.

"I don't want to cause you any pain, Anthea, but know this, I am only playing along to try and gain more time to find an alternative. I will *not* marry you. Not now, not ever."

As expected, the pain that racks through me takes my breath away, and a little part of me notices the prince grimaces, showing that he feels it as well. My pride has been wounded, but moreover, I feel as though I've failed my people. Breathing deeply through the waves of agony, I grip the pommel of the saddle to keep myself upright.

As soon as I feel as though I can ride without falling off, I attempt to sit up and meet his torn expression. I shake my head in disappointment and narrow my eyes. "You are a delusional fool."

Turning Shadow, I encourage her to gallop as fast as she can, leaving the prince behind. It's all I can do to lean forward and hold on for dear life, needing to put distance between us before I say or do something stupid. The world passes us in a blur, and I would usually love riding this fast, feeling the wind in my hair, but instead, I just feel numb.

The prince doesn't follow me.

Chapter Thirteen

Felix emerges from the barn as soon as he hears my approach, wearing a polite smile as he prepares to greet me and the prince. His smile quickly drops when he sees I came back alone, as well as the fact I'm practically draped over Shadow's back.

Any other horse would have dropped me, but Shadow and I have always had a connection that goes beyond that of a normal horse and rider. She looked out for me and changed her speed to make sure I didn't fall from my saddle.

"Thea!" Felix calls out, the alarm in his voice making me wince. He's at my side in a heartbeat, his hands on my waist as he helps me down. "What happened?"

Weak from the sun, exhausted, and sore from my escape and the agony of Havoc's rejection, I'm not quick to answer, my focus on staying upright. Felix curses and calls for one of the stable hands. I'm vaguely aware of him informing the boy to take care of my horse, giving very strict instructions. The next thing I know, his arm is around me, and he's leading me over to one of the barns.

As soon as we are out of sight, he shuts the doors behind

us, and I stumble over to one of the hay bales, using it as a seat. Felix turns and looks at me, anger simmering in his eyes. It's not aimed at me, but it's not an expression I see on him often.

"Did he hurt you?"

"No." I pause as I remember the pain of the rejection and wince. "Well—"

He leans over me and grips my shoulders. "What do you mean, well? If he fucking touched you, I'll—"

Rolling my eyes at his overprotective behaviour, I put my hand over his lips to stop him. It is my fault for letting the last part of my comment slip through, and I don't want him going on a rampage, especially over a misunderstanding.

"Don't be rash, Felix. He would crush you." Sighing, I lean against him for support. "He doesn't want me, Felix. He didn't lay a finger on me."

I know that Felix thought the prince might have hurt me, but for that to happen, he would have to get over his revulsion of me.

Seeing that my mood is only making Felix more unsettled by the second, I try to pull myself together.

"I'm fine. I just needed to get away and put some distance between us. The pain of his rejection was too much. The more distance there is between us, the quieter the bond is," I explain with a tight smile. "I can manage now. I'm okay."

This was supposed to comfort him, but it seems to have the opposite effect. He stills as though he's made of stone, his eyes locked on me.

"He rejected you?" The question is quiet, his voice deadly soft.

We are all taught about mate bonds when we are young.

This isn't just limited to vampires, but all races in the land. Race does not limit a mate bond. One of the main things we learn about these is that because they are so rare and all-consuming, it is very unusual for them to be rejected. When one does officially reject their mate, it is an extremely painful procedure for both, but more so for the one being rejected, and it often results in a shortened lifespan. Ceremonial words are needed, as well as shedding the blood of their mate, and then the bond will be broken for life. That does not erase it completely though. While they will no longer be bound, they will always feel as though they are missing a part of themselves.

Knowing all of this, I understand why Felix is concerned. I place my hand on his arm and smile sadly, shaking my head.

"No, he hasn't officially broken the bond. He only told me he will not marry me." A sharp pain like a dagger hits me as I speak, taking my breath away. I take several deep breaths and meet Felix's concerned gaze. "Considering how painful it was when he said those words, I don't think I would survive if he were to officially reject me."

This is a very real fear for me. If he officially rejects me, then I could die from the pain of the separation. If I die, then the prophecy will not be complete, and my people will suffer for it. All of my training and hard work will have been for nothing.

Sensing my line of thought, he pulls me against him, wrapping his arms around me in a comforting hug.

"You are the strongest female I know. If anyone could survive that, it would be you," he states firmly. Pressing his mouth to the top of my head, he kisses it before resting his cheek there.

Comfort and safety surround me, and in this moment, I

can pretend we are somewhere else. I take a deep inhale to settle myself further. He smells like home.

"Besides, that won't happen," he murmurs into my hair. "He's an idiot, but he won't doom the entire kingdom for the sake of his pride. Why wouldn't he want to be your mate? I would kill for that honour."

I don't think he's joking, and if he's speaking the truth, then this could change everything. Stilling, I pull back enough to look up at his face. His expression is serious, his eyes a complex mix of emotions.

"Felix, what are you saying?" My voice is a whisper, as though my volume will help contain the rush of feelings his words cause. I don't dare presume what he means in case I'm wrong and destroy everything.

Thankfully for my fragile heart, he doesn't leave me waiting. He cups my face with his hands, his expression softening as a gentle smile pulls at his lips. "I'm saying that I love you, Thea."

The world seems to shift around me, tilting on its axis as his words sink in.

I love you, Thea. The declaration rings in my mind, over and over, until those three words are all I can hear. *I love you. I love you. I love you.* The young, uninhibited part of me is overjoyed, my heart pounding in my chest, but that part of me was pushed to the back of my mind a long time ago. I don't have the time nor freedom to think like that, not when the fate of the land rests partially on my shoulders.

Felix's thumb gently strokes my cheek, and I realise he's still speaking. Shaking myself from my internal musings, I focus on what he's saying.

"I have for a long time, yet I said nothing because I didn't want to ruin our friendship when nothing could happen between us." His face darkens, but I know this change in mood isn't aimed at me. "We will never be accepted as a couple, and you have a mate, but I will not let you think you are unlovable. The prince is a prick for thinking otherwise."

He's right. A relationship between a born vampire and a changed vampire would never be supported, especially not when one part of the couple is the first bride. That's one of the reasons I have never let myself indulge in fantasies of the two of us despite the sexual tension between us. Geoff has always kept a close eye on us, noticing our connection, and has threatened to separate us several times because of this.

However, Felix has decided to end his silence on the subject. He truly believes that nothing will ever happen between us, but he has laid his heart out for me to see simply so I know I am capable of being loved. He doesn't expect me to reciprocate in any way, he's simply here to make sure I'm okay. It's selfless and something that sums up Felix perfectly.

I'm going to tell him how I feel. No, not tell—I'll show him exactly what his words mean to me. I might come to regret this later, as this will make things more complicated, both between us and the mess that is my relationship with Havoc. I am hurt and aching, though, from Havoc's rejection, and Felix is here, caring for me, just like he always has. If I allow myself to admit it, then I can admit I have had feelings for Felix that go far beyond friendship for a long time. We have walked a fine line with our friendship, knowing our circumstances would make a relationship impossible.

With him here now, comforting me and admitting his true feelings, it makes me feel brave enough to take what I have so desperately wanted for so long.

Our bodies are already pressed together thanks to the embrace he instigated, so it doesn't take much for me to push him backward until his back hits the wall of the barn. His eyes are locked on me, yet there is something in his dark, intense gaze that makes him appear... hungry. It makes me want him all the more.

Without waiting for him to say anything, I push up onto my toes and press my lips to his. They are soft and plump, making me want to sink my teeth into them. Felix kisses me back, his lips moving against mine gently.

"No, I don't want gentle right now," I whisper against his lips, gripping his shoulders tightly, my nails digging into his skin. "There will be a time for that. Right now, I want you to show me that you love me."

For a moment, he stares down at me, and I think he's going to say no. I have a mate, and Felix is the type of male who would never cross that line. He has seen how toxic the bond between Havoc and myself is though, as well as how he rejects me publicly. The prince wants nothing to do with me. All of this seems to flit across his face—Felix has always worn his heart on his sleeve.

However, before I can even take my next breath, he makes his decision and grabs my waist, flipping us around so I'm pressed against the wooden wall. Threading our fingers together, he lifts our hands above my head, pinning them there. His free hand cups my cheek as he gazes down at me.

"If I had it my way and the prophecy didn't exist, I imagine the two of us would live in the countryside of Trador, perhaps running a stable together. We would live there by ourselves with no one around to bother us. It would be peaceful and happy, a simple life." He smiles as he talks, but it turns into a seductive smile. "I could show you how much I love you every day."

"That is a beautiful dream, Felix." Looking up at him, I feel sad at the reality of our situation. "But I am never going to be able to give you that."

He kisses me slowly, showing me exactly what he thinks of my comment. "Any stretch of time spent with you is enough."

If I were the type to swoon, that is exactly what I would be doing. He's too good for me, he always has been, and I worry he's going to get hurt in all of this. Only a moment ago, I was ready to throw caution to the wind and let my feelings take the reins. Now, I'm lost in my mind, worrying that I might fuck this all up. He's one of the people I am closest to in my life, losing him because of this would destroy me.

Breaking the kiss, he arches an eyebrow. "I can feel you overthinking this, Thea. I'm not a naive little boy. I know the situation, and I'm prepared to face the consequences if needed. Now, kiss me and let me make you feel better."

He's giving me a choice—step back and forget this happened or kiss him and enter into a new life. It's terrifying. I have only ever grown up knowing that I will have to marry someone as part of the prophecy, and then as I got older, I learned Havoc was my mate. Felix has never been part of that equation.

Logically, I know I should step away, but my heart is making decisions for me now.

As soon as my lips touch his, he moves, releasing my hands and using his own to feel my body. Nicking his lower lip with my fangs, I gently work the resulting drop of blood into my mouth, humming as he continues to explore my curves. His blood ignites every nerve ending, and I know I'm playing with fire. Having sex weakens my control, and here I am, making him bleed and teasing myself with the scent of his blood. I'm walking a fine line, pushing myself to the limits of my control.

Sliding his hands up my tunic, he finds my breasts, working my nipples into stiff peaks. The sensation is everything, not to mention my feelings are heightened by the fact anyone could walk into the barn at any time.

Tearing at his shirt, I ignore the sound of ripping fabric and run my hands over his chest, his pale skin smooth and soft to the touch, yet the hard muscles below make his chest and arms feel firm. I always forget how much of a workout it is to work in the stables, constantly mucking out stalls and carrying heavy equipment. He might have a boyish look about him, but he is all man, something he reminds me of now as he presses against me, and I feel the hardness of his cock through his trousers.

Needing to feel him, I push the waistband of his trousers down, gasping as his cock springs free. He's not wearing underwear. I wrap my hand around his length, enjoying his noises of pleasure as he twitches in my palm. Pushing past my open skirt, he slides my leggings and underwear down, cupping my pussy before dipping a finger between my folds.

What he finds makes him groan with pleasure as my wetness coats his fingers. I'm so ready for him. Circling my clit, he uses various pressures until I'm a mewling mess. If I wasn't pinned against the wall, I would be slumped on the floor, my knees having given way at the pure pleasure he's bringing me.

The world tilts again, but this time, it does so literally as he lifts me and balances me over his shoulder. I feel safe and protected the whole time, even in our lust-filled state. Placing me on a hay bale, he gently pushes me back and opens my legs, muttering something that's distorted by a growl as he takes in my arousal for him.

He drops to his knees, his soft, warm breath blowing against my most sensitive areas, causing my back to arch. He's not even touching me, yet he's bringing me the most pleasure I've ever experienced. The moment his tongue flicks against my clit, I am unable to hold back my cry of pleasure, tilting my head back and threading my hands into his hair.

Chuckling against me, he dips his tongue into my channel, eating every drop of my desire for him. He slides a finger inside me as his tongue returns to my clit. My entire existence narrows down to this one moment, the pleasure he's bringing blocking out the pain of Havoc's rejection. This feels so *right*, so perfect. How is Havoc my mate, and Felix isn't? Why would fate be so cruel to pair me with someone who can't stand me?

All of those morose thoughts disappear as Felix adds a second finger, crooking them so he hits that sweet spot within me. I feel his devotion through his touch. Each flick of his tongue and movement of his hands are to bring me pleasure, his own needs put on the back burner.

Pleasure builds until it crashes over me like a tidal wave, sweeping me away on a tide of ecstasy. Spasming around his fingers, my body takes everything he's willing to give, pushing me to the very edge. It's only as I slowly start to come down from my high that I feel him lovingly kissing my hot, swollen pussy.

Pushing myself up so I sit on the edge of the hay bale, I pull him towards me, stretching up to press my lips to his. He tastes like my release, and strangely, I love that. My inner possessive darkness finds it sexy, like he is branded with my essence, warning off anyone else who might dare to look his way.

I want to feel him inside me, feel him fill me until I overflow with his cum. Reaching down, I take him in my hand, stroking the precum off the tip and directing him towards my eager pussy.

"Wait." His voice is tight with regret, making me freeze.

Why does he sound that way? Does he regret what we just did? My mind spirals, trying to push through the fog of hormones. He's looking down at me with a rueful smile, taking my hands in his and linking them.

Is this going to be another rejection?

My heart fractures a little.

He must see this, because his whole stance changes, his shoulders rolling back and a frown tilting his lips. "Don't you dare think I'm rejecting you." Lifting my chin, he presses a hot kiss to my lips, rubbing his hips against me so I'm able to feel his rock-hard cock.

"Do you feel how much I want you? How much I love you?" he asks breathlessly, kissing me between words. "As much as I want to fuck you, Thea, I won't do it like this. Not yet. Our first time will not be in a barn." He rests his forehead against mine, and his stare seems to penetrate to my soul. "I want you to be mine, and I don't want to have to share you with *him*."

Anxiety flips in my stomach, something I don't let most people see. He can see right through my masks, though, he has always been able to.

"I don't know what's going to happen in the future with Havoc." The admission feels like a failure.

He nods, not even a hint of judgement in his eyes. "Neither do I, but something in my gut is telling me to wait."

He's right. Now that the haze of my arousal has faded, I

can sense the same warning, my instincts telling me to wait. I have never experienced this before with any of my other sexual partners, so I have to assume it has something to do with Felix specifically.

"This doesn't reflect my feelings for you. I have waited for you this long, and I will wait as long as it takes." Each word is said with such conviction that I believe him. When he kisses me again, I allow myself to fall into it, kissing him as though he is the male I'm going to spend the rest of my life with.

He pulls back from our kiss and smiles at me sadly. "You should probably go back to the castle. They will be looking for you."

With a sigh of disappointment, I nod my understanding and jump from the hay bale, straightening my clothes so I don't look as though I've been fucking in a barn. He sorts his own clothes out, tucking himself away.

We share a final, silent kiss, and then I turn and stride out of the barn as though nothing just happened. A dark cloud has covered the sun, making my walk back to the castle feel longer than it should. The wind whips around me, signalling that a storm is coming. At least it will remove the scent of arousal from me before I get back.

My journey gives me a chance to think over everything and get my thoughts straight, so I keep my pace slow and even despite the turn in the weather. As rain starts to fall from the sky, I can't help but feel as though it is reflecting my own turbulent thoughts.

Chapter Fourteen

I attempt to duck the blade that slices through the air, but I wince as it nicks my cheek, a small trail of blood dripping down my skin. If I had been a fraction slower, it would have hit me, and I would be suffering with far more serious wounds than a cut cheek. He's a merciless instructor and doesn't hold back, forcing me to use my full abilities in our training.

He doesn't believe in practicing with blunt weapons or padded protection, making each sparring session just as dangerous as any real fight would be. Training this way forces me to put everything into protecting myself and coming up with creative ways of getting out of difficult situations. The only difference between training with Finnik and fighting a real opponent is that the fae male doesn't *want* to hurt me.

This morning, that feels different. Finnik is in a foul mood, his attacks more ferocious and ruthless than usual. He barely even grunted in response to my greeting when I walked into the training room, simply throwing a blade in my direction, expecting me to catch it. I did, of course, immediately dropping into a defensive stance as he lunged at me with little warning.

Seeing the blood trickling down my cheek, he stops his attack and steps back, putting a healthy distance between us as he scowls at me. Finnik is not the warmest of males, but today he's like a different person. It unsettles me, putting me on edge.

"I cut you," he snarls, stating the obvious as he jabs his dagger in my direction. He seems angry, irritation making his body stiff as he glares at me. What I can't decide is if he's angry at himself for cutting me or at me for getting cut in the first place.

"It's okay, I forgive you," I say in jest, although there is nothing comical about the tone I used. Reaching up, I smear the blood with my finger before popping it into my mouth and sucking it, the delicious flavour bursting on my tongue.

He isn't amused by my comment and bares his teeth at me. "You are holding back. I could have killed you!"

My patience is fried, and I don't have the restraint to hold back as I usually would. I step forward, my free hand balling into a fist.

"I am in *constant* pain thanks to Havoc," I spit out with malice. "The longer your friend continues to reject me, the worse it is going to get. I think you could cut me a little slack."

What I don't admit is that I feel weaker by the day. Gods, I can hardly even admit that to myself, let alone him. I feel so useless here, floating about like a spectre and hoping the prince changes his mind, unable to fulfil my purpose and protect my people.

"Then you need to master your power *now* before it's too late!" he shouts, gesturing widely. "I know you have more within you that you are too scared to let out, but you must. Your destiny is not an easy one."

The darkness. That has to be what he's talking about. Somehow, he is able to sense it. There have been a few occasions when we've fought where it rose to the surface, and I was so focused on my fight that I didn't immediately notice. It is possible that he picked up on it then, but he would have to be paying close attention to me. Other than those who have seen it, no one has guessed about the darkness I carry, and knowing that he suspects something makes my knees feel weak.

Standing straight, I take a deep breath and pray I can keep my voice steady. "I don't know what you're talking about."

"Coward," he spits, disappointment colouring his expression.

Outrage floods through me, scalding everywhere it touches, threatening to destroy the careful barriers I have in place. He has no idea, not even the slightest inkling of how difficult it is to control the darkness that hides inside me or how long it has taken for me not to constantly fear it breaking free of the cage I locked it in. He might see my actions as cowardice, but I'm really protecting them all. No one would survive the wave of evil that would destroy the world should I let the darkness out. It is a huge slap in the face for him to treat me this way, but I could never tell him, because he wouldn't understand.

Instead of an indignant response where I demand he take his insult back, I stifle my pride and channel it into something else.

"I have no idea who shat in your coffee this morning, Finnik, but do not take it out on me. You could have killed me with that move, and you know it," I snap, snarling at the fae and flinging my own dagger at him.

I don't even bother to aim, the blade flying through the air faster than the eye can track. He dodges the dagger of course, since my intention was never to hit him, but it makes a point. His eyes narrow into thin slits of rage, and he slowly walks towards me, crossing that careful distance he always keeps between us.

He's looking for a fight, wanting to hurt someone to ease his own pain, except it doesn't work. Him cutting me only made him madder, not giving him the sense of relief he's so desperately searching for. I don't know what emotion he's running away from, but the intense look he levels at me is making me nervous.

Each slow, deliberate step he takes towards me is filled with challenge. I should back down, since he's clearly going to take his feelings out on me. The smart thing to do would be to leave the room and speak to him again once he has calmed down, but I stand my ground, my body loose should I need to move quickly.

"Had you been paying attention, then it wouldn't have been an issue." His voice is deadly calm now, and that is somehow more terrifying than when he was shouting. He takes one final step, and we are so close I feel his body heat radiating from him. "Besides," he continues with a pointed look, tilting his head to one side, "you are a fine one to talk."

Blinking, I frown up at him in confusion. I already feel offended, and I don't even know what he's talking about.

"What in the underworld is that supposed to mean?" I demand. All of my intentions of not rising to his challenge go flying out the window.

"You were fucking some other male to get back at Havoc, knowing full well what that would do to him." His accusation is bitter. "I spent the entire night holding Havoc back from tearing apart the castle to find your lover."

My body seems to still for a moment in surprise, my brain digesting the ridiculous accusations. I don't know whether to be furious or to laugh aloud. Is he serious right now? This is what has him in such a twist? A single, shocked laugh escapes me, my brows raised as I stare up at him.

"Excuse me?"

Does he truly think so little of me? Firstly, I had no idea that Havoc felt anything through our connection, because he never seems to show any signs of discomfort when he's constantly rejecting me. I suppose I should have suspected that he might have been able to feel me, yet I was in such a tailspin yesterday that my thoughts were focused on surviving the day.

The biggest outrage to me is that he thinks I should stay celibate when I have repetitively been rejected. Havoc and I may be predestined to be together, but we are most certainly not a couple. He doesn't want me, therefore he gets no say in my romantic life.

Finnik's mouth twists into a sneer. "You heard me. He felt everything you were doing yesterday after the two of you parted ways. He was furious."

He moves abruptly, a flash of silver warning me that he has a blade. Thankfully, I was expecting something like this from him. Trust him to use this as a training exercise. As he attempts to get beside me, my weight is already on my toes and I duck, spinning around and kicking out to catch his legs. To my surprise, it works, and he stumbles, pushing himself into a forward roll and back onto his feet in a second, weapon in hand.

"He rejected me," I snap, circling him, my own dagger

glinting in my fist. "He told me he would *never* marry someone like me."

Finnik leaps forward, and I only just manage to block his attack, bringing us face-to-face once more, so close I can feel his breath on my cheeks. "He is your mate."

His anger turns his voice into a snarl, but I get the strangest feeling he's not actually mad at me when he says this.

"Oh, so I was supposed to stay celibate this whole time, was I? No one gave me that memo." With a burst of strength, I thrust him away from me and immediately go on the attack, leaping after him and slashing my blade towards his open side. "I suppose this standard is different for the prince, or are you telling me he's still a virgin?"

I'm so impassioned and bitter about this whole situation that I allow it to cloud my judgement, causing my reactions to be riskier than usual. In my move to catch him off guard, I leave my left side open. Taking full advantage of this, he leaps towards me and tackles me to the ground. I refuse to go down easily, kicking out with my legs as we both land with a thump. Finnik disarms me and pins my arms to the ground before I can even blink. The only benefit to this is that he no longer has access to his own weapon.

Vampires are strong and fast, but so are the fae, and I am completely pinned and at his mercy.

Lowering his face until we're almost touching, he shakes his head, a mocking smirk pulling at his sinful lips. "You allowed yourself to get distracted by your emotions. Again."

From this angle, with his wayward hair falling forward and the mischief sparkling in his eyes, he looks every inch a fae. I need not see those pointed ears. Despite being a panting mess, he still has an otherworldly beauty to him—

something I am currently being forced to look up at, making me all the more frustrated.

Thrashing under his hold, I make a noise of irritation when I hardly move, his smirk only growing at my anger. Fine, if he wants to keep me here to make a point, then I'm going to make sure he knows the truth about what happened. Something inside me has been twisting ever since he said I had been fucking someone else, and it seems important that he hears my side.

"I did not *fuck* anyone, so Havoc needs to get his facts straight," I spit out, my nose crinkling at the accusation. If he's surprised by my sudden tirade, then he hides it well. "Was I with someone last night? Yes, I was. However, we did not have sex."

I keep the rest of my encounter with Felix to myself. Finnik doesn't need to know what we *did* get up to. If he was with Havoc, then he will already know that *something* happened, so I'm not going into it. That is private and belongs only to Felix and me.

Looking back on it now, I'm glad we didn't take that step and go all the way last night. I would not want to regret my first time with him in any way, and the fallout from all of this would take away from the magic of our time together. Caught up in the hurt from Havoc and needing to feel loved, I would have gone all the way with Felix, but thankfully he was able to keep his head on straight. My feelings towards him haven't changed in the slightest, and he deserves to have all of me, not just the aching, broken pieces that were looking for a bandage.

"Not that I need to justify this to you *or* the prince," I challenge, my eyes flashing with rage and indignation. "He doesn't want me, remember? I do not belong to him, not yet, so I can do whatever I please. He cannot reject me and then be upset when someone else wants to be with me."

Finnik is watching me closely, some of his animosity draining away as he listens. He seems... relieved, yet I cannot figure out why. Even his grip on me seems to have lightened, and if I tried, I think I could escape his hold, but I still have one final point to make.

"There is a simple way for him to stop all of this confusion, and it is to face his destiny and marry me."

He opens his mouth to reply but is cut off as the doors to the training room slam open. I jerk my head around and find Havoc standing in the doorway, his face like thunder as his eyes land on Finnik pinning me to the ground.

Rage transforms his handsome face into someone I don't recognise as he looks between Finnik and myself. He vibrates with anger as his whole body seems to grow, his lips curling with disdain.

"You whore."

I have been called worse in my life before, but to hear my fated mate hurl the insult towards me like a weapon causes damage. This will take a long time to heal from.

It's the strangest sensation, because I feel as though I'm being pulled in two directions. Defiance and resilience are two attributes that have not always made me the easiest to shape, but they help me cope with setbacks. I am certainly not the type to cry over a male who doesn't want me, because my own sense of self-worth is greater than that.

However, there is also a part of me that was brought up being told she was going to save her people and had a mate who would love and cherish her forever. That type of thinking belongs in fairy tales, and this is anything but. Life rarely has a happily ever after. It was wishful thinking that I would come here, and he would instantly love me. The bond stirs up all of these feelings and brings them to the forefront of my mind, making it all the more difficult for me to see past them. It feels like a constant battle within me, and I don't know which side is going to win.

Consumed with loathing for me, Havoc's eyes blaze. All of this happens in a flash, and I clearly don't react in the way he wanted me to, because with a sharp gesture, he barrels towards Finnik and me.

Finnik is up in a flash, moving towards his friend, his hands up in a show of innocence as he steps in front of me, forcing the prince to look away from me. "Havoc—"

The prince turns to look at the fae, and with a snarl, he shoves him away. "Was it you? Did you fuck her behind my back?" he demands, pain lacing his words—not because of me, but because he believes his best friend betrayed him.

Finnik stumbles back a few steps, the shove having taken him by surprise. Pressing his hand over his chest, he stares at the prince with a wounded frown.

I sit upright, propping myself up with my arms as I watch the two males, shocked at how quickly Havoc turned on his closest friend. How can he truly believe that is what happened when logistically, it would not have even been possible?

My movement must catch the prince's attention, as he quickly spins to focus on me. Hands balling into fists, he prowls towards me. "It wasn't bad enough that you're whoring around, but you had to sully my closest friend too?"

That's enough. Any patience I had left is now well and truly destroyed. My body feels strange, twitchy, and suddenly full of energy, and as I stand, I notice a pounding in my ears that gradually gets louder until it blocks out all other sounds. Facing off against my betrothed, I bare my teeth in warning.

"How dare you?" I seethe, not caring that others can overhear us.

"Havoc, listen to yourself!" Finnik jumps between us, using his body as a barricade to keep his friend from getting any closer to me. Placing his hands on the other male's shoulders, he physically stops the prince and waits for him to meet his gaze. "I was with you yesterday, remember? It couldn't have been me."

The prince's posture changes, his body seeming to deflate in front of my very eyes. His head falls forward as he releases a long breath. When he looks up once more, he seems apologetic, yet I know none of this is for me.

"I'm sorry brother." Havoc claps his friend on the shoulder. "This demon is clouding my mind."

Demon, well, that is a new one. Shaking my head, I cross my arms over my chest. He cannot just waltz in here, insult me, and not get a mouthful back. I will not sit back and take his shit.

"Unless you have changed your mind about being my husband and mate, then you have no right to control if I sleep with anyone." Taking a step to the right, I make sure I'm within view as I speak, our eyes locking. "I could fuck half of the guards, and you still have no say as long as you're looking for a way out of this."

I don't tell him that I didn't have sex last night, or that it's been a long time since I did. No, my point still stands. Whether I slept with someone or not, I am not going to justify myself to him.

Havoc tenses, clearly trying to maintain the control he only just managed to regain.

Finnik steps in, blocking his view of me once more and

clapping his friend on the shoulder to get his attention. "Havoc, I am almost finished with her training. I will find you once we're done."

This is obviously the escape route that the prince needs, because he spins on his heel and stalks from the room, walking like one of those little wooden dolls with no knees. He doesn't even glance in my direction, and while I am not surprised, the bond weeps in my chest.

Finnik sighs and runs his hand through his hair, looking exhausted. It's still early in the day, many haven't even risen yet from their beds, but he looks as though he needs to go back to sleep. "That was a shit show."

I'm not sure if his murmured words are aimed at me or if he's talking to himself. Either way, he's right. The prince is not reacting normally to the bond. He's overreacting to anything that comes from my side and apparently not feeling anything when he's talking of ending our connection. He should be in agony over that. I know I certainly am. The second he suspected I slept with his friend, he blew up.

Finnik continues to stare at the door where his friend just left, a deep frown marring his perfect face.

"He's not going to change his mind," I say quietly. I'm not sure what made me lower my tone and why it almost sounds... gentle, but it shakes both myself and Finnik from the fog that settled over us.

"He might for his people," he replies firmly, finally looking away from the door, but we both know that is just wishful thinking. He rolls his shoulders and gestures towards the centre of the room. "Come on, let's finish this."

Holding back my groan, I narrow my eyes on him. "You really want to train after that?"

"Not really," he retorts with a raised brow, "but I want to talk to you about something."

This time I don't manage to hold back my groan, but I walk over to the centre of the room as instructed.

"If it's about Havoc—" I begin, but he cuts me off.

"It's not. It's about your fighting style." He gestures towards me. "You could have bitten me at any time and that would have given you an advantage. You don't reach for any of your abilities, and I know you're holding back."

His last comment causes me to stiffen up and look away, not able to look him in the eye. I'm sure he will take this as confirmation of what he's saying, yet I worry he will be able to see straight through me and into the darkness nestled within me.

From the corner of my eye, I see him arch a brow as he comes to his own conclusion. "Are you ashamed of being a vampire?"

"What?" I bark, completely dumbfounded by the question. How in the underworld had he managed to come to that conclusion? "No, of course not."

I was brought up differently than the other born vampires thanks to the destiny that marked my skin. However, I love being a vampire, and my own people are what keep me going through everything. Thinking over his words, I understand his point about the fact that I didn't use my fangs. I'm not sure why I didn't, it just never occurred to me to bite him. Despite my many years of training, violence isn't something that comes naturally to me.

Pursing my lips, I shoot him an exasperated look. "Perhaps I just don't like to hurt people."

Instead of reacting to the sly insult, his brows rise with clarity. "That's what it is. You very rarely ever go on the offensive, only defending yourself. You don't want to hurt anyone." He laughs, pressing a hand to his forehead in disbelief.

Grinding my teeth, I wait for him to stop laughing. "What's so funny?"

"You're a vampire, one of the most ruthless creatures in the eight kingdoms, and you don't like to hurt anyone." He shakes his head, his voice teasing. "You do drink blood, right? Or do you survive off plants?"

He's mocking me, and after the morning I had, I do not have the patience to put up with it, not when I don't fully understand why he's teasing me. What does it matter if I don't like to hurt others? I am still able to fight better than half the guards here.

"I drink from volunteers." My voice is curt, making it clear he offended me with his mocking. I should just mind my words and return to my rooms, but embarrassment and frustration make my tongue loose. "Why are you here anyway?" I bite out, letting my eyes trail over his body, noticing as it stiffens up. "Were you so terrible back in your home realm that you were thrown out and had to come here to terrorise us instead?"

As soon as the words leave my mouth, I realise I made a mistake, something that is only compounded as his face turns stony.

He stares at me for a moment with an intense look that makes me shudder. "Training is over."

"Finnik," I call, taking a step towards him, but he's already gone, using his speed to escape me before I can say anything else to offend him.

While I could probably chase him, my speed almost matching his, I know he needs some space from me right now. Groaning at my stupidity, I let my head fall back as I stare up at the ceiling, having chased off one of my only allies here.

Chapter Fifteen

As I stare out of the carriage window, I enjoy the feeling of the fresh air hitting my face. Getting out of the castle and away from the weight of the prophecy was the only thing I had on my mind this morning. It had taken a lot of organisation, yet as I get farther away, I know it was worth it. The city passes by in a colourful blur, the setting sun casting orange and pink hues on the white buildings.

As we get closer to the poorer part of the city, the colours dim, replaced by a darkness that has nothing to do with the setting sun. The distance from the castle seems to directly reflect the state of the dwellings, as though it's the palace itself that gives life to the city. By the time it reaches the outskirts of the city, that life force is drained, leaving cramped, crumbling structures.

Everything is closer together here, all of the buildings reaching up to the sky for any scrap of space they can find. None of them are uniform, although that does give it some charm, the mismatched shapes and structures making me want to look closer and see how they were made.

The carriage suddenly lurches, and I look out of the window in shock. We seem to have passed an invisible barrier, which is the only way to describe the sudden change in the land around us.

The slums.

As we roll into our destination, all my earlier happiness is dampened by the sight that awaits us. If I thought that the city we just passed through was cramped, then this is something different altogether. The dwellings are cobbled together one-room shacks, the walls made of anything they can find. Some of them are a little more structural and seem to have been here a while, and they even have walls and doors. My heart breaks as I see a young girl attempting to fix an old, torn piece of fabric that had been acting as a tent wall. It can't possibly offer her much shelter, yet that is everything she has.

It's not only the sights and smells that shock me though, but also the sounds that hit us. There are no calls of merchants trying to peddle their wares or the general hubbub of city life. No, the noise here is a cacophony of suffering.

Horrified by what I'm seeing, I lean back in my seat, a heaviness passing through my body. I don't know where to look, glancing from one sight to the next and struggling to process what I'm seeing. We hear how bad the conditions are in the slums, yet those reports are nowhere near enough to portray how truly awful things have become. Being here now, everything hits me in a sudden rush.

I had slowly been going mad in the castle. With Havoc refusing to see me, Finnik barely talking to me, and no obligations to keep me busy, I decided to do something useful. Helping rebuild in the slums had been Felix's idea, one I felt was a perfect distraction.

Felix has ventured into the city several times since we arrived and discovered that part of the slums was washed away after a flood. He makes friends wherever he goes, his happy demeanour making him easy to like and get information that locals wouldn't usually give to strangers. This meant that he was able to find out that there were citizens who need aid. There was a group of volunteers helping, but there weren't enough of them.

As soon as he told me this, I knew I found the perfect opportunity to assist. There is nothing for me to do in the castle, and I feel utterly useless, unable to complete my part of the prophecy while Havoc continues to refuse me, and I want to do something *good* with my time. If the prince gets his priorities sorted and marries me, then I shall be living here.

Unfortunately, it had taken a lot of organisation and permission gathering before I was finally allowed to go. The king and his advisors had not been keen on the idea of me wandering around in the city alone. The slums were considered dangerous, so in order for them to agree to my little mission, I require an escort with me at all times. One of the city folks has also been hired to liaise between me and the other volunteers to keep things moving smoothly.

The wheels of the carriage start to groan as the ground becomes broken and uneven. While I didn't need a carriage for this journey and would happily have walked into the city, it was part of the agreement I had to sign before I was allowed to leave.

"Are you regretting your decision now?" Geoff's voice is tight.

Glancing over at the male, I struggle to hide my amusement at the look of discomfort on his face. He clearly doesn't want to be here, yet he insisted on coming with me when I told him about my plan. He winces as we pass a pile of debris that someone had obviously been living in at some point.

My amusement dies as I follow his gaze.

"I told you that you didn't have to come." There's no accusation in my tone as I state the facts. This is not for the faint of heart, and I knew it would be something Geoff would struggle with.

His snort catches my attention, and as I look over, I see him pulling a cloth handkerchief from his jacket pocket. Looking offended, he dabs at his face with the material before tucking it up his sleeve and narrowing his eyes on me.

"As if I am going to let you waltz into the slums alone."

Geoff is like a father to me, and I feel very affectionate towards him, but he is going to be a fish out of water once we step from the carriage. In a political situation, I would not want anyone else by my side. Here, I fear he's going to be more of a hindrance. We are about to help rebuild in the slums, and he's wearing his finest clothing.

Raising my brow, I gesture out the window to the guards that surround the carriage. "I am hardly alone."

"Those meat heads..." He mumbles something under his breath that I don't catch, but a smile pulls at my lips anyway. Geoff has never been a fan of the king's guards, preferring our own. This was another condition of working in the slums though—we could only take the king's guards as our escort, not our own. Most likely so they can share our every move with the king.

My stomach drops when I see the devastation of the flood that washed away part of the slums. It is chaos. There are people everywhere, both humans and denizens from the other realms, all crushed together as they pick over the debris of what once would have been someone's shelter. The smell here is atrocious, a mixture of waste, stagnant water, and rotting food. It seems to permeate everything, and I know I'm going to struggle to remove it from my skin later.

"Look at the state of this place," I murmur in horror, my eyes wide. "How can the king allow his citizens to live like this?"

My heart breaks for these people. They had to carve out a life for themselves in a place like this, and then that was ripped away from them, leaving them with nothing. Nausea washes through me like the flood that destroyed these homes, consuming me whole. I have to do something.

I'm not really expecting an answer, my question more of a stunned statement that I couldn't keep within me, but when Geoff sighs, it's full of regret.

"The castle and his life are a long way from here, and royalty tends not to see further than the nobility who follow them. As long as the rich are happy, then all must be well within the city."

Anger makes me jerk back from the window. "That is just arrogant blindness." I throw my hands into the air as I fight my exasperation. I have to be careful of what I say. Any insult to the king is usually dealt with swiftly and forcefully.

No. This is something I will not keep quiet about. Should the king discover what I have been saying and decide to punish me, then so be it. I speak the truth.

"He cannot bury his head in the sand and pretend none of this is happening! If he wants to be the ruler of the continent, then he needs to take responsibility for *all* of his subjects. They are owed that much at least!"

Eyes widening in alarm, Geoff leans forward with a

stern hiss. "Keep your voice down, Anthea. While I do not disagree with you, we are not alone, and you know his dogs will report anything they hear."

"They should," I retort, feeling reckless with my anger. "Maybe he would do something about it then."

Geoff's eyes flash with warning, but he doesn't argue with me, just continues to watch me carefully as though he's not sure of my next move. I look back out of the window, my emotions turbulent within me. This is so much bigger than one person, so my help is going to be like a drop in the ocean compared to what is really needed.

Letting out a long, exhausted sigh, Geoff rests his hands in his lap, glancing out the window. "While I am not defending the lack of assistance in the slums, this is an issue that goes far deeper than the king ordering aid."

I look over and take in his defeated posture. Geoff is not the type of male who ever lets something beat him, so I find it very strange to see him like this. The weight of his fatigue makes him seem older somehow. He is old, I know this, but thanks to his vampire heritage, he appears middle-aged in human years.

"The slums continue to grow by the day," he continues wearily. "There aren't enough resources for everyone. It is how areas such as this are built, the lack of space forcing them to find shelter wherever they can."

I consider his words, mulling over the issue. If a surge in numbers is the ultimate problem, then a solution is needed regarding that. There would be a reason behind why the increase in population is happening.

"Why are all these people here?" I ask, seeing creatures from all seven races. Most of them appear to be humans, yet I see all seven realms represented here. Something must be pushing them from their homes. If there was only a small group of them, that would be one thing, but for a mass exodus from their home realms to live in the slums of Drathlor City is a whole different matter. They willingly gave up their homes and came here with no guarantee of anything. How bad must things be back in their home realms for this to seem like a better option?

Geoff sighs and looks away from the window, turning his attention to me, his expression tight and concerned.

"The prophecy." He says those two words like they are the answer to everything, yet I still have so many questions. Seeing them written across my face, he takes a deep breath and continues. "War was promised, but the lands are beginning to warp too. Life is being drained from the ground, slowly destroying the realms. I suppose they thought they could come here in hopes that being closer to the king would protect them longer."

Why have I not heard of any of this? The castle in Trador is right at the bottom of the realm, so I suppose it would be easy to miss something that was happening on the borders. However, the land dying is pretty big, and as one of the seven from the prophecy, I should have been told about this.

Staring at my escort, I open my mouth to give him a piece of my mind, but no words come to me. He knew about this, and he kept it from me. I should be worried about the life draining from the realms, and I am, but I am more upset that he's been lying to me.

The carriage rolls to a stop, and the door is opened swiftly by one of our guards. I don't say a word to Geoff, taking the guard's hand and exiting the carriage.

"Anthea," he calls out behind me, but I don't stop, taking in the chaos around me.

We seem to have stopped in front of the volunteers'

base, a large tent-like structure set up to act as a shelter and a place to organise the efforts. It's busy, everyone looking like ants as they scurry about, yet they all seem to know their place and job.

A middle-aged human spots us and peels away from a group of people who seem to be organisers, looking at a map. Once he reaches us, he bows deeply.

"Lady Anthea, it is a pleasure," he greets, his voice warbling slightly with nerves. I'm not sure if it's because of who or what I am, but I ignore it. "My name is Luca, and I am your guide while you are here."

I become aware of Geoff standing behind me, but I don't take my eyes off the male in front of me. "Thank you, Luca, put me to good use, I want to help."

He smiles tentatively and gestures towards the tent. "Of course, if you will follow me."

He leads me away from the carnage and towards the temporary structure that has been put up. The smell of cooked food greets us, yet it only mixes with the foul stench already in the air, and it makes my stomach turn. It doesn't seem to have that effect on anyone else though. Long tables have been set up at the back of the meeting point, and every single chair is taken as creatures from all different races eat from their bowls as though they are starving. Looking at how thin most of them are, that would be an accurate assessment.

Luca clears his throat to catch my attention. "We thought you could help give out soup."

My brows shoot up into my hairline with disbelief. "You want me to hand out soup?"

While there is absolutely nothing wrong with handing out soup, and I meant it when I said I would help with any job, they have clearly picked something they thought would keep me out of the way. Near the entrance of the tent are several large counters where a group of females and a couple of males are cooking and serving soup to those who wait. They have a good system going to keep the line moving, and there isn't space for me, so I would only get in their way.

I am physically able to help with the more difficult work, and my race gives me particular skills that will be useful here, yet they want me to hand out soup.

"Is there a problem?" He looks nervous, wringing his hands together as he looks between me and Geoff. It's clear Luca is terrified of me, although I don't have the slightest clue why. I spotted at least one vampire since I have been here, so I don't think it's because of *what* I am, but *who* I am.

"Yes, Luca, I'm afraid there is," I begin, turning so I can gesture to the devastation behind me. "I'm a vampire, I'm strong, and I want to help rebuild. Put me to good use!"

Looking completely dumbfounded, he blinks at me several times as though not understanding what I said. He frowns as he attempts to figure out what to say to me. "Well, we thought you might not want to—you see, it's very muddy—we just thought—"

His stuttering and stumbling reveal the true nature of the issue here. Whoever organised this excursion for me obviously assumed I would not even dream of tramping around in the mud and lifting heavy bits of debris. In fact, they probably believe I'm here just to look good. The first bride of the prophecy handing out soup in the slums—how lovely. No, that is not how I will be remembered. When I put my mind to something, I dedicate myself a hundred percent.

"You thought that I'm a pampered princess who wouldn't want to get her hands dirty," I say, cutting him off.

There's no malice in my words. I do not blame him for the assumption, since born vampires have a bit of a reputation for shunning physical labour. "Look, this isn't a publicity stunt, this is where I want to be. Use my skills, I want to help."

He stares at me intently for a few moments then nodes. "Follow me."

Dropping several broken pallets onto the growing pile in my section of the slums, I huff out a breath and brush back the silver strands of hair that escaped my braid. It feels so good to be physically active.

I look up at the sky to work out the time. We have been at this for around four hours now. Thankfully, the moon is bright without a single cloud around to obscure it, making the hard work a little easier—not that anything about this is easy. As soon as they pointed me in the direction of where they wanted me to work, I threw myself into it. I'm exhausted, and my entire body aches, but I don't mind the pain because I know I'm helping. The beauty of this is I don't have to think, and I'm able to switch off my mind.

Geoff surprised me and dove straight in to help once he saw what I was doing, and as I straighten and stretch out my back, I see him talking to a shifter child, gesturing towards the temporary base. It makes me smile, but my lips soon drop as I glance around and take in the destruction we still have to get through. We have barely made a dent.

Continuing to pick through the debris, I clear what I can, not concerned about the muck and filth that cover me. When I was given this section to work through, I was warned that we might discover bodies under the wreckage.

The search parties had been called off at this point, and recovery of the dead is now in progress. No one could survive being crushed under all this for that long.

While I have seen many dead bodies before, I desperately hope I don't find any today.

My heart aches again, twinging enough to make me wince. Pressing a hand against the pain, I focus on keeping my breathing even. The twinge happens again and again. Letting out a slow breath, I move around to see if that helps ease the sensation. Although I am just aimlessly wandering around, I quickly realise that when I move in a certain direction, it eases a little, becoming less of a pain and more of a pull. Frowning, I move slowly through the debris, following the instinct that's guiding me.

A figure appears in front of me, carrying a large wooden panel above his head, and I stop in my tracks, my chest no longer aching. In fact, warmth spreads through me. The male also stops, tilting his head to one side as though he's confused, his gaze still forward but his focus elsewhere. His eyes glaze over as he loses himself in his thoughts.

The moonlight shines down upon him, and I realise with a kick in my chest that there's a reason he seems so familiar. It's Eli, the mysterious fae who swept me away at the ball.

Eli, Eli, Eli.

My heart seems to pound to the sound of his name, my skin breaking out in goosebumps at the sight of him. Why am I having such a strong reaction to him? Even now, I feel myself being pulled towards him as though an invisible string ties us together and I'm being reeled in.

He appeared so suddenly that night, and after our magical dances together, he vanished once more, as though he was an apparition or a dream. If others had not interacted with him, I might have believed I was going mad. I would be lying if I said I hadn't thought of him since the ball, especially at night when I'm alone in my bed. In my dreams, he is always close enough for me to sense him, to want the promise of what he could offer, but is just out of my reach.

My recollections had not done him full justice, and seeing him here right in front of me causes my cheeks to flush—not an easy feat for a vampire. I need to go before he spots me. My clothes are dirty, and I am sure my hair is a mess of silver strands after digging through wreckage and debris for the last four hours.

I am in such a hurry that I jerk forward. He turns to look at me, his gaze locking on me immediately. As soon as our eyes meet, something comes alive within me, sparking and igniting a hope I didn't know was there.

I don't understand this connection between us. How can I feel so comfortable around a male I know nothing about? It feels so different from my bond with Havoc, yet just as powerful and binding. It's a promise of what could be, which makes no sense, because Havoc is predestined to be my mate. I feel a similar connection to Finnik, which only complicates that matter. Right in this moment, though, my only thoughts are on Eli, my mind utterly enthralled.

I'm locked into place as we stare at each other, hungrily committing every detail of him to memory in case I never see him again. It feels like fate has brought us together today, something I don't usually believe in. The fluttering in my chest tells me that this is *right*. He looks like I remembered, yet something about the moonlight makes him appear different.

The pallet is still balanced easily on his shoulder, and his bicep is flexed, showing off his strength. He's wearing dark trousers and a loose, dark green shirt that compliments the golden hue of his skin. His golden hair almost looks silver in this light, the long strands pushed back from his face as he works. This only highlights the golden markings on his face, going from temple to chin. I have no idea what the swirling symbols mean, but it's beautiful in a mysterious way. Altogether, he looks wild as he admires me back, his eyes glowing with an inner fire.

Dropping the pallet to the ground, he strides towards me, each step causing my heart to somersault in my chest. My breath catches in my throat as he stops before me, close enough to touch, but carefully leaving space for me should I need it.

"Lady Anthea," he greets, his voice low and smooth, a smile pulling at his lips. "I didn't think I would see you here."

"Eli." My greeting sounds far breathier than I wanted, and his eyes crinkle in amusement. He knows exactly what effect he is having on me right now. Taking a deep breath, I clear my throat and continue. "The same goes for you. I didn't think I'd see you again at all, to be honest."

This is true, I didn't expect it, yet what I'm not going to tell him is that I dreamed of seeing him again. It is becoming clear from his growing smile that my face is giving me away. He seems to get past all of my walls, exposing my true feelings beneath, knowing I've been hoping to see him again, even if I didn't believe it would happen.

"I promised we would meet again, my lady. I don't go back on my promises." He smiles, but I can see how serious he is about his statement, and despite only just getting to know him, I believe him.

I am commonly addressed as "my lady," yet when he says it, there is something about the warmth in his tone that causes it to sound intimate. I need to change the subject before I get distracted by this euphoric feeling and do something reckless, like kiss him. Searching my mind, I fumble around for a topic, my thoughts sluggish.

"Do you help in the slums often?"

He finally breaks eye contact with me and glances over his shoulder. "Yes, I like to be useful." When he returns his focus to me, there is a shadow over his expression and a heaviness that seems to hover around him, the weight of the despair he's witnessing leaving its mark.

"Tonight is different though." His tone changes, his gaze intensifying. "I was drawn here. Usually I help during the day and was expected on the other side of the city, but my instincts were telling me I needed to be here. Now I know why."

My eyes widen, and my heart beats fast as I try to come up with a suitable response. What are the chances that he would suddenly just decide to help the same night that I am, especially when he never works at night? It cannot be a coincidence, and once again I can't help thinking that fate has a hand in all this. My overwhelming emotions and confusion over what's happening leave me mute.

Pushing back some of the stray strands of hair that have fallen into his face, he looks conflicted, his smile wavering and his stance becoming restless. His eyes sweep across my face as he watches me closely. He nods curtly to himself, his jaw set before he takes a step closer, entering my personal space.

"I hoped to do this differently, but I can't ignore this opportunity."

I start to feel uneasy at the sudden change in him. I might feel a pull towards him, but I still don't really know anything about him. While I don't think he is going to hurt me, his rapid personality change is making me anxious. "What do you mean?"

Reaching out, he grips my shoulders, his expression intense. "Run away with me."

I open my mouth to reply, but I don't have a clue how to answer him, my mind still reeling.

Shaking his head, he curses when he sees my hesitation and blows out a long breath. "I am messing this up." He closes his eyes for a second, gathering himself together. Once they open again, he seems more grounded. "I know how to help you. I know how to break your curse, but you need to come with me."

Chapter Sixteen

Staring up at the handsome fae before me, I shake my head. He can't have said what I think he did. *I know how to break your curse.* The words spiral in my mind, and I think I go into shock. Stepping back to give myself some breathing space, I press a hand against my breastbone, attempting to soothe the ache there. Time seems to slow down as everything else falls away, leaving just the two of us and his words hanging heavily between us.

Eli is still watching me with an intensity that both ignites something within me and frightens me at the same time, and he clearly wants to close the distance I just put between us. He senses that I need a moment, though, and holds himself back, shifting his weight from foot to foot as if to expel excess energy.

Turning my attention inward, I let my tumultuous thoughts take over, desperately trying to figure out what is happening.

He wants me to leave with him right now. I have never dreamed of any other path but this one, because I knew there was no point. This is what I was fated to do, all for the good of my people, but now he's saying he knows how to break the curse. He speaks so matter-of-factly, as though he expects me to agree and skip off to goddess knows where. It's crazy. What is even crazier is that I *want* to go with him.

Pressing my fingers against my temples, I release a long breath and try to remind myself why I'm here. I meet his gaze and let him see the confusion in my expression. "What are you saying?"

He glances behind me, most likely making sure no one is around to overhear. "The prophecy that binds the land is in action, and I know how to break your part of the curse."

I have never heard of the prophecy spoken about this way, and it makes me pause. Is he suggesting that as one of the brides, I am cursed? The way it was described to me my whole life was that the prophecy was a look into the future, spelling out what was going to happen if we didn't do something about it. The seven brides would come together and complete what was needed, and we would save the land.

However, he seems to believe something different.

I hold my hands up to stop him from going any further, needing to clarify something. "Wait, you make it sound as though you believe we are all individually cursed."

Raising a single brow, he looks at me as though I'm being deliberately dense. "You are one of the brides of darkness, the seven females who are cursed and have to discover how to save their people."

Brides of darkness? I have never heard of us being called this before, but he has to be referring to the brides from each race, since it is the only thing that makes sense. He's from a land beyond the mountains, so perhaps this is just what we are dubbed, yet he seems to know so much about the prophecy that it makes me wonder how much is actually being kept from us.

Eli's expression shifts, and it's clear he can see I have no idea what he's talking about. Sighing, he glances around us once more, lowering his voice as he takes a step closer. "The prophecy is made up of seven curses, each relating to the land the female hails from. Together, if they break their curses, the land will be safe."

Screwing my eyes shut, I let out a sigh as I press my fingers to my temples once more, my mind aching from the intricacies of the prophecy. "How is that any different?"

At the moment, other than telling me that I'm cursed, everything else he mentioned still sounds relatively the same. If that is the case though, then why is his urgency making me feel so jumpy?

Eli twitches in front of me, and I get the distinct impression he wants to reach out and touch me, yet he holds himself back. "The time frames are different for a start," he explains. "You are all different ages, so some of the brides aren't old enough to marry yet. There was never going to be a way you could all complete it together."

This makes sense, and if I think about it, I realise the prophecy never stated that we all need to work together, it was just assumed. Eli takes a deep breath, seeming to prepare himself before he speaks again, which makes me nervous. He's had no issues speaking the truth so far, so what is he going to say now that makes him pause?

"I theorise that each land is tied to the fate of their bride, so your actions will directly affect Trador and the vampires. The longer it takes you to break it, the worse the consequences will be for your people." He speaks smoothly, and I hear the note of apology in his voice. He knows this news is difficult for me to hear and is trying to break it as gently as possible, yet he's making sure not to leave anything out at the same time. He glances at my hand and slowly moves to take it in his, giving me the chance to pull away if I want to. I don't.

"Anthea, I can break your curse and help you save your people at the same time. You wouldn't have to marry that brute, Havoc."

My breath catches in my throat at the notion of being freed from marriage to someone who clearly hates me. I cannot let myself get caught up in this idea or let hope bloom inside me when there is no chance of it coming to fruition. There are so many questions pressing for attention within my mind, but I force myself to focus on just one.

"How do you know all of this?" I ask, my voice tight with tension.

"Because I am fae, and one of my gifts is foresight. I can see glimpses of the future." He shrugs as though what he's saying is completely normal and a run-of-the-mill ability. Perhaps across the mountains, among the rest of the fae, this is the case, but here, foresight is an incredibly rare gift.

From what I know of it, foresight is a double-edged sword, as nothing comes for free. It can be difficult to differentiate between what is going to happen and what *could* be. Trying to alter what cannot be changed can lead to dire consequences for either the seer or the subject.

I'm not sure I want to know what is in my future, but there is one thing I need to know. Taking a deep breath, I prepare myself for the answer, telling myself it will not change anything, when really, it will mean *everything*.

"Do I save my people?"

He shakes his head apologetically, suddenly looking exhausted. "I am unable to see the outcomes of each prophecy. I have seen prophecies like this before, though, and know how they work." His eyes suddenly glisten, and a small smile pulls at his lips in a way that tells me he's sharing a secret. "I also have additional sensitivities around you."

Whatever has made him smile like that is a mystery to me, but I wish I knew how to recreate it. "Me?" I ask, my voice breathy. "Why me specifically?"

He raises a brow again, but his smile stretches into a grin. "Because you're my mate."

The warmth I felt in my chest suddenly turns cold, the sensation spreading throughout my body. "That is impossible," I croak out, a tremble running through my body as confusion, hope, and fear battle for a place within me.

I won't run from this no matter how much I want to. Something beyond my comprehension is happening here, but we were brought together for a reason, and I need to see this through. Just because I do not understand something doesn't make it dangerous. Terrifying, yes, but I have faced the unknown before, and I can do it again.

Eli stills, his expression dropping into one of careful neutrality, yet I know my reaction hurt him.

"You did not know." It's phrased as a statement rather than a question, and I realise this is news to him. He thought I was already aware of the fact we are mates, when all I knew was that I felt connected to him.

"Havoc is my mate." The words taste like acid on my tongue, and oh, how desperately I wish this wasn't true and that Eli really *was* my mate. There is something I cannot deny, however, and that's the mate bond between Havoc and me. As soon as my and Havoc's eyes met, we instantly knew we were mates, even though he didn't want to be. With Eli, I feel so drawn to him that it seems cruel to separate us like this. Physically, yes, he's gorgeous, but it is more than that, as though a piece of my soul recognises him and wants to be reconnected. If I'm going to be honest, then I would admit that I feel the same sense of connection to Finnik. These feelings are so different from the otherworldly assurance I have with Havoc, despite having no physical or mental desire to be with him.

"I do not know what happened there, or how the two of you are mates, but what I can tell you with certainty is that you are my mate. I am not mistaken on this." He certainly seems sure, his gaze unwavering, not feeling the need to demand my understanding. "Can you not feel the connection between us?" He raises the hand he's still holding and presses it to his chest. "Feel my pulse as though it was your own? You cannot tell me that you don't feel it too."

I do, and that is my issue. I shouldn't be feeling this way when I already have a mate. Everything that I have ever been taught says I shouldn't even want to look at another male, let alone want to run away with Eli. I stare up at him, feeling his warmth and the thumping of his heart beneath my hand.

"Come with me, Anthea. We can leave now before they try to stop us."

For half a second, I allow myself to imagine what it would be like if I just left with him, the two of us disappearing into the night. We could be happy together, travel the land, and perhaps even cross the mountains to his homeland, carving a life for ourselves where prophecies don't rule our lives.

That half a second is all I will allow myself to indulge in though. There is no way I could ever leave when it could directly have an impact on others. Eli might think he can help me break the curse, but it goes against everything I've been taught over the years.

"My part of the prophecy is tied to marrying Havoc. I can't leave." I hate every word that leaves my mouth, but I speak with a surety that cannot be swayed.

"Is it?" he questions, his mouth twisting. "Does it specifically state that you have to marry the prince?"

No, it doesn't state who I have to marry, just that I will marry. However, I'm exhausted, frustrated, and confused by all of this, and I'm not going to start debating the wording of the prophecy.

"He's my mate," I reply instead.

He snorts at my lack of an answer, anger in his eyes. "He doesn't want you, and I know you do not want to be tied to someone like him. You are my mate too, Thea, you need to believe me."

His words might be true, and I know for a fact that Havoc doesn't want me—gods, *I* don't even want him. Despite all of that, Eli's words still hurt, making me recoil. I try to hide my reaction, but judging by Eli's frown, I know he can see right through it.

"I believe that you believe what you're telling me is the truth, but I can't leave." I beg him with my eyes to understand. "Not yet. I have to try and fix things with Havoc. The fate of my people is on the line here, Eli. I have to try."

Tilting my chin up to look up at the sky, I shake my head. "I barely know you." Even as I say this, I know it's not true. Somehow, I *do* know him. I know his heart and that his intentions towards me are true. It is impossible for me to explain how I know all of this when we have only ever met twice, but the surety of it rings through me with such clarity that all else seems to fade away for a moment.

Warm, gentle fingers cradle my cheeks, pulling my face down so he can press his forehead against mine. "But you do know me, at least your soul does. You are mine, Anthea, just as much as I am yours." The gesture is so intimate and his voice is so torn that it makes my heart break.

Laughter fills the air, making both of us jump, and we look around for whatever the source of the noise is, only to realise it is just a group of males passing by. They pay us no mind, and I am quickly reminded of where we are. This conversation is far from over. I cannot let him go thinking that I don't care for him. If he is right and we are mates, I can't risk turning him away. I just need a little more time to get myself straight. The slums are not the place for a conversation like this though.

Biting down on my lip, I fight with myself over what to do. I close the distance between us and press my hands against his chest, staring up into his pained eyes. I only meant to comfort him, yet now I'm in his arms and emotions are high, and the rational part of my brain is no longer in charge.

"Meet me in my carriage in five minutes," I say, and although his lips twitch up at what could very well be read as a sexual invitation, his gaze searches my face carefully. "We need to speak about this more, but in private."

His brows furrow ever so slightly, and I get the strongest urge to lean up and kiss his forehead until he is no longer frowning. This is not a good idea, and I need to put some space between us before I do something stupid. I don't wait for his reply, already knowing he will come.

Spinning on my heels, I move through the rubble until I find Geoff, gesturing that I'm going to take a break in the carriage. He nods his agreement, waving me off and returning to his conversation with a young female centaur.

As discussed when we were planning our trip, the carriage has been moved to a quiet street between the bottom of the city and the slums, two guards standing vigil to make sure nothing is stolen. They snap to attention when they spot me, waiting silently for my instructions.

"I'm going to rest in the carriage, please do not disturb me unless there is an emergency." Reaching inside for my vampire traits, I keep my expression stoic and my voice even so I do not give anything away. The last thing I need is for them to suspect that I am doing nefarious things in the carriage with someone who is not my mate. I must manage it, since they salute me and step aside so I can pass.

"We shall wait at the end of the street, my lady."

Dipping my head in thanks, I pass them and walk straight to the carriage. They didn't suspect me in the slightest, and I have no doubt Eli will be able to sneak past them.

Now safely ensconced within the walls of the carriage, I draw the curtains across the windows and light the lantern before taking a seat on one of the plush benches. All I have to do is wait. Of course, with nothing else to do, my mind starts working over everything that happened between us, dissecting each interaction.

I'm not bringing him back to the carriage to have sex, even though both my body and mind are trying to convince me otherwise. Does Eli think that is why I invited him to the carriage? He seemed confused and conflicted when I left, so he could believe that I just want to talk... or he was conflicted because he doesn't want to fuck me until I agree to leave with him. If he's right and we are mates, then having sex will bind us together, at least, that is how it works here. Who knows if things work differently over the mountains.

Even so, there is one very important reason we cannot have sex yet, even though I wish it were otherwise. Other than the fact that I want to get to know him and not just jump into a lifelong relationship with him, I can't do this while I'm still trying with Havoc. As long as I am Havoc's betrothed, I will not have sex with anyone else. I almost went too far with Felix the other day, and I'm glad he managed to stop me before I crossed a line.

There is a light knock on the door, and then it slowly opens to allow Eli through. Closing it firmly behind him, he takes a deep breath before he turns to look at me.

My fangs ache in my mouth, desperate to taste him.

I am not sure who moves first, but our lips crash together, and our limbs intertwine. It becomes impossible to tell where one of us ends and the other begins. My aching need for him drives my actions, and I almost feel like a vampire in a feeding frenzy, but it's his kisses sustaining me rather than his blood. He tastes like sunsets and the smoke of fire pits, his warmth heating me from within. I could get lost in this sensation forever.

Time becomes irrelevant, and I don't know if I've been in his lap kissing him for minutes or hours. I am completely absorbed in Eli. Like this, everything else falls away, and the stressors and burdens that await me outside this carriage cease to exist. All that matters is him and me.

However, like all things, it must come to an end. I won't take the next step with him until things have been rectified with Havoc and me.

Eli slowly pulls back from me. His pupils are blown wide from his desire, and he's breathless. It is gratifying to see he feels this pull as much as I do. Looking at my face, he takes me in, the longing in his eyes clear to see.

"While I want to take this further, this is as far as we can go until you decide what you are going to do with Havoc."

He understands. His thoughts are aligned with mine, and while we might take things further if the situation was different, I have responsibilities I need to see through. My body slumps with relief, as though the tension in my bones has fled.

He's not trying to make me feel guilty with his comment, but I find myself explaining. "I have to try, Eli. I won't let anyone say that this was my fault if the bond between Havoc and me fails."

It also gives me time to research and discover more about the fae and their mate bonds. The fae are so different, and if Eli is right and we *are* mates, then they clearly have different bonds. I need to know the potential consequences of binding myself to him, and if there is going to be anywhere that documents this, it will be here at the Drathlor Castle library. Seeing as I am going to be here for the foreseeable future, I should make the most of my time.

"The only difference I can think of is that I am from another land, so perhaps our bonds are different?" Eli muses, his expression confused, but his stare is locked on me like he's afraid I might disappear if he looks away. "It is rare, but where I am from, it is possible to have more than one mate."

Rocked by this revelation, I sit back on my side of the carriage. My mind is spinning with questions and possibilities. Does that mean it is possible to have both Havoc and Eli as mates? Does that mean I am not defective because I repulse Havoc?

"Do you think that is why our connection feels so different than mine and Havoc's?" I ask tentatively, not sure how I feel about either answer.

I don't mention Finnik and how close I feel to him, and I certainly don't bring up Felix. I have no idea how my closest friend fits into all of this, because while I have feelings for him, true, real feelings, there is no sort of bond guiding me when it comes to him.

Could it really be that I have more than one mate? Is that why I'm drawn to him and Finnik this way? They are constantly on my mind, hovering in the background and never quite letting me free. Even my dreams are consumed with the two fae and Felix, not my mate who I'm supposed to love.

"It could be," he responds carefully, trying and failing to hide his excitement at the prospect. Something shifts in him, though, wiping away any hint of happiness. "You're not coming with me, are you?"

Despite how much I wish otherwise, I shake my head. There are so many possibilities with Eli, but my responsibilities are here, and there is too much at stake for me to be selfish. I open my mouth to explain again, to apologise, but he stops me by raising his hand.

"It is okay, I understand why you have to stay." Blowing out a frustrated breath, he runs his long fingers through his golden hair, pushing it back from his face. "It was rash of me to ask you to run away with me like we are teenagers and this is our first love." He grins, absentmindedly rubbing a spot over his heart. "I got caught up in the pull of the bond and being so close to my mate."

"I know the feeling," I reply, a small, damaged smile on my lips.

He watches me carefully, pursing his lips thoughtfully. "We need to research your curse so we can figure out how to save your people and get you away from here." His words end on a snarl, but he quickly carries on. "I can meet you in the royal library."

Raising my brows sceptically, I tilt my head to one side.

"How are you going to get in? I thought you weren't welcome in the palace."

"Oh, I have my ways." He grins cheekily, and it drags my own smile from me. If anyone is going to manage it, it will be Eli.

Noise from the slums works its way to us, reminding us of where we are. My heart squeezes painfully in my chest, but I know our time is running out. "You better leave before anyone comes looking for me."

He nods reluctantly, his hand on the carriage door.

"Good night, Anthea." He leans in and kisses me lightly.

It is sweet and promises more. Closing my eyes, I let myself enjoy the feel of his lips against mine, committing it to memory. The warmth of his lips is replaced by a cool breeze, and when I open my eyes, I am alone in the carriage.

Chapter Seventeen

The cold kiss of a blade against my cheek causes me to jump back a moment too late, and it nicks my skin. A tiny trickle of blood rolls down my face, and the darkness inside me surges to the surface, my fangs aching at the prospect of a meal. Apparently, even my own blood is appetising today, meaning I really need to feed.

"Hit," Finnik calls out, indicating that not only has he scored a point, but it's also time to take a break.

Cursing, I step back and sheathe my blade at my hip, reaching up to capture the bead of blood on my cheek. The wound has already healed thanks to my vampiric healing, and I cannot seem to stop myself from putting my finger in my mouth and sucking off the blood. It tingles over my tongue, and I almost close my eyes in bliss. It has been too long since I last fed, and I will not be able to ignore the need for much longer.

"You're distracted today," Finnik scolds as he walks over to the side of the training ring, grabbing his bottle of water.

He's right. Ever since I returned to the castle last night, my mind has been turning, not giving me even a moment of rest. Although I do not need much sleep, I've not had any at all, and partnering that with my hunger, I'm spacy and grumpy.

The gaunt, scared faces of the children who were living in the wreckage of their shacks and the sounds of wailing of mothers who lost their children in the disaster have stuck with me. It was a harrowing experience, and as soon as I can convince the king to allow me to, I will return to the slums to help once more.

Unfortunately, there is more than just that filling my mind and souring my mood. Everything Eli told me has been burning in the back of my mind, and I'm desperate to ask Finnik if what I learned is true. I know I cannot do this, though, as I remember his reaction to Eli at the last ball.

Perhaps there is another way to convince him to tell me.

"Can you tell me about the land you're from?" I blurt out, wiping the sweat from my forehead as I watch him drink from his canteen.

His entire body stiffens, and he turns his narrowed eyes on me. "Why would you want to know about that?"

The way he immediately clammed up and became defensive only makes me more curious. What about his homeland is making him react this way? It is not a secret that he is fae, something that would be impossible to hide, yet he's acting as though I just asked him to run naked through the castle. If I want to get any answers out of him, then I am going to have to act casually about this.

"I'm curious." Shrugging, I brush back several strands of my hair that escaped from my braid. "How did you end up living here with Havoc and the royals?"

"That is none of your business." His voice is ice cold, and his stare warns me not to keep pushing as he drops his canteen to the ground.

However, I am not in the mood to be turned down today, so I continue as though he never spoke. "You said Havoc was as close to you as a brother, which means you've been here for a long time."

With a face like thunder, he crosses his arms over his chest, and I know I have pushed him too far. "We are not here to gossip, Thea, but to train. Go through your drills."

Drills are the last thing I want to do, especially since we have been training for hours now, but I know I will not be getting information if I refuse. Groaning, I shift into start position and begin to run through the routines and sequences he taught me, first with blades and then without. It is just as important for me to know how to fight without a weapon, especially given that the prophecy hints that I'm going to be attacked.

One of the good things about running through these drills is that I am able to lose myself in the routine, my mind quieting and giving me some damn peace as I flow from one movement to another. Despite the physical strain, it is actually helping me restore my control over the darkness inside me.

The longer I am here and unable to complete my purpose, the harder it is to control. As I am continually rejected, it grows and spreads like a poison, being fed by my resentment and frustration. I'm almost afraid of feeding at this point, as I worry it might overcome me and turn me into a monster. Logically, I know I am weakening myself by not feeding, and that would in turn make it harder to control that part of me. However, the logical part of my mind is being overwhelmed by the constant feeling of failure.

"How did it go in the city yesterday?"

Snapped from my thoughts by Finnik's voice, I fumble with my blade and mess up the drill I was carefully working my way through. Annoyance floods me, as I'll have to repeat it, yet it slips away when I see Finnik's expression. He's frustrated, but more with himself rather than me. Amusement replaces my mood now that he's the one asking me questions, and I consider making a comment about gossiping after he snapped at me about it.

I think better of it, though, the question dragged out of him as he is unable to hold himself back from speaking. I don't think that he is particularly interested in the slums, so why is he asking me? Perhaps he was able to sense the direction my thoughts were taking me in.

Not wanting to linger on that particular idea, I shift my thoughts, bringing up images of the devastation I saw last night.

"The slums are..." I trail off with a heavy sigh, remembering the awful sights I saw. The heaviness in my limbs reminds me of their pain with every movement. "The destruction from the flood is terrible. Those poor citizens lost everything." I drop my gaze to the ground and let my weapons hang at my sides. The only help they were given was purely from volunteers. Where was the assistance from the rest of the city? It is an issue that goes deeper than that, though, because the citizens forced to live in the slums need desperate help, yet there is nothing there for them.

Righteous frustration warms my muscles, replacing the heaviness in my body. Lifting my head, I narrow my eyes on Finnik. "The rest of the slums are just as bad. They need help. Their basic needs are not being met, and most of them have no heating or running water. Why doesn't the king do anything about it?" Finnik doesn't make policies or decisions about what is done with the slums, that would be down to the king and his council, yet the fae is as close as I will probably get to anyone who can make a difference.

Finnik frowns, taken aback by the venom in my voice, yet there is resignation in his expression too. He's accepted that nothing will change. "There isn't enough space in the city to house everyone—"

Clucking my tongue, I cut him off. "Then expand the city and start reinforcing the buildings. The ones closest to the city are fairly substantial anyway, so it wouldn't take much."

"There is too much crime in the slums," he counters, crossing his arms over his chest. "They would never accept our help."

"That is a lazy excuse, and you know it," I accuse, snarling as my frustration gets the better of me. "If there is too much crime, then do something about it and send the city guard there. Let the citizens know you actually care about them too!"

His eyebrows rise as I get more worked up, and he realises just how much this means to me. Dropping his defensive posture, he takes a step closer and tilts his head to one side. "Thea, I don't have a say in any of this. I am just telling you what I'm told. Every time I bring it up in court, I get the same response."

Frustration laces his voice, and his body is tense, making me pay more attention to what he said. He *has* been speaking to the king about the slums, and the answers he gave me are what he was told when they rejected the motion, meaning he pays enough attention to know what happens to the citizens there. I was wrong, he *does* care.

This male is a perfect contradiction. He acts like he doesn't have a care in the world, and his best friend is one of the most heartless males I have ever met, yet he cares about the weakest citizens here. Drathlor is not even his homeland, he's a foreigner, but he still tries to help. I did not know he had this side to him, and it's making me look at him in a new light. The royals do not tend to care about the citizens who don't pay taxes and bring them nothing. In fact, I know many despise those in the slums for being a blight on the city. We have a less extreme but similar situation in my homeland of Trador, and I have heard similar excuses from my king.

"You have been fighting for the slums." It's a statement rather than a question, and despite myself, I hear the surprise in my voice. In my defence, it is rare to find anyone who cares enough to do anything to actually help those in need.

Thankfully he doesn't seem to be offended, and he lets out a long, weary sigh. "Not that it does any good. I get the same answers each time."

"Are there slums in the city you come from over the mountains?" I ask the question before my brain has a chance to register that this probably isn't the best thing to ask.

His whole body stiffens, and his expression turns flinty. "That's enough. Back to training," he barks, shutting down the conversation.

At least, he tries to. I'm not backing down on this though. I am finally learning more about him and the fae lands beyond the mountain at the same time.

"I want to know. I'm trying to get to know you better, and I'm interested in learning about the fae."

I don't know if it's my standoffish body language or the look on my face that conveys I won't be training until I get some information out of him, but it seems to have the desired effect.

Scowling, he looks away, indecision flashing in his eyes. I have never seen him like this before, and it is almost enough for me to apologise and drop the subject, but I hold my ground. Growling low in his throat, he turns back to me, his expression hard. "I'll answer a question if you can land a blow or disarm me. Deal?"

I don't even need time to think over it, agreeing instantly. "Deal."

Returning to the centre of the room, we face each other in our ready positions. I bounce on the balls of my feet, prepared to move as soon as the fight begins. Finnik is fast and highly skilled, and if I have any hope of scoring a hit, then I have to take him by surprise. My hand hovers over my hip where my dagger is sheathed, and as soon as Finnik barks the order to begin, I grab it, the blade glinting in the light.

In a move almost too quick to track, I pull my arm back and throw the weapon. The dagger flies towards Finnik, and it would have been a perfect shot had he not ducked at the last second and jumped to the right.

Ridding myself of my weapon so early in the fight probably wasn't the smartest move. However, in darting to the side to avoid being hit, it puts him exactly where I want him. Going for the unexpected, I leap forward, tackling him to the ground. Had he known it was coming, he would have fought me off, but I managed to catch him off guard.

He lands with a grunt, my weight on top of him as I pin him to the ground with my body. While he may be stronger than me, I have gravity and surprise on my side. It gives me a split second to reach for a blade I have strapped to my arm, although in doing so, I end up pressing my chest against his face. His body freezes for a moment, as he doesn't know how to react to such a close up view of my breasts, giving me an unexpected advantage. This was certainly not what I planned, but Finnik is always telling me to use every advantage I can, so I suppose I am just following his instructions. This strategy will never work on him again, but all I need is for it to work now.

I press my blade against his throat hard enough that should he so much as breathe too deeply, it will cut his skin —a hit.

"How did you end up in Drathlor?" I ask quickly, already having a question in my mind, ready to go.

Lips pinching together, he narrows his eyes on me, and I can practically hear his annoyed thoughts churning through his mind as he bristles at having been taken down so quickly.

"I crossed the mountain," he grits out between clenched teeth.

I wait pointedly for him to give me a complete answer, yet he just stares up at me with a brow raised in challenge. Oh, so he thinks he can get around having to answer my questions by giving me vaguely relevant statements.

"That is not a proper answer, and you know it! Give me more details." My comment comes out more as a demand, surprising me at the force of it.

For a moment, he continues to stare, and I think I am going to have to fight the information out of him, but he sighs and closes his eyes. The tension leaves his body, and when he opens his eyes again, I see a change in him, as though I'm looking at a younger version of him.

I shift my weight so I'm not hurting him and wait in silence. He's going to speak now, I can feel it. Whatever brought him here must have been traumatic to have this much of an effect on him, so I won't push him until he's ready.

"My parents were important in the fae lands," he begins, releasing a long, shaky breath. "They were murdered because of who they were, and I was sent away for my safety. My safe house was attacked, and I knew as long as I was alive and in the fae lands, I would always be under threat, so I crossed the mountains." His voice becomes matter of fact as he talks about the threat to his life, as if trying to distance himself from it. "I almost died, as it is not an easy journey. When I arrived on this side of the mountains, I had hypothermia and would not have lasted much longer alone. Havoc was tracking a mountain lion with a group of hunters from the castle. It turned out that the predator was stalking me, and I had not even realised it. Havoc came across me, lost and half frozen. He and the others took me back to the castle, and I told them everything. His family offered me a place among them, and I never left."

His eyes gleam with emotion as he speaks, and I get the impression this isn't something he ever talks about, the reminders of his past life only making him relive the pain of losing his parents and his home—not only his home, but his entire kingdom. I cannot imagine how difficult it must have been to flee his country and cross into a foreign, unknown land. His reluctance to speak of it makes more sense now, and I can understand some of his standoffish behaviour.

This also helps me understand his relationship with Havoc a bit better. While I am sure he sees a kinder side to the prince, I have always wondered what connected the two of them so closely.

Looking down at him, I scan his face, surprised by the emotion I saw when I usually see nothing more than a scowl. Although the emotions were negative ones of loss and reminiscing, it opened his face up and took away much of the battle hardened exterior that he carries around with him. Perhaps this is what he would look like had he not been through life-altering trauma.

"I'm sorry about your parents." I'm not trying to pity him, I can only imagine how he would react to that. No, I am trying to show that I know some of his pain. I lost my mother at a young age, and my father has always been distant. Thanks to my part as one of the brides, I don't have as close of a connection to my family or people as my peers do, so I know what it is like to grow up alone and leave your home behind. Of course, I am able to return to my kingdom every six months, but that place stopped being my home when my mother died.

His elbow comes up and hits my jaw, knocking me back. A hit. Damn it!

He crawls out from underneath me, the feat easier to do thanks to the fact I shifted most of my weight from him. "You get too emotional when fighting. It distracts you."

My ears ring, and I clutch my hands to my jaw to try and ease the pain, surprise and outrage making me see red. What a fucking bastard! He used my kindness against me. Any sympathy I had for him is long gone, his mental armour now fully back in place. Is anything he just said true, or was it all a lie to get back at me?

"Do you love Havoc?" he snaps, seeming both annoyed and curious at the same time. If I have learned anything about him, it is that he hates falling into unnecessary conversations, especially ones that involve sharing emotions. Something about me seems to get under his skin and make him ask things he would never usually dream of asking.

Irritated, I narrow my eyes on him as I rub my throbbing jaw. "I never agreed to answer questions." I pretend that it is the pain making me snappy, but really I know it is because he used my emotions against me.

"It is only fair that you answer my questions too."

Damn him. He's right, and while some people wouldn't care about something like that, I have morals.

Sighing, I straighten and prepare for any attack he might attempt while I'm still adjusting. "No, I don't love Havoc."

I try not to let myself think about why he's asking, and for a moment, I swear relief floods his expression, but it's gone before I can blink, and he's attacking once more. I have to drop those thoughts to protect myself from his barrage of strikes, his movements so quick that it's impossible to block him when he's this close to me.

A blade presses against my jugular, and I freeze so as not to get cut, cursing him for landing a hit so quickly after the last one. *Focus, Thea*, I tell myself, frustrated for allowing myself to get distracted.

"How do you feel about being one of the brides?"

His question takes me by surprise. I wasn't expecting him to ask something like that, and I'm not really sure how I'm supposed to answer.

"It is an honour to serve my land," I reply automatically, falling back on the rhetoric that's been trained into me while I stare at him, trying to keep still thanks to his dagger at my throat.

Scowling, he lowers his blade and steps back, pointing at me with his weapon. "No, don't do that. I want the truth."

Staring at him intently, I try to see past his scowl to the fae beneath. Why does he want to know so badly, and why is he so frustrated at my previous answer? It wasn't a lie, but it also was not the full truth. Does he really want the full, unadulterated truth? It is not pretty, and it's something I have only ever kept to myself for fear of being branded as selfish. This sort of knowledge could be used against me, especially if he told Havoc, yet for some reason, I want to tell him.

My anxiety flares inside me, although to my surprise, it is not because of what I am about to tell him, but because I finally have the chance to say something. These feelings have been locked up within me for so long, but now I might be able to get them off my chest. I might not get the chance again. My eyes scan his face, and I don't know what I'm looking for, but I must see it because I decide to take a risk.

"I hate it." The admission is quiet, shared like a deadly secret. Glancing around, I make sure no one else can overhear. When I look back at Finnik, he's watching me with an intense expression, nodding in a sign to continue.

"I don't fit in here, and I don't really have a place among my people." Taking a step back to put some space between us, I look away, staring into the distance but not really seeing. "Ever since the day I was born and they saw my silver hair, I have had the prophecy shoved upon me. While I am honoured to protect my land, I have never had an option in my life. This was the only path. Then I discovered I was mated to Havoc, and the only decision that was left open to me, who I was going to love, was taken away from me." Bitterness coats my words, years of keeping these thoughts to myself having turned them acidic. "I don't get a choice in anything that happens in my life, and I resent the rest of the world for it."

Whoa, I hadn't meant to be that honest. I felt comfortable enough around him to fall deeply into my feelings, and this is what came crawling out of the darkness in my soul. My eyes suddenly widen as I realise how blasphemous I just sounded, and panic immediately makes me want to take it all back, but Finnik must see this, because he holds up a hand, his eyes narrowed.

"Don't."

That is all he says, but I nod anyway, understanding that he's giving me a way out.

Raising our weapons in unison, we prepare ourselves. I am not sure who moves first as we become a whirling cyclone of limbs and blades. We move around each other flawlessly, and although we're sparring, it feels almost like dancing, our bodies twisting, bending, and leaping. The only sounds in the room are the clang of metal, the shuffle of feet, and our heavy breathing.

Finnik moves and leaves his back left side unguarded, giving me the opportunity to dive my dagger towards his kidney, stopping just before I pierce the skin. He freezes when he feels the cold tip of the weapon.

A hit.

I suspect he might have given me that one because of what just happened, but I don't fight it, taking the opportunity to ask a question.

"Do you miss your life in the fae lands?"

He doesn't try to protest answering this time, shaking his head as he steps back to take a breath. "Not really. I miss my parents, or I miss the idea of them. I don't really remember them, to be honest."

Nodding, I take several deep breaths and prepare to fight once again. Finnik comes barrelling towards me, no sign of his dagger as he soars through the air. I leap to the side in an attempt to avoid getting taken down. For a second, I think I manage it as the sound of him hitting the ground echoes from behind me, and I grin with feral pleasure, but then a hand tightens around my ankle and stops my escape, dragging me down.

I land heavily, and my breath is forced out of me by the hit. My mind can't quite work out what just happened, but a little voice is screaming in my mind to get up. Being on the ground is the most dangerous place to be. Rolling over so my back is now to the ground so I can see my opponent, I scrabble into an upright position. Before I can stand, though, he lands on top of me, forcing me back down to the ground.

He attempts to pin me to the ground, and I do everything to make him lose his grip, bucking my body and twisting violently, but I only succeed in hurting my wrists. His hold on me is like steel, and I know I have no chance of getting free while he has me like this.

Stilling, I take in his smarmy expression and snarl up at him. I expect him to release me and ask a question, but he doesn't, his eyes sweeping over my face as his expression changes into one of confusion. As I examine him up close, I cannot help noticing just how handsome he is. The upturn of his eyes and his pointed ears give him such a mischievous appearance, yet right now, he looks deadly serious. The pull in my chest is so strong that it almost takes me over completely, and had he not pinned me, I might have acted on my desires. I need to get out from underneath him and throw myself into a cold bath to cool off.

"Are you going to ask a question?" I ask quietly, my voice cracking despite my attempts at keeping it even.

"Do you feel as drawn to me as I do to you?" He looks pained as he asks, but his eyes seem to sparkle, needing to know the answer.

My heart flutters in my chest, knowing he feels the same way I do. However, I know this isn't a good thing thanks to the fact I am betrothed to his best friend. I won't lie though, especially about something like this.

"Yes," I whisper, almost afraid to answer.

Finnik releases my wrists and sits back on his heels,

allowing me to sit up. The two of us stare at each other. I knew about the connection, but this is new. This almost feels like... like what I have with Eli. Does that mean he could also be my mate? My mind begins to spin again at the possibilities. I don't know what to think, not wanting to give myself false hope.

Finnik leans towards me, and I think he's going to kiss me. For a moment, it looks as though he's thinking about it and then changes his mind at the last second. Reaching out, he tucks silver strands of my hair behind my ear.

For some reason, this makes me giddy, and to my immense embarrassment, my fangs extend. Vampire fangs are longer than our other teeth, yet when we are feeding or aroused, they extend farther, making it easier for us to feed. The urges can be controlled, and I have not had an accidental fang slip in over a decade.

Cheeks blazing with a blush, I try to move away, only to stop as he frowns and reaches out, lifting my lip to look at my gums.

Alarmed, I try to rear back. "Hey! Get off—"

He pulls back and frowns, not caring in the slightest about my chagrin. "You need to feed." He crosses his arms over his chest. "When was the last time you had blood?"

I look away, not wanting to get into this conversation. "I don't remember, I've been busy."

It's a poor excuse, and we both know it.

"You have to look after yourself, Thea. You're the key to our salvation," he scolds, sighing when he sees my stubborn expression. "We'll stop for now. It will give you a chance to feed."

I want to tell him to stop fussing and that he's not my mother, but a figure appears in the doorway. Geoff, my chaperone, spots Finnik and me on the floor, our bodies almost touching. His brow rises, and he meets my eyes, yet he doesn't comment. Instead, he steps into the room as though nothing about what he sees is compromising.

"Ah, Prince Finnik, Lady Anthea," Geoff greets, bowing at the waist once he reaches the edge of the training ring. "Prince Havoc has called a grand ball tonight in honour of his betrothed. Anthea, you have the rest of the day off to do as you please until the ball." He turns to Finnik. "The prince requests your company."

Finnik frowns, his expression severe. Something about what Geoff said is concerning him, his hands balled into fists at his sides.

My chest tightens. Something about this situation is wrong, my instincts warning me to be careful. Glancing at Geoff and then back to Finnik, I shift my weight and reach out, touching the fae's shoulder.

"Is everything okay—"

Before I can finish my sentence, Finnik pulls away from me and jumps to his feet. "I shall see you later, Lady Thea." He bows hastily and then marches from the room, leaving me alone with my advisor.

Chapter Eighteen

"I spoke with the eldest prince, and he doesn't know why the ball has been called. What do you think this is about?" Bliss asks, looking ethereal in her glimmering gown. I thought my dress was revealing, but she has me beat. The sirens and merfolk have always had a more open mind when it comes to nudity and sharing their bodies.

Her wavy locks are pinned back with two golden shells, exposing her pointed ears and sharp jawline. The top half of her dress is literally just large enough to cover her breasts, the pearl-lined straps more for decoration rather than having any structural purpose. The skirt is the showstopper, however, made up of layer upon layer of light, gauzy fabric. The colours shift between blue and green like the ocean, with darker purples closer to her body. Each time she moves, it seems to reveal a different shade, the iridescence making it seem magical. It would not surprise me if there was magic woven into the skirt to create that effect, and I cannot wait to see how it looks when she's spinning on the dance floor.

Bliss's question confirms something I had been suspecting. Havoc is acting on his own. I have not seen him all day, and something grand and public such as this when he usually doesn't want to be seen with me at all is out of character. What is the real reason he has arranged this ball, and why at such short notice? If Bliss is right, then his brothers know nothing about this evening, and even Finnik was taken aback by the news this morning. Fear claws its way up my throat, making it harder to take a full breath as all of the horrendous possibilities circle my mind. Out of instinct, I reach out and touch the bond between Havoc and myself, seeking comfort. If I realised what I was doing, I would have stopped myself, but I am so overwhelmed that I reach for my mate. There is no comfort waiting for me. As though it's a coiled snake waiting inside me, ready to pounce, the connection between us seems to strike me as Havoc viciously pushes me away. Pain radiates throughout my body, and my breath is momentarily stolen away.

"I'm not sure," I croak out, my voice scratchy.

Bliss is watching me closely, her eyes shining with concern, yet she doesn't comment on my long pause and wince of pain. She sees everything, so I know she's aware of each lash of pain I experience from the bond in my chest. Some might think it strange that she doesn't ask how I am, yet Bliss knows me well enough that she understands I don't want to talk about it.

"It seems strange that he would throw a ball in your honour when he hasn't been particularly kind about being your mate," she comments, pursing her lips with distaste, letting me know exactly how she feels about Havoc and his behaviour.

We are currently in my rooms, so the two of us can speak without fear of being overheard. Even so, Bliss keeps her responses measured, an old habit we all quickly learned when we were first brought here all those years ago. Loose tongues do no one any favours here.

I am determined to go into this with a good mindset. It is hard not to expect the worst, considering my interactions with the prince so far, but perhaps he has finally realised this is our fate.

Besides, Finnik never returned after our sparring session this morning. While his abrupt exit worried me, he would have warned me if something bad was about to happen, right? As Havoc's confidant and closest friend, the prince would tell Finnik before doing anything too drastic—of that I am sure.

"He wants all the nobility to attend, along with the entire royal family. This has to be a positive thing, right?" I ask, trying to convince myself more than anything, my stomach tying itself in knots.

"Oh, yes, I'm sure it is." She smiles brightly as she steps forward and brushes back a stray piece of my hair. "The prince is probably doing this as an apology for everything so far."

"Yes, I'm sure that is it," I reply, forcing my own, tight smile, but even I don't sound convinced.

Bliss's hand drops, her smile quickly following it, replaced with a serious expression. "Thea, I will do what I can to help if you need it." She puts her hand on my arm, squeezing it in a gesture of support.

Warmth spreads through my chest as I smile at her in return. We might have only met through circumstance, but I found a true friend in her, one that I know would step in to help me even if it jeopardised her position here.

"I know." I allow my expression to soften. "Thank you, friend."

There is a light knock on my bedroom door, and we both know our time is up. Our presence is required. Nerves flutter like butterflies in my stomach, causing a riot with their tiny wings. I straighten my posture and adopt a placid expression, watching in fascination as Bliss does the same. Gone is my friend, and in her place is the third bride—unassuming, innocent, and completely mouldable for her position. Little do they know, her personality is like the sea, calm one moment and deadly the next.

Bliss runs a hand through her hair and checks everything is still in place. "I best go, but I shall see you in the ballroom shortly."

Smiling at the demand in her voice, I nod and watch her leave. The moment the door shuts behind her, I am surrounded by silence, like the quiet before a storm. My mind starts to fill the space, all of my fears and darkness clawing at my insides to be let out.

No, I refuse to fall apart. I am the first bride, and I am here to save my people. The ball tonight, as far as I am aware, is a celebration, so I shouldn't go in expecting the worst. I shall be composed yet careful, as I always am.

Determined, I stride over to the mirror to check my appearance. Tonight's dress is my favourite of all I have worn since I have been here, and it is sure to cause a scandal, but I don't care.

The fabric is a deep mauve crossed with gold, shimmering as it moves. Wrapped around my body in a toga-like fashion, it is draped artistically over my bust, and a waterfall of pleats crosses down from my shoulder to the cinch at my waist. More fabric drapes over my legs and tucks up under a pleated waistband, the remainder rippling down the opening, which exposes most of my left leg. A gold chain hangs from my waist, and two cap sleeves have been added that are made entirely of golden chainmail. It's delicate and beautiful, but it makes me stand out, giving me a feminine yet powerful appearance. A half cape made of the same gauzy material as the dress hangs from my left shoulder, flowing gracefully behind me as I walk. My silver hair is pulled back and braided with additional golden chains woven throughout, causing the strands to shine even more than usual.

I look like a warrior.

Another light knock pulls my attention away from the mirror, and I turn to see Felix walk into the room. He takes one look at me and frowns in concern before crossing the room to me. "Thea, is everything okay?"

"Felix." I whisper his name like a breathy prayer, not realising just how much I needed to see him tonight. He is my rock, my link to my home, and a constant reminder of exactly why I am here.

Stepping forward to meet him, I place my hands on his chest, holding him close. I press my forehead against his chest and take several deep breaths, inhaling his scent and grounding myself.

"I think something bad is going to happen tonight," I whisper, keeping my face buried against his chest. "My instincts are screaming at me." The admission costs me, making me wince as Havoc's bond flares within me, as though he is able to tell I am questioning going to the ball tonight.

His fingers brush against my chin, gently lifting my face until our gazes lock. "Everyone is going to be there tonight, including me. He wouldn't have brought us all together if he was just going to shame or hurt you. It would make him look bad. The nobility is on your side here. Besides, I would never let that happen," he tells me, staring into my eyes and making sure I understand what he's saying.

I only now register that the shirt I am currently clinging to is a smart white shirt, nothing like the loose beige overshirts he usually wears. Glancing down, I see he's wearing fitted black trousers that hug his frame in a way that makes my fangs ache.

He notices, his eyes narrowing suspiciously. "When was the last time you fed?"

Damn it. Sure, it has been a while since I had a full feed, but the fact that people keep pointing it out makes me wonder what they are seeing that I don't when I look in the mirror. Perhaps I am a little pale, and I look as though I could use a good night's sleep. Even so, they should not be able to tell. Perhaps it is only those who know me well, as only Finnik, Geoff, and now Felix have mentioned it.

"I had a couple of shots earlier," I confess, raising my chin, daring him to say something.

Shots are donated blood that has been taken and bottled, allowing for a quick feed when there is no time to find a donor. They are generally kept for emergencies, and most vampires prefer to feed from the original food source. Bottled blood tastes different, probably the anticoagulants they put in it to keep it from clotting.

I didn't have time to feed properly earlier thanks to having to get ready for the ball, so I took a couple of shots to top me up. I am nowhere near close to being full, but it's enough to stop me from trying to bite anyone at the ball.

He frowns as he crosses his arms over his chest. "You know those aren't good for you."

"I know, I know." I do know, as Geoff tells me every time he brings me one with a disapproving frown. "Anyway, do you really think you could stop the prince from hurting me if it came down to it?" I turn the spotlight onto him.

It's an unfair question to ask, as it sounds like I'm doubting him, which I'm not. I'm simply stating that Havoc has been trained in fighting and defence since he could walk, not to mention he has guards all around him who would likely stop Felix from getting to me. Felix is a stable hand, so although he's strong, I don't know how he would manage against the prince. Really, I am simply trying to take the weight of the conversation off me because I am uncomfortable and don't know how to manage. Unfortunately, that has turned him into my unwitting target.

He doesn't seem offended by my question, though, sensing my turbulent emotions and knowing I do not mean it like it sounds. Instead, he takes my hand in his and pulls me close, looking down at me with an intensity that makes my knees weak.

"Thea, I would do *anything* to get to you if you needed me. I may not be the most powerful male around, but do not doubt the strength of my feelings for you. I love you and shall *always* have your back." Every word is said in earnest, and I can feel the truth in what he said. He would move mountains and fight impossible battles to get to me, give up everything he possesses, and live life on the edges of society to be with me. I know all of this simply from the way he looks at me and the way my heart responds in my chest.

What have I ever done to earn a love like this? He is not my mate, yet I love him fiercely. This shouldn't be possible, and I am only just allowing myself to admit that, the force of my feelings for him too strong to deny any longer. It's an unrestrained love that is not controlled or predestined by fate or the gods or any other mystical force. It is simply him and me.

If only it were that simple.

I am betrothed to a prince who is also my fated mate. There is a fae male who tells me he is my mate, which, although impossible, is getting harder and harder to deny. That mystical pull inside me is also dragging me towards Finnik, another fae and the best friend of my betrothed. Even if I am able to work out that complicated mess, there is no possible way that any of them would allow Felix to have a relationship with me, our feelings be damned.

Gripping his shirt, I screw my eyes shut and press my face against his chest, my eyes stinging with unshed tears. Everything is so complicated. How can I fall in love with someone who is not my mate?

Felix sighs and wraps his arms around me, resting his chin on top of my head. We stay this way for several minutes, making the most of these few stolen moments, as we both know as soon as we leave this room, everything will go back to the way it was before.

"Seeing you like this makes my heart hurt," Felix whispers into my hair, rubbing my back in soothing motions. He untangles himself from my hold and steps back, brushing his fingers against my cheek in an intimate gesture. "Try to enjoy tonight. I will be there if you need me."

Stretching up onto my toes, I press a whisper of a kiss against his lips. "Thank you, Felix."

He smiles down at me sadly before turning and exiting the room, leaving me alone.

The party is in full swing when I arrive, and even outside the ballroom, I can hear the buzz of excitement from the attendees. Standing by the open doors, I peep in and see flashes of brightly coloured dresses as couples dance in the centre of the room. Goblets of wine are being handed out by servers, and there is a mostly untouched buffet at the back of the room, the tables laden with food.

A glimmer catches my attention, and I spot Bliss spinning with a handsome horned male. Are all the other brides here too? A quick scan of the room confirms what I thought —everyone is already here.

Glancing at Geoff, who is gracing my right arm, I frown and tilt my head towards the packed ballroom. "Am I late?"

"No, we are here at the instructed time." Grimacing as though the words leave a bad taste in his mouth, he gives me a sympathetic glance. "I believe the prince wishes to announce your arrival to everyone."

Wonderful.

The brides are usually all introduced together. By announcing me on my own after the festivities have begun, Havoc is bringing even more attention to me. He is already throwing a ball in my honour, so is it really necessary to have me announced too?

Three loud banging noises cut through my internal grumblings, the staffs of the four guards by the door slamming into the ground. The music cuts off, and the dancers quickly hurry to the sides of the room to create a path from the doors to the foot of the dais. Everyone's attention turns to the open doors, focusing on me standing a few paces back.

The last thing I want to do right now is enter this room, my instincts telling me something is wrong. I ignore it, though, and allow Geoff to guide me to the threshold of the room.

A male steps forward, taking up position by the left side of the doors, and clears his throat. "The first bride of the prophecy, representative of the vampires and betrothed of Prince Havoc, Lady Anthea of Trador." The steward's voice rings around the room with the assistance of his magic, the telltale markings of a witch written into his skin.

Holding my head high, I allow a small smile that I don't feel to pull at my lips as I follow my cue and enter the room. This is all a farce. I do not want to be here, but for my people, I will. I force a semi-smirk that is expected of a vampire and stalk the length of the ballroom, Geoff at my side.

All eyes are on me. My dress is so different from all of the classic ballgowns with large, netted skirts, although I notice a few female vampires in the hall who wear a similar silhouette to me. Somewhere in this room is Felix, and from the light pull in my chest, I know Eli is also here, although not close. He is most likely lying low somewhere in the castle until an opportune moment. However, I keep my gaze straight ahead.

The king and his queen sit on their thrones, watching me with neutral smiles, while Havoc stands at the foot of the dais, waiting for me. It is not him that my eyes are locked on, though, but Finnik at his side.

He looks particularly fae-like tonight. His hair is tousled, the delicate pointed tips of his ears peeking through. Mischief shines in his eyes, and his smile practically promises mayhem. His stare is as stuck on me as mine is on him, his gaze taking in every inch of skin my dress reveals.

Havoc quickly realises I'm looking at him and glances at his friend. When he spots Finnik's expression, he frowns and mumbles something to him in a low voice. Finnik quickly snaps out of his staring match with me and says something in response, keeping his gaze away from me as I continue my walk to the thrones.

The fact that Finnik doesn't seem concerned is a huge relief. He would warn me if he suspected something bad was going to happen. In fact, he seems to be in a remarkably good mood, and I am not quite sure how to take that. I suppose I shall soon find out if my worries were for naught.

Reaching the prince and Finnik, I drop into a shallow curtsy, Geoff bowing at my side. Havoc takes my hand and links arms with me, leading me to the foot of the dais so I can greet his parents. I curtsy once more, although much deeper this time, and then I wait for their words of approval before standing and glancing at Havoc. He's looking at me differently tonight, and for the first time, he smiles at me.

For a moment, I think my heart is going to stop beating in my chest at the shock. Our bond expands within me until it's taking over everything, my thoughts becoming flooded with happiness at the possibility that we might finally be united.

Wait, a small voice in the back of my mind calls out, making the smile I give in return freeze on my lips.

No, this is not happiness. At least, it is not *my* happiness. This feeling is like a drug, artificially telling me that I am overjoyed at the prospect of being together with my fated mate. In another circumstance, I might have gone along with the feelings until they reflected my own, but Havoc has done *nothing* to earn this from me. He has been unkind, cruel, and wanted to damn us all because he did not want to marry one of the brides.

My expression doesn't change, so Havoc must sense my change in emotions through our bond, because he frowns again, absentmindedly rubbing a spot on his chest as though it aches. That is a pain I know well, one he causes me almost constantly. It is not nice being on the receiving end, and he is finally coming to realise that.

He lets out a long breath, squeezes my arm, and turns us to face the guests, a perfect, princely smile etched onto his face. "Enjoy your evening," the prince says simply, dismissing everyone and releasing them to their previous activities before I entered the room.

I am surprised by the length of his speech, and most of the ballroom seems to be too, yet that does not seem to bother Havoc who is already on the move. With my hand in his, he pulls me over to the side of the room, and I have to lift my skirts to hurry after him so I don't trip. Finnik, Havoc's brothers, and other members of the royal family are gathered here, present yet separate from the rest of the ballroom. I am not sure if this is intentional or not. When we reach them, he releases my arm, and I don't miss the fact that he drops it as though I might burn him.

The music begins, and I sense the movement of people behind me as they return to their drinking, dancing, and gossiping. I would love nothing more than to slip into the crowd and disappear among the masses, but I stay with Havoc, waiting to discover why he brought me here.

He seems to be making an effort to be civil to me, even going as far as flashing a tight, quick smile my way. It doesn't reach his eyes, and his entire body is stiff at being so close to me. His whole attitude is so different, though, and he seems to finally be trying. Perhaps all of my fears were wrong, and I can work alongside him. Did the king speak with him? Something must have happened for this dramatic change in behaviour, not that I am complaining. Havoc and I do not need to have a romantic relationship for this to work. Many arranged marriages within the nobility are not love matches, and they still live out many happy years together.

I get the impression that Havoc wants to say something, his jaw clenching and unclenching. An anxious energy surrounds him as he shuffles his weight from foot to foot, almost as though he's about to flee, which is very unlike the strong, stubborn prince I am used to. The other princes are watching us, speaking conspiratorially to each other in low voices, and it puts Havoc off whatever he was going to do next.

Huffing out a frustrated breath, he runs his hand through his perfectly neat hair, messing it up in his annoyance. He glares at his brothers then gives me an abrupt twitch of his lips that I believe is supposed to be a smile.

"Enjoy the party." Spinning on his heel, he stalks away and disappears in the throng of people.

I am so confused that I have no idea what to do next. He has been nothing but awful to me since I arrived, and today he is acting like a nervous teenager around me. Unsure what is expected of me now, I glance around until I see Finnik. He's frowning and staring into the spot where Havoc just disappeared.

My feet move before I register what I'm doing, walking towards the fae male. His gaze meets mine before I reach him, his expression smoothing out as he tries to hide his confusion. Once again, I find myself worried about what is happening, and I need to know the truth. If anyone will tell me, it will be Finnik.

"Do you know what any of this is about?" I ask, getting straight to the point and not bothering with pleasantries.

Finnik looks at me for a moment, deciding if he's going to tell me what I want to know. Letting out a long sigh, he glances around to make sure no one is listening. "No. He's not acting like the man I know."

"You make that sound like a bad thing." I give him a half

smile, attempting a joke to lift the tension in the air between us.

I'm not quite sure how I feel about the fact that even Havoc's closest friend has no idea what the prince is doing. He's unpredictable, and in my world, that makes you dangerous. He left me feeling... adrift, unable to fulfil my purpose.

Finnik is staring at me with a raised brow, knowing exactly what I'm trying to do and seeing straight through my deflection with humour. Before he can say anything in return, though, movement at my arm draws my attention.

A nobleman I vaguely recognise is holding his hand out to me expectantly. "Lady Anthea, will you do me the honour of this dance?"

Unable to say no without seeming rude, and secretly glad for an excuse to escape Finnik and his piercing gaze, I smile and place my hand into the male's before being drawn onto the dance floor.

I spend the next hour or so moving from partner to partner, dancing around the ballroom and answering the same questions over and over. The nobles do not particularly care about me, yet I hold information they want, so I am in high demand. Of course, they all act as though they are honoured to spend time with one of the brides. Really, they just want gossip of what is happening between Havoc and me, asking carefully phrased questions to try and trick answers from me. Most of them leave disappointed, as I know next to nothing anyway.

Dipping my head in thanks to my last dance partner, I move away, hoping to hide in a corner for a while to recover from having to be social. A figure appears in front of me, and I bite back my sigh. When I look up, though, I see Finnik holding out his hand to me, wearing a crooked smile.

"You wouldn't deny me a dance, now would you?" he teases.

"It depends," I quip, smiling as I place my hand in his, automatically, falling into step with him as he leads. "Last time we danced together like this, the evening ended up being pretty disappointing."

His lips twitch, remembering the ball I'm speaking of—when Eli arrived and danced with me over and over.

"Ah, that was because I had to put out the trash." His grin is feral, flashing those sharp teeth of his.

If there really is anything between Finnik and me, then he is going to have to learn to accept that Eli is a part of my life too. I might have thought he was joking about putting out the trash when he was referring to the other fae had it not been for his grin. He was showing entirely too many teeth for it to be an innocent comment.

"Finnik—"

Whatever I am going to say next is cut off by Havoc, who's standing on the dais and clapping his hands together to get our attention.

"Attention one and all," he shouts, stamping his foot loudly. His hair is even more tousled than before, where he has clearly been running his hands through it, and a manic gleam shines in his eyes.

Finnik freezes and steadies me as I bump into him, cursing violently as he takes in the state of his friend. He doesn't let go of me, though, holding onto me tightly.

Low muttering fills the hall as they sense that something is wrong, the king and queen frowning as they watch their son. In fact, the king is hastily whispering something to his steward. Havoc is either completely oblivious to this, or he just does not care.

"I know you must be wondering why I called this ball. I

have an important announcement to make, which is why I extended the invitation to all who work in the castle, as well as the nobility of Drathlor City."

People shuffle awkwardly. This is not how things are done in this world, and change is not usually for a positive reason—not to mention the prince has been outwardly hostile towards me in public, then today's strange behaviour. It feels as though that has all been leading up to something.

"Anthea, my betrothed," he calls brightly, gesturing towards me on the dance floor, my arms around another man. "Oh, and with my closest friend too. Wonderful. Please join me."

I walk slowly towards the prince. Finnik is stiff at my side, but he walks forward with me as well, something I am grateful for. I am not sure why, but the fae's presence is helping to keep me calm. The prince doesn't sound like he's speaking sarcastically when he mentions Finnik being with me, yet I get the distinct impression that seeing the two of us together triggered him.

Havoc says nothing as we walk up, but he watches us closely. Finnik is very careful not to touch me, picking up on the same vibes I am. You could hear a pin drop in the room, absolute silence surrounding us. No one wants to draw attention to themselves in case they incur the prince's wrath.

My instincts are warning me not to step up onto the dais, and I listen, pausing at the bottom and looking up at my betrothed expectantly. People shuffle around behind me, closing the gap on the dance floor and moving closer to hear better, while keeping a bubble of space between them and us.

"You are the first bride of the prophecy, and the gods

decided to bind us together, making you my mate," Havoc begins, his warm expression changing in the blink of an eye as he glares at me. "They chose wrong."

Gasps fill the hall. Not only is he breaking the prophecy, but he is insulting the gods and their decisions. A fated mate is an honour most never receive, and he is rubbing that into everyone's faces. Havoc's brothers look furious, and one of them, Chaos I believe, makes a move towards his younger brother, but he is held back by the others.

A part of me was expecting insults. What I was not expecting was how painful hearing those words would be. I press my hands against my abdomen as cramping twists my insides. I feel nauseous and devastated that I am going to have to go through public humiliation once more. The worst thing, though, is the fact that I allowed myself to hope that things might have changed.

"Havoc," Finnik calls, staring up at his friend like he doesn't recognise him.

"I will never bond with you, and I knew I had to make this as public as possible, otherwise you would never leave me be," Havoc continues, either not hearing his friend or not caring. He sneers at me, his true hatred for who I am finally breaking through the control he was attempting to hold over himself.

King Darth stands, his hands braced against the armrests of his throne as anger lines his face. "Son, stop this now, before things get out of hand."

I was expecting the king to march over and shake some sense into his son or order him to do his duty. Drath is not known for his kindness, so why is this all he is doing? Why is no one stepping in? Why are his brothers holding Chaos back? Am I just cannon fodder, a commodity they are disappointed to lose but not willing to go out of their way to save? Is there something about the prophecy I do not know? None of them are doing anything to help. In fact, the queen is just staring at me with sympathy, like she knows what is coming.

"No, Father." Havoc spins, jabbing his finger viciously towards the king, his teeth bared and words clipped with his anger. "You cannot force me into this. I tried for your sake, but the more time I spend around her, the worse things are getting in the kingdom. *They* are the ones who are tearing us apart, not some mystical prophecy."

They?

At first I think he's talking about all of us who are watching, and then I realise that it is just a select few—the brides. He's back to blaming the brides again, now taking the time to find and point them out in the crowd. Muttering fills the room, and people shuffle away from the brides until they all have an empty circle of space around them, as though they are diseased.

He is blaming disasters and awful happenings on spending time with me, like the prophecy is in reverse. He is saying it's not our union that saves us, but ridding the world of me. It's madness. How could I be responsible for natural disasters or the poor decisions of others? He is picking and choosing what happens around us to fit his narrative.

"If you do this, you will be harming your own people." My voice is annoyingly shaky, and I clear my throat to try again, putting more force behind my words.

Finnik goes to move towards me, only to pause at the last moment, pain flashing through his eyes. He's stuck between a rock and a hard place. Thankfully, Geoff is at my side in a flash, supporting me as he glares at the prince.

"Have you no heart, Your Highness?" my advisor barks

Kingdom of Broken Bonds

at Havoc, his fangs flashing in the low light of the ballroom. "Can you not see what this is doing to her?"

"Me? I don't have a heart?" Havoc laughs manically, shaking his head in disbelief. "Keeping her alive is what will kill us!" He jabs his finger towards me, almost shouting. "You must have heard about the vampire attacks. They only started happening when she arrived here. I do not think that is a coincidence."

Vampire attacks? If I had the strength, I would ask what he meant. I am using all of my energy on staying awake and upright. Are my people okay?

"Havoc, let's talk about this." Finnik steps towards him, his hands raised.

"No, there has been enough talk." For a moment, he looks regretful, weary almost, but it changes the moment he turns to face me. "Anthea of Trador, first bride and representative of the vampires. I hereby dissolve our betrothal and cast aside our mate bond."

A stabbing pain slices through my chest and abdomen so fiercely that I am speechless, my breath taken from me. I look down at myself, expecting to see a knife jutting from my chest, only I am completely uninjured. At least, physically I am. If it wasn't for Geoff holding me up, I would be on the ground.

"Havoc, stop." Finnik is striding towards the dais now, shouting up at his friend, anger transforming his face into someone unrecognisable.

Havoc does not stop. He continues to stare down at me, disgust etched into his expression. "I reject you, Anthea. I reject our bond. I refuse to take you as my wife, and I shall no longer acknowledge your presence in my life."

Pandemonium ensues around us—shouting, screaming, and what I swear sounds like fighting as everyone in the room seems to move at once. I do not know for sure, though, as a pain unlike anything I have ever experienced before takes away all logic. It feels as though my soul is being ripped to shreds and torn from my body one small piece at a time. My heart is shattered like a useless glass ornament, jagged pieces stabbing into my vital organs. The pain is so intense that I feel it pulling me under, the call of darkness within me oh so tempting to give in to. Beyond that, though, is a fuzziness that promises rest and relief from the pain. I almost give into it, but a tiny fraction of my heart flutters, a small golden glow to light up the darkness. It's faint, yet it is enough for me to fight. I am not ready to give up yet.

My eyelashes flutter, and it takes me a moment to realise that I'm lying on the floor. Someone stands over me in an immaculate suit, snarling as he protects me. Geoff, the snarling male is Geoff. I have never seen him like this, and if I wasn't drowning in pain, I might feel honoured by his behaviour.

I can hear a voice calling my name. He sounds like he is in so much pain that I fight against the fatigue and pain holding me down, frantically looking around for him.

"Finnik!" I try to call back, but my voice is a broken whisper.

Agony obliterates all else, my body convulsing in pain. As I fall into the grips of unconsciousness, the last thing I hear is him calling my name.

Chapter Nineteen

All I know is pain—searing, agonising pain that seems never-ending. My body twists in torturous anguish, writhing in excruciating suffering. I feel like I'm burning alive, my skin too tight for my body.

What hurts the most, though, is the empty, gaping hole in my chest where my bond with Havoc once resided. He might as well have physically carved me open, tearing my beating heart from within me.

Desperate to alleviate the pain, I scratch at my chest, needing to relieve some of this pressure to do something, *anything*, to find a way to end this agony.

Alarmed voices speak around me, but I'm unable to make out what they are saying, crying as my hands are restrained.

Time seems endless, and my tear ducts are long since dried up, my body weak and dehydrated. I'm dying, and with the strength of my suffering, that might just be a blessing.

"Don't you dare give up, Thea," a voice snarls, laced

with what sounds like fear. Did I speak aloud? I don't have the energy to care.

I recognise that voice, but I can't force my eyes to open. Something warm flutters in my chest for a moment, almost like a frantic heartbeat, but I am no longer able to focus on it as the pain racks through my body once more.

I begin to become aware. My chest still feels raw, my metaphorical wounds still open, although I no longer think I am dying.

I'm warm, surrounded by a hot male body, my face pressed against his neck. He smells delicious, my stomach groaning in agreement, but I am still too far under to attempt feeding. I know who I am lying next to, and while his name does not come to me instantly, I can imagine his handsome face in my mind—golden hair that falls to his neckline and golden symbols written across his face.

Eli. His name is Eli, and he belongs to me.

When this revelation came to me, I don't know, but this is a certainty I feel in my blood. He is mine, and he is the reason I am still alive.

"She needs to feed." It's a male voice I recognise, the same one I heard while I was in the throes of agony. Somehow, his voice broke through the pain. He sounds different now though. When I last heard him speak, he was terrified, his voice high and tight as he forced the words out. Whoever he is speaking to now, though, is getting to see a different part of him—a sharper, unforgiving facet of his personality.

Eli stiffens beneath me, his arms tightening around me possessively. "That is exactly what I have been doing—

feeding her." Each word is sharp as he replies to the other male, so different from the caring fae I know him as. "What are you even doing here anyway?" I assume his comment is aimed at the familiar male close to us, but I am becoming aware that there is at least one other person in the room.

A low hiss of anger sounds beside us, the male affronted at the question. "She called out for me."

His face appears in my mind, and his name suddenly comes to me—Finnik. He's the male who has been at Havoc's side during all of this, and if I'm honest, his presence was probably the only thing keeping me together during those awful meetings.

Eli snorts, his hand moving in small circles on my back. "Then why did you come running for me, saying it was *me* she was asking for?"

I can imagine the sneer on his face to match his tone and get the distinct impression that his current actions are done with the intention of proving that I am his. He's trying to provoke Finnik, but I cannot figure out why.

From the snarling and heavy steps that move towards the bed, I can tell it worked. "That was after," Finnik snarls. "During the fight, before she passed out, it was me she wanted." There's a heavy emphasis on his last words as he makes his point. He sounds... jealous.

Before the two of them can say anything else, the light tread of footsteps sounds from the other side of the room—the third person in the room. His scent reaches me as he moves, and I instantly know it's my Felix.

"Why isn't she awake yet?" he asks, his voice so quiet and broken that it stirs a part of me that had been slumbering until now.

I might not know what has happened since the ball, as I only have snippets of memories, and they were all filled with pain and make little sense to me. Not to mention my brain is still reeling from Havoc's rejection, and the agony my body has suffered. However, I know that my current state is causing Felix distress, and that is enough of an incentive to have me fighting into consciousness.

It takes a monumental effort as I fight through the fog and heavy weight of heartache, but I know the struggle is worth it. Felix is hurting, and although they might not be as obvious with it, Finnik and Eli are too. They need me.

"She has been through something most do not survive," Eli explains quietly, the low rumble of his voice vibrating through my chest. "Her body and soul need time to heal." Shifting his weight beneath me, he pauses and brushes some of my hair from my face. "Wait, I think she's waking up."

"Thea, can you hear me?" Felix's voice is like a siren's song, calling me through the turbulent, murky waters of my mind that try to keep me submerged.

My eyelids finally flutter open. They feel as though they are made of lead, but I force them to stay open, my gaze going straight to the male kneeling at the side of the bed.

"Hey, Felix," I whisper, my voice scratchy, but the small smile on my lips is genuine.

The heavy tension in the room suddenly seems to lift, like a balloon that is popped with a pin, quick and startling. The males seem to come alive, an air of positive excitement that gives me strength. Felix continues to kneel at the side of the bed, content with his position thanks to his proximity to me.

"How are you feeling?" Finnik asks, frowning with concern as he scans my body. If his expression is anything to go by, I look a sorry state.

"Like my heart has been torn out and stomped on." I

attempt to make a joke, but it falls flat as I cut off with a hiss of pain. I roll my eyes up to Eli. "What happened?"

"You almost died, that is what happened." Eli's clipped tone is so unlike him, a complete contrast to the gentle way he cradles me.

I turn in his arms as much as I can, agony lancing through my body and restricting my movements. My eyes widen as I take in Eli's feral appearance. He looks like a warrior, his gaze menacing as he looks at the other two males in the room. When his attention shifts to me, his expression softens slightly, but he still looks as though he could tear through the room at any moment.

Several raised red marks on his neck have me frowning. I didn't notice them at first, as I must have had my face pressed against them. They are fang marks, and not neat ones. Whoever fed from him was in a hurry and could not control themselves. A horrible feeling rises within me as I suspect who might have been responsible for them, but I push that thought aside, not ready to face it now.

Instead, I realise I am pressed against Eli's naked chest, and that I am also without a shirt. In fact, I am completely naked beneath the bed covers other than a pair of underwear. Fighting against my fatigue, I manage to raise a questioning brow.

"Why am I naked?"

"You needed skin-to-skin contact with your..." Finnik starts, only to trail off, his jaw tight as he glances away, unable to say whatever word is causing his problems.

"Mate," Eli supplies, his voice forceful and full of authority as though reminding the others of his position. "You needed skin contact with me while you were feeding. It was the only way we could think to stop Havoc's bond from killing you."

I must look as confused and taken aback as I feel, because Felix sighs, taking my hand in his and rubbing his thumb across my palm. "You should start from the top," he suggests, and although he looks at me the entire time, I know he's really talking to the others.

Fatigue pulls at me, still making it impossible for me to move from Eli's chest, but I manage a small, grateful smile for Felix, hoping he knows how much it means to me that he's here.

Finnik sighs loudly, rubbing his hands through his hair as he nods, gathering his thoughts. There's a haunted look in his eyes, and I prepare for whatever horrors the three of them witnessed.

"When Havoc severed your bond, it was going to kill you. You collapsed, the pain overwhelming you completely," Finnik begins, pacing the length of the room, unable to meet my gaze as he explains what happened. "Havoc's actions had drastic consequences though." He hisses out a frustrated breath, his expression tight. "A fight broke out amongst the nobles due to fear of what would happen now that the prince was not going to complete his side of the prophecy—not to mention he had potentially destroyed the first bride at the same time."

The kingdom has been so focused on the seven brides and the prophecy that Havoc going against it must have seemed catastrophic to them. Finnik is right, not only did he fail the prophecy, but in severing the bond, he could have killed me. That would have destroyed the prophecy as a whole, not just the small part I play. *All* the brides need to survive for the prophecy to be fulfilled.

"It was chaos," Felix comments, resting his chin on my hand as he leans against the mattress for support. "It did not seem to matter if you were nobility or working in the castle.

If you believed the prince was right, then you were going to be destroyed."

Finnik pauses in his pacing, seeming to get lost in his memory. "Geoff and I had to physically lie over you to make sure no one crushed you while the guards stormed the hall and attempted to bring about order."

Gods above. It must have been terrifying to witness, and I hope the other brides were not caught up in the madness. The king's control over his people is not as firm as I believed it was. A riot broke out all because of his son's actions—a son who had too much power, and ultimately, he could not control. Will the nobility lose faith in the king now?

Finnik turns to face me, finally meeting my eyes. I see pain, guilt, and fear shining back at me. "You were dying. Havoc's rejection was so fierce it was tearing you apart." His voice croaks, and he stops to clear his throat. "You were in and out of consciousness, and there was nothing I could do. That's when you called out *his* name."

I would have known whom he was talking about without the jerk of his head thanks to their interactions. I called out for Eli. If what they are saying is true, my body must have found enough energy to call out for him, knowing instinctively what I needed.

The male in question shifts beneath me, his hand running down my bare arm and making the hair stand on end.

"I was already making my way to you," he explains, murmuring the words against my ear. "I could feel your pain and knew you needed me, but Finnik found me and told me you were calling for me."

He was able to feel my pain. I can only imagine how awful that must have been, desperately searching the castle for me.

"We brought you back here, and we knew you needed to feed, and at this point, it was pretty obvious that you and Eli share a mate bond," Felix states factually, managing to keep himself stable despite the tension between the other two males in the room. "You might not have completed your bond, but his blood was enough to keep you from dying."

Guilt floods me as I glance at Eli's neck and the many vicious bites that tore his skin. He's no longer bleeding, his fae blood making him a quick healer, but hunger stirs within me being this close to his arteries. There is no hiding from it anymore, I'm the one who caused those marks.

I reach up and brush my fingertips across his damaged skin. The movement hurts and makes me gasp, but the fact that I became so feral and bit him like this hurts more. "I did this to your neck?" I ask, needing to hear it aloud.

Eli meets my eyes as he captures my fingers in his hand, stopping me from pulling away. "You needed to feed, and I am your mate. I will do whatever I need to for you to survive." Pressing my fingers against his neck, he kisses my forehead lovingly. "Everything I have is yours, my blood included."

Even though my heart is battered and bruised, and missing a literal part of myself now that Havoc has rejected me, I feel warmth in my chest at Eli's commitment. I hear what he's not saying—that he would sacrifice every last drop of blood to me if I needed to, not caring that it would kill him in the process. This type of devotion, along with Felix's declaration of love, is enough to keep me going. I will fight the nagging voice in the back of my head that I am not enough and that I will be rejected again. It is different with them. It is real.

Eli's hand stops stroking my arm, and I feel him tense up. "I have something to admit to you."

The feeling in my chest quickly disappears, replaced by dread. Those words are usually never followed by good news, and I am not sure that I can survive bad news right now. Sensing my sudden discomfort, he slips an arm underneath me and helps me sit up, leaning me against a stack of pillows to keep me upright.

I glance at Finnik and Felix to see if they know what Eli is about to say, but their expressions give nothing away. Swallowing the lump in my throat, I tilt my head towards my mate, waiting for him to speak.

"When we first met, I was cursed." He gestures to the golden markings on his face. "I was unable to speak, doomed to be mute for the rest of my existence. The only way to break the curse was to find my mate. I had no idea it was you, all I knew was that when I first saw you, I knew I needed to dance with you. When you asked me my name, I realised I was finally able to speak." He pauses to run a hand across his face. When he looks at me again, his expression is open and sincere. "I knew from that first day that you were my mate. I should have told you then, and I should have told you about who I was. There was a reason I was banished. I have done bad things in my past, and I won't lie, I would do bad things to keep you safe."

I was vaguely aware that the marks on his face were a punishment, thanks to what Finnik told me about him and the King calling him a 'cursed one'. However, I thought his punishment was banishment, not taking away his ability to speak. Fate is a strange thing, for Eli had to be cursed and banished from his homeland for him to find me. He might never have made the perilous journey over the mountains otherwise, and we might never have met.

Eli is more rugged than Finnik's sophisticated bearing, but I have never felt unsafe with him. In fact, he is one of the people I would go to if I was feeling unsettled, despite the fact that I have not known him long. Time doesn't matter, what matters is that I know, deep in his soul, that he is a good person despite his poor choices in the past. It doesn't matter to me what happened before.

"You are mine," I confirm, my voice steady for the first time since I woke up. It might be Eli's blood in my veins that made me realise this, but I know for sure now. He is my mate.

The look of relief that passes over his face at my declaration is like the sun lighting up a dark day, his smile wide as he leans forward and presses a kiss to my lips. The pain in my body is momentarily dimmed thanks to my bond with Eli struggling forward. Looking inside myself, I see the golden light that surrounds the bond, noticing how much stronger it looks now. Our lips move together in a passionate kiss, and I only pull back because I am completely breathless.

It only occurs to me as I fall back against the pillows that Finnik and Felix would have seen us kiss. I am not so worried about Felix, because he knows about my situation, and we have discussed this before. While it might not be comfortable for him to watch, it isn't something that was completely unexpected.

I am almost afraid to look at Finnik, and when I do, I see his angry expression. He doesn't say anything. In fact, he looks jealous. Could this be my moment to ask him? I feel the same pull towards him that I did with Eli, meaning we could also share a mate bond. I want to ask, since it's clear that he feels something too, especially now that my near-death episode has forced him to evaluate his feelings for me.

No, I cannot do it, not today. I could blame it on my

pain, but really, I'm too afraid to ask in case he rejects me. There is no way I could survive a second rejection.

There's a knock on the door, saving me from having to explore those feelings any deeper, and Geoff walks in.

When he sees that I am awake, his entire body seems to droop in relief. The controlled male who appears emotionless to some falters before me. Geoff prides himself on his even nature, not letting anything crack his sense of decorum, so seeing relief cross over his features moves me.

"Anthea, you're awake." His voice trembles. He doesn't try to hide it, which just goes to show how upset he truly is. Moving over, he stops at the foot of the bed, looking as though he wants to throw his arms around me. That is probably why he also looks so uncomfortable. This is a behaviour that is very out of character for him, and any displays of extreme emotions make him uncomfortable.

"Geoff, is everything okay?" I ask quietly, wishing I could sit up by myself and not have to rely on Eli and the cushions.

Seeing me alive and upright seems to have rattled him, and it takes him a moment to get his emotions under control. He slicks his hair back and brushes down the front of his jacket before speaking. "Everything here is a mess. I have petitioned the king to take you home to Trador where you can heal. You have been grievously injured because of his *son*. He cannot deny you time to recuperate."

I arch a brow, only able to hold the gesture for a second before the pain of the movement becomes too much. Geoff has never seemed so dominant before. Sure, he was strict and commanding during my years growing up, when I needed structure and rules to ensure I became the young lady that was expected of me. This is something on a different level though.

He follows the rule of his king, and therefore, the rule of King Drath, to the letter. Breaking rules and orders is not something Geoff does, nor would he even question it until now. Seeing me on the brink of death seems to have moved something inside him, making him more forward and forceful in his actions. He is *telling* the king that we are leaving, not the other way around.

"You're leaving?" Finnik asks sharply from his position at the edge of the room, his crossed arms falling to his sides.

It is clear he is about to argue this point, but Geoff spins and pins him with a glare, causing him to close his mouth. I do not blame him for faltering at Geoff's current expression —he's terrifying.

"Why should she stay here any longer when your *friend* tried to kill her?" my advisor and father figure asks pointedly, his fangs flashing as he speaks. "There is nothing she can do here now. Havoc has seen to that," Geoff bites out. Taking a deep breath, he attempts to regain some of his composure, glancing at the other two males in the room. "It is my job to protect Anthea, and I cannot do that here, not any longer."

Silence follows his declaration, and I know everyone is processing his words. If all is well, I shall be returning home. For how long, I do not know. Will the king call for me again? Will I still be expected to spend six months of the year here in the city? Geoff is right, I cannot fulfil my purpose, so what will become of me now?

Geoff clears his throat, breaking the heavy silence in the room. "The king has requested your presence as soon as you wake, but you are in no state to see him right now. He can wait."

Again, I am surprised by his attitude, but I am so

exhausted and relieved that I am not required to move that I don't question it.

"Agreed," Eli rumbles, holding me closer. "She needs to stay here with her mate to recover."

Geoff nods approvingly, clasping his hands together before him. "I will let you rest and send the healer in to check on you." He begins to leave, only to pause at the door. "Anthea, it really is good to see you awake."

If I was not so emotionally raw at the moment, then I would probably be touched by his comment. As it is, my eyes sting with tears, the words meaning so much more when they come from someone who is not sentimental.

Exhausted from the interaction, I lean my head back against the pillows, slumping to one side and resting against Eli for support. Someone says something, but I am already being dragged back into sleep, my body telling me it needs to rest.

Just as I'm about to fall asleep, I manage to send up a quick prayer for a dreamless sleep. Thankfully, my prayer is answered, and the darkness of unconsciousness pulls me under.

Chapter Twenty

Several days have passed since that first awful day when I woke up after Havoc's rejection, and I am finally beginning to feel a little stronger. The wound in my chest is still a constant ache, but I am learning to live with it. Without Eli practically pressed against me at all times, I would have died. I do not understand why the fae's bond and the mate bond we have in Drathlor is so different, yet it saved my life, so I am grateful for it.

Sitting on Eli's lap in front of the mirror, I brush my long hair and take in my reflection, my expression blank. Ever since the ball, Eli has been my one constant, always there to help me, even if it is just to hold me while I weep at the loss of the bond. It is a strange feeling, because I don't miss Havoc, nor am I particularly heartbroken over what could have been. Instead, I feel as though my emotions are being driven by the bond, or in this case, the loss of that bond.

The whole experience seems to have affected Eli pretty harshly too, causing him to become even more possessive and protective. Wherever I go, he is not far away, touching me constantly. I suspect he fears that without his touch, I will deteriorate, and he would be at risk of losing me again. My body, soul, and mind feel much more stable now, even if I am still in pain, so I do not think there is any danger of that happening. Whenever we are together, warmth fills my chest, especially as his arms wrap around me.

I look at him through the reflection, and I cannot help but smile softly at his expression of adoration as he stares at me. His chin rests on my shoulder as he rubs his nose against my cheek, inhaling my scent.

A flash of movement catches my attention, and I watch through the open door as Felix, Geoff, and my guards move around, gathering our possessions. Every time Felix passes, he pauses in the doorway and searches for me, his expression softening when his eyes land on me. I have not moved, yet he still keeps checking that I am okay.

Gratitude and love swell in my chest, helping to fill the gaping void Havoc left behind. I am so blessed to have Felix here, my old friend anchoring me. He may not be one of my mates, but he helps me in ways they are unable to. He *chooses* to love me, despite all the difficulties being associated with me comes with.

Shifting forward on Eli's lap, I gather together the top part of my hair and pull it around to the back, braiding it while leaving the rest down. I drop my arms to my lap and stare at the wraith in the mirror. I've lost weight, and there is a tightness around my eyes that wasn't there before. Pale skin might be expected for a vampire, but mine is almost transparent. I lean back against Eli, disappointed by what I see.

I need to get up and finish getting ready. Before we leave for Trador, we have to speak with the king. Officially, I need his blessing to return home during the six months I am supposed to be here, but I have been assured that he would not stop me after everything that happened.

Standing slowly, I glance down at my hand with a smile, which Eli has commandeered. I open my mouth to comment on his protective nature, but pause as a presence hovers in the doorway. Glancing up, I see Finnik. His gaze roves over me, a hint of panic flashing in his eyes that does not dim when he sees me. Instead, he looks around the room and notices the folded clothes in the trunks by the door, waiting to be transported to the carriage.

"You're going to leave." Finnik glares at me, his words an accusation. In fact, he is acting as though I'm going back on a promise or that I'm unreasonable for wanting to return to my homeland to heal.

I nod slowly in agreement. "If the king allows it, yes."

With a predatory expression, he begins to walk towards me, his body vibrating with tension. I stiffen and prepare for an attack, shifting my weight to the balls of my feet so I am ready to run should I need to. It is an automatic reaction, my instincts simply responding to the situation. I do not really expect Finnik to hurt me, but I am still battered and bruised from everything that has transpired over the last few weeks.

Eli is behind me in the blink of an eye, wrapping his arm around my waist and pulling me back against him. A low snarl sounds from above me as he bares his teeth at Finnik in warning.

This quickly brings Finnik to a stop as he looks between my reaction and Eli's overprotective arm. His expression smooths out, and a grin pulls at his lips. Only... I swear I saw a flash of pain in his eyes. Did my reaction offend him?

He crosses his arms over his chest, doing a very good impression of looking unimpressed. "You seem very keen to get away from me."

Frowning in confusion, I tilt my head to one side as I rack my mind for what he could be talking about. Is this strange behaviour linked to his pointed comment?

"What do you mean? I'm not trying to get away from you." Is that what this is about? He thinks that I don't want to be here with him? I ache at the very thought of us being parted, that strange pull in my chest begging me to step forward and reassure him. I do not have the energy, though, so I stay where I am, wrapped in Eli's arms.

"Yes, I am leaving," I begin, not understanding his frustration, "but you will come with—" Realisation suddenly hits me. "Oh."

He won't be coming with us.

I had never even considered that he wouldn't come with us, although why I thought that, I do not know. We never had a conversation about us being together or him leaving, yet after everything that happened with Havoc...

Finnik's expression softens, and he takes a step forward, his hand outstretched as if to touch me. He stops at the last moment though, the space between us so small, yet it feels like a chasm. He came to the same realisation I have—I thought he was coming with me.

Torn, his face contorts. "My place is here, Thea. I cannot leave, especially not with the mess Havoc has gotten himself into."

I am so fucking stupid for getting carried away, making assumptions that I really shouldn't have, and now I look like a fool. A hot blush colours my cheeks. Suddenly unable to meet his gaze, I look away and try to find something else to focus on.

"Of course, I shouldn't have assumed." I give a wan, fake smile and laugh breathily to try and cover the heartache the thought of leaving him behind produces.

Pushing from Eli's arms and moving over to the trunk, I refold clothes that don't need it just for something to do. My shoulders hunch forward as I try to keep myself upright against the emotional onslaught.

I feel him behind me, and my body aches to lean back and burrow into his warmth, but I keep my focus on the clothes. A large, warm hand lands on my arm, tingles shooting through my fingertips at the feeling.

"Is that what you want, Thea? Me to come with you?" he asks quietly, but there is a weight in his voice that tells me my answer is important to him.

The rest of the room falls away, and everything narrows down to this one question. I so desperately want to say yes, but as I open my mouth to tell him, I find myself suddenly without a voice. Of course I want him with me, but Felix and Eli are part of the equation, so would he ever agree? We still haven't spoken about this thing between us, and I know there is more to our relationship. I want to explore that when we are away from the craziness of Drathlor and Havoc, in a place where we can simply be who we are and get to know each other in a way we cannot here. However, I can't face another rejection. It would tear me apart and set me back. All of the hard work I have done with Eli's and Felix's help to recover could be destroyed with one word.

"Does it matter what I say?" I reply instead, my voice cracking with suppressed emotion. My answer will not change anything.

Finnik seems to believe otherwise, his hand tightening slightly on my wrist as he steps closer. He's so close to me now, I can feel his heat against my back. "Yes, it matters."

The emotion in those words has me turning around to look up at him, grabbing onto the trunk behind me to support my shaking legs. Frustration courses through me, and I narrow my eyes at him as I speak. "Then yes, Finnik, I want you to come with me. I do not want to be separated from you. But you won't come, will you?"

I sound far more aggressive than I meant to, my surety that he's going to reject me lining each of my words with agony and disappointment.

He seems to be taken aback by the force of my words, his breath even catching in his throat. He wasn't expecting me to be so honest, but I have stripped back all my masks and guards and let him see the raw emotion beneath it all. He wears a look of longing so intense that he actually looks like he's in pain, then he huffs out a frustrated breath and runs his hands through his hair.

"Thea, if I could, I would, please know that." Taking a step forward until we are almost pressed together, he reaches out and places his hands on the tops of my arms, looking earnestly into my eyes. "I am tied here by more than just loyalty."

His comment makes me blink. What does that mean? I assumed he stayed with the king and other royals because of loyalty thanks to them accepting him into their family, like he told me before. Now, though, he makes it sound as though there's another reason, something that is stopping him from leaving with me now.

Before I can formulate a question that makes sense, he is already moving on, shaking his head. "Is there anything I can do to convince you to stay?"

Eli snorts loudly, breaking his silence. I'm impressed he's managed to last this long without needing to touch me, especially with Finnik in the room. The two of them are pretty competitive with each other, and I'm the new shiny toy. Storming forward, Eli pulls Finnik's hands off me and squeezes between us.

"She needs to heal," Eli growls, and as I skirt around him so I'm at his side, I see he has his sharp teeth on display as he snarls at Finnik. "Surely you can see how bad the city has been for her. She is skin and bones. You can thank your prince for that. She needs to get as far away from this cursed place as possible."

To my surprise, Finnik doesn't start pushing or fighting as I expected him to, reacting much better to Eli's accusations. His frustration seems to be aimed more at the situation rather than my mate. "I know that, but my hands are tied! What about the prophecy? You cannot break it in Trador." He throws out the question like a lifeline, his tone hopeful as he searches for a reason for me to stay.

My chest constricts at the reminder of my failure, and I have to grab onto Eli's arm to keep me upright. His attention is quickly shifted to me, his expression concerned as he wraps his arm around me and pulls me against his side.

"We don't actually know that," Eli begins, distracted with trying to take care of me.

"Stop," Felix orders, stepping into the room and looking between the fae with a frown. "The two of you are acting like bulls fighting over a female. This is not helpful, and it is not good for Thea. Let her get ready in peace."

Felix always takes me by surprise when he stands up for me. Usually, he is fairly placid, happy to take life as it comes at him and step back when there are stronger males around. Both Eli and Finnik are very dominant in their personalities, so naturally he is quieter around them, focusing on making sure I am happy and safe. However, every now and again, when I need someone to back me up against the fae's strong personalities, he seems to become a different person. It just makes me love him all the more.

Raising a single brow, Finnik looks at my friend in shock. For a moment, I worry that he's going to snap back, but he seems to take Felix's words to heart. "You are right. I'm sorry, Thea." He dips his head first to Felix, and then back to me, taking my hand in his and raising it to his lips. "I need to return to Havoc, but I shall see you in the king's office later," he murmurs against my skin before kissing the back of my hand.

I smile slightly, the tingles from his kiss shooting up my arm. "Bye, Fin."

I don't know where that came from, as I have never heard him being called that before, and I have certainly never used the nickname. He stills, and I think I offended him. In some of the cultures in Drathlor, it is an offense to change someone's name, as names have power. The witches are particularly strict with this.

"That's the first time you've called me that," he says, his voice low.

That's it, I have blown any chance of friendship or something more thanks to a slip of my tongue.

Finnik smiles, his eyes sparkling as he tilts his head to one side, that mischievous look returning. "My younger brother used to call me Fin."

Storing the information away for another time, I feel tentative relief begin to work its way through me. From his expression, I am guessing he isn't gravely offended by the nickname, but I need to be sure.

"Is that okay?" My last word is stretched out, unsure as I watch his face.

"Yes." With my hand still in his, he raises it once more to his lips, keeping his eyes on me the whole time as he kisses my hand. "I would be honoured for you to call me Fin."

A heavy weight lifts from my chest, and I smile softly. "Then I shall see you later, Fin."

Flashing a smile again at the name, he turns and leaves the room, nodding to Felix on the way out and ignoring Eli completely. That was a dramatic, intense couple of minutes, and I need a moment to process what just occurred. Emotions shifted and changed so quickly during the conversation that I cannot remember how it even started. Fin left with a smile on his face, while my heart still aches knowing that he will not be leaving with us later today.

Can I cope without him, or will it cause more damage to my fragile heart?

Chapter Twenty-One

"You look exhausted, Thea. How do you feel?" Felix asks quietly, taking a step closer, clearly wanting to reach for me. However, Eli's presence seems to discourage him.

Chuckling at the question, I rub a hand across my face before answering. "Exhausted."

Eli looks down at me and frowns, the golden symbols on his face shimmering in the light. "Lie down for a bit, you need to rest."

The whole world suddenly shifts and tilts as he scoops me into his arms as though I weigh nothing. Yelping in surprise, I grip his shirt as he crosses the short space, placing me gently on the bed.

"I am capable of walking," I chide, but I am not really mad, because I wasn't exaggerating when I told Felix I was exhausted.

"I know." Eli shrugs and smiles, running his hand over my hair. "I was also capable of helping." Leaning in, he presses a kiss against my head, and panic flashes through me. Is he leaving?

"Wait, don't go. I don't want to sleep. That is all I have done for days. Come sit with me."

He must hear the panic in my voice, as he is instantly by my side, sliding onto the bed next to me and letting me rest against him.

"What would you like to do instead?" Eli asks with a crooked smile.

I know he's joking, but little does he know that his hint is closer to the truth than he thinks.

"That's what I wanted to talk to you about." I pause, glancing down at my hands in my lap. "I almost died from the rejection, and I know we are stronger together."

It is not the clearest of explanations, and I wince at how it sounds. Eli must pick up on where I'm going with my comments, though, because he stills. Felix's attention feels heavy on me, and everyone in the room seems to be waiting with bated breath.

"What are you saying, Thea?" Eli asks quietly.

Looking up, I allow him to see the truth of what I want in my eyes, no longer holding back my longing.

"Fuck me." I grip his arm tightly. "Bond with me."

"Thea..." Looking pained, he removes himself from my side and climbs off the bed, hissing out a long breath. When he turns around, he leans forward and grips the bedpost as if to stop himself from returning to me. "I want you more than anything in the world, and the idea of you being bonded to me so I can make sure you are never hurt again is pounding in my head." He gestures towards his temples. "It is so strong that I am having to physically hold myself back from pouncing on you right now." As if in response, the wooden bedpost he is gripping groans under the force of his hands.

He wants me, yet there is something holding him back.

If he feels as strongly for me as he claims, then why not give into his instincts? I don't understand what's stopping him. Unless... Unless the force that is driving him is the bond and not his true feelings. Is he fighting with himself? A single rejection is one thing, but to be rejected by two mates... There must be something wrong with me.

He must feel my doubt and dejection, because he frowns and leans forward, gripping my chin firmly so I'm unable to look away. "Stop it," he bites out, shaking his head sharply. "Do not ever doubt my feelings for you. You are my *everything*, Thea." With a grumble of annoyance, he releases my chin and seems to force himself to take a step back. "I don't want our first time to be because you are scared of being rejected again. I will never do that to you. Plus, I don't want to hurt you, and you're injured."

Rolling my eyes, I shift my position. "I'm not injured, at least, not physically. This is a way you can make me feel better." I smile coyly, looking up at him through my lashes. "I want you to bond with me because I *want* you, and I want to be able to call you my mate."

Just saying that word aloud in that context seems to do something to him, his chest expanding and his pupils dilating with desire. To be honest, even I feel something, my body tingling and easing my aching heart, giving me relief for the first time since I was rejected.

I can see how much he wants this, and despite him trying to hide it, the light tremor in his hands gives him away.

"Are you sure?" His voice cracks, and I realise I am going to have to be the one to push this forward.

I shift into a kneeling position and reach up to press a long kiss to his lips. It is deep and passionate and shows him exactly how I feel for him. My hands caress his face gently as our lips move, and somehow, the motion seems to help restore some of my strength. It makes no sense, but with each kiss, I feel stronger. My whole world has narrowed down to the feel of the male beneath my hands, my lips, and his scent surrounding me in a heady, addictive perfume that washes away my pain.

An awkward sounding cough comes from somewhere in the room, footsteps following it as though they are backing away. "I should, um, give you guys some space," Felix says.

Breaking through the fog of desire, I gasp for air and turn my upper body to find him, an immediate sense of panic racing through me.

"No, Felix, wait," I call out before I even realise what I am doing or what the potential repercussions of my actions could be. All I know is that if he walks out that door, it will irrevocably damage our relationship. He needs to know that I love him and want him just as much as Eli. It is easy to get caught up in the pull of the bond, yet that does not take away my desire for him. He was the first male I ever felt attraction to, and he has stayed by my side as my friend all these years.

Thankfully, Felix stops his retreat, looking at me with a soft smile that tells me he's okay with this situation. He is not offended that I am going to pick Eli over him. I might not have a mate bond with him, but I am able to read him just as well. He genuinely thinks that, and he is willing to step back so I can be happy with another male.

No. I will not let him believe that. I just need to work out a way to make this work harmoniously between the two males so it does not put a strain on my relationship with Eli.

Taking a deep breath, I tilt my head up to focus on Eli. He is watching me questioningly, but as I scan his face, I see it is without judgement, so I take the plunge.

"Felix loves me and has loved me for a long time. There is no bond holding him to me, yet he stays by my side despite the difference in our rank," I explain, begging him with my eyes to understand. "I love him, Eli, and I could never choose between you."

What I'm saying is dangerous if the wrong ears hear me, because I am going against everything we have been taught about mates. You have one mate, and you are completely tied to them, never so much as looking at another male or female with lust. Not only have I done that several times now, but I also survived a mate bond being severed *and* I love someone who has no mystical ties to me.

I think it has been pretty clear during this healing period that Felix means more to me than just a stable hand or friend. He has hardly left my side, only leaving to check on the horses and to feed. He is just as dedicated to me as Eli is and has proved his loyalty time and time again.

Thankfully, Eli is truly another part of my soul and can sense how much he means to me. The golden symbols on his face crinkle as he smiles and cups my cheek softly. "I would never ask you to, my heart." He presses a kiss against my forehead, soothing me just with his presence. "There are so many facets to you, and he can offer you something I cannot. In the fae lands, we believe that everything happens for a reason. He has been placed into your life for a purpose." Pulling back from our embrace, he glances at Felix, smiling at him as he gestures to the door with a tilt of his head. "Shut the door and make yourself comfortable."

My brows rise. Wow, I was not expecting this. Felix seems just as stunned, but when his eyes shift to me, there's determination in them. He seems to change, something about him almost shifting as he shuts the door and stalks forward, crawling up onto the bed with a grace I have never seen in him.

Moving behind me, he places his hands on my body and gently turns me towards Eli, pressing himself against my back. Eli seems to immediately understand what the other male is doing and closes the gap between us.

I am sandwiched between the two men I love, and for the first time since Havoc broke our bond, I do not feel pain. My mind starts to go into overdrive as I begin to overthink how this will all work. However, Felix's hands start moving across my body, caressing me with soft touches. I feel his hands move around to my back and start to undo the laces of my gown. I gasp as his fangs scrape across the delicate skin of my neck, and Eli is quick to press his lips against mine, capturing the sounds as though they fuel him.

With strong, desperate kisses, Eli flicks his tongue against mine, his large hands gripping my shoulders and keeping me steady while Felix undresses me. I still cannot believe this is happening. I must be in a dream, as things like this do not happen in real life.

My gown puddles around my knees on the bed as it slides from my body, leaving me in my underwear. Almost as soon as I think this, my panties are torn from my body. I am so deep in my kiss with Eli that I only vaguely notice it from the change of temperature around my most intimate parts. The moment Felix's fingers reach around and slide between my legs, though, I am fully aware. I pull back from Eli and tilt my head back, exposing my chest in the process. Eli quickly uses this as an excuse to palm one of my breasts with his large hand, kneading the sensitive flesh and pinching my nipples into stiff peaks.

All the while, Felix flicks my clit and drives me mad, bringing me to the brink of pleasure only to pull away at the last moment. Somehow, he seems to know the right moment to pull back. My gums ache, and my fangs fully extend, desperate to sink into one of them. I force myself to hold back, though, attempting to keep a tight grip on my control.

That quickly goes out the window as Felix slides two fingers into my pussy. He's not rough, but he certainly is not gentle, brushing the spot within me.

My whole body feels alight with sensations. I am hot, oh so hot, and every place they touch tingles. I am so lightheaded that I feel as though I could float away, and these two are the only ones anchoring me to the ground.

"Someone needs to fuck me right now," I gasp out, unable to take it any longer. It was meant to come out as an order, but it sounds more like a desperate plea. Thankfully, I am not kept waiting, and the two males lock eyes, having a silent conversation about how this is going to work.

"You should go first," Eli bites out, clearly struggling to say the words. "Once we fuck, it will seal the bond, and I won't be in control of my instincts. Seeing you fuck her would be too much."

He stops there, but I know what he isn't saying. His mating bond will make him extra possessive of me, particularly for the first few weeks. Watching a male who isn't my mate have sex with me would probably push him over the edge, and I do not want to see what happens if we were to try. The fact that he can acknowledge this just proves that he is a good male, no matter what Finnik says.

Felix nods, accepting this without question, and moves farther onto the bed. Sitting upright and leaning against the headboard, he reaches over and pulls me onto his lap, his hard flesh standing proudly between us. He takes my hand and wraps it around his cock, watching as I stroke him as something akin to awe glitters in his eyes. I can hardly believe that I am finally touching Felix like this, and that we are able to take this step. His cock gets harder in my hand as I pump his length, changing speed and grip until a shiny droplet of precum glistens on the tip.

It would be so easy for me to lift my hips and sink onto his cock, but his hands on my legs keep me in place. Eli shifts behind me, placing his hands on my hips as he guides me up and positions me over Felix's cock. Desperate for friction to ease my pulsing need, I attempt to impale myself on Felix. Something is stopping me though—Eli. Whining with frustration, I wiggle in his arms, his deep chuckle making the hair on my arms stand on end.

"Oh, my heart, so desperate for some relief." His new endearment for me makes me shiver with pleasure, especially as he leans in to whisper in my ear. "I will always give you what you need, what you want..." Oh so slowly, he lowers me down until the head of Felix's cock stretches my entrance.

I throw my head back, savouring the stretch as I take each rock-hard inch of his flesh inside me. I feel Felix's eyes on me, watching my every movement, but I focus on the feeling of him, my heart beating rapidly in my chest.

"Fuck," Felix mutters as I sink down onto him. His curse almost makes me laugh aloud, as I don't think I have ever heard him swear before, but I am too preoccupied for that right now.

Finally, after what feels like a lifetime, I am fully seated on his length, his heat feeling so fucking delicious inside me that I can no longer wait. Desperate for friction or any sort of relief, I rock my hips, the two of us moaning in unison. After all this time, after all of the looks of longing and flirtatious conversations, we are finally joined together in a way that is far deeper than the physical act of sex. My eyes are locked onto him, giving him my attention despite the fact that my mate is here. I need to show him he is just as important to me as Eli.

Of course, the fae is never one to be outdone, and as he presses up against me, he matches my movement, rocking his hips with mine. His hard cock is pressed between us, and I feel it move against me as I pleasure Felix. It does something to me that I cannot explain, only turning me on more.

One of Eli's hands slips around my hip and goes straight between my legs. I startle as he presses his fingers to my clit. Felix doesn't seem to mind the other male's involvement. In fact, he watches me with hooded eyes, lost to the magic of this moment.

The three of us work together, all receiving pleasure in our own ways. Mine is building within me, a slow, winding type of pleasure that I know will be explosive when it finally hits me.

"Feed on me," Felix begs, his voice cracking with his desire, and I know he is close to coming.

Licking my lips, I lean forward and latch onto his neck, the darkness within me walking beneath my skin. Rich, deep blood floods my mouth, the flavour intoxicating as I suck hard against Felix's neck. More, I want more. The darkness is greedy, pushing within me for more blood, more power, and thanks to the recent weeks, I am weak, and my guard is not as strong against it. It almost takes control, but I remember who is beneath me, a wave of pleasure bringing me back to the present.

Yanking my fangs from his neck, I hear Felix hit his climax a moment before I feel it. Gripping my hips tightly, he holds me still as he thrusts up into me, burying himself as deeply as possible. I feel every flutter and pulse as he comes inside me.

High on his blood, I quickly follow, my channel squeezing down on Felix's cock. I was right about my orgasm hitting hard, my whole body alight with the overwhelming sensations. I rock harder against Felix, trying to extend my orgasm for as long as possible.

Chuckling from happiness, I lean forward and press a long kiss to Felix's lips. He kisses me back, his hands soft and gentle now that he had his release. He also looks a little pale thanks to me feeding on him.

Eli doesn't rush us, nor does he make a single comment as Felix and I share this moment, but I can feel his desire for me. The bond is aching and pulling. We have been so close, our bodies rubbing together, but we have not crossed that boundary yet, keeping us from having a fully completed mate bond.

With a final kiss, I slowly climb from Felix. Eli places his hand on my lower back to support me as I turn around to face him. He's kneeling on the bed, sitting on his heels as he watches me. He holds out his hand. Without having to think about it, I take it and let him pull me closer. I am not sure at what point he removed his clothing, but he is now fully naked, his cock arching towards me. I take in his member with wide eyes. He's larger than any I have ever had before, and although it makes me a little anxious, I know he would never hurt me.

Spreading my thighs, I sit on his lap. Even just the stretch in my legs tells me this is going to be a tight fit. Wrapping my hand around him, I groan softly, loving the velvety smoothness of his cock as I stroke him—only to be stopped a moment later.

"No, I have been waiting for this moment ever since I

realised you were my mate," he tells me breathlessly, rubbing his cock against my entrance. "I am not wasting any more time."

I chuckle breathlessly and lift my hips to give him access. Surprisingly, his cock slides into me fairly easily. He still stretches me, and I have never felt so full before, but there is no pain. In fact, it feels as though he was made for me.

I must have spoken aloud, because he smiles at me, his eyes sparkling as he presses his forehead against mine.

"I was, my heart. I was created to be your perfect companion, just like you were created to be mine."

My heart.

The new endearment is perfect. Together with him, especially like this where there is nothing between us, my heart feels... not quite whole, but I am filled with life and hope again. Something is still missing, and I think I will forever be a little broken because of Havoc, but Eli does something that Havoc never did—he makes me happy. This happiness cannot be forced. It is the sort of love that is genuine and comes from two souls being truly right for each other.

Our bodies rock together with a synchrony only lovers know, my heart pounding to the beat of his name. *Eli. Eli. Eli.* I become lost in him, his scent surrounding me, his love and honesty blanketing me. The bond between us tightens bit by bit with each thrust of his hips, like we are wrapped in fishing line and slowly being reeled together.

He begins to kiss my neck, and although I came not too long ago, I can already feel another orgasm growing. This one isn't going to be as shocking, but still just as meaningful.

"I love you, my heart," Eli whispers into my skin, thrusting upward to meet my hips.

This is all it takes to push me to the brink. Gasping, I grip his shoulders and hold on for dear life as I rock on his cock, my orgasm flooding through my body, healing me in the process. I am still a broken mess, but I know I can survive this with Eli and Felix at my side. Eli must have been holding back, because as soon as I come, he comes too. Hissing a curse, he thrusts deeply into me with a shudder of pleasure.

Our bond fully snaps into place, and pleasure unlike anything I have known pours through my body and into Eli's, binding us irrevocably. This is it, a bond stronger than marriage has tied us together, his presence filling my mind. I assume he can feel the same sensations I can, bliss still setting my nerves alight.

I am not sure how long we are together like this, but eventually, Felix helps me off Eli's lap. The bond is so consuming as it settles, I am unable to do much but bask in the sensations, so Felix being the amazing male he is, cleans me up with a wet cloth and helps me into bed, curling me up against a silent but smiling Eli. Felix then gets into bed beside me and wraps an arm over my waist, then the three of us drift off to sleep.

Chapter Twenty-Two

"Lady Anthea, how are you feeling?"

The king's rich, commanding voice greets me as I straighten from my curtsy. Embarrassingly, I require Eli's assistance, my strength still reduced despite the new bond helping to restore me. The monarch notices the movements, his keen gaze locking on the grimace on my face and the hand around my waist, his expression pensive.

We are in his private study. The king sits behind his sturdy wooden desk, while several of his advisors hover close by on his left side. To his right, one of his sons watches me closely, his hands clasped behind his back. I cannot remember the name of this son. I think he is third or fourth in line to the throne, so I have never really paid him much attention.

I start to open my mouth to reply when the side door pushes open. Somehow, I already know who it is before he even steps foot in the room. Finnik. Fin. I am almost certain at this point that he is also my mate as my eyes track his every movement. He doesn't look at me until he reaches the king's side, bows, and then takes up his place beside the prince. Now that my bond with Eli has locked us together, I can feel my connection to Fin even clearer, my entire focus on him. He seems to be just as transfixed as I am, his body taut as though he is attempting to hold himself back.

There is a long, heavy pause in the study, only broken by Geoff's cough beside me, startling me into action. Clearing my throat, I force my attention onto the king.

I do not smile like I usually might, but I do incline my head slightly in acknowledgement. "I am slowly recovering, Your Majesty, thank you for asking."

Of course, this is not what I really want to say. Bottled up and contained, my feelings have become a pressurised, seething mass inside me, just waiting to explode. If I were able to speak truthfully, then I would tell him the agonising details of what happened when his son destroyed our bond. That is without considering the embarrassment of it being done so publicly, or the shame of the fact I cannot complete the prophecy.

I am still feeling delicate post bonding with Eli, the connection wrapping around me tightly. I know it is the same for Eli. His heightened fae senses are on overdrive thanks to the bond. I am happy with the way things worked out between us, as I am not sure I would have the strength to be in this meeting with the king without Eli's bond bolstering me.

Felix is preparing the horses, and I already miss his calming presence. However, the sooner this meeting ends, the quicker we can leave, and then I will be surrounded by both Felix and my mate. The time together will allow me to heal, both physically and mentally. In time, I shall return to Drathlor and see what can be done for the prophecy, but being here now is only causing me more pain.

Of course, none of this can be said to the king, so I adopt

the stoic expression expected of the vampires and bite back on my remarks. I need his permission to return home. Without it, I am stuck here, meaning I need to stay on his good side.

Despite my comment regarding the fact I am recovering, the king frowns as his eyes drag over me, taking in the gauntness in my cheeks and how my skin is almost transparent. I certainly do not look well, and that is a direct result of his son's actions. Obviously thinking along the same lines, he blows out a long breath and shakes his head, leaning back in his throne.

"This whole situation has been a mess, and I know you have been caused pain due to my son." He growls in frustration as he speaks, yet I get the impression he is more annoyed by the fact his plan did not work rather than feeling truly sorry for me.

"She almost died, Your Majesty," Geoff comments, his voice uncharacteristically snappy. "We may be in trouble with your son not accepting the prophecy, but we are all finished if the first bride is killed."

My bruised and battered heart warms a little at my guardian standing up for me. King Drath is not the type of male you want to push, yet here is Geoff, standing his ground.

The king focuses on my guardian. "Yes, I am well aware of that, Geoff." He speaks through gritted teeth, his patience running thin. I know Geoff has been spending a lot of time with the king's secretary, trying to get me home to Trador, and that he is a stubborn male. Perhaps he has been pushing a little too far.

"It is only thanks to my new mate, Eli, that I survived," I comment, stepping in before things escalate. Glancing back at said mate, I smile up at him softly, unable to stop myself as warmth and love move throughout my body. His eyes are already locked on me, something about his face softening as we share a moment together. "Without his bond, Havoc's rejection would have killed me," I finish, ripping my attention away from Eli and facing the king. It is one of the hardest things I have done today, yet I know how important it is.

The king's eyebrows rise, and silence falls across the room. "New mate?" He looks between Eli and myself, taking in how close the fae is behind me and the protective, possessive hand on my shoulder.

However, it is not his reaction that I care about, but the other male in the room whom I feel inexplicably drawn toward. Finnik is staring at me, his expression unreadable, yet I can feel his distress. He knew Eli was my mate, but for the two of us to have bonded, we had to have sex. He must have known that this was going to happen eventually, but now it has actually occurred, it has shocked him. He looks like a statue, barely even moving to breathe as he fights to control his emotions.

While I do feel bad he discovered it this way, I refuse to apologise for bonding with my mate. Finnik has been so hot and cold with me, hinting at but never truly confessing his feelings, and I am not going to wait around for him to make up his mind.

The king is still waiting for my answer, his brow raised. Clearing my mind, I return my focus to him and nod. "Yes, Your Majesty. The fae mate differently, and it turns out that I share a mate bond with Eli." I keep my head high as I speak, because there is no shame in this.

King Drath frowns and glances to his right to look at Finnik, silently asking for his opinion on the matter. After all, fae are rare in this land, so who better to ask than another fae?

"She is speaking the truth," Finnik grinds out, his posture still rigid.

Surprise colours the king's face, his doubt and scepticism replaced by a thoughtful look. Pressing his hand against his chin, he hums aloud as he takes in this new information. "Well," he comments after a few silent moments, "this is a turn of events." The words are muttered, so I get the impression he is speaking to himself more than us.

He seems a little warmer now, so I think this is the perfect time to bring up the real reason I am in his office today. "Your Majesty, I wish to return to Trador to recover. Being around Havoc is going to be detrimental to both of us. The prophecy has been broken, so I am no longer needed here." My emotions overtake me, and despite the earlier promise I made to myself that I would keep myself in check, my voice cracks. I take a deep breath and lean back against Eli for strength.

Of course, he is already there and wraps an arm around my waist, tucking me tightly against him. I hate the fact that the king might think I'm struggling because of Havoc, and he is a factor, but the real reason for my emotions is the disappointment I feel in myself because I was unable to complete the one job I was born for.

Unaware of my internal battle, King Drath sighs and scrubs a hand across his face. "Yes, your escort has been petitioning for you to be pardoned from the agreement keeping you here for half the year." He shoots a small glare in Geoff's direction, confirming my earlier suspicion that my advisor, guardian, and escort has been bothering the king with constant requests.

Tapping the arms of his throne, he looks at me with

what I believe is supposed to be sympathy but just makes him look uncomfortable. "While I understand the reasons you wish to return to your homeland, I am afraid I cannot allow it."

Stunned silence fills the room. I do not think that anyone, including the king's advisors or middle son, expected this reaction.

Trador is going to be in an uproar when they hear of Havoc's rejection. We are a proud nation, and honestly, our egos can be large. All of vampire kind will be offended by the situation, Havoc's actions reflecting on the king, and therefore, the whole of the land. A way to get us back on his side would be to allow me to go home to recover, show my people I am still alive, and that I am willing to return to Drathlor City. By refusing my leave, he is effectively keeping me prisoner. For what reason, unless this is all about power, and he is lording this above us all?

"Your Majesty," Geoff interjects, taking a step forward. I have never seen him look so angry before, his fangs extending over his lower lip. Geoff, the perfect example of an unfeeling, stoic vampire, has lost control of his temper.

Thankfully, before he can get himself into too much trouble, Eli reaches out and pulls him back. If he looks like he will attack the king, he will quickly be put down, the hidden guards in the room not leaving anything to chance, especially with how frustrated the king seems to be with him at the moment. For a second, it looks like Geoff might throw off Eli's hand and continue storming forward, but when his eyes land on me, he lets out a long breath and nods, brushing down the front of his jacket.

Sure that my advisor is not going to get himself killed, Eli releases him and clears his throat, addressing the king. "Thea has been nothing but compliant to your rules and this *prophecy*," Eli hisses, showing exactly what he thinks of the situation. "She has handled all the prince's rejections with grace and dignity despite the enormous amounts of pain it causes her. The very least you could do is let her recover in the peace of her own home."

The king glares at Eli but turns his attention back to me, effectively ignoring my mate. "You deserve better than what happened to you, Anthea. You have behaved as the perfect first bride, however, I cannot allow you to leave." His expression hardens as his decision is made, and all sympathy is lost as the might of the king enters his voice. "I need to think on how your new mate impacts the prophecy. I need you here so I can study any changes in you, not to mention the vampire attacks. It is not safe for you to return. Here, you are safe, and we can work on a solution."

He makes me sound like an experiment, something he can examine, poke, and pull apart, not a living being. This is how he is going to repay my sacrifices and loyalty? How am I to—something he said suddenly sticks in my head, over-riding my outrage.

"Wait, vampire attacks?" My instincts are telling me this is more than just one or two random attacks, and I am instantly on guard. What happened while I was recovering? Several weeks have passed, which is hardly the blink of an eye to vampires, but things move quickly here. I glance over at Geoff to see if he knows anything about this, but he looks just as mystified.

The king sighs. He was hoping that I wouldn't pick up on that, or perhaps he thought I already knew. Either way, he does not look happy to be explaining this to me. "Vampires appear to be turning feral. We believe it is a disease and that it is tied to the prophecy." Short, succinct, and without elaboration, he told me as little information as possible. Why? Does he not know, or is he trying to keep more from me?

Fear strikes my heart, and my knees feel weak at this new piece of news. Is this restricted to the city, or has it spread to Trador? The king thinks this is linked to the prophecy, so is this the consequence of my failure? Havoc had shouted about vampire attacks at the ball, but I had put that down to the odd incidents that occasionally happen, added with the ravings of a crazed male.

"My people..." I gasp, trailing off with horror as I think of home. Is everyone okay? My king? My father? "Why did I not know about this until now? This is something I should have been told."

I am speaking out of turn, in fact, I'm being impertinent and could very well be punished, but I don't care. Everything I say is true. My life has been forfeited for the good of my people, and this is something I accepted as I knew I was doing what was necessary to save them. Years of my life have been spent here, learning about the other lands and how to be the perfect bride instead of spending time with my family or making friends like other young vampires. Now, it was all for nothing, and my kind is suffering regardless.

Raising a brow at my tone, the king clears his throat as though to remind me who is in charge. "We decided it was best not to tell you with everything going on. Plus, we have not made this public knowledge, and we plan to keep it that way."

While I understand it is important to keep news of this calibre under control until they know more about what's happening to avoid panic, I can read between the lines. They want to write this off as a few random feral vampire attacks and nothing more.

I'm utterly horrified, and even Eli's steady hand on the small of my back does not help settle me. My eyes shift to Finnik. His expression is hard, his body seemingly frozen, but as our gazes meet, I can feel his anger, horror, and frustration at the situation. Without our tentative, fluttering connection, I would never know the turbulent storm going on within him or know with pure certainty that he had no idea about this.

A heavy pause falls over us, the king intending for us to feel the weight of the unspoken order in his words. We are not to tell anyone of what he told us.

Drath strokes his chin as he watches me. "I have scholars working on the prophecy to see if there are any other ways we can fulfil your part with or without Havoc." He might not have said it aloud, nor did he mean to give himself away, but his anger at his son and his catastrophic actions bleeds through his composure and into his voice.

I never understood why the king would choose to name his sons such names. Princes Desolation, Ruin, Anarchy, Chaos, and Havoc. He is certainly living up to his namesake. His name causes me pain, making me want to wither away into nothing, but Eli's bond strengthens me, bolstering me against the onslaught of the rejection.

I take a moment to make sure I am in control of my voice. Havoc has made me look weak enough, and I will not allow that to continue. Clearing my throat, I meet the king's gaze. "Where is he?"

The king scowls, and his advisors shuffle anxiously behind him. "He has absconded, but when he returns, I shall deal with him." The dark promise in his words is laced with animosity and bitterness. "I am sorry I cannot accept your request, but you may rest here, in the safety of the city where I have access to you as needed." He glances down at the papers on his desk, waving a hand in my direction. "Return to your bed, you look exhausted."

It's a clear dismissal, and I know better than to argue with him, especially with the dark mood he seems to be harbouring. I glance at Finnik, and his gaze tells me the same—do not push the king, not now. I do not want to leave the study without him, yet I am getting the strong sense that I need to go now. Finnik will find me later, and we can speak then.

Dipping my head and lowering into a shallow curtsy, I turn and leave the room, my entourage following close behind.

Disappointment weighs on me like a heavy shroud, clouding my mind and view of the days ahead. However, what stirs in me the most is the sense of dread and fear over the vampire attacks. I should be with my people during this time. If this is truly linked to the prophecy, then there is a possibility that I can help them, but instead, I am stuck here. There is not a single doubt in my mind that the king would hunt me down and drag me back if I were to leave without permission, so that is not a viable option.

What is becoming clear to me, however, is that I need more information, and if I cannot leave the city, then I will discover as much as I can from here. First things first, I have to know how much my companions know.

We slowly make our way back to the vampire wing of the castle, seeing less and less beings the closer we get. By the time we reach the bridge that attaches the wing to the main castle, we are alone. I look at Geoff and find him frowning, lost in thought.

"Did you know about the attacks?" My voice is quiet, but the question is strong, demanding an answer.

"No," he replies instantly with a shake of his head.

Thankfully he doesn't seem offended by my direct question, instead, he continues to look thoughtful. "I heard of one attack at the castle back in Trador, but I assumed it was a one-off incident—a turned vampire going feral and attacking. It is not all that uncommon for the changed. I never would have thought..."

He is right, occasionally there is an attack, usually one of the newly changed vampires. On its own, although tragic, that information would not be anything to be worried about. Knowing what we do now, it's a horrifying factor. If there was one and this... disease is spreading across vampire kind, then who knows how many were affected.

Everything he said adds up with his shock and outrage when the king told us, but I had to be sure. A weight I did not know I was carrying lifts from my shoulders now that I know he was not concealing anything from me. Yes, I almost died, but I needed to know this information. I pause at the entrance to the bridge, leaning against the stone wall.

"No one knew?"

"Not as far as I am aware, Anthea. It was kept from us all." Geoff is clearly outraged.

Eli moves over to my side, leaning against the wall and looking down at me with an intense expression. He says nothing, but his body shelters me from view, and I know he is silently assuring me that he will do everything he can to protect me.

At this moment, protection is not what I need, but answers.

Closing my eyes, I take a deep breath as a wave of exhaustion washes over me, making me lightheaded. My mind spins with ways I can help my people while being stuck here, and as I open my eyes once more, I look at Geoff.

"We need to know more. I need to speak to some of our people and find out if they have heard anything."

My attendant shakes his head, his frown growing impossibly deeper. "The king will not allow you to leave, and the vampires who live within the castle are loyal to the king. They either will not tell you what they know, or they will genuinely know nothing at all."

These were all facts I anticipated, and a plan begins to form in my mind. Humming to myself, I press my hand to my chin. Yes, I will do anything for my people, and I know a way I can do that whilst still following the king's rules.

"Then we speak to the vampires in the city." A small smile stretches my lips, the action feeling foreign as I look between Eli and Geoff. "I know exactly the place."

Chapter Twenty-Three

Despite weeks having passed since I last visited the slums, there is still much work to do from the floods. Everywhere I look, I see people in need. Disease has been spreading among the camp, the water supply contaminated. Enough have died that the king was finally forced to admit he needs to do something to help. Thanks to his money, physicians have been set up in several stations dotted throughout the area, where they are able to treat all ailments.

It had not taken much to convince the king to give me permission to continue to help in the slums. I had managed it before without issue, and it keeps me out of his way. He still has not located Havoc, and I know that he is getting tired of my daily attempts to get more information from him. I have spent many hours in the library, trying to work out what this curse that has fallen upon vampire kind is, and how we can treat it.

There are several faces I remember from before, and they greeted us and pointed us towards the area that needed the most help. Working in the slums gives me a great sense of gratification, because this is something I *can* do, unlike my part of the prophecy. However, I have another reason for coming out here.

I glance at the female I have been paired with as I continue sorting through the mounds of donated clothes, folding and placing them into piles to go to those who lost everything in the flood. Felix and Geoff are helping in the food tent just opposite, and Eli hovers close by, cleaning up debris with a group of minotaurs. I know my mate is struggling to hold in his possessive, protective mate instincts, and I am really proud of how he is putting his feelings aside to help others.

Today, I have been placed with Ama, a siren who lives in the city by the harbour. Many of those in the outer slums are sirens, driven here by destruction in their homeland, and Ama wants to help in any way she can. She is very knowledgeable about the city and the workings of the slums, seeming to know everyone—the perfect person for me to ask some quiet questions.

Glancing around to make sure we are out of supernatural earshot, I step closer to the pretty siren. "Ama, may I ask you something?"

She glances up from the clothes she is folding, her bright coral hair shifting with a life of its own. "Yes, my lady."

"I told you, please call me Thea," I insist with a small smile. She has been friendly, if not a little wary, but has given me a far warmer reception than many here. If anyone is going to give me answers, she will. "Is there a section of the slums where the vampires dwell?"

She stiffens at my question and shoots me a look as though suddenly remembering I am a vampire. Doubt plays across her face, and she bites down on her lower lip, finding the clothes before her very interesting. For a moment, I think she is not going to answer me, but then she drops her chin and clears her throat.

"Not many vampires like to live in the crowded conditions of the slums, so they live in the city or hide underground when the sun rises. There were a few vampires who resided here though." She glances up at me then quickly back at the clothes once more, seeming anxious. "That has all changed now."

She was hoping I wouldn't hear her last comment. I can tell from the way she ducks her head and murmurs it under her breath. Noting this, I store the information away for later and do not question it. Instead, I go over what she just said. It makes sense. Vampires are hurt by the sun, so they would not want to dwell in a shelter that could not protect them from it unless there was no other option. I thought it strange I hadn't seen many around, but that explains it.

We continue sorting the clothes in silence, both of us lost in thought. I have more questions, but she is nervous. If she were branded a snitch for telling me anything, it could put her in great danger. Is that what the issue is here?

"Do you know where I can find them?" I ask quietly, not looking up from my work so I do not draw attention to us. "Where is the underground entrance?"

Ama stops what she is doing and faces me, grabbing my arm tightly. I turn to look at her but see she isn't trying to hurt me. No, her expression is full of fear and concern—for me. In the background, I see Eli move closer, instinctively following his protective needs, but he refrains from closing the distance between us completely.

"You do not want to go there, my lady." Ama's eyes are wide and full of caution. "Even before all of this, it was a dangerous place to go, even for fellow vampires. I strongly advise you stay away."

Again, the ominous mention of change. The transformation in her is dramatic, meaning that whatever I said triggered something within her. It makes the hair on my arms stand on end. She knows something. I may be forbidden to tell anyone of it, but if she already knows and tells me, then I am not breaking any rules.

"Before all of what?" I probe gently, fearing scaring her off if I press too hard.

She stiffens at my question, realising she said too much.

"Is this about the changes with the vampires?" I am very careful with how I phrase my question, not directly giving anything away, but enough to hint that I already know a little. If I were to be questioned, I could innocently say that I was querying why the vampires all left the slums. However, when her eyes widen, I know I asked just enough to encourage her to talk.

"What do you know of the attacks, my lady?"

This is it, the information I was looking for. My heart pounds wildly in my chest. "Call me Thea, please," I remind her, letting my lips turn up as I look at her. To all the world, we appear like two young females in light conversation. "Not much, to be honest," I reply, "but I want to help my people. If there is an affliction hurting them, I want to know."

Her movements still for a moment as she looks up at me, *really* looks, like she is seeing into my soul, and whatever she finds clearly surprises her. Sighing, she returns to her folding, shaking her head.

Resigning myself to the fact I am not going to get any more answers, I try to control my disappointment.

"They say it is a disease." Ama's lyrical voice is soothing, like a peaceful lake, only I know that there is a dangerous current beneath the surface that could sweep me away. My whole focus is on trying to maintain a casual posture while she reveals what she knows in quiet whispers.

"Infecting only vampires, it turns them into bloodthirsty beasts. They lose all sense of reason and attack without discrimination. Once they have caught the affliction, there is no going back." Blowing out a breath, she shakes her head again and raises her hands in a stop gesture. "I have said too much. Take no heed, all this is just rumours."

We both know that is not true. Whatever is happening in the city is real and dangerous. Everyone is on edge, yet no one is willing to do anything about the threat hovering over them. The king is only harming his people by doing nothing. Those in the slums already know, and it is only a matter of time before those in the city learn of it too—gossip travels quickly.

We are still being watched, and wary looks are still being sent in my and Felix's direction. No one is outwardly avoiding us, but our every move is closely monitored.

"Please, Ama," I plead. "I need to know more. How can I help?"

My sincerity must come across, because her expression softens. "You really do care about your people." This is said as a statement rather than a question, so I stay quiet as she ponders my query. "Go to the west dock." Her voice drops even more, and I have to strain to hear her despite being so close. "At the end of the far pier, you will see an old boat. It looks abandoned, but it is not. Board the vessel, and you shall find Harvey. Tell him that Ama sent you." Holding up her hand, she gives me a wry smile, stopping me from speaking. "Do not thank me for this, and do not expect him to be friendly."

Eli narrows his eyes as he stays hyperalert, looking for any signs of danger. "This is a bad idea," he mutters, his voice low as he takes in all of the possible escape routes should we need them. The bond is tight in my chest, letting me sense his wariness. It is not his safety that he is so concerned about, but mine, fearing that something might happen that will put me in danger. I am much more capable than he gives me credit for, though, and besides, I know he would never allow anything to happen to me.

Placing a gentle hand on his arm, I draw his attention to me. "We need to know more, and Harvey is supposed to be able to help us. We did everything to make sure we will not get caught."

Once we returned to the castle after our visit to the slums, we made sure to take the more public route back to our wing of the castle so we passed the palace gossips. Eli and I went about locking ourselves in my room and made sure it was clear how tired we were from the excursion. I feel bad about lying to Geoff and Felix, but I need them to remain in the dark in case we get caught. They will not go down with me.

After that, Eli and I managed to give our guards the slip, and we entered the city. While I feel bad they will get punished if it is discovered that we left the castle, there was no other option. We need to find Harvey, and although my guards are loyal to me, the king has assigned me additional guards to keep me safe. If they knew I was going to meet someone to get more information about this sickness, then they would report me, and I would be in a world of trouble. These new guards are positioned outside the door to our suite, noting everything. We all know the king is having me watched, ensuring I am not going to leave the city.

Luckily for me, I can scale walls.

It was surprisingly easy for Eli and me to escape the castle and move through the city. We still have several hours of darkness to cover our tracks, and our plain black cloaks help hide our identities in case we are spotted. Thankfully, we didn't come across anyone, and we have reached our destination without any problems.

The docks are large and make up a huge part of the infrastructure of the city. The business it brings to the city is vital, and as such, they are busy at all times, even in the dead of night. The west dock is where the local boats are kept, that of small fishermen and pleasure vessels as opposed to the large ships that carry goods and creatures to other realms and continents across the sea. This means that at night, the west dock is far quieter.

The moon is covered by a thick blanket of clouds, perfect conditions for sneaking around. Squeezing Eli's hand in encouragement, I check my hood is firmly in place and stride across the dock, following the instructions Ama gave us. Running only draws attention, but two figures walking with confidence is far less suspicious, so even though it feels wrong and exposing, I force myself to keep going.

The boats here are obviously used much less than ones on the other piers, with little to no care of the vessels. Green algae grows on the hulls, and dust and debris coat the windows. The farther we walk down the pier, the worse condition the boats seem to be in.

Right at the end of the pier and away from any of the other vessels is a boat that looks as though it's about to crumble apart. Looking at the state of it, I am surprised that it is still afloat. Without Ama's direction, I never would have known anyone stepped foot on that boat in years, let alone be living on it.

"Are you sure about this?" Eli asks quietly, resting his hand on the small of my back as we hide in the shadows of another boat.

This seems crazy, and I fully understand that and any of his misgivings. I only just met Ama, and she has led me to a secluded place away from my protection. However, my gut is telling me that I can trust her and that I need to be here. Explaining that to someone else is not easy though.

I let him see the surety of what we are about to do in my expression, sending him my feelings through our bond. "I do not know how to explain it, Eli, but I need you to trust me on this."

I can only just make out the golden shimmering marks on his face, the ridge of his nose, and the slight upturn of his lips as he leans forward, pressing his forehead to mine.

"I always do, my heart."

His whispered words patch that hole in my heart that Havoc created, helping build me back up by supporting me with every fibre of his being. The love he feels for me flutters in my chest like a butterfly, spreading its wings and gently moving through me, filling me with warmth.

I stroke his face lovingly, not needing to share any more words. What we feel is beyond the capability of being explained by words alone. Taking a deep breath, I turn back to the dilapidated boat and go over our plan. There is no sign of anyone on the vessel, but Ama assured me Harvey would be here.

We move over to the boat, my senses on high alert as I climb on board, using every scrap of vampire grace I possess to avoid making noise in the process. Although I might be supernaturally quiet, the boat seems to groan with every movement. There is no need for magical wards when your intruders announce themselves simply by placing their weight against the broken flooring.

The inside is just as broken as the rest of the boat, with upturned furniture and fabric and debris strewn across the floor. There is not a single sign of anyone living here. It looks as though the boat was ransacked and no one has been here in many years. Was Ama wrong? Did Harvey get attacked and have to move? Glancing over my shoulder with a frown, I clear my throat to ask Eli something when his eyes widen at something behind me. I turn back around and see a crooked figure.

Dropping into a defensive position, I take in the male before me. There must be a hidden door somewhere that he was hiding behind, as there is no way he was here with us the whole time. He is probably about my height, but it is difficult to tell with the way he stoops over. His clothes are worn and ragged, his brown hair curling around his slightly pointed ears. The fangs that peek through his lips identify him as a vampire, and as he lifts his dark eyes to meet mine, I see a cunning, clear mind. We do not move, waiting to see what the male will do next. The way he stands makes him seem far older than his smooth, wrinkle-free face suggests.

"Well, well, well... Look what has stumbled into my lair."

The hair on my arms stands on end at the scratchy sound of his voice, rough from lack of use. His shrewd gaze narrows on us but settles on me. This male is sharp and intelligent, which is probably how he is able to survive in these conditions.

"Harvey, I presume?" I ask quietly.

The fact that I know his name and have come looking

for him seems to have a negative effect on him, his posture changing. Rolling his shoulders back, he stands upright, coming to his full height and baring his teeth.

"Who the fuck is asking? How did you find me?"

I realise what is happening here. He's afraid. He is hiding from something, someone, and if we were able to find him, then others could. I need to explain why we are here and how we found him, that his whereabouts are not common knowledge. Eli has moved closer, pressing against my back, and he growls quietly at the vampire, clearly not liking his behaviour.

"My name is Thea. I am from Trador—"

"Shit, you're her, the vampire bride." He cuts me off, looking horrified before his features settle into anger, his body swelling with rage. "Get off my boat. You're going to bring the whole fucking king's guard down on me!"

Panic races through me as I realise we might have to leave here empty-handed. Inadequacy, a feeling that I have been experiencing a lot lately, rears its ugly head, mocking me in the back of my mind. I cannot even get a fellow vampire to talk to me, yet I seem to believe that I can single-handedly solve the prophecy.

"No, please, hear me out! I am here with my mate, and the guards don't know we are here," I say in a rush, desperate for him to hear me before we are ejected from the boat. "My friend Ama sent me. She said you could help."

"She did, did she? I am going to have to have words with that one." His expression turns crude, yet he does not move forward to force us out. "Well, what do you want?"

I have to stop myself from smiling, as I do not think the vampire would take kindly to it, thinking I am mocking him.

"I need to know what is happening to the vampires in the city."

"Ha," he scoffs. "It is not just the city, girl. Vampires everywhere are turning feral, and there is nothing any of us can do to stop it—at least not now that the prince has fucked up our chances."

His words are like the hammering of a nail into a coffin, dread settling around me. *No, he is just being dramatic and pessimistic. This is his prediction, not a true vision into the future*, I tell myself. Everyone can have opinions, and this is his. However, Ama sent me here for a reason, so there must be something he can help me with.

Pushing away the panic, I focus on what he said. He brought up Havoc messing up our chances. I never mentioned the prophecy, nor my reason for being in the city, which means he also thinks there is a connection. The king suspected this too. Perhaps this is why I am here.

"Havoc? You think this is linked to the prophecy?" I try to keep my voice even, not wanting him to know how badly I need this information.

He snorts and looks at me like I am the most stupid being in the world. "Strange things have been happening for a long while now, tensions building between the different races as time passed and the prophecy remained unfulfilled, waiting for the brides to come of age. Things have been escalating since you were called back to the city. Now, there is a disease that affects only vampires as you fail your task?" He bares his teeth at me, his face contorting. "You were supposed to save us, but you failed, and now we are all doomed for insanity or death."

I don't deny it, after all, he is right. Through no fault of my own, I did fail, and I will have to carry the weight of that for the rest of my life. His words hurt, opening old wounds and insecurities. The dark whispers in the back of my mind are vicious, welcomed forward by the harsh words thrown back in my face.

I am convinced that there is another way, though, or at least something I can do to help my kind. Hiding my hurt, I stand tall and hold his gaze.

"I am trying to find another way to fix the prophecy. That's why I need to know about the disease," I explain, needing more information. "You said things have been strange for a while. Can you tell me what you mean?"

He lets out a defeated sigh and clears his throat. "Strange happenings, disappearances, feral attacks among the vampires that were being written off as one-offs." He shakes his head like he doesn't believe it in the slightest, a suspicious gleam in his gaze.

"Vampires were going missing, so I decided it was time for me to disappear," he continues. "I could not return to Trador, since I am not welcome there, so I created a new life for myself on the docks. I have the gift of knowing when storms are coming in, so I share my predictions with several sirens in return for food. They then pass the news on to the main docks. I do not have to leave the boat, and only a handful of people know about me." His gaze went distant as he spoke, but now it narrows on me. "Until you came along."

He told me far more than I expected, yet I do not know how any of this is supposed to help me. Was I led here because of his gift? No, that does not seem right. Storm predictions, while useful, will not turn the tide in helping the vampires. The growing disturbances, disappearances, and general animosity within the city all sound like the buildup of trouble we were promised by the prophecy if the brides were unable to come together.

"How can I stop this? Can I prevent the spread of the

disease without fixing the prophecy?" There is a growing sense of urgency in my gut, and without meaning to, it comes out in my voice.

"Do I look like a fucking crystal ball? I do not know about any of that." Despite his insistence that he knows nothing and has nothing to do with any of this, his frustration seems to be growing—a frustration that is not aimed at me. He is annoyed with himself, perhaps because he is unable to help. Yes, I think that deep down, he wants to do something to help, he just does not know how.

He grumbles to himself under his breath, muttering about cursed prophecies and feral vampires when he suddenly looks up, his hands held wide in a hopeless gesture. "The only thing..." He trails off, something clearly playing over in his mind.

My heart leaps in my chest. "Please, if you know something, tell me."

He grumbles under his breath again, rubbing a hand over his face and mumbling about uninvited guests.

Eli clears his throat, his voice rumbling from his chest and through my back where he is pressed against me. "Have you always been this antisocial, or are we just lucky?" He's stayed quiet until now, and I know it was an effort for him to hold his tongue when the vampire has been so vocal about how useless I have been.

Harvey bares his teeth in a snarl, his eyes narrowing on my mate. "Fae," he growls and spits on the ground. "I have never trusted them, and I never will. Get him off my boat."

Wonderful, just what we need. Ama warned me that he would not be welcoming, but this is a step further than I expected. I am surprised Eli has held himself back until now, yet it is clear the animosity between them is just too much.

"He's my mate, he is just here to protect me," I explain, attempting to calm the situation down.

Harvey's gaze swings back around to me, his eyes blazing. "If you want any more information out of me, then you will get him off my fucking boat!"

I look up at Eli, having a silent conversation with our eyes and the bond. He does not want to leave, but he knows how important this is. Decision made, he sighs quietly and turns to the vampire with the promise of pain in his eyes. "If you touch her or hurt her in any way, I will make sure that your remaining days on this land are filled with misery and torture."

"Mates and their dramatics," Harvey mutters with an eye roll as my mate removes himself.

I can still feel Eli, and although he is off the boat, he is not far away. This probably benefits us, as he can keep a look out while I talk to Harvey. At least, that is what I keep telling myself. The darkness that lurks within me seems to pulse, reacting to the stressful situation, and although I have full control over it right now, it feels as though it is ready to leap into action should I need it.

"What do you know?" I ask once more, putting emphasis into my words to show the urgency of this. The longer I am away from the castle, the more chance I have of being caught.

Harvey looks thoughtful now, staring into the distance, and I can see that something is troubling him. Holding back the urge to demand answers, I bite my tongue. When he finally meets my gaze, the look he gives me fills me with dread. His expression is grim, as though he has come to a harsh realisation.

"I think we have been looking at the prophecy wrong," he starts, his frown deepening. "A thirst for blood will twist the tide," he quotes, shaking his head as though he is stupid for not having realised it before. "A thirst for blood? The rabid attacks? The prophecy warned about this. You may be a bride, but the prophecy said nothing about your marriage to the prince breaking it." His voice gets louder and more passionate as he stalks towards me, grabbing my shoulders to emphasise his point. "Blood, my lady. I think the prophecy requires your blood. The question is, are you willing to pay the cost?"

Chapter Twenty Four

The words blur on the page before me, and my tired eyes ache. A long, exhausted sigh escapes me, my shoulders sagging and head hanging forward as my sore neck protests the hours spent in this stationary position. Closing my eyes, I rub the bridge of my nose and curse the tellers of the prophecy for making it so obscure.

No one truly knows what the prophecy means, and those who created the prophecy died. The power that such a large vision took killed the seven females who made it. If only they were still around now, we could ask them for more information or to confirm our thoughts, which could help us turn the tide.

It has been a week since I was last allowed into the slums, the vampire attacks now deemed too dangerous for me to leave the castle. Although I have protested this and tried to explain to the king that this will only negatively affect the vampires, he will not hear anything of it. As well as potentially being attacked, there is concern that my entourage or I could catch this new mystery disease. Since I am no longer welcome to meet with the other brides, due to suspicions from the others that I will curse them and they will be unable to marry, I have been spending almost all of my time training with Finnik or here in the library.

I am convinced there will be something in here that will help me, and that is the only way I am able to get through tome after dusty tome, day after day.

The attacks are increasing at an alarming rate, and the fear of vampires is rising with this, the other races terrified that we will maul them out of nowhere. Humans who live in the city have begun to evacuate, heading towards other lands where there will be less vampires. Out of all the races, the humans are the most defenceless and have the least rights, so I do not blame them for uprooting their lives and moving.

With each of these attacks, the ball of tension inside me increases, my mind focused on this one and only task. There is nothing else I can do, Havoc has seen to that, and the king refuses to let me leave. Instead, I turn my frustrations on myself, pushing myself far beyond my limits. Sparring with Finnik has been a great distraction, allowing me to burn off some of my annoyance, yet I am hardly getting the opportunity to see him at the moment as the king keeps requesting his presence. Finnik tells me this is for emergency meetings and searching the city for Havoc, who they still have not been able to find, yet I cannot rid myself of the feeling that the king is trying to keep me separated from Finnik.

Although I have no proof of this, I have become suspicious of everything that is happening around me. Geoff has been in countless meetings, sending message after message back to those in Trador, and even Felix has been kept busy recently. If it was not for Eli, I would be spending most of my time completely alone and isolated.

I have been in the library for hours now, and I am still

no closer to an answer. Eli's gaze has been heavy on me. Although he has not voiced his concerns yet, he will. We always reach a point where he insists it is time for us to stop. Honestly, if he did not, I think I probably would not leave, my overwhelming sense of duty keeping me back.

Shaking off my fatigue, I blink my eyes several times until the words come back into focus, and then I try to make sense of what the old text says. I have already searched all of the books here on diseases that affect only vampires, but there are so few that it did not take long for me to rule out that avenue. Now, I am searching through the seemingly endless supply of books that discuss the prophecy and the many different theories behind it.

"Thea, please, you are exhausted, let us go to bed," Eli pleads—not for his own sake, but for mine. Everything he thinks, says, and does is always for me. He would stay awake for a week straight if it would benefit me.

Sighing once more, I shake my head, keeping my eyes locked on the page. "Just a little while longer. I need to figure this out."

"Mate, you are pushing yourself to a breaking point." His large hand rests on mine, and I finally look up to meet his gaze. "This is not good for you, my heart. You cannot help anyone if you are too unwell."

At this point, I care very little about how *I* am when the world is falling apart around us.

"My people are dying, Eli. I have to do something to help them. I will not just be shoved into a room and locked away while all of this is happening." Frustrated, I slap my hands down on the table, totally at a loss for what to do. "There *has* to be something I—" My voice cracks, breaking off as tears sting my eyes. I am being torn apart inside, and this time it is not because of Havoc's rejection, but because I am majorly lacking in my own sense of self-worth. Loyalty is what keeps my heart beating and gets me through my day—loyalty to my king, my people, and the promises of the prophecy. Currently, I am failing in that duty. Without my loyalty, what am I?

Eli pulls me into his lap, wrapping his arms around me and holding me against him. He can feel all of my doubt and has been a solid anchor for me during this last awful week. What I love about him is that he does not try to force me into believing differently about myself. While we have had conversations where he has told me exactly how strong he thinks I am while worshipping my body to prove it, he does not make me feel bad about the fact I am struggling to believe him. What he does do is send me constant reassurances and praise through our bond. It is impossible to lie through our connection, so I know every thought and feeling is true. Between him and Felix, I know exactly how loved I am.

We stay cuddled up like this on the library armchairs for some time, just silently resting in each other's company while he reminds me of my worth with soft touches and warm thoughts. I am not sure how long we stay like this, but I grow sleepy, so I push up into a sitting position, rubbing my hands across my eyes to keep me awake.

"Okay, my heart," Eli murmurs, helping me reposition on his lap but not releasing me. "Let us go over it again."

I smile up at him and reach forward to pull my notes over.

"A thirst for blood will twist the tide," I begin, quoting the line of the prophecy that has been plaguing us for the last week. "We always assumed this confirmed that it was the vampire bride who would fulfil that part of the prophecy. However, if Harvey is right, then it could be that my blood is needed as a sacrifice." Something in this feels right, as though I am on the correct path, but something is holding me back from putting my everything into this line of thought. If I must sacrifice myself, then so be it. I am not afraid of death for the right purpose, but that's not why I am unsure. Something in my gut, deep down inside me, is telling me that I am missing something.

"How is that linked to the brides though? Why do you have to be a bride to give your blood? Why the need to marry Havoc? I do not think that option makes sense."

No, he just does not *want* it to make sense, terrified of losing me. He does have a point though, and I feel him shaking his head behind me, preparing to stand his ground.

"Maybe being a bride ensures that I am in the right place at the right time?" I suggest, twisting in his lap so I can see his expression as we talk.

His brow rises, and his lips curve up a little, making the symbols on his face glimmer in the lamplight. "That brings me on to my next point. What if that line is actually describing a particular situation? That something involving blood will happen, and the outcome of that will decide if that part of the prophecy is broken or not?"

This is something that has been thought of before, documented in minute detail in the scholars' notes who picked the prophecy apart bit by bit. It seems like a plausible idea, yet none of them could decide what this was, or when this event would take place.

"If that is the case" —my eyes drop as my heart sinks with disappointment at the thought of more unknowns— "then there is nothing I can do but wait and hope I am prepared when it comes down to it."

The sound of the library doors flinging open have the two of us stiffening, Eli ready to react if we are under threat.

Quick footsteps move towards us, putting us out of our misery as Geoff appears around a stack of bookshelves. He looks dishevelled and almost out of breath, something Geoff has *never* looked. He takes pride in appearing together and poised at all times.

I stand, feeling Eli copying my action. "Geoff, is everything okay?"

He takes a half second to take a breath, brush down the front of his jacket, and dip his head in greeting. "Lady Anthea, the king requests your presence immediately in the throne room. An emissary has been sent from Trador. It is your father."

We do not bother to change or wash up first, instead heading straight to the throne room. Given the unexpected nature of the visit, I do not think it necessary, and I am sure I shall be forgiven for the social faux pas. All that I can wonder as we stride through the castle is why my father is here. Has something happened in Trador? Is this about the attacks?

When we arrive in the throne room, we are quickly announced without fanfare, and I hurry over to the throne. The only people present are the king, queen, their heir, the advisors, and the new arrivals. Thankfully none of the other nobility are here. I am guessing that also means this has something to do with the vampire attacks. Although everyone has heard the rumours, the king has kept quiet and not announced anything official.

My father stands at the foot of the dais with his hands behind his back, his expression giving nothing away. Four of his own guards stand back a respectable distance. My throat tightens as I notice he is still wearing his riding clothes. This must be an emergency for him not to wash up beforehand—that, or he is planning on leaving as soon as he gives whatever message he has been tasked with.

"Your majesties," I greet the royals, curtsying low, then I turn to my father and bow my head respectfully. "Father."

Eli greets the royals similarly, standing a step back from me. He is not greeted in return, but I see my father eyeing him for a brief moment before dismissing him with an upturned nose. I wondered what he might think of my mate, knowing his feelings on other races, and that one glance tells me all I need to know.

"Anthea," he greets without a hint of warmth in his cold eyes and inexpressive features. I should know better than to expect him to be anything else, but the short exchange is more painful after everything that happened.

"Lady Anthea, thank you for coming so quickly," the king says, pulling our attention to him at the head of the room. Lifting a hand, he lazily waves it towards my father. "As you can see, we have an emissary from Trador, and he would not speak his message until you were present."

Surprised, I raise my brows and look at my father. His court manners are impeccable, so for him to refuse to speak to the king until I was here is both unusual and alarming.

"Thank you, Your Majesty. This message concerns the lady, and I am short on time and cannot delay." My father's well-spoken voice is familiar and brings up unpleasant feelings. I only used to hear it when I was not doing as well as he hoped I would. Praise was a hard thing to obtain from him.

"Our mighty King Trador has sent me as his emissary to give you this message. As you are aware, there is a disease spreading among the vampires. Our land is being ravaged and torn apart by our own people." He pauses as his grand voice takes on a tight edge. The well-being of our people has always been a top priority for my father, so he must be taking this hard. "As you have failed to provide any help or return our bride to us as requested, I am here to take her back to Trador. We believe she is the key to fixing all of this. The way you and your son have treated her is appalling, and as such, a great insult to Trador as a nation. Now, we are dying in large numbers, and you are refusing assistance. If you try to stop me from taking Lady Anthea back to Trador, then we shall take it as an act of war."

Stunned silence fills the throne room, the weight of my father's words falling heavy over us all. The king will be declaring war if Drathlor refuses to allow me to leave. It sounds as though they believe I can help with the disease. I want to fall to my knees and beg the king to allow it. This is my chance to properly help. Even if there is nothing I can do about the prophecy, there has to be something I can do about the destruction of my homeland.

The whole room seems to hold its breath as it waits for the king to reply, his queen looking aghast by the sudden nature of this new threat. This is a serious situation, one that could easily dissolve into all-out war, exactly what we are trying to avoid with the prophecy. The king is being forced into a decision without any time to deliberate. While it is a clever strategy, as it gives him no time to find a way out of this, I am also worried about the repercussions of forcing a male like him into conceding.

The tension is so thick I could almost cut through it with my dagger, and from the awkward shuffling of the guards stationed around the room, I know I am not the only one who feels it. The king shifts his eyes from my father to me, scanning me from head to toe before returning his hard stare to the emissary.

"I do not take kindly to being threatened in my own throne room." The power he infuses into his voice rattles my bones, forcing many of those witnessing this to their knees. From the corner of my eye, I notice Geoff on one knee, his head bent, and I see my father struggling against the power directed at him.

"Due to the recent circumstances of this new disease among the vampires, and the unfortunate events involving my son, I shall allow Lady Anthea to return to Trador for a month." The way he accentuates the final word tells me that even delaying my return by a single day would have severe consequences. "Then," he continues after a heavy pause, "she is expected to return here. This is extended as an act of friendship." His voice is as sharp as a knife, the last word drawn out to make his point. He does not want a war, but he is not happy about being pushed into this decision.

My father bows his head, and without a further word, he takes this as a dismissal and gestures for me to follow him as he turns and strides towards the doors.

Stunned, I look at the king. His expression is enough of a threat that he does not need to repeat his words. I have a month, and then I am expected back. I do not even want to contemplate the repercussions of disobeying. I curtsy deeply and see Eli bow in my periphery, and then I turn to join my father who is almost out of the door.

Chapter Twenty-Five

As soon as we leave the throne room, I jog down the corridor to catch up with my father, Eli keeping pace with me. I have so many questions, my fear hardening me as I prepare for whatever is necessary of me. This is no time for uncertainty or anxiety. The distant sounds of Geoff huffing behind us tell me he's trying to catch up, but I do not slow, needing to learn the truth of what is happening.

Trador is a proud nation, but we do not act in haste. This—whatever *this* is—is completely out of character. The beat of my heart is so rapid that it aches, feeling as though it is going to pound its way through my ribcage. Although dread fills me, I have been prepared to deal with a crisis within my land. First, though, I need to know how bad the situation is.

Finally reaching my father's side, I place a hand on his arm to slow him down. "Father—"

He shakes off my touch, his stride not faltering in the least as he powers forward as though nothing just transpired. He does at least deign to glance at me, shaking his head.

"We are being listened to. Wait until we are outside." Short and sharp, his words are an order he clearly expects to be obeyed.

I am a little surprised that we are not going back to our suites to discuss what is going on, and it is only as we leave the castle and start moving towards the stable block that I realise he means to leave immediately. It is not a short journey from Trador to Drathlor City, so he must be in need of a rest, yet he is already striding towards his large dark horse.

"Wait, you are leaving now?"

I know nothing of his plan, why I'm leaving, or when he plans for me to travel back. Can he not spare a few minutes to discuss this with me before racing back to our king? I try not to pay attention to the fact that this might be hinting at just how bad the situation in our homeland is.

Striding straight up to his horse, which is being fed by Felix, my father adjusts the saddle and stirrups, preparing to mount. "No," he bites out, the word tight as he glances at me with raised brows. "*We* are leaving now. We need you in Trador immediately. This would not be happening if Drath had not refused your requests to return to us."

I understand the frustration in his voice, as it is the same I felt when the king told me of his decision. What takes me aback, though, is the fact that they were willing to threaten war against King Drath if I was not allowed to return to Trador.

"Father, what is happening in Trador that our king is willing to declare war over?" It is a question, but I ask it with the authority of one of the brides, demanding he answer simply with my tone.

He checks his saddle bags. "I will explain on the way, but our people are losing their minds. A disease has overtaken us, making us lose control. Rabid vampire attacks are tearing our society apart, and the humans are terrified of us. They have even begun hunting our kind." He shakes his head with disgust. "Humans hunting *us*. It is an affront and an insult."

My father's attitude towards humans is, unfortunately, in line with most of what the born vampires also believe. They are a necessary source of food and labour that we require to live the quality of life we do, but in that sense, they are thought of as little more than cattle. The changed once started off life as humans, and they are also looked down upon by most of the nobility, which is made up of born vampires. I have always believed otherwise, my friendship and now relationship with Felix is proof of that.

Hearing that the humans are beginning to hunt us is disturbing. While we may be far more powerful, they are much greater in number.

Finished arranging his saddle, he turns to address me. "Our seers believe that you are directly connected to healing us of this affliction, and we need you before things escalate further."

His expression is neutral as usual, yet I swear I see something glimmer in his eyes that looks like uncertainty. He may be trying to hide it, but he is concerned about what is happening. I do not bother to wonder if his concern is about me and what I might be expected to do in my role—I know better than that.

I nod, my mind already spinning with everything I need to do before I can leave. He is clearly in a hurry, but there are some things that cannot be left, Finnik being one of those.

"Give me an hour," I inform my father, running my hands through my hair and pulling it back into a tight braid. "There are several matters I must tie up before I can leave."

My father bares his teeth at me and begins to move towards me, only stopping when a low warning snarl sounds behind me—Eli. I am so used to his constant presence now that it did not even occur to me that he would not be there. Pulling up short, my father balls his hands into fists but says nothing about the towering fae behind me.

"We do not have that time," he bites out, his words clipped. "This is critical, Anthea."

The situation is so dire that he cannot wait a single hour? The dread floating through me breaks through the damn, and a tidal wave of it washes through my bloodstream. It threatens to overwhelm me, but I do not let it, bracing against the force of it instead. Adrenaline fills me, along with Eli's love and support, strengthening me. Felix is watching me intently, his silent but steadfast presence a comfort. He knows exactly how much my people mean to me and the strength of the sense of duty that drives me. While he stays silent, knowing his input would only inflame the situation with my father here, I know in my heart that he will do anything to help me.

I will do anything for my people, including leaving without saying goodbye to Finnik. It feels as though I am tearing off a piece of myself by departing without him, especially after I promised I would not leave without him before. We have spent so little time together recently that I worry how he will take the news that I'm gone. That does not mean he cannot join me later though, and I shall be back in Drathlor City soon. I am needed, this is part of my role. He will understand that, won't he?

My heart clenches painfully in my chest, stealing my

breath away. Trying to reach for the strange connection between us, I press my feelings down it, hoping he can feel my... love. It is the strangest feeling, the possibility of our love, but I won't deny my feelings for him anymore. It might not be a traditional relationship, but I am sure there is more to us. There has to be, and I know he can feel that too. Hoping he knows I have not abandoned him, I blindly reach for him. I feel nothing back other than a vague warmness in my chest, so I will have to just hope he understands, not able to waste any more time.

Blowing out a long breath, I nod at my father, moving onto the next obstacle. "Okay, what about the others—"

"Felix, Geoff, and the others will follow behind us," he interrupts. "We need *you* right now."

Grumbling, I press my hand to my temple but do not bother to argue. My horse, Shadow, is being brought out, and I know we shall be leaving any moment. There is one non-negotiable issue that we have not yet discussed. I hold my hand out, which Eli immediately takes as he steps forward.

"Father, this is Eli. He is my mate and will be riding with us." There is no room for argument, and before he can say anything, I turn to Felix. "Could you prepare a horse for Eli please?"

"Of course, my lady," he answers respectfully as he dips his head in acknowledgement before leaving.

"I shall be back in one moment," I tell my father and share a quick look with Eli in the process. He nods ever so slightly, indicating he understands what I need him to do without me having to ask. I feel torn in so many different directions—my duty, saying goodbye to Finnik, and my love for Felix that my father most definitely would not approve of.

I follow Felix, forcing myself to walk at a normal pace and not chase him like I long to do. As soon as I enter the stable and am away from my father, I pull Felix into an embrace. My whole body trembles at the idea of having to leave him behind as well. We do not have the same magical connection that tells me he is alive and well, something I have come to depend on with Finnik and Eli. What if Felix catches this disease or they get attacked on the way to Trador? There would be nothing I could do.

Despite not having that metaphysical connection, he already knows what I am thinking and frames my face between his hands. "I will see you soon, Thea," he promises, his eyes locked on mine. "I will travel back with the others. We shall only be half a day behind you."

Am I so bad at hiding my feelings? No, Felix has always been able to see through my masks, getting right down to the root of my distress. We have spent years together as friends, and the bond formed by time cannot be reproduced any other way.

My body trembles slightly as I adjust to the overload of information, becoming my true self in front of Felix. I release a long, shaky breath. "I love you, and I am sorry I cannot take you with me now." Pressing my forehead against his, I lean against him and absorb his warmth. Our time is running out, but I have one last thing to ask him. "Could you please find Finnik and tell him I have gone, and I did not have a choice about leaving? I do not want him to think I left him behind."

Any fears I had of upsetting Felix by asking him to seek out the other male were unfounded, as my love simply smiles sadly, picking up on my stress. Running a hand over my hair, he kisses my forehead.

"Of course." His reply is immediate and without any jealousy or frustration. "Travel swiftly, Thea. I love you."

Now that it is time to leave, I am overcome with a rush of emotions. My gut is telling me that all of this is wrong, and that the next time I see him, everything will be different. I have to close my eyes for a moment, breathing through the tightness in my throat at the idea of something happening to him.

"Be safe, please," I beg, gripping his shirt. "I cannot lose you."

I seal my words with a kiss, desperately needing to feel close to him. Our kiss deepens as our tongues twist in a dance known only to us. I breathe him in, his scent wrapping around me like a blanket, keeping me warm with the depth of his feelings. I am feverish, manic with energy that I do not know how to release. Our kiss feels as though it could be our last, like we are saying goodbye.

No, I refuse for that to be the case.

Breaking off from the kiss, I back away, knowing if I stay a moment longer that I will not leave. I point at Felix. "I *will* see you soon."

Spinning on my heel, I exit the stable before I do something I might regret.

Shadow's long legs eat up the ground as we canter through the outskirts of Drathlor City, leaving the castle. Refusing to think of the people I left behind, I focus instead on the journey. We are going to have to push our mounts to the limit to reach the centre of Trador before the sun rises.

The land between Drathlor City and the wall separating

it from the other nations is barren and desolate. No one lives out here, and we do not see a soul as we ride. Two guards lead the way, then my father, myself, and Eli ride in a triangular formation with the final two guards protecting our rear.

This gives me very little to do while we race forward, my thoughts going over everything my father told me, dissecting every detail and trying to make sense of it. The human hunters are a huge concern, but I am feeling more positive that I might actually be able to help in Trador. The seers mentioned me, so that must mean this illness is related, confirming my suspicions.

Seeing into the future is an ability that is not typically gifted to vampires, and what our seers do manage to glean is usually more of a possibility of what is to come. Even so, they have seen nothing significant for many years, so the fact that they had a vision with me is big news.

I hope that when it comes down to it, I am strong enough to do what I have to. The weight of responsibility is tight around my chest, and if I am being honest, having my mate at my side is the only thing keeping me going.

The wall begins to appear before us, stretching out as far as the eye can see. I always thought it looked foreboding and ugly, the dark stone separating the city from the rest of the land. For a king who proclaims he wants all of the lands to be united as one, he sure knows how to separate us. I suspect there is some form of magic on the wall, as I always feel nauseous when we pass it, and today is no different.

Only, as we approach, I notice one big difference—there is no one manning the gate that leads to Trador. There are seven gates built into the wall, each leading to the seven lands beyond, all of which are heavily guarded. However, I cannot see a sign of a single one of them. Usually there would be several guards stationed a hundred meters or so before the wall, who would check our identities and our business for passing through the wall. More guards would be by the gate, monitoring the comings and goings of those passing. The other side has the same amount of vigorous inspections, yet I can see straight through the open gate, and not a single soul approaches.

We slow our horses as we reach the checkpoint, and I sense my companions' confusion. Our personal guards who are leading the way seem wary, but one climbs from his horse and jogs forward, passing the empty checkpoint and moving swiftly towards the gates.

"Where are the guards?" Eli asks me quietly, moving his horse closer to mine. His eyes flit around us, checking for threats, his fae senses picking up something I am unable to.

"I do not know," I reply softly, unable to ease the queasy feeling in my stomach. "Something does not feel right."

My father seems to be thinking along the same lines, his face tight as our guard runs back and reports that there is no one manning the gate. Nothing seems to be out of place, they just seem to have... vanished.

"We proceed with caution," my father announces grimly after a momentary pause. He is clearly disturbed by this turn of events, yet he is having to choose between putting us at risk for the whole of our kingdom.

"Is that wise, Father?" I cannot help asking the question even though I know he will have weighed all the options, not one to make a rash decision.

This time, when he looks at me, I see a flicker of emotion in his eyes. "There is no time to waste, daughter."

Biting back my retort, I nod in agreement, feeling the desperate need to get back to Trador as soon as possible. We pass through the gate without trouble, not a soul to be seen. Our entire party is on high alert, and everything is eerily quiet, yet we do not have time to investigate. Once we are past the empty checkpoint on the other side of the wall, we move our horses into a trot, still keeping our eyes on the barren land around us.

We have been riding for around five minutes now, and nothing out of the ordinary has occurred, so we allow our horses to canter, taking us towards the capital city of Trador.

Something appears on the road ahead of us, at first appearing like a dark stain across our path. As we get closer, I see it begin to take shape. It looks like a carriage, but it's on its side.

"What is that? Has there been an accident?" I call out, glancing over at Eli for his verdict. He is frowning, looking intently at the apparent wreckage.

My father calls out, and we slow our horses to a trot, approaching with caution. Although not common in Trador, bandits do occasionally attempt to rob people on the main road to the city, yet this does not have the same feel as that. We get closer, and I see that it is not a carriage, but some strange wooden contraption. It lies on its side, exposing the wheels at the front and back, but where you would expect the body of a carriage, there is nothing. At least, from our vantage point, that is how it appears. The strangest thing about it all is that there is no one around to be seen. The landscape is empty and barren, the life drained from it, so there is nowhere for anyone to hide.

Slowing to a walk, we close our formation. Something is off about this situation, and I am not the only one who senses it.

A blast of bright, dazzling light cuts through the darkness ahead of us, as though the sun has been concentrated into a single beam. Our horses rear up in fear, and my skin burns as the light touches me. Dazed and shocked, I fall from my mount, landing on the ground with a heavy thump, my shoulder taking the impact. Pain rips through me, my right arm dangling uselessly at my side. I suspect it is dislocated, but I am in so much agony I cannot even think about putting it back into position.

"Thea!" Eli's voice cuts through the chaos.

My eyes stream, the bright light making them sting and water. Attempting to shield my face, I desperately look around to see what is happening. Blurry figures run across my field of vision, and I hear the sounds of fighting. If I am being burnt by the light, then my father and our guards will be as well, disabling us. Thankfully, Eli won't be damaged by the light, but can he fight off all of our attackers?

It is clear that this was all a trap, designed specifically to target vampires. Did they know the first bride was among this travel party or were we just unlucky?

The warmth of many bodies surrounds me, their scents strange and unfamiliar, disorienting me all the more. When one of them touches me, I jerk away violently, making my shoulder scream with pain as I snap my teeth and snarl in warning. I draw my dagger and hold it before me threateningly. However, whoever is attacking us is clearly not a vampire, because they approach me, unbothered by the beams. Baring my teeth and hissing, I begin to descend into my primal self, my fangs extended as I blindly thrash around. The figures in front of me are just blurry shadows. They close in, and I feel surrounded. The sounds of fighting appear far away as the guards rush to defend us but are drawn farther from me. From the sharp tugs on our bond, I know Eli is attempting to fight his way towards me, using our connection as a compass.

They are separating me from the others. This was a trap, and we rode straight into it.

"Anthea!" my father shouts, panic lacing his voice. That, more than anything, fills me with fear. Strong emotions are not proper in the world of vampire lords. I do not think I have ever seen him display fear before.

The light is still shining on me, making it impossible to see clearly, and my skin burns, keeping me disoriented and confused. The mystery, carriage-like structure must be part of the light-making machine. I do not know how they are doing it, but it is stronger than any sun I have experienced before, as though it has been magnified and directed straight onto me.

Pain explodes on the right side of my face as a fist meets with my jaw. My body is thrown to one side with the force of the blow. I try to scrabble upright, my damaged shoulder making it almost impossible. As I struggle, a pair of boots appears in my blurry vision, and without warning, those boots kick out at me, slamming into my stomach, my back, and my face. They kick me over and over, taking it in turns.

Agony encompasses me until it is all I know. Is this how I'll die? After everything I have done to try and save us from war, I'll die from a beam of sunlight. There are many times that I could have died in my past, yet I survived. Dying now when I am so close to fulfilling my purpose seems like such a waste.

My damaged, burnt, and beaten body screams in protest as hands grab me roughly and proceed to drag me across the ground. They are taking me away—away from my family and my mate, and thanks to the concentrated beam of light aimed at me, I am unable to fight back. Pitiful.

Somewhere in the distance, I hear Eli roar as he tries to make his way to me, but there are too many of them. Through bleary eyes, I see my father fighting his way towards me. As a pair of boots steps into my view, I brace myself for more pain, expecting to be beaten once more. The male crouches down in front of me, and just the scent of him twists something within me before I even see his face. I know exactly who orchestrated this whole attack.

Lifting my gaze, I stare at the male who once could have been my mate.

Havoc.

"Well," he says with a wide smile, his cruel eyes scanning me with manic glee. "Hello, dear Anthea."

The world goes dark around me, and I fall into unconsciousness.

Chapter Twenty-Six

*D*rip. Drip. Drip.

The noise is the first thing I notice. It is irritating, catching my attention and pulling me from the dark space in my mind, dragging me back into reality.

Pain slams into my body, waking me with a jolt. I am aware of people talking and movement around me, but I am unable to see anything past the agony that fills me. The mind is funny that way, able to block off pain, yet as soon as it is acknowledged, there is no way to push it back.

My skin is tight and feels burnt, sensitive even to the air around it. My dislocated shoulder is causing me the most discomfort. I am tied up between two pillars, with rope tightly wrapped around each wrist and ankle, spreading me wide. My right arm is hanging awkwardly where the bone is no longer in its socket. The circulation to that hand is clearly being affected, the purple colour of it concerning. I am sure my abdomen is a mess of purple bruises thanks to the beating they doled out to me, and my lip feels swollen. Breathing, although painful, is not agonising, so if I did break any ribs, they healed while I was unconscious. A small blessing.

Other sounds begin to filter through, and with tremendous effort, I lift my head.

The room I am being kept in looks like an old bunker, and from the damp, earthy scent, I would guess we are underground. Five males are all staring at me with a variety of expressions ranging from disgust and anger to glee. The only one I recognise is the male in the middle of the group —Havoc.

Instinctively, I reach for my bond—not the one with the male in front of me, but to Eli, my true mate. I cannot feel it though. It is as though there is a block stopping the connection—magic, I am sure of it. I try to touch my connection to Finnik, and I desperately hope he can feel me, even though I hit that same wall of magic. There is no way for me to reach them.

Adrenaline pumps through me at the thought that my mates could be in danger, and that gives me enough strength to face the man who destroyed everything. My eyes lock with Havoc's, and his smug smile only grows wider.

"You are finally awake," he remarks, as though I overslept and kept them waiting.

I want to spit and curse and bellow at him, let him feel my anger and sense of betrayal—not only for kidnapping me now, but for everything he put me through in the city. That is exactly what I would do if I was not so drained. Part of my mind is screaming at me that it's worth it, that he deserves to hear how much agony he put me through, but I know I need to conserve my energy.

Finding as much strength as I can, I roll my shoulders back and glare at him. "What's going on, Havoc?"

He raises his eyebrows as though he's surprised by my

attitude. Does he really think he can break me so easily? I might have appeared demure at the castle, but I have claws and fangs, and I know when to use them.

Snorting, he shakes his head and crosses his arms over his chest. "The brotherhood and I are taking matters into our own hands, seeing as cutting off our bond did not kill you as planned."

Havoc has truly gone off the deep end. At one point, I thought I might be able to convince him that I was not cursed and we needed to work together, but now I realise he has been too brainwashed to see anything past his fevered anger. The growl in his voice makes it obvious that he believes cutting our bond would have solved his problems. If it were not for Eli and Finnik, then I would have died from Havoc's rejection.

"If I die, then the whole prophecy will fall apart," I argue, ignoring the mumbles of the other males in the room. "It warns against trying to harm the brides, and that is exactly what you are doing!" My attempt at staying calm is rapidly failing. I should probably be worried about what they have planned for me, but I have to try and convince Havoc he is wrong, even if I know it is impossible.

"We do not believe in the prophecy," one of the males behind Havoc spits out, his dark eyes narrowed on me.

"We believe the brides are the ones causing the unrest in the land," Havoc continues as he gestures at me. "Look at the vampires, they are killing people!"

My anger overtakes me. Havoc is never going to change his mind. They brought me here to hurt me, and I will not baby him any longer.

"That," I hiss, pulling at my bindings, "is because you messed with the prophecy!" Glaring at each of the males in the room, I plan their deaths in my mind. "The brotherhood has brainwashed you. They are a group of fanatics who spread rumours and cause discontent. It is you who the prophecy was warning us about!" I have completely lost control of my temper. Growling, I attempt to rein myself back in. "Just let me go. I need to help my people."

Looking at me as though I am a child, he shakes his head. "The only way you can help anyone is by dying. You are an abomination." He turns to one of the males and crooks his finger. "Bring the light."

The light. That must be what they used when they attacked us.

"Havoc," I start, my fear rising as that strange wooden device is brought into the room. I feel my limbs begin to tremble as I remember the pain and disorientation it caused. Of course Havoc could not just kill me, he has to torture me in the process.

He walks over to the device and gazes at it fondly, placing a hand on top of it. Looking up at me, he stares with an eagerness that makes me sick to my stomach. "Sunlight will purify your soul."

"No!" Any further protests are cut off as a beam of light lands on my skin.

Already burnt and vulnerable, my skin is scorched, my exposed nerve endings making me cry out in agony. Contorting to try and get any semblance of relief, I desperately fight against my bindings. I am too weak, the rope holding me tightly. The previous attack and beating drained me, and now the light only makes it worse. I am being burned alive.

Fighting with every ounce of strength, I scream and tear at myself to try and get free. My agony in my shoulder is excruciating, the movements only enhancing the pain I feel, yet I know if I stay here, I will die.

As suddenly as it turned on, the light turns off, and I cry in relief, hanging forward against my restraints. Despite the fact my whole body feels ablaze, I shiver. This is a bad sign, and my vampire healing seems to have slowed down, being affected by the sunlight. I do not know the reason they stopped using the light, but I am grateful for the respite.

I only just finish my thought when Havoc calls out, "Again."

Pain envelops me.

This goes on and on. My alabaster skin is blistered and peeling, each of my breaths laboured as I desperately fight for air. There is also a silent battle in my mind. During the short gaps between torture, I have to remind myself why I am here and that I must survive for the good of my people, my mates, and Felix. However, it is getting harder with each passing minute, and my energy levels dip, pain draining me. It is not only my energy that is dropping, but my blood too. They made a simple cut to my arm and pressed a silver coin into the opening to stop my body from clotting, so my blood dips slowly onto the ground beneath me.

Silver doesn't kill or wound us like some myths would have you believe, and I can touch it without being harmed, but when ingested or it's inside our bodies, it slows down our healing process. It is a smart way of keeping me weak, however, I do not know why they are keeping me alive. They said I need to die, so why not just kill me?

I glance at the far corner where Havoc and another male are talking in low voices, their eyes on me, gleaming with sick pleasure. That is why I am still alive—they are taking great enjoyment from this, my pain and suffering giving them a sense of godlike power.

I attempt to lick my cracked lips, but my tongue has dried up, the world spinning around me. I feel almost as bad as when Havoc rejected me. At least then I had my mates with me to help me through it. Now, I am completely alone in this, and the weaker I get, the more exhausting it is to hold on to my sanity. I am unable to feel my bond, completely cut off from Eli and Finnik, and I struggle to stay grounded because of this. In my sparse moments of clarity, I come to a conclusion.

I cannot wait around for someone to rescue me. If I want to survive, then I have to save myself.

The darkness within me is begging to be let out, my control slipping as it pushes against my boundaries. I know that releasing it is the only thing that will save me, but I fight against it out of instinct. I do not know what sort of monster I will become when it is released, or if I can call it back and return to myself. A pained noise between agony and frustration slips between my clenched teeth.

"How are you feeling, mate?" Havoc calls out, appearing in front of me with a wide, twisted smile.

Snarling, I jerk forward and snap my teeth in his face. "Do not dare call me that. You do not deserve the honour." The word is an insult on his lips, something he is making a mockery of. Besides, he is no longer my mate, he has seen to that, severing the bond and the possibility of any type of life together. Just hearing the word revives me, giving me strength as anger courses through me.

"It is clear the gods were testing me when they made *you* my mate."

Disgust makes his upper lip curl, and he shakes his

head. He's trying to offend me. For what purpose, I am not sure, but all he does is make me see just how deluded he is.

I attempt to hold back my anger and reason with him before I turn to my last resort. "I am giving you one last chance. Release me."

Havoc just laughs, and the others in the room do the same, clearly finding my words amusing. They have no idea what they are about to face.

"Enjoy the sunshine, my dear." Havoc turns from me and waves his hand in a gesture that I now know means pain is on the way.

This time when the light hits me, instead of trying to escape the agony, I absorb it, letting the darkness within me devour it as it grows, pressing against the boundaries of my skin. It pauses, and it takes me a moment to realise what is happening. It shimmers in my mind, waiting for something.

Permission. It is waiting for permission, one final barrier still in place across my mind. Even though I am writhing in pain, I take a shuddering breath and let a small, tight smile pull at my lips as I stare at Havoc. I narrow my eyes on him, and he has the decency to look uncomfortable. Good.

I drop the final barrier and release the darkness.

My body shifts and ripples, the pain replaced with a burning sensation as I become something... other. My eyes shift, and the light they direct my way no longer burns them, allowing me to see their faces clearly, including the looks of shock as they watch my transformation. My limbs extend, and my skin appears to become darker, and I swear I notice an iridescent sheen. My body feels stronger than I ever have in my life, and as I slip from my bindings, a phantom wind blows through the room, my wayward hair surrounding me in a silver halo.

Shouts of terror and confusion fill the room. Havoc

looks horrified and lunges for the door, trying to get away. Coward. Several males jump forward with blades, all aimed at me. Now that their light is no longer affecting me, they are having to resort to physical weapons instead.

Not a problem, because I now have weapons of my own. The nails on my fingers have extended into long, vicious claws, and my fangs are far larger than they usually are, ready to feed. Their torture drained me, and I need blood. This body is stronger now that it has transformed, yet it will not stay so for long without refilling myself. Dispatching my kidnappers and feeding at the same time will be easy enough. They might as well be useful for something after everything they did to me.

With a speed I have never possessed before, I whirl around and I slice at the two males attempting to attack me. The tallest assailant gets too close, and I catch him in the gut. He falls immediately, uselessly clutching his stomach as he tries to hold in his internal organs. The other male is faster and manages to dodge the blow. He spins his sword in his hand, showing off his skills and demonstrating just how cocky he is, not caring that his companion is dying on the ground. He believes that he is going to kill me, and it is this attitude that will be his downfall.

Jumping forward, I back him into a corner, knocking away each of the blows of his sword with my claws, somehow instinctively knowing they will hold against the blade. He leaps to the left, leaving his right side open in the process and giving me the perfect opportunity to latch onto his neck. My fangs sink into his delicate flesh, his blood filling my mouth in an instant. I want to groan in pleasure as I drink the rich liquid, his life force restoring me.

Unfortunately, I do not have time to indulge as I wish, not when two more males are coming towards me, their swords raised. They are my next targets and will fall beneath my feral attack, death the only option available. As I spin around the room like a hurricane of teeth and claws, it occurs to me that while I am fully capable of creating this destruction on my own, the darkness takes away my more human sentiments and allows me to do what is necessary.

It isn't some monster inside me or something I have been cursed with carrying like I always believed—no, this *is* me. It's a dark, powerful part of myself I have pushed down and refused to acknowledge out of fear. If I learned to embrace this all along, then I could have been so much stronger and achieved so much.

Perhaps this is the hardship I had to get over to complete my part of the prophecy—learning to embrace this part of myself. I also feel the potential of something else within me. I have not discovered what yet, but when I do, it will change everything, I know it.

A sense of clarity has come over me. Finnik is my mate, just as Eli is, and holding back is not only hurting us, but the land. We are supposed to be together, all of us, Felix too. I need to get back to them and complete my bonds, sealing us together. Before I can do that, though, there is something I need to do first.

Bodies fall around me, and now that I am alone, I drop to the floor and latch onto the dying males, drinking deeply. I feed like a glutton, taking more than I need and revelling in the feeling of indulgence.

Full and finally sated, I stand and wipe my mouth with the back of my hand. I'm a mess, my dress torn and covered in blood, but I do not care, not when there is one more person who needs to pay for their crimes—Havoc.

I stride up the stairs of the bunker, my hands tingling with power. The door to the outside is locked, but when I place my hands on it and give the lightest push, it buckles in on itself.

Light streams down on me, but it does not even make me wince thanks to the change in my eyes. Looking around, I try to get a clue as to where I am. We seem to be on an old, abandoned farm. I stand at the edge of a courtyard with a farm building lining the square, open space. My inner compass is telling me we are still in Trador, but I have never seen this farm before, so they must have taken me far from the main road. There is no one to be seen, and it is quiet. A loud caw rings out, startling me.

Looking up, I find a large crow perched atop a weathervane, watching me with far more intelligence than I would expect in a bird. It tilts its head to one side and seems to be watching me. I bow my head to it. I am not sure where this idea came from, but the darkness is telling me it is important to respect the creature. When it lowers its head in return, I feel shock, but the darkness is not surprised at all. It caws loudly once more before leaping from the weathervane and disappearing into the sky.

Back in the moment, I scan the area around me once more.

"Havoc," I call, my voice carrying across the deserted space. He is here, I can feel him, but instead of facing the consequences of his actions, he is hiding like a child. "Come out, you coward!"

A flash of movement catches my eye, and I see him run into what looks like a stable block. Pushing that strange dark power into my limbs, I soar across the courtyard and am on him in an instant. It is the oddest feeling, because for a moment, I swear my feet did not touch the ground. This is not the time to be thinking about this, though, as I knock him through the stable doorway, and we go crashing down to the floor.

He cries out in alarm and tries to struggle away from me, holding his arms up in protection. I have seen him duel before, he is well trained, yet he seems to have lost all of his confidence and bravery, resulting in him being a quivering mess beneath me.

"Please, do not kill me!" he pleads. "I am a prince!"

It is my turn to look disgusted. The darkness in me wants to get this over with now and take his life, not bothering to waste a single moment more on him, but I have something I need to say first.

I dig my claws into his shoulder and neck, watching thin trickles of blood form where they puncture his skin. Good. Leaning closer so our faces almost touch, I lift my top lip and growl, enjoying the sensation of him shaking beneath me.

"You are a scumbag who was happy to sacrifice his people over a superstition," I growl, allowing the dark part of me to enter my voice. "You are a danger to our safety, and you will continue to be for as long as you live."

I raise my hand above me, ready for the final blow. This is it. I do wonder how it will feel when he dies given our broken bond, but he has already killed the connection between us, so I am sure I will survive it. I am stronger now. I can do this.

I go to move, but a strange feeling in my chest makes me pause, quickly followed by a scent I know well.

He is here. He came for me.

Finnik.

"Thea, wait!" Havoc's best friend and my mate to be calls out as he steps into the stable, his face contorted into a frown of disapproval. "Do not kill him."

Chapter Twenty-Seven

"Finnik!" Havoc cries, relief filling his eyes as he jerks beneath me, trying to throw me off him, but it is no use. "Brother, save me from this lunatic. She is trying to kill me!" He attempts to sound fierce, snarling up at me threateningly, but it has no effect on me. We both know that only moments ago, he was running away and begging for his life.

I shift my weight so I am still pinning Havoc to the straw-covered ground while turning to look at Fin. He is wearing hastily thrown on travelling clothes, as though he grabbed the first items of clothing he could find and rushed straight here. Perhaps that is exactly what he did after Felix told him I left for Trador. I have so many questions, but I hold my tongue.

"Fin," I greet, and although my voice is smooth, hiding my true emotions while Havoc is listening, I use his nickname, knowing how much he enjoys hearing it from me. It will also tell him that the changes to my body and mind have not changed how I feel about him. In reality, all I want to do is race forward into his arms, hold him close, and never let go, but something in his eyes stops me. He watches me closely, taking in my burnt, bruised, and broken body, along with the changes the darkness has caused. There's a stillness inside him and a coldness in his expression that makes my heart race. I thought he was here for me, but now my brain is processing signs I did not want to notice before—the way he holds himself back from me, the almost indifferent attitude towards me, the lack of anger at Havoc. He cannot possibly be here to help the former prince, could he? My heart is telling me to trust him, the whisper of our bond brushing against me now that I have left the bunker.

Staring at his friend, Finnik raises a brow and glances around, not moving from his spot in the doorway. "I thought you might be hiding out here."

My head jerks around to look at him, a frown pulling at my brow. "Wait, you knew where he was this whole time? Why didn't you tell the king? Tell me?"

I feel a little betrayed that Finnik was aware of Havoc's location. He could have been here sooner, but he arrived after I was tortured for so long I descended into my darkness to escape. Havoc tried to kill me, sabotaging our chances at surviving and saving the whole kingdom. Finnik knew but said nothing.

Something strokes across the partial bond, like a warm, gentle breeze as he looks at me. There is a disconnect between his flat expression and the warmth he is sending me, and I find it difficult to know which one to trust.

"I did not know for sure," Finnik begins without any emotion. "He once told me about a hideout he created in Trador years ago. When we could not find him in the city, I assumed this was where he came. I did not know where it was, only a general location. I have been searching for an entire day."

My hurt and confusion must be on my face, because his composure shifts.

"The reason I did not tell you was..." He sighs and shakes his head, his eyes moving to take in the pinned male beneath me. "Some lingering sense of loyalty I suppose. I also hoped he would give himself up, and I was giving him the opportunity to do the right thing."

Finnik is here for me. He came for me. He searched the land and found me. He does not spell it out for me or say it directly, but the words he uses when talking about Havoc tells me he is trying to keep his anger controlled. Why the ruse? I assume he is trying to get some information out of Havoc before I kill him. At least, I hope that is what this is, and I have not been fooled.

"You were behind the abduction, Havoc?" he asks his friend, his voice smooth once more. "You were the mastermind behind it?"

"Yes, friend. I planned with the brotherhood. We knew she would leave soon enough with everything happening with the vampires." The words fall out of him quickly now that he believes he is about to be rescued. How he has deluded himself into thinking Finnik is going to rescue him when not a single step or action has been taken to do so, I do not know. I think he is so certain in his relationship with Finnik that he believes it will automatically override any loyalty to me, ignoring the signs.

"You attempted to kill Thea twice then?" Finnik asks slowly, his voice deadly calm.

I do not know if it is the question itself or his tone that twists his words as he speaks, but Havoc frowns, catching onto the fact his friend has not jumped to his rescue. The question could sound innocent, but the tension in the air says it is anything but.

I take the opportunity to drag Havoc to his feet and pin him against the stable wall. With my new strength, it is like dragging a rag doll. He grunts at the force and glares at me before turning his attention back to his friend.

"You know my views on the brides, my friend. Nothing has changed," he explains slowly, frowning as though he doesn't understand why Finnik would believe otherwise. He takes a sharp breath and smiles at his friend. "Help me fight her. We can do this together." Havoc seems more cautious now, having picked up on the strange tension in the stable, but a manic fervour shines in his eyes as he gets swept away by his extreme views once more. He truly believes he can convince Finnik to help him.

Finnik steps inside the stable, his boots clipping against the stone ground, one measured step at a time. "You rejected your mate, almost killing her, then you ran away like a coward. Now, after trying to kill her again, you want me to help you kill her?" He lists off each action on his hand, counting his sins for us to see. He comes to a stop several paces away and snarls viciously. "My mate?"

Havoc feels like a statue beneath my grip at this new revelation. When he finally returns to the present, he blinks several times, but horror has entered his eyes. The stale stench of fear wafts from him as he contemplates the consequences of his actions.

"What?" He starts to shake his head viciously, but I plant my claws against his neck, and he stills. "She cannot be your mate. She was mine." Accusation, worry, and pride all coat his words. How chauvinistic of him to believe that I *belonged* to him, like a possession no one else could own. It makes me sick to my stomach. Although I wish the circumstances were different, I know a bond between Havoc and I would not have been a happy one. In a way, things have worked out better, because I have found the loves of my life, which I wouldn't have if Havoc accepted our bond. If only the rest of the land did not have to suffer.

"I can only assume fae bonds are different. We also have multiple mates in the fae realm," Finnik explains as I bring myself back to the present. "Her bond with Eli was the only reason she survived your rejection." Anger simmers beneath the surface of Finnik's neutral expression, and I know it will not take much for him to snap.

"I did not know she was yours, my friend," Havoc replies quickly, sounding genuinely sorry as he shakes his head.

All he would need to do to make us waver is leave it at that, and I think the two of us would find a way to rehabilitate him, far away so he couldn't hurt the land any longer. However, Havoc is not capable of leaving anything alone.

"I am sorry for that, but we still have to do this. We need to rid the land of the brides so we can all prosper!"

Havoc just dug his own grave, and he does not seem to realise it.

"No, Havoc!" Finnik snaps, flashing his pointed teeth and hissing with anger. "You were like a brother to me, but you have committed treason and are a constant danger to my mate!"

He paces behind me, his hands balled into fists as he attempts to calm down. At this point, I am surprised he has not struck his old friend for everything he has done, but they were close, more like family than friends. Hurting someone like that is like wounding a part of yourself, even if they deserve the punishment. No one benefits from it. For that reason, I am glad he is holding himself back. Although I know he would do it for me, it would hurt him too much to kill Havoc.

"What happens now then?" Havoc asks, bravado in his voice as he scowls at my mate, attempting to appear unbothered by his impending death. "You are going to kill me?"

"No," Finnik replies, surprising both of us.

I whip my head around in confusion. Is he going to try and convince me not to kill Havoc? We do not have a choice in this, not when he is determined to destroy the prophecy. If we do not kill him today, then he will attempt to take my life again.

My prisoner's eyes light with hope once more, and he struggles against my hold. It is pointless, he does not budge me in the slightest, yet I can see he believes he is about to be saved.

Before either of us can say anything, Finnik takes a final step forward, resting a hand on my shoulder and glaring at Havoc. Side by side, we stand against the prince.

"No," he repeats, his eyes narrowed. "*She* is going to kill you. After all the hurt you caused her, the rejection and torture—she has earned this."

It is now or never. I do not give Havoc a chance to reply, slicing my nails across his throat in one quick movement. Shock flashes in his eyes, but that quickly fades as he becomes limp in my arms, his face going slack. I feel the exact moment he dies, as his soul passes from this life to the next. A jolt like that of a skipped heartbeat thumps inside me, the absence of something I did not know was still there making me feel hollow. There is almost an echo of remembered hurt, both physical and emotional. It is nothing like what I have experienced before, and although it is uncomfortable, I finally feel Havoc leave my soul. I will never be fully complete, thanks to him, but he is no longer lingering within me. The shadow of his rejection and hatred lifts from me, allowing me to stretch my wings and be the female I was always destined to be.

With a gasp, I jerk backwards, slamming into Finnik's chest as we both watch Havoc's body fall to the floor. His blood drips from my hand, and I am covered in the blood of those I killed before him. I am sure I look awful, but Finnik's steadying arm wraps around me and holds me against him. My breathing is rapid as the realisation of what I just did finally hits me.

"Breathe," Finnik whispers in my ear, his warm breath tickling the sensitive skin.

Focusing on that feeling, I take several slow, deep breaths, allowing my new body to settle. The smooth, gentle brush of his breath helps guide my own breathing—in, hold, and release. After a while, I forget about my breathing and focus on how his teeth graze my earlobe and the hair on my skin stands on end, tingling from being so close to my mate. That triggers other feelings within me, warm sensations that have no place here considering the body that lies just a few feet from us.

Shaking my head to clear my mind, I turn in his arms and look up to examine his face. He appears different, his expression harder than the mischievous fae he was before. He still carries the beauty that all fae seem to be blessed with, and he is just as handsome as he has always been, but he has a ruthless edge to him. He would do anything to find me, even if it meant killing the male he thought of as his brother.

"Thea, I was so worried." Cupping my face gently, he examines me. "Are you okay? What did they do to you?" His final words end in a growl as he takes in the damage to my body and face. I have not seen myself in a mirror, but his reaction tells me it is not a pretty sight. His hand runs down the length of my arm, the touch against the sensitive skin making me shiver.

"You transformed." He sounds reverent as he looks me over in awe. A tiny part of my mind dreaded how he would react to the changes in me, to the darkness in my soul that now cloaks my body. The fact that he looks at me as though I am something wondrous and not to be feared helps heal a little of the damage my soul took on over the last few months.

"I let the darkness out of me," I begin, attempting to explain the separation of myself in a way that makes sense. "The power in me was mine all along, not a monster or a curse after all. I pushed it down and hid it for so long I grew to fear it when there was nothing to fear." I pause, contemplating what I just said, and raise my arm with my claws. "Well, perhaps I am a monster, in appearance anyway, but I am in full control, finally, after all this time."

He shakes his head, his expression earnest. "You could never be a monster. You are kind and smart and beautiful. I shall love you the same in every form. Your appearance is just different, but that does not mean it is bad."

My heart slams in my chest at his casual use of the word love, but I do not bring it up or question him over it like I want to. He has never admitted his feelings like this for me. Without our bond being complete, it leaves things more open, giving me only a vague sense of his strong emotions. Hearing that he loves me out loud is enough to make me want to sing out in happiness.

Finnik has not finished, though, and a cheeky grin spreads across his lips. "The addition of the feathers and tail might take a little getting used to though." He's grinning widely, his forehead pressed to mine, but I am too distracted by what he said.

A tail? I must have heard him wrong.

"What?" Spinning around, I try to look behind myself, and sure enough, there is a long, black feathered tail. I stare at it in shock and blink several times, waiting for the hallucination to disappear, but it does not. This is not a dream, but reality. I have a tail.

"How the fuck did I not notice that earlier?" I curse under my breath, shifting my weight from foot to foot and watching the tail move.

"You look like a bird," Finnik comments helpfully.

A sarcastic retort is on the tip of my tongue when a cawing sound reaches me from outside—the crow from earlier.

I knew then it was unusual, but now I realise what it was. It wasn't just a strange coincidence, it was communicating with me. While I cannot fully understand what the creature is saying, I know it is here for me, and I know I have something to do with its appearance.

"Not just any bird," I whisper, still trying to understand. "A crow."

The darkness in me *calls* to the crow. With my power released and blending with my body, it has taken on a form. For me, it has manifested as a crow. Do all of the brides have this sort of power within them? Can they transform too? I have so much to learn about myself.

My body suddenly shudders, the world moving around me as I seem to shrink, every part of me tingling with magic I did not know I possessed. Finnik watches in fascination, taking half a step back to give me space for whatever is occurring. When I take a deep, steadying breath and glance down at my body, I notice I am back in my usual form, no tail to be seen. That answers my question about whether I can return to myself or if the darkness permanently changed me. I may look the same, but I feel different. Something in me is altered, and I finally feel more at home in my body. I have accepted a part of myself I always shied away from and blocked.

I am glad to be back in my usual form, and when I look up at Finnik, I'm surprised to find he has a horrified expression on his face.

"Thea, your skin..."

His whispered words are tight and clipped, as though he's trying his hardest not to explode in anger.

Since my transformation, my skin actually feels a little better, as though it kick-started my vampiric healing. His stare is making me uncomfortable, so I try to make light of what happened. "Oh, this is nothing. They used sunlight to torture me, along with a good old-fashioned beating." I chuckle, but there is no humour behind it.

Finnik's hands tighten on my arms, and I watch his expression go dark with feral rage.

"Fucking bastards." His growl is low and long, and his teeth are bared, looking more animal than fae. "I hope you killed them all." There is a gleam in his eyes, one I cannot help but react to.

Grinning, I expose my fangs. "Every last one of them."

His expression turns smug as he watches me proudly. He licks the front of his teeth, his stare heating. "Why do I find that incredibly sexy?"

My body reacts to his words, warmth moving through me, causing my body to come alive. Fucking him here in this stable while I am covered in blood should be a huge turn-off, but for some reason, it's the opposite. Perhaps because we have been apart for so long and been through so much, our bodies know this is what we both need.

"Even with Havoc's body in the room?" I am not sure

what makes me say this, and as soon as the words leave my mouth, I regret it, but it is too late to take back now.

Finnik stiffens, the moment between us gone, and I think he's going to shut down. This conversation needs to happen whether or not he will admit it. I just killed someone he loved, and no matter the reasoning, he is going to need to mourn. If this is bottled up, then it could negatively affect us in the future. He could come to resent me for it, so even though it is uncomfortable, we need to talk this through.

Sighing deeply, he glances over my shoulder at the body. "It was the only way. I regret that things happened like this, and I wonder if I missed something in all those years we spent together. I never would have thought he was capable of the atrocities he committed this last year. That was not the male I knew and loved." He nods his head towards the body. "That is not Havoc. My friend died a long time ago when the brotherhood got their claws into him."

My heart aches for him as he speaks. I had no idea he was carrying this guilt around with him. He used to tell me Havoc did not usually act like he did with me, and he just brushed it off, but now I am beginning to understand that something deeper was going on with Havoc.

Taking Finnik's hand, I pull him from the stable, wanting to get him away from the body, only for him to drag me into another stall several down from where we were.

"You are magnificent," he whispers as he pulls me deeper into the stall, his lips crashing onto mine.

My arms wrap around him, one across his back and the other threading into his hair. The soft, messy waves are finger-length and perfect for grabbing. Arousal and need courses through me, my body needing my mate as soon as possible.

"You found me," I murmur as I tear at his shirt, trying to pull it off him, needing to feel his skin against mine. Against all odds, Finnik found me, and that makes me want him all the more, my entire body filling with a delicious warmth.

"Of course I found you, you are my mate." As he kisses the length of my jaw, he speaks between each kiss, the rumbling of his voice vibrating against my skin. "I would travel the lengths of the world to find you."

A thrill shoots through me when he calls me his mate. I miss Felix and my other mate, but Finnik and I need to be together. There have been a lot of differences between us, and many trials we have had to work through for us to get to this point.

Humming with pleasure, I take his shirt off, scraping my nails over his bare chest and enjoying his deep grumble of pleasure. "You sound pretty sure about that."

"It took me a while to work out, but I have almost lost you twice, and I cannot do it again. I need you, Thea." His final words are a plea. He needs me just as much as I need him. Some might think this is a poor place to seal a mate bond, but it is clear the two of us need this.

"Finn," I gasp as he gently bites my neck, pinning me against the stable wall. While he does not draw blood, something about the act of *him* biting *me* is a real turn-on, especially while I'm trapped by his body.

We are not gentle, tearing at each other's clothing, pulling and tugging, desperation driving us until we are completely naked. We have been apart for too long, we need this bond between us.

Sliding out of his grip, I drop to my knees and take his cock into my hands. I have wanted to taste him for so long, and as I stroke his length to get him hard and ready for me, my mouth salivates. As my tongue flicks out to taste him, Finnik groans, sliding his hands into my hair. His salty taste settles on my taste buds, and I know I need more.

I have a sudden realisation. I am a vampire, and I have fangs. There is no proper way to give a blowjob without cutting him, and no male is going to want to risk his favourite body part. He must see the devastation on my face, because he reaches down and lifts my face to meet his gaze.

"Do not worry about hurting me."

"But I will probably cut you."

"It is okay, just do not bite me." He grins and winks, but I am still not convinced. "Pain does not scare me, Thea."

I see the arousal in his eyes, brighter than it was before. The thought that he could get hurt is turning him on. He likes pain. Not needing any further instruction, I shuffle closer. His cock is longer and thinner than the others, so this might work. Opening my mouth, I carefully slide onto his length, hollowing out my cheeks to create suction. I love the way I feel him hardening and shifting, and I quickly figure out what he likes. I grip the base of him tightly, twisting and squeezing to the rhythm of my mouth. He jerks as I accidently graze him with my teeth—not enough to cause injury, but sharp enough to remind him that my fangs are razor sharp.

His hand lands on my shoulder and stops my movements. "Thea, stop, or I am going to come in your mouth." Pulling back, I look up at him through my eyelashes. "As much as I would enjoy that, I need to make you mine."

He helps me to my feet and presses me against the stable wall once more. There is a feral look in his eyes again, and it sets my insides alight. I need him right now.

"Yes, make me yours, Fin."

His hand cups me, his thumb instantly finding my clit and rubbing it in rough circles. His fingers slide down and find my entrance, and he pushes a thick, calloused finger inside me. Groaning, I bite down on his shoulder to stop me from shouting out loud. This sets Finnik on fire, and he growls as he adds two more fingers. It is rough, the stretch burning as he keeps pushing in and out of me, not giving me time to adjust. It is the rush of two mates about to bond for the first time, and it is so fucking hot.

My nails dig into his back as I release his shoulder and take his mouth, kissing him roughly. The angle is awkward between us, because I struggle to stay upright as his fingers furiously pump inside me, and with a frustrated growl, he pulls his hand away, grabs my ass, and lifts me, pinning me against the wall as my legs wrap around his waist. I am open to him, and he thrusts his fingers back into me. I do not hold back my yell this time.

His fingers suddenly disappear, and I feel his hand moving just before the hot press of his cock is at my entrance. He slides his long cock into me as I moan against him. He keeps going until he is fully sheathed in my pussy, and it feels like his dick is pinning me to the wall more than anything else. He feels incredible. Slowly, he begins to move, his eyes scanning my face to make sure I am okay before upping the speed and force of his strokes.

All I can think about is Finnik, the rest of my troubles falling away as we sink into the rhythm created by our bodies and our love for one another. His touch, taste, and smell surround me, encompassing me completely. There is a light inside me, one that grows with each thrust, and the closer we come to completing our bond, the brighter it becomes. Possibilities wait for us on the other side, I can feel them, and I know there is so much more happening now than just two mates forming their bond.

Finnik is close to coming, but he does not want to until I reach my climax first. I am so close now to finishing, but I just need a little bit... Just as I think it, Finnik presses a finger to my clit, changing the pressure between fast and slow.

"I love you," he whispers against my lips, and that is all I need to fall over the edge.

As soon as I clench around him, he finally loses the battle and lets himself finish, his cock expanding and then pulsing as he comes inside me, burying himself as deeply as possible. My orgasm hits me, shattering my mind as pleasure moves through me. A bright light appears in my vision, growing until nothing is visible and I am completely bathed in light. I have never experienced anything like this before, and as the mate bond finally settles in place, something shifts inside me. I feel like I am lifted from my body as my mind expands and I am moved to another realm.

Complete.

The word rings through me, settling the restless part of me that always felt as though she was not doing enough. *Complete.* My part of the prophecy is now complete. Bonding with Eli and Finnik sealed the deal. My challenge was dealing with Havoc, and now that I have completed mate bonds, I can become a bride and save my people. Everything becomes very clear to me in this moment. I had to suffer and survive to prove myself. Clarity washes through me without a single drop of doubt. The power that lingered in my body had a purpose—I am the cure to the curse affecting the vampires. It is in my blood.

Armed with this new knowledge, I return to my body, pleasure still coursing through me as Finnik finishes emptying himself inside me. No time has passed while I was having my epiphany, and as I blink and come out of my pleasure-induced thoughts, I find Finnik grinning at me. He has an arm above me and a look of adoration in his eyes.

Reaching out with his free hand, he caresses my cheek. "Mate."

"Mate," I say with my own smile, wishing we had more time together to enjoy this moment.

I cannot hold back my excitement any longer, not when I have such important news to share with him. "I am sorry to ruin the moment, but we did it. I have completed my part of the prophecy. Our bond unlocked everything within me." My words are fast and jumbled together, but from the surprise in his eyes, I know he understands me. Taking his hand in mine, I squeeze it hard. "Fin, I know how to cure my people."

Chapter Twenty-Eight

Following the aching pull in my chest, I direct our stolen horse towards Eli, who is waiting for me. If it was not for the bond, I do not know how we would find each other. Trador is a large kingdom, after all.

After Finnik and I completed our bond, and I realised what my purpose truly was, I knew we needed to find Felix and Eli, not to mention my father who was attacked during the ambush that led to me being kidnapped. Thankfully, as soon as we left the abandoned stables, I was able to feel Eli again. There was some sort of magical shield blocking the bonds, only allowing me to feel the connections of my mates who were actually *inside* the shield.

The two of us were able to sprint to the nearest farm and steal a horse. Unfortunately, we lost a lot of time, as the borderlands have been drained of life for a long time now, causing the ground to be poor for farmers.

Now, we are on the back of a galloping horse, Finnik's arm wrapped tightly around me, allowing me to act as our compass. My mind is focused on getting to them and making sure everyone is safe. They are my top priority, and then we shall plan how to help the vampires. Returning to the main city where my king resides is still a priority, and once I have explained everything to him, we can begin the process of figuring out how to heal everyone.

Out of the gloom of the night, I see the silhouette of a building—an inn. The two-story building has a thatched roof, and had it not looked as though it needed some love, it would be charming. Where roses once grew up the walls, weeds now replace them, and the windows are thick with dirt. Two guards are stationed outside, keeping a wary lookout.

We must have reached the main road, as no one would dare to run a business such as this in a secluded area. There are only a handful of places you can stop between Drathlor City and the capital city in Trador. Once upon a time, it used to be safe to travel all the back roads and businesses bloomed, but unfortunately, those times are now long gone.

I am not particularly keen to stay here or even step foot inside, however, Eli is inside, and that overrides all else. As we approach, a stable boy hurries outside, guessing that we will be stopping. We climb from the horse and pass a coin to the stable boy. I take Finnik's hand, intertwining our fingers before hurrying towards the entrance of the inn. The two vampire guards watch us with twin glares, silently assessing us.

Finnik stiffens behind me, his newly awakened mate instincts hyperaware of every threat, and in this moment, he is attempting not to react to the looks the guards give us—give *me*. They are simply doing their jobs, albeit a tad judgementally, yet this seems to offend Finnik. It probably does not help that they are both male. They do not give any indication that they want anything from me, but the mating bond is a little chafing when it first begins. A low warning snarl emits from him, and I have to squeeze his hand to silently beg him to stop. We should not be pissing off the guards, as they could make life difficult for us, especially when Eli is *so* close.

Thankfully the guards decide we are not going to cause trouble and stand to the side, allowing us entry. I step forward to reach for the door when it flings open, Eli standing in the threshold looking like a male possessed.

"Thea," he exclaims, leaping forward and scooping me into his arms. The air is forced out of my lungs as he crushes me against him, and emotion wells up inside, making me choke up. I hadn't realised how much it hurt to be apart until we were back together and I could feel the fullness of our bond. I knew the bond was gone, and now that I can feel it fully once more, I am shaken with how much I missed him.

Given the circumstances of our parting, I think this is probably an accelerant to our extreme reaction, and I feel his pain and fear as though they were my own. I was so worried he was injured, as I know he would have given his all to get to me, so seeing him unharmed and in one piece makes my eyes sting with unshed tears.

"I could not feel you. Our bond was so quiet, and I began to think the worst..." Eli buries his face in my hair, inhaling deeply, his voice tight with emotion. "I was so fucking scared." He cuts himself off, and my heart aches for him. He is really struggling, and that tears me up.

I pull back enough so I can look up at him, lifting his chin until he meets my eyes. "I am here now. I am safe," I assure him, keeping my voice as even as I can.

As he scans my face and the red, healing skin on my arms, his feral fae side begins to rise and take over. "They took you from me. They hurt you." It is a statement, not a question, anger flashing in his gaze.

Placing my hands on his cheeks, I hold his face and force him to look at me. "And they paid for it with their lives. I killed them." There is a promise in my words and a ruthlessness that is new to me. When you have been attacked and hunted, I suppose it changes you, and I cannot find it in me to feel sorry.

"Havoc?" Eli asks tightly, not even flinching at the fact I just told him I murdered my attackers.

"Dead," I reply matter-of-factly.

Eli nods his approval as he absorbs this information, and after a moment, his face softens and the feral part of him sinks down, and my mate returns to me. "Are you okay? Did the bond cause you any problems?"

He is asking if killing a male who was supposed to be my mate caused me to lose a part of myself. After Havoc rejected me, Eli saw how badly it affected me, so it makes complete sense that he would fear something similar when that male died.

"Any issues were minor, and now I am free of him." I am suddenly very aware of the fact that we are standing in the doorway of the inn where anyone could overhear us, including the two guards who do not even try to hide that they are listening in. "Where are the others? I need to talk to all of you."

Eli shifts his weight and frowns as he becomes aware of the public space we are currently in. What we are going to talk about is critical, and the king should hear it before any rumours begin to spread. We need privacy.

Nodding, he gestures to the inn behind him. "They are waiting inside. We did not want to overwhelm you, as we did not know what state you would be in." Wincing at how that sounded, he places a hand on my shoulder and begins to guide me inside. "Come, you look exhausted."

He lifts his head, his nostrils flaring slightly as he sniffs the air. Glancing at Finnik beside me, he raises a brow before dipping his head. "Congratulations on your bond." I can tell he truly means it, but there is a roughness in his voice that indicates he is not happy about the arrangement. However, I know he will not cause any problems, not when he knows the pain of being separated from your mate.

Finnik has stayed silent this whole time, watching closely and guarding my back, keeping an eye on the guards and surrounding area. We are not safe outside, yet I was so lost in reuniting with Eli that I completely forgot where we were. I am grateful to have Finnik around, making sure I am safe at all times. From the jealousy swirling in his chest, I suspect his silence is also part of his strategy in keeping his overprotective mate bond under control.

Eli leads us inside, and I run my eyes over the cosy interior, the couches placed in a semicircle in front of a large, burning fireplace. The small dark wooden tables and chairs are empty, with only one male vampire sitting at the bar, nursing a beer. We walk across the room, Eli nodding to the bartender as we pass. A short corridor leads to three identical doors, and Eli heads straight to the door on the right.

I am exhausted and aching, but knowing that Felix and my father are waiting for me gives me the motivation I need. Eli knocks on the door once, and someone opens it for him, allowing us through. To my surprise, the room is filled with people, far more than I was expecting. Two of my guards stand by the door, bowing deeply as I walk into the space that is clearly one of the bedrooms the inn rents out. Magic tingles over my skin as I step over the threshold—most likely a spell that only allows someone to enter if they have been let in by someone already in the room.

My father and Geoff stand together near an unlit fireplace, stepping forward to greet me. At the back of the room, standing in the shadow of a large four-poster bed, is Felix. He smiles at me but hangs back as the others rush forward. He is probably just giving me some space, but an uneasy feeling settles over me, giving me the sense that something is wrong.

"Lady Anthea," Geoff exclaims, stepping forward and taking my hand in his, kissing the back of it respectfully. "Thank goodness you are safe." He is acting by the book, most likely because of my father's presence, yet I can see emotions swimming in his eyes. Squeezing his hand, I meet his gaze and let my lips twitch up into a half smile, silently communicating that I understand.

"Daughter." My father's voice sounds the same as always, cold and to the point. He has never been one to waste time with flowery words or feelings, deeming them unnecessary. However, I saw a different side of him when we were attacked, so I know he is capable of feeling that way.

"Father," I greet with a shallow nod of my head. I run my gaze over him, and I am relieved that he seems unharmed, but I say nothing, knowing he would only feel uncomfortable.

He also appears to be assessing me. "I am glad to see that you are still in one piece."

My eyes widen in surprise. This is probably the most emotion he has expressed to me since my mother died all those years ago. I must be too obvious with my shock, though, as he clears his throat and brushes down the front of his jacket, his go-to when he is uncomfortable. "After all," he continues, "you cannot possibly complete your purpose if you are dead, and then where would we be?"

Ah, that is more like what I expected from him. I do not feel disappointed by his comment, this is just how the vampires are expected to act, especially among the nobility. The smallest smile crosses my face. "It is good to see you too, Father."

"What happened?" Geoff asks, taking another step forward, his face twisted with concern. He looks as though he wants to touch me and confirm that I am really here, but he stops himself, most likely because of the weight of my father's stare. "Your father said you were ambushed and they kidnapped you. Who were they? How did you get away?"

Images of the attack flash in my mind, the pain of the light, the disorientation, and then realisation that I was separated from Eli and my father. My heart rate spikes, and panic flutters in my chest like a thousand butterflies demanding to be released. I fight against the anxiety that tries to overwhelm me. No, Havoc is dead, he cannot hurt anyone ever again. *You are safe, you are free.* I repeat those words to myself, my mantra. I fought for my life and came out the victor. I will no longer allow Havoc to cause these feelings within me, he does not deserve to take up space in my mind.

Both of my mates make low grumbling noises as they feel my distress, stepping closer as though they can shield me from the memories. Taking a deep breath, I clear my mind and focus on Geoff's question.

"Havoc and the brotherhood were the ones behind it. All of my attackers are now dead, including the former prince." There is a heavy pause as they digest this information. How King Drath is going to take the news that I killed his youngest son, I do not know. There will probably be consequences, but I did what I had to. I can only hope he realises I did what I had to.

"They tortured me," I continue, "and in the process, it caused me to fully embrace my powers, the good and the bad. I transformed, finally able to access my full powers. I was able to escape and kill them." My voice is even and disconnected from my emotions, simply telling them the minimum details.

I glance at Felix at the back of the room, wanting to see his reaction to what I said. I know none of this is easy for him, being the only one of my loves who is not bonded to me. My heart aches as I take in his distressed expression. He seems to sink into the wall, as though wanting to become invisible.

Wanting to make him smile, I take a deep breath, knowing the news I have to share will please him—will please everyone.

"In more important news," I begin, "my position as the first bride is now complete."

As expected, shock ripples through the room and exclamations fill the air. Even the guards seem surprised, sharing a look between them.

"You solved your part of the prophecy," Eli whispers, awe making his eyes bright. "How? I thought it was linked to Havoc."

"We read the prophecy wrong. We misinterpreted it all." I laugh, everything seeming so clear now. "While I was Havoc's mate, my real purpose was to survive Havoc and find my true mates, Eli and Finnik. That is what lifted the final block on my powers—my powers that will save our people."

Before anyone can comment, my father sneers and

makes a noise of disgust. "The fae are your mates? You were supposed to marry a prince."

Of course this is what my father would pick up on—the status of the males I surround myself with, not the fact that I have discovered how I can help Trador. My metaphorical hackles rise, my overprotective instincts running high. I should not let him get to me, and I am going to blame it on the new bond between Finnik and me.

"We are meant for each other. It is fated," I grind out between clenched teeth, as civil as I can manage.

Geoff clears his throat, pulling attention his way to stop an argument between my father and me. "Why is the vampire disease still spreading if you completed your purpose?"

Geoff always asks difficult, hard hitting questions, even if they might sound offensive to some. I do not take his words as a critique or a sign of doubt though, knowing he is simply trying to get to the bottom of what is happening.

Feeling a little breathless at the responsibility, I smile as I meet his gaze. "Because my purpose *is* to heal the vampires. I *am* the cure."

His eyes widen in surprise and understanding. "How do you know this?"

"It was revealed to me when I unlocked my powers." I wish I could explain the certainty within me in a way they could understand, but without feeling it themselves, it is impossible. They just have to trust that I am right. "I have not quite figured out how to do that just yet, but I know this is what I am supposed to do."

I sense Eli's surprise through the bond, but it quickly settles into a glowing appreciation. He is proud of me and what I am capable of doing. He knows I am at my happiest when I am helping others, and it makes sense that my true purpose is this. Finnik already knew about all of this, yet he is still brimming with pride as I explain. Geoff is watching me with a considering look, and when he nods his head in approval, accepting that what I say is true, I release a quiet breath of relief. My father is unmoving, probably still trying to get over his aversion to the fae and the fact I have mated with two of them.

Finally, my eyes settle on Felix—my friend, lover, and anchor to reality. Only he seems like a shadow of himself. The feeling of something being wrong surges within me once again. I need to speak to him and make sure he is okay.

"Could I please have a moment alone with Felix?"

My father grumbles and looks as though he is going to argue, but Geoff stops him by placing a hand on his arm, shaking his head slightly.

"We shall be in the bar," my advisor replies, steering my father from the room.

I turn to look at Eli and Finnik, the tension on their faces telling me just how unhappy they are with this request. However, just as I can feel their needs, they can feel mine too. Taking their hands, I squeeze them tightly and let them sense how much I need to do this, not just for me, but for Felix. They leave reluctantly, taking the guards with them, the door shutting with a quiet click.

Silence fills the room, and the sour stench of fear reaches my nose—Felix. He is afraid, but of what? Surely it isn't me. We have been friends for decades, and I share everything with him, so why would he be scared of me now? Because of what I did to escape? He was totally silent when I explained how I escaped, so perhaps I disgusted him with the lives I took.

"Felix, is everything okay?" I walk towards him, my

hand reached out to touch him, but he shrinks back and bares his teeth.

"Stay back," he hisses, his hands pressed against the wall as if feeling for a way out.

I jerk back as though I have been stung, feeling sick to my stomach. He is afraid of me, of what I can do. *Do not overreact, you do not know this for sure. Look at him,* the sensible part of my brain tells me, and I have to force myself to take deep breaths. I automatically assume I have done something wrong, but he was looking off when I first walked into the room. He did not know the details then, so he was disturbed by something before I arrived.

Scanning him from head to toe, I take in every little detail, desperately looking for a clue. He does not even sound like himself, his words harsh. Sweat beads on his forehead, something that's not common for a changed vampire. In fact, he does not look well at all, the colour drained from his face.

"Felix, what is going on? Are you feeling—" I cut myself off as I have a disturbing realisation. "You are sick."

He caught the disease. This must be the early stages, as he has not gone feral yet, but I would say he is close to descending into the madness. I try to look at him objectively, calmly noting the symptoms and making a plan to treat him. In reality, that does not work in the slightest. This is Felix, my first love and best friend. I was terrified he would catch this, and now my worst nightmares have become a reality.

Ignoring his earlier plea, I step forward and attempt to pull him into my arms, only he avoids me with a hiss, holding his arm out to block me.

"Thea, please, do not come any closer." His entire body seems to shudder as he fights against the disease working its way through his body. He grips onto one of the bedposts, the wood groaning under his hand.

"I cannot control myself," he cries out, his voice shifting into a deeper timbre I have not heard from him. He is clearly in agony, both emotionally and physically. Tears of blood leak from the corners of his eyes, and a terrifying growl leaves him. He lets out a howl of pain, and when he looks up at me again, I see a flash of mania.

"No," I whisper, realising I am about to lose him. I do not worry for myself, only my first love who is suffering before me. I take a step towards him. My bonds are pulling in my chest, both of my mates feeling my distress and trying to reach me, but I block them out, needing my full focus to be on Felix.

"No!" he shouts, the bedpost cracking under the force of his grip. He jerks his hand away, and a large chunk rips from the wooden frame. It looks like... like a stake. Vampires are hard to kill, but a stake through the heart will do it. Felix stares at the sharp wood in his hands, his body stiffening. When he looks up at me, all traces of my lover are gone. His face contorts as he watches me like I am a threat. His stance changes, dropping into a defensive, animalistic position.

He has gone feral.

Banging on the door startles me, and I make the mistake of glancing away. In that moment, Felix leaps for me, knocking me to the floor and startling a cry from me as we land in a heap.

"Thea!" Eli shouts from the corridor, his voice urgent. "We cannot get in without you opening the door. Let us in!"

"Mate!" Finnik calls, his voice descending into panic. I can feel their emotions, the panic and frustration in them making it difficult for me to manage my own fear.

There is no way I can get up and let them in, as I am too

focused on keeping Felix's teeth from my neck. I do not want to hurt him, yet if he kills me, I can never heal him. If only my new gifts came with instructions so I knew how to use them. Bucking my hips, I try to throw him from me, but we only end up tumbling across the floor, fighting for dominance as we try to stay in the top position.

He pins me to the ground once more, snarling down at me, and I see my death in his eyes. I can only hope that when he strikes, my blood will cure him. I do not want my death to be in vain. I am devastated that this is how I am going to die, and I will never get to experience a full life with my mates. Most of all, if Felix does survive this, I know my death will destroy him.

"I love you, Felix," I whisper, my quiet goodbye full of my love for him as I stop fighting, simply staring up at him with a sad smile as tears roll down my cheeks.

Something flickers in his eyes, and all of a sudden, Felix is looking back at me. Horrified, he looks at our position and realises what he was about to do. Jumping to his feet, he backs away, his hands shaking. "What have I done?"

Overwhelmed by the sudden change but overjoyed that Felix managed to fight his way to the surface, I sit up and watch him carefully. His movements are erratic, and I am guessing he could be overcome once more, so I need to be careful.

"Felix, it is okay. Let me help you." I want to jump up and run to him, although that is probably one of the worst things I could do right now. Startling him would likely bring back the feral side bubbling under the surface.

"No." His eyes go to the large stake that was dropped during our tumble. Before I can react or fully take in what is happening, he crosses the room and grabs it. His eyes meet mine as those bloody tears continue to roll down his cheeks, but it is his smile that truly makes my blood run cold. "I am so sorry, Thea," he whispers. "I wish there was another way. I will see you in the next life."

My eyes widen, and I push to my feet as I realise what is about to happen. Everything seems to move in slow motion, and there is nothing I can do but watch helplessly as he lifts the stake and impales himself in the chest.

"No!" I scream, a potent wave of my power ripping from me like a tidal wave, turning over furniture and blasting through the magic on the door, flinging it open. The whole building seems to shake around us, yet I do not care. Scrabbling towards Felix, I catch his body as he goes limp, his infected blood dark as it oozes from his chest.

Eli, Finnik, and the others hurry into the room, stopping when they see the destruction and Felix's bloody body in my lap. Only my mates approach me, slowly standing on either side of me as they place their hands on my shoulders in support. I feel as though I am going to fall apart. No, I do not have time for that, I need to save Felix. I am the first bride, this is my purpose.

"Do not do this to me, Felix. I need you. You cannot leave me," I order him, stroking his hair from his face.

He gives me a beautiful smile. "I love you, Thea."

I can see him fading before my very eyes, his life force bubbling from his chest.

No. No, this cannot happen. I am supposed to save the vampires. *Blood will turn the tide.* That is what the prophecy said. The cure is supposed to be in me, my blood. Without question, I lift my wrist to my mouth, tearing through the skin so blood pours from the rough wound. I shove my wrist against his mouth. "Drink, Felix, it will help you." My voice chokes off, unshed tears stinging my eyes.

He doesn't drink, the blood running down his lifeless lips.

"Damn you, Felix! Drink!" My voice cracks, going high-pitched. It is not working. I do the only thing I can think of and tilt my head upward, closing my eyes and praying to whoever is listening.

"Please, whatever powers watch over us, help me bring him back to me. Help me heal him and banish the disease from his body," I beg, needing someone, something, to help me. "I will give anything, I just need him back. Why did you give me this power if I cannot use it?" I shout, my desperate emotions twisting like a storm churned ocean. "Heal him. Heal him!" I demand, looking down at the limp body in my lap.

Warmth moves through me, and at first, I think it is my mates and they are pouring their strength into me, but the darkness rises within me, called by my plea. I do not fight it as it moves through me. Something changes then, a shift in myself, almost like a glowing sunrise in my mind, lighting the way. It glimmers and shows me where to go, and I close my eyes as I push my will into the writhing power I now control.

Finnik gasps behind me, and I hear the quiet murmurs of exclamation from others in the room. "Silver surrounds her," he whispers with realisation.

A tug on my arm has me opening my eyes, and I cry out with joy as Felix clutches my arm, drinking my blood like a man starving. It is only now that I realise all four of us are surrounded by a silver glow and that I am the source.

Finnik's comment makes sense now, and I realise he is referring to one of the lines from the prophecy. We always assumed the silver referred to my hair, but now I realise it is because of my powers.

With my mates supporting me, I let Felix drink from me. He is firm but gentle, nothing like a true attack from a feral vampire. This gives me hope that whatever is happening is healing him. I know there are others around us, all wanting answers, but the four of us stay like this, not saying a word until Felix finally stops drinking and opens his eyes—eyes that now have shimmering silver irises.

It changed him not just by healing him, but in another way too. There is a slight pull in my chest, and I realise it is him. Looking within me, I see a silver thread now connects my heart to his. We may not be mates, but we have the connection I know he was longing for.

"Thea, I'm—" He slowly sits up and looks down at himself before looking back at me, laughing with bewilderment. "You healed me."

Movement has me turning, and I watch as Geoff, my father, and the guards move farther into the room, their expressions ranging from shock to fanatic awe.

"You truly are our saviour," my father whispers, pressing a hand against his chest.

I look up at him and nod. I have always hated being called a saviour, but I suppose he is right. I just proved myself, not only to him, but to myself too. We have a lot of work to do, and we still need to get to the capital before we can begin to start planning how this will work.

With my mates at my side, I know we can heal the land together.

Chapter 29

Three months later

"Are you sure we have to go?" Finnik asks for what must be the tenth time, a petulant expression on his face.

I do not blame him for not wanting to go back after everything that happened. Visiting his old home will be difficult, especially because part of the reason we are going is for me to get a formal pardon from the king for killing Havoc.

"We cannot delay any longer, you know that." We reached the end of the three months King Drath granted us to help Trador with the feral vampires. "Besides, there are vampires in Drathlor City who need our help."

It has been three months since that awful day when I thought Felix died in my arms. I still have nightmares about it. We managed to survive, though, and get back to Trador Castle without any further incidents. After many, many meetings with the king detailing everything that happened over the last few months, he finally agreed to let me start treating those who turned feral.

The city was in an awful state when we arrived, with

curfews in place and guards everywhere. The market was deserted, and bodies were piled up in alleys. It was heartbreaking. It also went to show just how quickly the disease spread between vampires.

With the help of my mates and Felix, we created a treatment centre. All feral vampires are detained for their own safety before they are healed by me. It is a slow process, as there is only one of me and many with the disease, but we discovered that drinking blood from one of the healed vampires can help stem off the worst effects of the disease.

Now that I have to return to Drathlor City, I worry about the state of the treatment centre, but I left some of my blood for emergency treatments. There is also a host of volunteers who have been healed and help with blood donations.

Glancing over the large room the four of us stayed in over the last three months, I feel a slight pang of sadness, but I know we will be back soon. I have obligations in Drathlor City, and then we shall return and help rebuild Trador. Assured I have left nothing behind, I hold my hand out to Finnik, who instantly takes it before we leave the room.

Descending into the large entrance hall, I see Felix and Eli loading boxes into a carriage through the open doorway.

"The silver lady," the servants whisper as we pass.

That is a new moniker I picked up, thanks to the silver glow that appears when I am healing and the silver light in the eyes of those who recover. It makes me feel awkward, but I smile slightly and nod my thanks. I suppose there could be worse designations. Dragging Finnik behind me, I practically skip across the entrance and throw myself into Felix's arms, giving him a kiss in greeting. I then move over to Eli and push up onto my toes and give him a kiss too.

"Are you ready to go?" Eli asks against my lips, sneaking an extra kiss before releasing me.

I have already said my goodbyes, and I know Geoff will be joining us in a few days, giving him a chance to train a new manager for the treatment centre, a job he has taken over since we got back. I look up at the castle I called home and smile, knowing my real home is with these males right here. No matter where we go, I am at home with them.

"Yes," I reply with a smile, turning to the carriage that will take us to the next part of our journey. "I am ready."

The End

The curse continues in A City of Embers and Brimstone.

Coming soon.

Author's Note

As usual, it takes a whole village to create a book, so thank you to everyone who helped pull my crazy ideas together and make it into a readable story that actually makes sense. If writing was the only part of being an author, things would be much easier, but there is so much that goes on behind the scenes, and I am in debt to those who helped to keep my on track, reminded me to leave the writing cave to eat, and made sure that I went to meetings that I agreed to and then promptly forgot.
Nikki and Kat, my PA goddesses, you are amazing. Jess, Kaila and all of my alpha/beta readers, thank you so much for everything you do for me. Your cheerleading is what keeps me going.
Of course, a huge thanks goes to Connor, my partner, for putting up with me and pretending to be interested when I talk through my story ideas. My family and close friends also deserve a thank you for their constant support.

Most of all, a huge thank you to my readers. You are all

Author's Note

amazing and I hope you love this book and the beginning of a new fantasy journey together.

Lots of love,
Erin xoxo

About the Author

Erin lives in the UK with her cat and works full time as an independent author. Now a *USA Today* bestselling author, she began writing in 2018 when she published her first book, *Hunted by Shadows*. She specialises in writing fantasy and reverse harem paranormal romance.

She met K.A Knight in 2018 when they became partners in crime and began writing together. In 2019, she became co-authors with Loxley Savage, writing fantasy reverse harem. She's Disney obsessed, loves cookies and baking, and is always planning her next story.

Make sure to follow her on her social media pages for updates on what she's currently working on:

Facebook Group:
https://www.facebook.com/groups/ErinOKanesShadowRealm
Facebook Author Page:
https://www.facebook.com/ErinOKaneAuthor
Newsletter:
http://eepurl.com/gJhSd9
Instagram:
https://www.instagram.com/erin.okane.author

Also by Erin O'Kane

The Shadowborn Series:

Hunted by Shadows

Lost in Shadow

Embraced by Shadows

The Shadowborn series- the boxset

Born From Shadows Series:

Demons do it Better

The War and Deceit Series:

Fires of Hatred

Fires of Treason

Fires of Ruin

Fires of War

Fires of the Fae:

A Lady of Embers

A Spark of Promise

A Legacy of Hope and Ash

The Cursed Women Universe:

Venom and Stone

Betrayal and Curses

Fractured Wings

Bloodlines series:

Midnight Magic

Midnight Trials

Midnight Deception

Midnight Conviction

Midnight Ascension

The Complete Bloodlines Series – omnibus

The Brides of Darkness – interconnected standalones:

A Kingdom of Broken Bonds

A City of Embers and Brimstone – coming soon

Standalones:

Second Chance

Love Bites

Co-writes

By Erin O'Kane and K.A Knight

Her Freaks Series:

Circus Save Me

Taming the Ringmaster

Walking the Tightrope

The Wild Boys:

The Wild Interview

The Wild Tour

The Wild Finale

The Wild Boys Series- The boxset

Standalones:

Hero Complex

Dark Temptations

By Erin O'Kane and Loxley Savage

Wicked Waves Duet:

Twisted Tides

Tides that Bind

Printed in Dunstable, United Kingdom